T0368091

FORGIVE AND LIVE:

RWANDA FROM GENOCIDE TO PROSPERITY

WENDY STANLEY MILLS

BALBOA.PRESS
A DIVISION OF HAY HOUSE

Balboa Press books may be ordered through booksellers or by contacting:

Balboa Press
A Division of Hay House
1663 Liberty Drive
Bloomington, IN 47403
www.balboapress.com
844-682-1282

Because of the dynamic nature of the Internet, any web addresses or links contained in this book may have changed since publication and may no longer be valid. The views expressed in this work are solely those of the author and do not necessarily reflect the views of the publisher, and the publisher hereby disclaims any responsibility for them.

The author of this book does not dispense medical advice or prescribe the use of any technique as a form of treatment for physical, emotional, or medical problems without the advice of a physician, either directly or indirectly. The intent of the author is only to offer information of a general nature to help you in your quest for emotional and spiritual well-being. In the event you use any of the information in this book for yourself, which is your constitutional right, the author and the publisher assume no responsibility for your actions.

Any people depicted in stock imagery provided by Getty Images are models, and such images are being used for illustrative purposes only. Certain stock imagery © Getty Images.

Scripture quotations marked KJV are from the Holy Bible, King James Version (Authorized Version). First published in 1611. Quoted from the KJV Classic Reference Bible, Copyright © 1983 by The Zondervan Corporation.

Print information available on the last page.

ISBN: 979-8-7652-5487-5 (sc)
ISBN: 979-8-7652-5486-8 (e)

Library of Congress Control Number: 2024917188

Balboa Press rev. date: 12/27/2024

CONTENTS

Dedicated to the memory of Fredrick D. Mills, Jr. and to the memory of Nellie P. and Thomas B. Stanley, Jr., my parents, and to all the people fallen in struggle for freedom and peace throughout the world, due to the devastation of colonialism, racism, fear, and greed.

ACKNOWLEDGEMENTS

Thanks to Spirit for guidance, inspiration, and the words. I thank Fredrick Douglas Mills, Jr., my husband for the freedom to write; Candace Stanley Pinn, whose computer background set the stage; Sandra McMullen, ever present positive force in my life; Noel, for her encouragement; my editor Jennifer Monahan; and my publisher Balboa Press. I also thank, fellow writer Brenda Bakari who made it so easy by purchasing the <u>Rwanda History of Genocide</u> for me; Dorothy Hunton who wrote <u>Unsung Valiant</u> about her husband, Dr. W. Alphaeus Hunton, who authored <u>Decision in Africa,</u> and was head of the Council of African Affairs, in New York; and my guide to truth Rev. Saundra Porter Thomas.

I am indebted to the authors of the books on Africa: Cecil Niles who wrote <u>Black Heart</u> about the Congo and his trip which gave detailed descriptions of this area of the world; Rwanda Touristry published <u>Rwanda</u>, a beautifully colored photo book with descriptions of the country and the people; <u>Rwanda Today</u> by Jean-Claude Klotchkoff; Michael Crighton who wrote <u>Congo</u>; and <u>The Rwanda Crisis, History of a Genocide</u> by Gerard Prunier. The most stirring authors were, Immaculee Ilibagiza who wrote <u>Left To Tell</u>, a genocide survivor story and Gael Faye, who wrote <u>Small Country</u>, a novel about his life in Burundi before and after the genocide war there. They witnessed firsthand the holocaust and through their young innocent eyes saw the brutal murdering of their people by their people.

<u>A Course in Miracles</u> and the <u>Bible</u> and many spiritual

teachers guided my vision to finally complete this book after almost 30 years.

I give special acknowledgement and thanks to The Charlotte Observer whose Associated Press (International), and Kidder Press reports of the war inspired me to write the book in the first place, in 1994. And my last resource *Africa Now,* and *Africa Online* gave me the African perspective along with the *NY Times* articles on the last days of the bloodshed in Rwanda.

Online is where I learned about the Forgiveness Project that started in Rwanda in 2004. I also learned about Project Hope started in 1958; and Doctors Without Borders that has been in existence since 1971, placing power in the hands of local health care workers to save lives around the globe and especially in Rwanda after the Genocide. These three organizations have helped the Rwandese people see each other in a different light and bring peace and forgiveness to the country.

AUTHOR'S NOTE

With the permission of my genius niece, Candace Stanley Pinn, the information about her high school and college endeavors, including NOAA, along with other computer related enterprises, are factually related in this book.

Also, the information about the Original Council of African Affairs and Sierra Leone is factual. All other information about the main character Cheyenne LaTour and other characters are historical fiction or imagined by the author.

<u>The Characters</u> as they appear in order in the book: Cheyenne LaTour- Computer genius, quits her job to go to Rwanda with AT&T to place fiber optic cable for the internet; Dava Love, Cheyenne's best friend from childhood who goes with Cheyenne to Rwanda; Stacy, Cheyenne's secretary in NY at Duran, Inc. Web and Aunt Wen are siblings; Leon Virgo, Cheyenne's love of her life, Journalist on assignment in Egypt in 1994; M.H. Duran owner and founder of the Duran Corporation; U.S. Chairman Fossil Gatt, predator, and member of the malicious Organization; Woodrow Falt, Gatt's assistant and the person who warns M.H. Duran of the Organization's plot to destroy Rwanda.

GranNellie and Tommy, Grandad, are Cheyenne's grandparents and original members of the African Affairs Council in the 1940s and 50s; Tombe is President of the African Affairs Council, Sim, Nefertari, Wynt are friends Ali and Ca are sisters of Cheyenne; Henri, Marie, Dominique, Eugenia and Iramania are Rwandese who are the host family for Shy and Dava.

ONE SET OF FOOTPRINTS

One night a man had a dream. He dreamed he was walking along the beach with the Lord. Across the sky flashed scenes from his life. For each scene, he noticed two sets of footprints in the sand--one belonging to him and the other to the Lord. When the last scene flashed before him, he looked back at the footprints and noticed that many times along the path there was only one set of footprints in the sand. He also noted that this happened during the lowest and saddest times in his life. This really bothered him, and he questioned the Lord;

"Lord, You said that once I decided to follow You, You would walk all the way, but I noticed that during the most troublesome times of my life, there was only one set of footprints. I don't understand why, when I needed You most, You deserted me."

The Lord replied, "My precious, precious child, I love you and will never leave you. During your times of trial and suffering when you saw only one set of footprints, it was then that I carried you...."

Anonymous

FOREWORD

The most current Nast Conde's, Travelogue, June 2023, of the beautiful Rwanda of today is thriving and new. Forgiveness and love propel the President and the Rwandese to manifest their hopes for their beautiful country.

This book is about the people of Rwanda, whose lives and country I depict in my story, set in 1994. This is an historic fictional work; however, some of the incidents are directly related to newspaper reports, a war survivor's tape recording, and various books used to describe this part of Africa from 1994-2010. In addition, a future of possibilities, and the present are encapsulated within the last pages.

Rwanda lies near the heart of the Congo which has always served as a challenge to outsiders. The Africans there, for the most part, had been protected from slavery since they were sheltered by the rainforest of the Congo. In the 19th century, Stanley and Livingston were disturbed by the presence of the African, the Twa in particular, living in a part of the Congo never seen by a white man. Rwanda, which used to be part of the Congo, was beautifully laid out by nature. This was because it is believed that human life developed in this region, near Malawi.

Rwanda was fought over by Germany, then France and finally it was Belgium that claimed the country in the 19th century and reclaimed it again after World Wars I and II. The beautiful beaches along the rivers in Rwanda were already the proud possession of the Belgians, and they lent their European appendages to them by calling these African beaches the "Riviera of Africa."

xv

These Europeans also possessed the Volcanoes National Park in the Virunga Mountain range in which "Gorillas of the Mist" was filmed. The story of American Dian Fossey who sacrificed her life to save the gorillas of the Virunga. This movie can still be watched and there are many books written about this American zoologist. However, the focus is on the animals, not the human civilizations in Rwanda. Fossey lived in the wild amongst the gorillas and she was eventually killed by poachers.

My book has two opposing groups who entered Rwanda in 1994: the African Affairs Council, the helpful one; and the Organization, the harmful one. The Organization is from my imagination.

The problem, in 1994, as the Organization members saw it, was that in Rwanda the soil was so rich and the weather perfect for growing food, the Rwandese people became healthy and happy farmers. Their life span was raised from 39 to 50 years of age. The birth rate doubled, and the people needed more land for farming and for the increased population. There came to be more people farming and wanting to farm than there was land for them to farm. They would try to take some of the National Park area but would be fought by the Bureau of Tourism to go back. This was supported by the Europeans there. Rwanda is rich in gold, and many minerals needed for technology.

Ethnic warring developed over who rightfully should live and rule in Rwanda. Both the Hutus and Tutsis thought they had the right when it was the Twa people who had lived there since almost 8000 BC. The Twa were descendants of the first Homo sapiens found near this area in Malawi. The (Ba) Hutu came to the Congo area from the west in around 1000 AD, the (Ba) Tutsi came during the 16th century from the north. Hatred between the ethnic groups was started by the Belgians and instigated by the Organization (a fictitious group from the author's imagination).

PROLOGUE

In a protracted struggle of more than 140 years, the people of this region had to come in accord with guidelines established by a unified leadership to live in love, peace, and harmony regardless of ancestral background, tribal or religious differences, or ethnicity. The Arusha Accord in 1993, was written to promote this unification.

The Arusha Accord was never put into effect and life in Rwanda sank to the lowest ebb of human travesty possible, from this place of sheer and utter depravity in the year 1994...

In the green steamy rainforest of Rwanda's Akagera Park, the hiss and squeal of the jungle animals is now quieted by man's murderous presence. There is only the unnatural sound of the shouts and commands of the government's death squad leader. Under the leader's orders a Hutu beats a Tutsi civilian to their death. The people that kill prepare to do their worst while the Gods of the forest look on in anguish...

CHAPTER 1

La Raison D'être

"If thou wilt return, O Israel, saith the Lord,
return unto me..." KJV Jer. 4:1

With the certainty of her uncertainty, she melted into her surroundings for, perhaps, the last time. As she stood motionless, overlooking Fifth Avenue, with a slackened posture Cheyenne LaTour gazed from her fifty-fourth-floor window of the Duran Building. Her anticipation of this afternoon's meeting with her boss, M. H. Duran began to overwhelm her.

Cheyenne disengaged herself from this fear by quickly focusing on something different. As she looked around, she began to think about leaving this place behind. It made her more cognizant of the effort she put into her office to make it beautiful and functional.

She strategically placed her gift from Leon of the Waterman pen and pencil set that matched the grain of her desk. She remembered when she bought the solid marble desk in Italy. It was placed catty-cornered to the window so that her chair could easily swivel to the two computers on her desk in the surrounding circumference.

The soft ergonomically designed chair was placed so that she was a swivel away from facing the huge window. Everyday Cheyenne positioned herself in the chair so that she faced the window as she worked.

As she watched the sky and clouds Shy (her nickname) imagined what the weather felt like outside. This view often gave her the motivation to continue to squeeze out the transmissions that led to her VP status in operations. She opened the window and with a deep breath, felt the cool air against her face. Then immediately closed the window.

'Sea breeze' scented potpourri awakened her sense of the slightest scent of an ocean in her office. It helped stimulate her work which would begin before sunrise and finish well after the sunset.

Her diffidence disappeared instantly as she regained her composure. Her mind was wide open and racing joyously in frivolity as she began to fathom the adventure that awaited a few days away. Her cell rang and she knew who it was.

"Hi Dava, do you believe this is our last day here?" Cheyenne said to her lifelong friend.

"Shy, it is like a dream. We have had a good run at Duran, Inc., but my friend we are about to venture into the unknown, now," Dava answered with hesitation.

"I can't say I haven't enjoyed working in the heart of the city, right in the middle of Fifth Avenue in New York City. I can afford and enjoy the best New York has to offer; I know there is no place like New York for the variety of food. The only redeeming thing about missing the tasty international cuisine here is the fact that I can reduce my weight with the food I get in Africa. I know I'll do a vegetarian thing there, maybe? Then again..." Cheyenne mused to herself her secretary knocked while Dava spoke.

"Look dreamer, I have a million things to do before I leave tonight. I'll see you at the house. I will be a little late. I know you can handle the heat!" Dava said as she hung up

"Good morning Miss LaTour," said Stacy as she knocked and opened Cheyenne's office door at the same time with coffee and pad in hand.

Stacy came into the office later than usual and looked troubled. Cheyenne knew something was amiss. Her natural reaction with any friend was to find out what was wrong.

"Good morning, Stacy. What is hiding that wonderful smile today?" Cheyenne asked with genuine concern. She intuitively knew Stacy so well. Stacy didn't seem quite herself. She had become very dear to Cheyenne not only as an administrative assistant, but as a friend. Even though Stacy was older with children close to Cheyenne's age, Cheyenne felt maternal toward her; some older people are like that. They complimented each other in the most spiritual sense, so it worked out wonderfully.

"Oh, nothing really, Miss LaTour," said Stacy unconvincingly.

"Come on now Stacy, I know you a little too well to try to hide this from me," Cheyenne said, not allowing her to let this pass. Stacy had a difficult divorce a month ago.

"Thanks for asking. Maybe we could have lunch today after your meetings," Stacy said, averting direct eye contact with Cheyenne.

Stacy tugged at her inherited suit. It was tapered to fit Cheyenne's body, but because Stacy was thin it fit her nicely even though it was handmade. The sky-blue silk/wool blend made the suit delicate yet elegantly serious. The jacket sleeves fit the arms to the perfect length above her wrist then gloved her body to the top of her hip. The short, fitted skirt looked like an extension of the jacket. The jacket had a round neckline high, so that no jewelry would distract the person with whom business was being done. She wore it the way Cheyenne would with no jewelry, no glitter. The jacket was fastened by a bib front with four navy roped trimmings that met the wide opening in tiers.

Her shoes, also previously Cheyenne's, were black leather, pointed toe with two skinny straps above the leather enclosed toes. The four extra inches of skirt that rose above the knees made her look tall. There were no wrinkles or creases in this attire. Cheyenne worked hard to get this look every day so that she could say what she had to say with the greatest confidence, and this quality was soon instilled in her administrative assistant, Stacy. There is something powerful about looking good and feeling good.

"Sure, we'll do lunch, remind me." Cheyenne knew there was something urgent Stacy needed to discuss and wrote herself a reminder. She'd be there for Stacy. First Cheyenne had to take care of business

Cheynne said, "One of the most important things today is my meeting with Mr. Duran. I want to know as soon as he calls. I'm glad this morning's schedule is light."

"Please confirm my apartment rental with Mr. and Mrs. Fred Cheltenham's attorney. I want to make sure my aunt and uncle complete the transaction before I go away and then they can move in while their house is renovated," Cheyenne said to Stacy.

As she left Cheyenne received an unexpected phone call.

"Hi Shy, this is..." Aunt Re started.

"Aunt Re what a surprise. I haven't talked to you in months. How are you?" Cheyenne asked, wanting a conversation.

"I'm fine dear and yourself?" Aunt Re did not want to get into small talk.

"I am great and ready for my big move. I know you've heard about it."

"Yes," Aunt Re seemed ill at ease for the moment. "Look sweetheart, I know you are busy at work, and I never bother anybody on their job, but I needed to let you know I won't be able to get there for your big family meeting tonight.

"However," her aunt stated slowly and deliberately, "my dear Miss Cheyenne LaTour, I need to know how you thought of this one? What went through your mind while you were planning to go off on this extreme tangent?" asked Shy's aunt from North Carolina. "You know I truly don't understand why you are going so far away and for so long. I'm sorry but I need a good explanation."

"There are many reasons for me to go to Rwanda now, Aunt Re," Cheyenne began; she knew all her aunts were so concerned for her welfare and took pride in her success.

"With AT&T opening up their telecommunications systems in Rwanda the opportunity was given to me to head up the fiber optic cable installation and remote connection for them. I will be able to train Rwandans and other Africans how to run their internet and global systems. It's exciting introducing this country into the 21st century! Also, one of the absolute best reasons is that the love of my life will be in Africa for the same amount of time I will be there. Leon and I have never been far from each other for any significant stretches of time. I know it sounds trite, but I love him and prefer to see him now and then. While he is in Egypt for his journalism internship I will be down the Nile in Rwanda."

"Well, you know I believe that you should be as close to the man you love as possible. I have learned over the years separation creates more problems than whatever purpose it had. My sister lost her husband because he didn't take her with him when he went off to get his MBA degree in another state," said Aunt Re with recollections of a sad time in her life.

"Not only that but I have been doing my homework. This Central African country, Rwanda, goes to the heart of

5

the world's energy and peace solutions. We, the West, are not its saviors but its destroyers. In my studies while seeking information about Africa and her history, I found that the West's interest in Africa is far greater than the news media tells the public. There are people in the world that are plotting the future for all of us. I'm determined to contribute to a good future outcome. We have technology that can possibly save Central Africa from going into oblivion in the next century. The people of Rwanda have an ancient story to be told. I believe that if they aren't saved there will be an episode of history lost forever."

"You can make your contribution and do that research from here can't you?" Her aunt asked tepidly. Steam had been blown out of her argument from Cheyenne's first comment about Leon.

"Not really, auntie. There is a certain group of people indigenous to Rwanda that are so great, and no one has really studied them and their origin in depth. Now they are becoming extinct. They were eight feet tall and there were thousands more of them at the beginning of the century. Even before the genocidal massacres in 1959, they were being destroyed. They fought for Belgium in World War II, because of their warlike characteristics and height, they presented themselves as formidable foes against German invaders. They were called the Watutsi," Cheyenne began...

"I've heard of them. I remember when we were in elementary school, we saw a film in black and white about this African group of warriors who were eight feet tall. They looked magnificent as they carried their spears and ran, or pranced was more like it, through the tall grass. They had a unique hairstyle also. There was a movie...hmm "Solomon's Mines" back in the 1950s about them," Aunt Re stated with authority.

"Yes, they were the Watutsi. They have been in Rwanda, Uganda, Zaire, and Burundi since the 13th-16th centuries. The Watutsi came from the north to Rwanda and then spread out to the other Central African countries. It is unclear whether it was Egypt, or some other area of North Africa or maybe Ethiopia from which they came. My guess is that they came from Egypt as the original Nubian builders of the pyramids, Luxor monuments, and the Sphinx. I say this because the Nile River's source is in Rwanda. My belief is that since Rwanda is where the Nile River begins, the Tutsi followed its flow south through Egypt through Sudan to Uganda and Central Africa where they were protected from the white and Arab enslavers for centuries. The Nile flows up from Central Africa to the Mediterranean Sea. In Karmac, Egypt where they came from are all statues and monuments of giants.

"All this evidence proves my theory more and more. In times of danger why wouldn't these original builders of Egypt, the Tutsi, or Watutsi, instinctively return to their ancestral home in Uganda and Rwanda. Rwanda is where the Tutsi settled after leaving the north …".

"Yes, I see where you are going with this, Shy."

"Anthropologists and archaeologists have found that in 50,000 B.C. "Sangoan man" a hominid named for the Sango Bay in Uganda, spread across Africa. Not only that, but this same hominid settled the Nile Valley in Egypt, at about the same time, 50,000 B.C. There is truly a link between the ancient people of the Nile and East and Central Africa." Cheyenne was so enthusiastic, she couldn't stop.

"The great civilizations in Egypt and the Sphinx have been estimated to have been built between 2600 and 2500 BC. The ancestors of these Sangoan or Homo sapiens from Central

Africa are, in my opinion, responsible for building ancient Egypt," Cheyenne said with excitement.

"Uganda is right next to Rwanda and at one time these two countries were one country. Today it has the same population make-up. I want to go there and learn more about who these people are," Shy added with passion.

"You seem to know more than most of us mere mortals know now. What else do you want or need to know?" asked Aunt Re reluctantly.

"Aunt Re, I want to know the truth. What has been hidden from the world for eons? What happened in between the oldest Homo sapiens's bones being found in East Africa to where Africa is today? What happened to the ancient Africans and their civilizations? What lies between the first man of African descent and today's African diaspora?"

"Your pursuit is noble, indeed; however, we will still worry about you no matter what you say. Africa has been made unstable by colonialism, slavery, and general plunder of its people and its land forever. Americans, especially Black Americans are not always viewed as friendly to the people there since a few Black Americans were paid to disrupt governments in Africa in the 1960s, I'm sorry to say. When your Aunt Wen went to three countries in West Africa in 1972 and performed, they were not allowed in Nigeria because they did not trust them. So please be careful and watch everything around you," Aunt Re pleaded.

"I will use the utmost discretion and caution. It never fazed me that I was venturing into what might not be a safe journey."

"The rest of us have thought about the perils of Africa, you can believe that", said Aunt Re. "Well anyway how did this big presentation develop that we are all invited to at your grandparent's house tonight? Of course, I won't be there. New York is not on my schedule at this time."

"It happened that sometime in mid–1993, thoughts of my adventure became a reality. I knew I had to face the facts of telling my boss and later my parents and grandparents. So, I arranged that one month before I left, I would let them know. One month is all I want to hear of the warnings, and any prolonged worry or talk of trying to stop me. It would be too late to stop me. After careful planning and assuring my future at Duran when I return from Africa, I made up my mind to tell everyone at one time and just get it over with at one time," Shy said, attempting to comfort her aunt. "And so, I leave next month."

"I can only argue on an emotional level. Go with God and do what you've got to do. Fly as high as you can, girl, and with your brain you can soar like an eagle," said Cheyenne's aunt lovingly and sincerely. Round one was unanimously won by Shy.

After they hung up Cheyenne's mind was reeling again. She saw a great gap in history between the builders of the ancient pyramids and the enslaved African, Cheyenne knew there existed a link. She knew that link of time and people lay in Central Africa and probably where she was headed, Rwanda. The only conclusion that lay ahead was to go investigate for herself, while at the same time make progress for the people of Africa, but Cheyenne felt there was more; more to do in the world, more to her and more to her life and much more than what she was doing at her job.

★★★★★★★

Thus began her sojourn into the unknown. She needed to experience this perplexing point of history that could not be overlooked, and she believed this would change the face of Africa forever, and maybe the world.

Cheyenne felt that as a twenty-eight-year-old African American woman executive, working for one of the greatest most successful companies on earth at Duran, Inc., there had to be only more and greater things ahead. She was fortunate every step of the way in her success. She was able to get this job through a friend, who mentored her from undergraduate and graduate school and is still with her today. It was time for Cheyenne to give back.

There was one obstacle that under ordinary circumstances would have kept her home. She thought back to that day, last summer when she told Leon. Leon Virgo, the man she had loved since childhood, had to know about her plans to go with the African Affairs Council to Rwanda. Leon took it well.

"In one month from now I will leave for Rwanda and Leon will be going to Egypt to do hands-on journalism on terrorism. I am fearful for him, but I love him too much to burden him with these concerns. He probably feels the same about my going to Rwanda. We both have a mission and purpose in our quests for truth," Cheyenne envisioned the future.

Speaking with Aunt Re put Cheyenne back into a state of deep concentration. She didn't hear or see Stacy come into her office and walk to her desk.

"Is there anything else Miss LaTour?" Stacy asked sadly. Cheyenne noticed her nervous fingering of some leftover confetti on the desk from the Bon Voyage party she threw for Cheyenne two days ago.

Stacy knew that any day Cheyenne would be leaving her, so it was hard for her to go over the daily routines. They built a kind and trusting relationship in the two years Stacy worked for Cheyenne.

Stacy is newly returning to work after being a stay-at-home mom for years. She was pulling herself and her family together after her divorce. Cheyenne and Stacy both demanded the best from one another and were never disappointed. They both had mutual respect. Cheyenne admired the fact that Stacy was putting herself through college and had helped her husband with his business when he left her, while raising a teenage man-child. Stacy forgave her husband, eventually healed herself, and moved on, but her son did not forgive his father for leaving him.

After their usual morning meetings and computer relays their lunch was quite memorable that day. Cheyenne had to get to Stacy's story before lunch ended and preferably before they entered the restaurant.

Finally, the truth came out about Stacy's trouble. Her son was with street boys who had stolen articles of clothing from a department store. He was taken to the precinct. Stacy had to get him. Charges would be dropped when four thousand dollars were paid to the store. He pleaded his innocence. When Stacy was with her son, he promised to move on from his father's mess, and live with self-love and forgiveness.

Before the lunch began, Shy was able to get a lawyer who looked at the store's footage that proved Stacy's son's innocence. After clearing up the entire disagreeable mess with Stacy's teenage son, he would be vindicated. They walked briskly to their favorite sandwich shop on Park Ave.

Stacy ordered pizza for two and Pepsi knowing it would be some time before Cheyenne indulged in junk food again. They finished eating feeling relieved and happy to know they shared and solved another problem in the world that day.

As they walked back to the office, they talked about the times Cheyenne and Stacy worked into the night with new computer users around the world who had the weight of hundreds, sometimes thousands of lives in their hands and would rely on Cheyenne's expertise to make their computers work efficiently.

Stacy reminded her of when Leon sent those huge bouquets of roses on special occasions like the night after a date or for any reason big or small. Stacy talked about all the other men at the office who questioned her about Cheyenne's availability and how she screened them. Cheyenne never knew about some of the interest that was paid to her, and she was grateful to Stacy for saving her the trouble of politely telling these men she was not available; Stacy was discreet yet diplomatically persuasive in her approach.

"Well, I guess we should get started with the rest of our workday. And don't forget, please ring Mr. Duran's office to let me know when he can see me this afternoon?"

"Thanks again for all your help. You will have our prayers everyday you are away, and I know God will bless you," Stacy said tearfully as she left Shy's office. Stacy's job at Duran, Inc., was secured for as long as she wanted it. Her computer knowledge was invaluable.

Cheyenne began talking as she cleared her desk of only a few more transmissions she had that day.

"I used to really enjoy the job, especially when I was sent to various places around the world to fix major companies' computers and equipment. The money has always been excellent but lately the routine of the office work has been the same. Working with machines all day, day after day, has become monotonous especially since I like working with people directly. I used to have five to six computers talking to each other around the world at one time sometimes. Nothing the COO asked of me seemed impossible by his standards and I always seemed to find a way for him to do whatever he deemed mandatory at the time. When did things turn?"

Suddenly a pigeon smashed into her window, half blinded by the snow. The noise jolted her back to the reality of the present situation. This would probably be her last day of work and being with the people she has come to know and love. The thought that this was not just another winter day in New York seemed to crush down upon her. Cheyenne prepared for the rejection she might receive from Mr. Duran.

The snow suddenly became gray, and the air turned hostile. Looking out from her office window she observed how busy New York was at this time, especially on Fifth Avenue, always so rushed and congested regardless of the weather. She peered down at the people trudging along through the snow; there must be one hundred thousand people moving along on one side of the street alone, she thought as she watched the madness below.

The people appeared like rodents below. This in no way concerned her, she was oblivious, and her mind was set on much more important matters.

"Today may be the turning point in my life, the next half an hour could determine my entire destiny. I am committed to my goals; however, everything rests on what this man that I am waiting to see did next. I wonder how the impact of his words will affect my decision. This meeting with Mr. Duran would either validate or nullify my dream. Reality certainly was about to set in.

"Mr. M.H. Duran did not become a multi-billionaire and world-renowned financier making foolish decisions, nor did he deny himself his dream. However, now it was time to put my own dreams into fruition. I am young, healthy, and attractive by most standards and more than capable of making a dent in this world..." she mused with consternation.

"Buzz", the intercom interrupted, "Mr. Duran will see you now, Miss LaTour," Stacy said, "He asked that you go up to his office."

CHAPTER 2

Fear is Hate, Hate is Fear

"…you have united with your source…; This
level cannot be attained until there is no
hatred in your heart, and no desire to attack."
<u>A Course in Miracles</u>, Healing

Stateside in 1994, in Chairman Fossel Gatt's office in the heart of Dixie, the Chairman's assistant, Woodrow Falt, pleads with him to stop a massacre before it begins.

"Why do this horrible thing, for God's sake? These people are the most harmless, innocent people in the world," Woodrow Falt began to beg Chairman Fossel Gatt, as he sickened with the thought of Gatt's intended crime.

"Listen boy, I don't want that kind of talk around here and you know it. Why hell, as we speak those jungle bunnies are practicing how to kill their own kind in the worst conceivable way. Needless to say, we couldn't stop this thing from happening if we wanted to. And since we started it, we don't want to stop it under any circumstances." Chairman Gatt loved listening to himself, as he stared down disapprovingly at Woodrow Falt.

"You know our mission is and always has been to dominate the world. You as a white man should know better, Woody. We have control of almost every land mass in the world including the French Indonesian Islands, and the natives of the Pacific region near Hawaii are totally under our control. Their life span is negligible with France testing nuclear bombs in the Pacific Ocean, anyway.

"Our Organization controls South America economically and politically and has taken possession of the rainforests, where the native Indians live within these jungles, through attrition. Drug wars keep us there.

"Africa is our only nemesis. It is the only continent where the native inhabitants still have most of the control over their land. Of course, our concerns and European businesses own the lumber, gold, diamonds, cobalt, silver, and most of the oil there, but some of it is still in the hands of the indigenous people, the Black Africans, especially West and North Africa. Africa is still the richest continent in the world for natural resources. Even with centuries of destroying and killing, they still have millions of savages there growing stronger and stronger.

"We want to control all of Africa even more so than the enslavers of the last six hundred years did. Africa without those jungle bunnies would be the gateway to paradise with the Mediterranean, Indian, Atlantic, and Antarctic Oceans surrounding it. We can control every other continent including Asia as long as the dragon continues to sleep. If we had the African continent, we could threaten Asia and the Middle East with our nuclear weapons lodged from Africa and pose a real threat and thus, economically rule the world. But we can't nuke Africa because of the treasures there," Chairman Gatt looked at a hot button he had on the panel of his phone, Woody shrunk with fear and nausea at the thought of this madman having so much power.

"Why shucks Woody, between Pakistan and India setting off nuclear bombs right on their own land, we don't even have to wait for them to destroy each other. They will eventually end life over there all by themselves. However, Africa is a friendly power to the U.S., and we cannot bomb it especially since we want their natural resources, and our investments are there.

"In other parts of the world we can generate enough hate of terrorism in Iraq, Syria, Jordan, and Iran to bomb these countries. Our Organization can't touch Egypt now that Israel has no war plans and is in control. So, you see, genocide is the fastest, easiest, and most uninvolved way we have of destroying the sub-Saharan Africans. And we have the means of making Civil Wars in these countries from coast to coast and from north to south right now.

"We have armed the savages in many countries in Africa for years and years to fight each other. We have it so that they don't even have to fight another country; they kill off each other in the same country. Somalia and Eritrea are our best examples. Their people are starving, there is famine, and yet they keep fighting each other. And if you ask me, they are the same people. We did well there," Chairman Gatt smiled to himself.

"In the other African Islamic countries north of the Sahara, we plan to destroy them openly ourselves in defense of the series of terrorist acts about to happen around the world. Some of these acts the Muslim terrorists will actually cause themselves and some we will generate and make it look like a terrorist enacted bombing," Chairman Gatt boasted in his almost flamboyant southern accent. He sat way back in his chair, folding his hands on his protruding stomach, looking at his assistant Woody Falt. Chairman Fossel Gatt was a Southern Senator for decades and had been newly appointed Chairperson to the Foreign Affairs Committee. He had intentions of crushing all non-white ruled countries, while he was in power. He knew he had considerable pull in the legislature, and with the Organization, he would stop any power or agency, including the United

States President that tried to impede this destructive end by any means necessary.

"I can't believe the power and range of the Organization..." Woodrow tried to say something that would bring some sense to this conversation, but he was cut off by the Chairman.

"Don't even think of saying what is in your head. You know these non-white people are nothing." Chairman Gatt had no tolerance for what he claimed was cowardice and feelings of compassion for dark people. Gatt was against any humane thinking and sympathy for any brown, black, red, yellow, or olive hued people and despised any white person that didn't agree with him. His hatred was innate as certain brain damage is inbred from incest. Woodrow was as usual ignored by the Chairman.

"Doggoned it to hell Woody, it's not safe to think any other way but ours. These blasted militia and Nazi groups we hired will kill as many whites as they will the others if their way is not honored as the one true way for white people. Look our hate white terrorist groups here in the U.S. are still hunting for the white families that gave them nigger slaves here shelter when they were escaping in the Underground Railroad more than one hundred years ago. That is how deep this hate thing goes. After this African thing goes through, we have painful things for those people of color here in the good old U.S. of A., which includes the reservation Indians that took our land. We will be a white country like our forefathers wanted it to be. Africa is the beginning."

Woodrow Falt knew only too well the power of the Organization. He wanted to ask what this hate thing was really about. The people of color in this world are no damn threat to anyone. In fact, Woody knew they were the friendliest people when a foreigner visited their countries. But he knew the history of the Organization, there was no reasoning with this dangerous group. It was established by prominent figures in the world who sent representatives from different countries around the world. The members all strived for similar goals - mainly world domination through elimination of the indigenous people of the world. They worked individually and in groups for their goal. The name of the plan for the Organization was 'Protocol 2000'. By 2001 hate and fear would be so instilled in the U.S. that the dominant political party in the Presidency and Legislative branches would have full reign over foreign affairs without dissent. Even Bilderberg had no control over them.

"Now look here Woody, this killing in Africa has been going on for centuries. Even today, those jungle bunnies, mainly those Muslims, use the poisonous gas the Germans in the Organization gave them, for their border skirmishes. They were encouraged to use these gasses against neighboring countries or Western countries that stood in their way. They also sold land mines in Angola and other African and Asian countries, and these people have been blowing themselves up ever since then, ha, ha. The only problem would be if these people decide to unite instead of killing each other.

"Heck we don't even really want Europe to unite. They are talking about one monetary unit, the Euro or something. That's not so good for us. But if Africa united, they could economically be a superior power in the world. Then what would we do for exploitation? I shudder to think about those damn Chinks over there and Japs and Koreans getting together in economic harmony. If that happens, we might as well surrender all our power. They would be unstoppable. Their sheer numbers alone would devastate us. Imagine a United Nations of Asia or Africa fighting for their people. I don't want to dwell on that too much. Plus, it ain't never gonna happen. They hate each other as much as the Organization hates them all."

"Yes, sir," Woody replied, too intimidated to say anything else, his heart slowly breaking. He was frozen in fear by his boss.

"Our biological and chemical warfare has already put diseases in these third world countries that they will never cure. We will watch out for their air borne diseases like smallpox, flu, and the like. We have more Africans with AIDS than anywhere else in the world. Two thirds of the sub-Saharan population are infected. And the dummies keep spreading it without protection. The men think screwing a virgin will cure them of AIDs; instead, they infect and impregnate another generation.

"No, my friend we are too close to think of these inferior people of the earth. Someday we shall have a pure earth with only a few of these darker kinds as servants or worse, to do our dirty work and be our guinea pigs for science, and maybe entertain us with their primitive customs." Chairman Fossel Gatt, lll, was immensely proud of the success and accomplishments of the Organization's agenda. He was especially pleased with his major effort for the last fifty years, of the Organization's dissolute birth, in the Senate where the most significant racist legislation was his doing.

The Chairman personally plotted much of the havoc the Organization caused. He began with seeds of destruction after World War II with his fiendish plot to poison the will and trust of the nations of Africa while they started gaining their independence in the 1950s and 1960s. He was very instrumental in keeping the war alive during the Indonesian countries' fight for freedom against European colonization, Christianity, and communism. Later he involved the U.S. in Vietnam. His racist and anti-communist legislation helped quell any activist movement against the policies of the U.S. in foreign or domestic affairs, especially in the 1950s.

Chairman Gatt eased back in his leather chair, knowing he'd get no argument. He spat in his spittoon angrily, as if Woodrow Falt, his loyal assistant, would dare not see things his way. His office was permeated with reminders of his beliefs and hatreds. His mentality was immersed with relics of an uncivilized, violent, and barbaric old southern lifestyle.

He had a confederate flag placed next to the American Flag, on the left and right of his chair, respectively. The Confederate Flag recalled for him the time when Blacks were treated as if they were childlike animals and knew their place, and killing one was as unpunishable as stepping on an ant. He believed it was more profitable to work a nigger to death, rather than killing one, though..

This was a tobacco state so smoking, even in this day and age, was not only permitted but nearly required. By the door he had a two-foot-tall black jockey statue holding an ashtray instead of the lantern southern homes still have on their lawns; beside the jockey stood a painted sculpture of a Native American with ceremonial feather headdress holding a cigar box in his hand. These were what made Chairman Gatt happy, as he looked forward to seeing these oppressive relics again in his version of the south.

But his proudest monument and testimony of his true convictions was the painting of his grandfather, a boorish slave owner, Confederate Colonel Fossil J. Gatt, pompously mounted between the paintings of Jefferson Davis and General Robert E. Lee. Other faded symbols of truculence and uncompromising bigotry surrounded the old, dying senator during the last five decades in his worn, faded, decrepit, creased leather chair, an attribute of the chairman himself.

Chairman Gatt always engaged in his daily work of trying to hold onto something that should never have been sanctioned in the first place. His office was full of strife and suffering for the two groups who helped make America, first the Native Americans, whose land was stolen, and second the African Americans, whose free labor brought the wealth that made America what it is today.

★★★★★★★★★★

Woodrow Falt understood his position, sad as it was. Yet he was torn between what he knew to be right and the fear of being eliminated permanently. He had to keep silent and not let it be known what was going to happen to Rwanda and the world. So, he smothered his guilt with hard drink and the prestige and perks associated with being an assistant to the chairman. He was confident of his ability and knowledge, yet deep down inside he longed to be someplace else working with someone other than the senator. Like a maggot sucking on a rotten piece of pork, here he was, sucking up to the senator and this Organization that still secretly and continually permeates and destroys the innocent.

Woody also knew that Rwanda was chosen next for genocidal homicide by the Organization because the Rwandese population was growing too fast and the land has valuable minerals, like coltan used in computers, and other precious minerals, as well as a potential for fuel. This was cause for alarm to the European power brokers since Rwanda had the world's richest iron supply and it was called the "Riviera of Africa" by Europeans who frequently vacationed by Rwanda's beautiful Kivu Lake.

He wondered how the rest of the world would forgive the Organization this time for infiltrating and devising havoc and mayhem on innocent people. He recalled the gentle movie from Rwanda 'Gorillas of the Mist', filmed in Rwanda's Volcanic Mountain National Park which permanently enshrined and protected the gorilla. Even this movie generated strife for the Rwandan people, whose land is used to grow the food their growing population needs, as they began pushing the boundaries for the Gorilla National park.

"Desolation is inevitable for all of Africa since our European brotherhood has generationally destroyed and taken from Africa," the chairman interrupted Woody's thoughts.

"Africans are totally inferior to us, you know this, Woody. We have gone from thinking Africans had tails to dealing with them as half animals and half children. We have treated them this way from the moment we set foot upon the rich ancient civilizations of Mali and Egypt to the Primitive African societies of today. Furthermore, this war will help us initiate wars within almost all sub-Saharan countries. We want their natural resources, and their corrupt leaders are willing to sell their people back into slavery to get power and wealth for themselves," Senator Gatt was happy to have a rich destructive history to back him up.

"Yes sir."

"Rwanda is an easy target because of the ethnic strife Europeans have helped manifest for centuries there. Once Rwanda goes into its fatal final civil war, the whole of central and east Africa will be decimated, especially the Congo. The bordering country, Congo, has a particular mineral that the Western world will take.

"As you know, Woody, Rwanda exists on a fragile curve of privilege for the minority ethnic group, Tutsi, over the other indigenous majority Hutu and Twa people. This has caused the Tutsi to be massacred since the end of WWII when Germany lost and France and lastly Belgium took over permanently.

"The third ethnic group and first to populate Rwanda were the Twa, who are of no consequence at all and are powerless against both the Tutsi and Hutu. For the present, Rwanda is under the leadership of the majority Hutu. The Hutu president wants to have peaceful, equal partnership with the Tutsi. However, to his eventual demise, we have persuaded his Hutu comrades to overthrow this peaceful coexistence."

"Yes sir."

"Rwanda has become a healthy country despite the colonialism imposed by the European governments that took control. The population has increased to the point that they need to expand into the Volcano Mountains for farmland for their people. You know we'd rather protect the gorilla than make room for those people to farm. Their life span goes beyond forty years old, and this is bad for us because that is the time men and women really start thinking about the world around them. Their tea and coffee crops are becoming popular around the world, not only in Europe.

"Yes, this is a suitable time for the Organization to begin to destroy this country. We have an advantage especially now since these two groups are finding excuses for small fights. The Hutus could easily be swayed to hate each Tutsi, literally to death. This ethnic death will spread into the Congo, Burundi, Uganda, and other Central African countries because they are the same people. The Organization wants Rwanda, and we are going to get it no matter what it costs. And with the destruction of Rwanda would come the destruction of Sub-Saharan Africa from the Atlantic to the Indian Ocean.

"These wild tribes are so caught up in their different ethnic cultures, they will continue fighting and killing each other to keep their own beliefs dominant. This is not even a religious battle as 90% of the Rwandans are Catholics. They will fight Christian against Christian throughout Central Africa, for no reason, mark my words. They will think it is over power, but they have none. They won't even notice us taking over again. Then the Muslims will take a shot and we will destroy them, legitimately," the senator was off on a tangent and Woody paid little attention.

Woody was glad of at least one thing, alerting his friend M.H. Duran, to this latest of tragedies to be initiated by the Organization. He looked forward to being dismissed for the day so he could make his phone call.

So, with the self-confidence and assuredness that his flunky would obey and not betray him, after lunch the senator bid Woody a fond farewell for the rest of the day. With that Woody immediately got on the phone to his friend, M.H. Duran.

"Hello, M.H. this is your old friend Woody. What I have to tell you is so sensitive we must meet someplace in private immediately. But let me tell you, it's about Rwanda, I'm afraid there is trouble brewing."

"Here we go again, eh? Another civil war, different country, after Somalia I thought the U.S. would be finished. At all and any costs, Woody, let's get our people out of there, not like we did in..." M.H. was interrupted by one of his protégés entering the office, Cheyenne Latour. M.H. had an idea of what was going to happen, he needed to know when it was going to happen.

Woody knew Duran had business interests in Rwanda and thought he might be able to protect his people and business concerns there before the horror began. For Woody knew this was the next country slated for destruction by the Organization.

They had Liberia on their knees, and even Libya was being troubled.

After discussing the destruction about to befall the Central African countries with M.H. Duran, Woody felt dispirited and melancholy. Later that night, Woody drank himself into a stupor. His heart would not forgive. Depression compounded by the chemical changes hard liquor brings to the body and mind made Woody succumb to an even deeper state of wretchedness. He saw no escape for the people he befriended and enjoyed on his safaris and visits to Africa. This beautiful continent will fall to destruction and mayhem before the takeover, he thought.

He realized this when he danced and played with the beautiful Polynesians on their islands of the Pacific who could not surmise or elude their ultimate outcome. He also couldn't understand why anyone could hate the indigenous people of the rainforests around the world who don't even know their destroyers exist. He wrote down everything he knew and mailed it to M.H's home. The cold black night seemed endless to Woody. Not being able to stand the grief any longer, he tried to end his life with the gun the Chairman gave him. This weapon was intended for Woody to protect his life, not take it.

If Woody had only known of the one obstacle that could perhaps hold back the tide of destruction ahead. One African American group and M.H. Duran's large conglomerate would attempt to pull Rwanda together and bring the country into the modern world with telecommunications and computer technology. They believed the placement of advanced technology and the promise of a brighter future would bring the people of Rwanda together.

At the forefront of the turmoil and war that would inevitably lie ahead would emerge an unlikely survivor, M.H. Duran's protégée, a young African American woman, Cheyenne Latour.

CHAPTER 3

Self-Determination

"... if you have faith as a grain of mustard seed,
you can say to this mountain 'Move from
there,' and it will move. KJV Matt. 17:20

The intercom buzzed, jolting Cheyenne out of deep thought.
"Mr. Duran will see you now, Miss Latour," Stacy said, "He
asked that you go up to his office."

Cheyenne reminded herself she had nothing to worry
about. Mr. Duran liked her. He told her often how he admired
her intelligence, poise, and determination, and he did not want
to lose such an indispensable asset to his company. Though
Cheyenne had been telling him of her plans for a long time,
she knew her departure would be difficult whether it was
temporary or permanent.

She took the elevator up to the eighty-eighth floor and
turned right to Mr. Duran's suite of luxurious offices and
mega-sized conference room. The elegance spewed forth
as soon as the elevator opened to his floor. Revealed to the
fortunate few who were privy to be invited to this floor was a
dazzling spectacle of lush opulence of the thick carpeting and
marble flooring, and beautiful masterpiece paintings by an
array of international artists. One could stand around and gaze
as if in an art museum admiring the color and brilliance of a
Picasso, the complexity and movement of Marcel Duchamp,
the campiness of Roy Liechtenstein, the mythical and haunting
African ceremonies portrayed in Zombie Jamboree's paintings,

and the absolute artistry of Dr. John Biggers bringing the ancestors to life in the present with ancient African symbols.

Cheyenne walked the familiar yet exciting hallway down to the offices devoted solely to Mr. Duran's personal business, and his beloved collection of African art. Within these walls one could find works of art from Mali, South Africa, ancient Somalia, and Egypt.

Mr. Duran's secretary greeted Cheyenne and silently motioned for her to proceed directly into his office. Mr. Duran was on the telephone. This was more like a mansion than an office. It had everything including a grand piano for his personal delight. He often played it to contemplate a particularly troublesome thought to solution. Cheyenne smiled as she was reminded of Sherlock Holmes, who would pensively play his violin to solve mysteries.

As with any great and true connoisseur of art, his office displayed only the finest sculpture in the world. Elizabeth Catlett's gracious and curvaceous marble and onyx works graced his wall along with large pieces by Henry Moore, Ed Dwight and one Julio Gonzales' sculpture. In the center of the room were the great pieces by Richard Hunt and David Smith. These pieces seemed to dress the room impeccably framed by the huge panorama of New York City, shown through ceiling to floor windows. The lighting was brilliant yet not a single bulb was visible to the eye, and the color of the walls and carpeting blended, only to accentuate the art and the man.

Overseas again, Cheyenne thought as she looked at the back of his chair listening to the commanding yet softly spoken voice of her boss as he commanded his intention in some covert plan.

"Now look, Woody, let's at all costs protect our interests and get our people out as soon as possible, the moment before trouble starts. Don't wait until the last minute as you did in..." M.H. Duran's back was toward Cheyenne, but when he swiveled his chair around and noticed her, he stopped his conversation flat and tilted his face with a suspicious eye in her direction, wondering what she might have gleaned from the conversation.

"I'll call you back shortly, Woody." Duran hung up abruptly and turned his attention to his favorite protégée. Without hiding affection, he smiled broadly at Cheyenne; he openly loved her as a daughter.

M.H. Duran was a towering six-foot four inch, slim and slightly graying man in his mid-fifties. His slender physique looked magnificent in his custom-tailored Versace suit and shirt. His shoes were the most beautiful color leather ever seen. His tie matched everything, even his eyes, ever so subtly.

"Well Shy, my dear sweet child, what can I do for you?" Duran asked in his fatherly, yet non-condescending tone, and one could see that he wondered if Cheyenne heard part of his call.

He continued before she could respond, "I heard about your going away bash on the fortieth floor the other day. How was it? I am sorry I didn't come, but I was in Japan; heard it was the best," Duran asked and answered.

From the time he met Cheyenne, theirs was more than a boss-employee relationship. One night while she was working late, sometimes until 3 a.m. in the morning Duran would come to her with a problematic communications relay he received about his interests in Liberia and Mauritania. Cheyenne didn't know he was the heir of the Duran Corporation the first time she talked with him. Cheyenne helped him through his problem as she would anyone else who asked her. Over time she was able to explain to Duran how to send the information through the computer. She taught him the system so that he could program the computer himself if necessary. They worked after hours for months.

Cheyenne was the only person he trusted in aspects of his software skills training. She taught him how to use the million-dollar programs he had installed for his personal business use. She carefully explained the operation of the systems to him, and he was forever grateful.

Finally, one evening while they worked Mr. Duran told Cheyenne who he was. She reacted in her usual casual way and asked, "Do you understand a little better Mr. Duran?"

He had expected a little more of a reaction. But then that would have been unnatural. Cheyenne was not the star struck kind. Since they had worked for so long together on a first name basis and she was his teacher, so to speak, she was comfortable with him. Her honesty and self - assurance were the two things he had never seen before in anybody other than himself.

He genuinely liked Cheyenne. She was the only person of color he could honestly relate to and not feel superior over as some other people made him feel. They had a relationship based on trust, admiration, and kindness, with a touch of love and respect. So, today was a difficult goodbye.

"Mr. Duran, you know how I appreciate your wisdom and the knowledge you have shared with me. I know I would never have this information without being in the old boys' network. I thank you for the bonuses and the promotions." She remembered one Christmas she received a thirty-five-thousand-dollar bonus aside from her salary checks. What pleased her most about her entire situation at the job was that she was autonomously employed with no immediate supervisors, basically him and his administrative assistant.

Cheyenne went on to say, "How can I express the way I feel toward you? I believe you are the magician who can change straw into gold and a young Black, M.B.A. degreed woman, into a world class businessperson confident enough to deal with any world leader. You have been my guru, and the private tutelage you gave me with investments could never be appraised. What I'm about to say is the toughest thing in the world for me. Even though I really could see myself retiring here in another forty years or so, extraordinarily rich, and very connected, right now my lifelong quest is to go to Africa. I feel led to seek out the true beginnings of humanity and offer my humble services to Rwanda's new fiber optic cable, internet business. It's my life's mission. I feel I know my true purpose here on earth. As it is everywhere, I look only at the so-called primitive indigenous people of the world as living according to God's plan, simple, loving communities of family and friends. I need to know why and how they continue. There is a spirit within me that tells me that I must share my knowledge with my people, first in Africa and then back in the U.S."

This was more difficult for her to say than she thought it would be. Mr. Duran was looking heartbroken as he listened. She could tell from his glance that she no longer had to say anything. Mr. Duran was taking it all in his way.

There was a pensive silence between the two of them. Suddenly both Cheyenne and Duran simultaneously said, "Do you remember when we met for the first time here at the office?"

At her interview Cheyenne never saw Mr. Duran. The two of them recalled different events that brought them close to each other. She could tell Mr. Duran had a flashback of Cheyenne's file that journeyed across his subconscious. Everything she told him and everything he found out from her school, her mentor and his contacts became a pictorial filtering through his mind's eye, as Cheyenne sat admiringly before him.

Cheyenne could almost feel Mr. Duran's thoughts as they compiled the history that shaped her destiny and molded her youthful endeavors. Her blessings were abundant from earlier lucky and well guided choices encouraged by her parents. By the time she graduated from Brooklyn Tech High School, New York's best technical public school at age 16, everything seemed to fall into place for her. She majored in industrial design engineering. She excelled beyond her expectations in high school and received a full scholarship to Tufts University with an additional $1000 award for maintaining an A average in high school.

Cheyenne LaTour Curriculum Vitae

I. *Academic honors and achieving entrance into Brooklyn Technical High School*
   A. *Outstanding Academic Scores; Above average SAT and Regents Scores*
   B. *Full participation in academic, political, and social school activities in and out of high school*
II. *Tufts University full four-year scholarship student*
   A. *Worked part time at Department of Health of Massachusetts*
   B. *Petitioned Dean at Tufts for academic credit and succeeded*
III. *Sophomore year summer-took five courses in Public Administration*
   A. *Worked in Computer Communications in Engineering Department*
   B. *At Department of Health showed psychologist how to measure brain waves (biofeedback) with computers*
IV. *Junior year received graduate minority fellowship in engineering*
   A. *At Department of Health collaborated with Epidemiologists*
   B. *Helped lobby for prenatal care using computer data*
V. *Senior year wrote technical instruction manuals with engineers from prestigious New Jersey company*

A. *Took classes at Rutgers University*
B. *Received full fellowship to Washington University from the School of Engineering*
VI. *Internship at NOAA (National Oceanic and Atmospheric Administration)*
   A. *Programmed communications data for the national weather service*
   B. *Used COBOL, a computer programming language, fed mainframe for real time stock market data*
VII. *Graduated January with a Master's in Computer Science Polytechnic University NY*

The seed for Cheyenne's desire to go to Africa began with her exploring the epidemiology of the U.S.. Epidemics were much more prevalent in Africa, Asia, and the Central American countries. These countries were the most exploited, but the people were helped the least.

Mr. Duran looked over Cheyenne's credentials and again was reminded of the determination in this young woman. She did it not because she is a revolutionary, but from needing to be expedient and practical.

She gave the best reports her previous bosses had ever seen, and this information and her reputation for sending quality work preceded her working at Duran. She was hired instantly.

Now M.H. Duran peered at this genius protégé who achieved so much before the age of twenty-five years. On the job Cheyenne started out as a communication analyst. Her work in data collection was later implemented in sale calls and later used in election campaigns.

It was clear once again, that left to her own initiative she would develop and invent great strides in communications. Her job then expanded to talking to the mainframe. She created programs that linked computers all over the world. As a result, management positions opened up in other departments as well. Word spread rapidly about her helpful interest in getting people to understand complex computer programming.

She was sent to Australia, Stockholm, Geneva, and Zurich to name only parts of the world she visited. When the computer didn't work after she spoke to the users over the phone, she'd fly out to fix it. Later her newly appointed manager got word from Duran to keep her around the office more. With Cheyenne nearby Duran could learn more about computers.

However, the people in Geneva and other places wanted Cheyenne to come back. She was sent one last time. She sat with an older woman in Geneva over the computer, in a Mom-and-Pop type of company. It was then that she realized how good she was at training people and how they enjoyed learning from her. This was a turning point in her career.

When she returned to the office, the manager gave her tedious work, and the traveling stopped. She ended up back where she started, and something clicked for her. She could use her skills teaching and training instead of fixing other people's problems on the computer.

After working almost three years at Duran she sought out her old Brooklyn contacts. They participated in setting up telecommunications in Africa with AT&T. AT&T was establishing satellite communications to link up all of Africa, eventually, on cable.

The African Affairs Council, having members in the engineering and telecommunications departments at AT&T, decided to create the foundation for this African Communications endeavor. They, of course, told Cheyenne about it. The prospects of working with an entire country in Africa to set up telecommunications and cable was exciting to her.

She wrestled with conflicting thoughts of her fervent desire to lean into this project in Africa and staying in the comfort of life in Brooklyn and Manhattan. It took months to make the choice to move forward and go with the African Affairs Council to Rwanda and help set up telecommunications and cable, via satellite. She knew they could use her expertise. Settling for lesser work at Duran's lost out over moving to an unknown challenge.

Mr. Duran listened soberly, then realized for the first time that she was really going to be leaving him and gave a sigh of loss and pride as she stood humbly before him. Even if the odds were against her, God was with her always, as Mr. Duran knew. She would not be destroyed.

Mr. Duran had this strange, yet kind look in his eyes and tears began to well up as he looked into her eyes and saw the certainty, the confidence, and that she knew exactly what she was doing. But he knew another fate for Rwanda that he could not reveal.

"Say no more Shy. I know what your heart is saying and what you are about to tell me. We have already discussed your need to pursue your gift for helping people to understand the complexities of the computer world. After all, look what you have done for me."

Duran pointed to an adjacent room with mainframes buzzing and computers flashing that he alone could manage..

"I do understand," Duran looked at her admiringly with a smile.

"Thank you, Mr. Duran, I....," Cheyenne said, words eluded her as a rush of warmth enveloped her.

"When you complete your work would you be willing to come back to us with an upgraded salary, retroactive to date?" Duran had to ask.

"Yes, of course I would, Mr. Duran," Shy answered.

"Believe it or not, before I got into business and made millions, I set out to right the wrongs of the world, physically, alone, trying to help in my own way. The world being the way it is, taught me a lesson, and I knew that power and money can effect change."

Mr. Duran continued, "You may not always find things in a state of balance. Sometimes your efforts are thwarted by outside forces that have nothing to do with you or your mission. People may appreciate your efforts, but the only true reward is your own internal satisfaction in fulfilling the universe's purpose for you. Don't always look for others to be grateful or acknowledge your sacrifices. Do it because you are concerned and doing what you feel is right in this world. I believe the spirit within you is leading you to Rwanda, Shy. It may not be for the reasons you think. I believe in you, so I give you my blessings and I won't stand in your way. I may want to stop you for your own safety, but it is not what the world wants."

"Thank you, Mr. Duran, you have confirmed my convictions."

"My last words to you are from Og Mandino's, The Greatest Salesman, 'You have mastered the art of living not for yourself alone, but for others, and this concern has stamped you above all, as a special human among all humankind'." Duran was in another sphere of reality now; a peaceful calm was transfixed over his demeanor.

"I understand sir." Cheyenne was fascinated, she had never heard him say things like this before to anyone. And she never saw him go into this trance-like state as he did now; it was both exhilarating and scary at the same time.

"Shy, another phrase from Mandino's book will serve you well if you remember it when things go wrong, '...Each struggle, each defeat, sharpens your skills and strengths, your courage and your endurance, your ability and your confidence and thus each obstacle is a comrade forcing you to become better or quit'." He knew he may not ever see his protégé again, but he could not hold her back. This was not about him and forgiving her, it was about letting go and letting God.

They hugged and tears flowed freely from them both.

"Let my secretary draw up the papers for your return. If you want to come back to the job when you return from Africa, your job will be waiting. AT&T provided me with one of their experts for now. You can have the rest of the week off to take care of your business. I know you've been looking forward to this for a long time and nothing should stop you from your heart's desire."

★★★★★★★★★★★

She walked carefully through the snow to the subway, mentally preparing to break the news to her family and friends at home. Cheyenne gathered strength and held on to the validation she received from Mr. Duran. She dazedly traveled to her grandparent's home on the subway, resolute in her mission.

The rush hour had not yet begun, so the consistent muffled, noise of the metal wheels hitting the metal tracks that filtered through her subconscious did not disturb her thoughts. She knew that if her parents felt the strong will within her and knew that a consciousness had determined her way, they would only pray for her success and know that this is the will of a greater force other than their own.

★★★★★★★★★

Little did she know that Mr. M.H. Duran's business interests were in the very country to which she was going. Cheyenne could have never guessed that Duran had knowledge, from Woodrow Falt, Chairman Gatt's aide, that civil war was to break out soon in that country. While Mr. Duran helped prepare materials and transportation for her departure, contributing to the African Affairs Council, he also planned for her and other American's evacuation. Deep inside he wanted Cheyenne to succeed, but he knew her mission was doomed from the start.

Other than sister city groups in the U.S., this was the first and only African American business/education sponsored group to go to Africa to work. Dr. Alphaeus Hunton, a founding member of the African Affairs Council, was living in Ghana when he began writing the Encyclopedia of Africa. Dr. Hunton helped initiate the distribution of food and supplies to South Africa in 1946 and helped Kwame Nkrumah gain independence for Ghana in the 1950's. However, today, this was the revived Council's first effort since the original African Affairs Council was shut down by the US government in 1955 for gaining momentum against the Jim Crow laws and racism experienced by Black soldiers after WWII and southern Blacks. Unbeknownst to the new Councils' ideas, this trip to Rwanda would change the African Affairs Council's mission forever.

Mr. Duran covertly arranged for his own special forces unit to be ready for military maneuvers and secure all of his operations in Rwanda. He wanted more time, but time was not to be factored into this plan.

This war was imminent; months or days away, no one really knew when it would begin. He could do one of two things; sell his interests in Rwanda to a German or Japanese concern or abandon everything until after the war and resume business when the Rwandan government was secured again.

The Organization and other groups like it already knew the results of this soon to be conflict. Duran was helpless in preventing the war and helpless in warning people of it. It didn't matter what he decided to do. If he tried to warn friendly forces of the impending war the information would be intercepted, since all international data was filtered through certain countries and the Organization would know first.

Major General Dallaire's, from the U.N. peacekeeping force, messages were intercepted long before the U.N. received them. Kofi Annan in the U.N. was given a diluted version of the atrocities about to happen and clearly asked the Major General to not intervene or disarm the stashed armaments. The Organization would either stop the data from going any further or find out the source of the data and eliminate it. Mr. Duran hated the Organization. His fight was greater than anyone could imagine. Personally, he could forgive the individuals in the Organization, but as a whole they were a malignant virus.

Duran focused on the most important part of this equation that mattered, protecting Cheyenne.

"I don't want to disillusion her, and I cannot confront her with what I know. Race wars would break out everywhere in the world with disproportional dimensions and results. Because of the powerlessness of the oppressed people of color, the Organization would still continue their efforts to foster a genocidal war in central Africa and watch it reach from ocean to ocean across Africa.

"No, an outright confrontation might result in the world taking sides and at this time most people would lose to this hatred driven group of minority whites. Things had to be done differently, events would have to take their course," he thought out loud. However, he knew how he would manipulate the results. It would be different than what the Organization was expecting. He must wait for the right time and then expose the Organization once and for all!!

CHAPTER 4

The Announcement

"...Ye are Gods." KJV St. John 10:34

It was a typically cold January 18th day in New York. As usual the snow was relentless and nasty, as snow becomes within minutes after falling to the ground in Brooklyn. There was a peaceful calm over the old neighborhood. She could only hear her own footsteps crunching through the snow as there was no traffic in sight. The sidewalks were without the usual throng of pedestrians, and Cheyenne could see only the snow capped building roofs and snow encased storefront windows, as she headed for her grandparents' house.

The curbs became sinkholes of snow and wet slush as this trip entailed walking eight long blocks from the subway. Driving had been out of the question because she knew parking in Brooklyn after a snowstorm was impossible for at least three days. Cars looked like an extension of the sidewalk, as the snowplows encased them in a hill on the passenger side. Cabs did not run in inclement weather and were difficult to get in mild weather in this neighborhood. Mindfulness for Shy was on overdrive while walking in the ice-cold snow mounds.

Unlike any other part of the city, the streets of Bedford-Stuyvesant Brooklyn took on a country almost rural feel. In Manhattan, the retailers and hotel staff cleaned the snow from the curbs and sidewalks immediately, but in Brooklyn, sometimes the shop keepers would wait until it melted and warmed up enough to soften before they shoveled the snow.

The snow may be patted down into small mounds or narrow pathways by the feet of the consumers before it was shoveled, days later.

The long blocks were tranquil and quiet. With the sidewalks empty the Brownstone houses were lined up in straight connected rows as far as the eyes could see. The snow engulfed her feet with each step. It sounded like she was stepping on Styrofoam cartons, and it felt like the eggs were inside the boots.

The drifts were remarkably high, and most people decided to leave their cars parked where they were. Since there was no alternate street parking, cars were parked on both sides of the street, safe for the moment from the ticket dispensers and tow trucks. The cars were covered with snow up to the windows and the front and back windshields were completely white. The only way you could recognize your own car was on the sidewalk area, the snow partially revealing a door handle or side fender. Cars were covered by the drifts revealing only big white bumps in the snow. The next day people would try to remember where they parked or wait until the snow melted a little so they could find their vehicles.

Nearly everyone was inside enjoying their own cozy warmth. Those few outside on the main thoroughfares walked in the street. People seemed to have a friendlier look during their snow walks. It's like everybody was saying, "Hey, you live in New York, so you got to deal with toughing it out now and then."

Cheyenne observed that the snow was clean and white as she sank into the bog of snowdrifts covering her parents' street and sidewalks. Children were playing in the middle of the residential streets, sleighing on garbage can tops, and shoe-skiing and sliding on cardboard. Small children were throwing snowballs and yelling for no apparent reason except that it was fun. Cheyenne remembered doing similar things when she was a child, especially when schools closed for snow days.

Those were the best times when everyone had time off from school and would dress their warmest and then go outside to scream and play and laugh until their fingers began to freeze. Then go in all rosy cheeked and get some hot chocolate and warm up in bed or with a blanket on the couch, while the moms would rub warmth into their cold extremities.

Suddenly, Cheyenne felt a twinge of guilt. Her internal dialogue took over. She felt slightly reluctant about telling her parents and grandparents of her plans to go to Africa. She knew they would hate the idea of her leaving. Cheyenne's parents loved her so much, and she had never let them down. They were grateful for her as much as she was grateful for the two of them. Especially since they saw five of their friends' children fall prey to some Bed-Stuy neighborhood fears: drugs, lethargy, disease, and death. Cheyenne has avoided that fate by receiving academic scholarships to Tufts University and a fellowship for graduate studies at New York Polytechnic for her master's and worked during her entire college experience. She now pensively strolled up Malcolm X Boulevard to Hancock Street.

"Jiminy Crickets!" GranNellie exclaimed as Cheyenne whizzed through the door from the freezing cold to warm herself. She pecked her grandmother on the cheek and ran inside.

Cheyenne thought, "Nothing has changed with GranNellie and grandpa especially knowing they have been married for fifty-six years."

She knew her granddad was undoubtedly glued to sports, or sensationalist journalism show on TV in his favorite recliner and GranNellie was in the kitchen as usual. Shy's two sisters were playing. A big crash echoed from their bedroom as if on cue. Her grandmother waited for crying, and with no distinguishable sound, she kept doing what she was doing. She knew nothing in that den of an iniquity room of theirs was of any value.

Cheyenne came out to the kitchen where her grandmother was preparing dinner. Her grandmother, Mrs. Nellie LaTour fixed dinner for her husband, Tommy, every night for all fifty-six years of their married life at the exact same time at six p.m. She kissed her grandmother again and grabbed a piece of a chicken wing already carved, and then went in to see her granddad.

She kissed him, and he fanned his hand, as if her chicken breath bothered him, and had small talk with him. Her grandmother called everyone in for dinner and they sat down. They all ceremoniously blessed the food and ate dinner in the kitchen around the table as always. The usual silliness went on with her younger twin sisters and lecture from granddad on how to behave. Grandmother had to tell Ali, the perkiest twin, about food.

"Shy, we had a good laugh today, Ali asked me what the difference between lettuce and cabbage was, Ca answered, 'one you cook.' I had to laugh at my two preteen cooks." Her dazzling smile infected all and even Ali had to laugh at herself.

As soon as dinner was done, as if in an unwritten script in a play, everyone rose and placed their dish in the sink, washed it, put it into the rack, and vacated the kitchen in a sudden wave. The girls anxiously disappeared to their quarters to play loudly and rudely as twelve-year olds must do and her grandparents resumed their positions watching the TV and reading the paper simultaneously.

The kitchen had been remodeled when Cheyenne's father

was still in high school. Web married young and had one daughter. Web was what everyone called him because his parents named him Wendell, after Oliver Wendel Holmes, his middle name Edgar, after his mother's favorite Edgar Alan Poe, and his third name, Bakari after Abul Bakari the African Navigator who sailed from Mali and began the Olmec Empire in Mexico with the Mayan Indians in 1350 B.C. They are all great names, but it's a mighty big load for your average African American young man.

The house was over one hundred years old, and nothing had been done to it when her grandparents moved in after their wedding. Years later they remodeled. The bathroom was moved from the unheated shed leading to the backyard and modernized for inside the house.

There was a tin ceiling in the den that was repeatedly painted. Cheyenne later found out that was a prized New York feature in homes.

She remembered her best friend Dava Love, when as children they would run through the front yard gate and into the kitchen to hide under the counter or get water, or peek into the den, then run out again to play some more.

Cheyenne confided nearly everything to Dava and vice versa. When they were five years old, they became mercurochrome sisters, in the shed bathroom before the renovation. They didn't have the nerve to cut themselves to become blood sisters. They promised to never keep secrets. As much as they could, they would tell each other everything. There are things that never needed to be repeated was Cheyenne's belief. But Dava didn't mind telling Cheyenne the most intimate of intimate things, which was all right.

Being in this house, memories began to fill her thoughts. Her third-grade teacher was Dava's mom. This was the only year of her school life they separated and were not placed in the same class. For some reason, the Board of Education, City of New York, did not allow a parent to teach their own child in public school. Most people disagreed with the idea. And one day, Cheyenne raised her hand in class and said "Mommy" to Mrs. Love, Dava's mom. The whole class laughed.

Cheyenne remembered this for the rest of her life not that she called Mrs. Love 'mommy', but that the class laughed. She will never forget how the next day Dava ran into her classroom and told the class that they were sisters, and her mom was as much Cheyenne's mom as hers and dared anyone to laugh. Dava hated to see her friend hurt even for a childish minute.

They don't make them like Dava anymore, Cheyenne thought as she looked around the house as if it could be her last time recalling old memories. She knew when she left for Africa she would never be the same again. The time was right for telling her mom and dad. Now she had to begin her defense for going to Africa.

The doorbell brought Shy's parents into the fold. The girls came roaring downstairs hugging them then escaping back to play.

"Mommy, Daddy, GranNellie, Grandpa, I have to tell you something very important concerning my future," Cheyenne blurted out after the small talk and when there was a minute between the commercials. They turned, slightly startled, but seeing her smile, they were assured she was all right, not sick or hurt.

She knew the news she was about to tell them would be astonishing and a little frightening to both parents and grandparents of hers. They both were brought up in households with depression era parents. They knew none of the people in their lives would ever quit an excellent job and seek a new

45

destiny like their daughter was about to tell them she was going to do.

Shy was always encouraged by her Aunt Wen. Her aunt had some experiences in civil rights and protesting that were family lore. Aunt Wen gave the speech Robert Kennedy spoke at her Erasmus Hall High School graduation in 1967.

"Before I say what I need to say, remember when, R. Kennedy said, 'The world which you enter is a world in revolution, and war,...for uncounted centuries they have lived with hardship with hunger and disease. For the last four centuries they have lived under the economic, political, and military domination of the west.'

"He went on to say, 'This revolution is directed against us, the successful and the rich and the mighty, against the established order of which we are the principal part.

'The Democratic system of government is subversive in a few countries. Our choice is whether to support the status quo, or the forces of change; whether to sit content in our storehouse or share our wealth with our fellow human beings around the world.

'Fulfill the promise in the world or within our gates, the revolution will fulfill the promises of the Constitution for all America.

'Our answer is the world's hope. In your hands, not with presidents or leaders, is the future of your world and the fulfillment of the best qualities of your own spirit.'

Cheyenne added, "Robert Kennedy was killed just before M.L. King, Jr. was killed, Aunt Wen, you and students at Howard took over the administration building, and after "Eyes on the Prize" Black people were elevated to a new level of respect in the world."

Cheyenne encompassed this passionate speech in her

changing the world. "For the last six months I have not been completely happy with my job. I think I might have hinted at this a few times." Cheyenne said with that Cheshire cat grin. They knew she wasn't as happy with her job as she had been in the beginning. They knew too well how she felt from the frequent phone calls all day. Before that when the company sent her to Europe, she'd call and tell the family she was happiest when she was instructing people about the computer, not remotely fixing them. Working much of her day with a computer and a telephone began to bore Cheyenne after a while.

"Well, you know I wouldn't jump into anything without first investigating the pros and cons of the matter carefully over and over in my head and on paper. I have been researching this matter intensely. I have mentioned my intentions to our Pastor, and he said pray on it and the answer you need to know will appear. So, I did, and my decision is to leave next month with the African Affairs Council for Africa. We will live in Rwanda working with the people there, for the next two-three years."

This big announcement required a thoughtful pause on her part. Cheyenne gave them time to recuperate from the apparent shock of having their prized daughter going off to a remote region of the world. They feared the Africa of today and were mindful of the lack of sanitation facilities, and much more knew the danger the unstable governments presented there.

This was a different Africa from the one her grandparents' friends, Alpheus and Dorothy Hunton lived in for years. The Huntons were founding members of the original Council for African Affairs and lived and worked in Ghana. Dr. Hunton worked with W.E.B. Dubois on the Encyclopedia Africa in the 1950s and 1960s, until his death. During the 1940s and 1950s in Ghana, before and after independence, all the indigenous people worked together for their country.

The Huntons were good friends of Kwame Nkrumah before and during his leadership. After independence and the assassinations of the leaders such as Lumumba and Nkrumah, the African people reverted to their tribal or ethnic cultures, reinstated their differences, and fought each other prompted by the West with arms and promises of riches and power. This is a similar scenario to when the U.S.S.R. disbanded all the countries under their former dictatorship and resumed their independence, then these countries began the reinstatement of their differences and they began to fight among each other like Bosnia, Kosovo, Sarajevo, Afghanistan, and others.

"You're crazy. I worked forty years in the same job and didn't need to go to Africa when I got a little bored," was the promised remark from granddad. He was often predictable with his statements.

"Shy dear, do you realize the drastic move you are making? "Mother started. "Have you any idea what it entails to go off to some God-forsaken country in Africa and risk being attacked or becoming susceptible to disease and most of all leaving everything behind you have built up for yourself." Mother was almost pleading now.

Of course, her mother was referring to Cheyenne's condominium which she waited one and a half years to acquire, and her new car, which was the first time anyone in the family owned a brand new one, and the most important reason of all, Cheyenne was leaving her potential husband, Leon Virgo. Cheyenne's mother and Leon's mother, Mrs. Helen Virgo, had been trying to arrange this marriage since Cheyenne and Leon were six years old. Little did she know Leon and Shy had their own plans.

"GranNellie, granddad, mom, dad, I know this is a bit of a shock..." She started again to explain.

"A bit of a shock," Dad blasted. "This is ridiculous. How the hell are you going to leave a job that pays over two hundred fifty thousand dollars and your home which costs fifty or one hundred thousand I imagine; I have to guess since you won't tell us and fly off to Timbuktu without discussing it first." He said this with considerable impatience.

Then realizing he said the words "...discussing it with us first," he had to pull back. This was the weakest thing he could say, since Cheyenne rarely discussed anything before, she did it, even when she was under their supervision. They could trust her unconditionally, and they knew it.

"Wait!" GranNellie anxiously wanted to turn this argument into something more pleasant.

"You finally have all the things you wanted and a new car. Shy, remember that old Peugeot with the rip in the roof, and you had to keep patting the stuffing back in as you drove in order to see. It flew around the car when you had the windows down because there was no air conditioning in the summer. Please think this over, baby. Have you given notice or canceled or sold anything yet?" Mom moved right in before Cheyenne could tear apart her father's authoritarian argument.

"Yes, I have." Cheyenne had to admit this fact before she really wanted to, timing is everything.

"Shy, you know we both love you," Mom continued, anticipating Cheyenne's response, "And we will always want what is best for you. You know I always say if you are happy and trust in the inner God it will be alright....," Mom was speaking rapidly now. She was a great speaker; even Cheyenne's friends liked talking to her.

"But listen, we are terribly concerned about your decision.

You know we have been getting along in years now..." Her mom was getting desperate, she thought. She never mentioned getting old; in fact, she always looked ten to fifteen years younger than she was (especially after a diet) Cheyenne thought. It was time to jump in and relieve the tension.

"As I said, I've investigated the matter quite extensively, plans are being made and preparations are in the works for closing down my life here for the next two or three years and going to Rwanda, Africa!"

There she thought, it is said, and she felt the excitement in saying it. It was real and a definite go from now on, especially now that she told her parents. That was that! The matter was done and over, they had no more to say, or so she thought. Without sensing that wisdom and oratory prominence comes with age, her mom and dad were not through with the matter, yet.

Mr. Web and Mrs. Marilynn Latour fruitlessly continued arguing their point of common sense, which usually worked, except in matters where their oldest daughter knew her heart. It was this she followed. This was one of those exceptional times.

"Shy, did you read the paper this month?" her grandfather said calmly, thumbing through the Times hoping to find another article.

"The two tribes had a skirmish this very month, in which hundreds of one group were killed by the other," while her dad looked at her as if this were all he needed to say.

"Grandpa, dad, I know they have had this centuries' old ethnic, not tribal, problem. That's one of the things we hope our presence will diminish. We want them to move on from there. We hope that by them looking at us and how mixed we are they can see past their minor physical differences. The groups are the Tutsi formerly the Watutsi, the tall slender cattle herders, and the Hutus, from the south, mixed with BaHutu, from the Bantu people. The other inhabitants of Rwanda, the Twa are a petite people hidden in the forest; they used to be called Pygmy."

Cheyenne told them how happy she was to finally be doing something that mattered. She was going to change people's lives for the better. The people in Rwanda really wanted and asked for the skilled workers in the African Affairs Council to come. This was going to benefit the Africans in Rwanda, but also African Americans over here, as well as Africans throughout the world. They were going to do more than put in fiber optic cables for computer operations and telecommunications; they were going to help Rwanda become self-sufficient.

"The Rwandese people are growing fast in population. Farming was the only means of sustenance there, and it was fading due to lack of land. They need and want to begin industry. The Council could see in the future, Africans mining and refining the vast iron and copper deposits there and making machinery for all of Africa to use. Plus, fiber optic cable will allow for internet jobs.

"They can eventually mine the gold there and get into the big financial markets of the world. Finally, Africans could be producers of the vast minerals and wealth in their own country instead of the West who come there and take the land. The Council could help them build their infrastructure. Make schools, roads, car manufacturing plants, housing, clothing and increase the potential of the existing farms, by the next millennium, 2001," Cheyenne felt exuberant now.

★★★★★★★★★★

Before she knew it there was a large family meeting with cousins, aunts, and uncles present. She had some more explaining to do before this group would be satisfied. She began at the beginning.

"My thirst for knowledge of who Black people are and therefore where my ancestors originated led me to try to find the answers from the beginning of civilization as we know it. When I started to study the other ethnic people in Rwanda, I really got fascinated. First the Hutu or Bahutu farmers settled in Rwanda 1000 B.C. I learned that the Watusi now called the Tutsi may have been the original people of Egypt whose ancestors built the great Sphinx, some of the Pyramids and the ancient city of Karmac in ancient Thebes. They may have been the original Nubians."

"So how did they get to Rwanda? That is a bit of a stretch even for you," Uncle John said smiling.

"I read that an Italian explorer went through the doors at Karmac and commented on how these ancient people must have been giants. The Watutsi have been known to be over eight feet tall. But after the continuous invasions the Watutsi migrated to the southeast from the North around the 13th century B.C. I also noted in history that in 640 A.D., the Arab invasion and destruction of many Egyptian monuments happened. No great monuments were built of any consequence since the Arab invasion.

"The Watusi were a regal people always decorating themselves and kept their rituals when they arrived in Burundi and Rwanda. In written records there is no exact information about from where in the north the Watutsi came. The Europeans speculate that the (Wa) Tutsi came from either Somalia, Ethiopia, Senegal or some other African nation north of the Sahara, denying any possibility they could be the descendants of the builders of the ancient pyramids in Egypt. "

"Well, that figures. When we went there, they tried to tell

us people from outer space built the pyramids and other great temples in Egypt. We laughed at them and told them we knew the Nubians built these monuments. They didn't smile so much at us after that," her cousin Wynt blurted out.

"Not only is that denied, but history and further study of the Nubians is unattainable. Ancient Nubia is now under the Nile River, dammed up by President Mubarak during his time in office in Cairo. Why did he flood the Valley of the Kings? Was there a great secret that would forever put the Black Man of the Nile in his rightful place in history? The pastoral scepters always held by the Pharaohs show that herding cattle was a high honor. The Belgians knew this and gave the Tutsi herding cattle and the Hutu, farming in Rwanda. The Watutsi, now called Tutsi, are known for being cattle herders." She had her audience spellbound at this time.

"You're a regular encyclopedia," Aunt Cornelia began. "You know..."

"You mean microfiche. That's what we use today, auntie," said Sima.

"This along with the fact that the Watutsi migrated from the north led my curiosity to seek more facts concerning these great people. Upon further study I found that they actually had monarchies in Rwanda that rivaled the Egyptian nobility. How can a so-called 'nomadic people,' as the Tutsi were called, reign so supremely if they did not have similar Kingdoms in their history? I believe in ancient memory and my ancient memory is leading me to Rwanda."

"So, let me understand this. You are going to a place of potential war to find out if the Watusi are the builders of the pyramids?" questioned Uncle Shotgun.

"Today they use the shortened name of Tutsi. Yes, it is true, I believe the Tutsi are the original Nubians that built the Pyramids and Kemet. These are the same people that were massacred in the 1960s and then slayed in 1990 by their Hutu brothers who didn't like the superior stance the Tutsi took. They retaliated, but soon wanted peace since the Hutu outnumbered them."

"Yes, and…," started Aunt Bullet.

"The passion for going to Rwanda was motivated when I began to ponder past and present circumstances there. They say meditation is good for the soul, yet too much thought over an issue may tend to mislead one's instinctive wisdom. I was led to thoughts that I too, like the Belgium and French before me, was attempting to put a superiority label on the Tutsi, which after all, was the cause of their problems. My desire is to bring this part of the world into the 21st century with cable optics and telecommunications.

"Peace can be attained when everyone is on an equal footing, when there is no fear of lack. Then all of the history of these three peoples, the Twa, The Hutu, and the Tutsi can be brought out without any superiority or hate. Just like African American history came to the public after we had a more equal stance in this country."

"A luta continua!" shouted Cousin Nefatari. After this speech, the relatives applauded and then the questions began. Cheyenne had helped various members of the family from time to time and they were sincerely concerned about her.

"Ok say you go there and put in the fiber optic cable for the telecommunications, what happens next. AT&T is not going to leave this material and technology. When do you think the Rwandese will have control of this and AT&T relinquish their investment?" J, one of her uncles from Washington DC asked.

"There is no guarantee of anything except the telecommunications are set to go and the African Affairs

54

Council is skilled and qualified to help implement this plan. We were chosen to do this because of our record as Pan-Africanist and the African people have had trust in our group since the 1940s."

"Since the guys from your group are going, why do you have to go and stay so long?" This came from her favorite cousin from Queens. Cheyenne was waiting for this question all night.

"I was the person initially contacted because of my work at NOAA and Duran. It was my work with telecommunications which started the Weather Channel that caught the attention of AT&T."

★★★★★★★★★★

Needless to say, she championed her cause with vigor and remarkable success. Cheyenne brought out pamphlets and told of her immunizations and other precautions she'd taken. She brought a video of Rwanda and its people and how the Council was going to help bring about change in Africa for the Africans. Cheyenne was well prepared.

Her friends called, they too had to see this and become convinced that she needed to go. They stopped by the house that night, which was a natural thing for them to do since they had been coming by all their lives. Along with Shy's relatives they covered every detail of the trip.

Dava's arrival brought to the evening's festive yet serious purpose, even more evidence of the soundness of this venture. She had a large stake in the final results of this too. She was going with Cheyenne. This way they would both look out for each other and what one lacked the other had covered.

Dava was happy. Dava hugged her best friend, as Cheyenne kissed her lightly on her scar near her left eye. Cheyenne made a point of doing this every time she saw her best friend. After the ordeal with Ben, Dava felt self-conscious about her scar and her life. Her life had changed for the better since she left her old love forever. While the AT&T video of "Africa Two Project" went on Dava and Cheyenne had coffee in the kitchen quietly looking expectantly at each other.

CHAPTER 5

||||||||||||||||||||||||||||||||||||||||||||||||||

A Friend in Need is a Friend Indeed.

"The sun shall not smite thee by day; nor the
moon at night." KJV Psalm 121:6

Cheyenne recalled briefly Dava's sad affair with Ben. As Mr.
Duran said, "if we don't quit we are made better by challenges
and setbacks."

Dava met Ben at a Pan-Africanist fundraiser for Mandela.
This happened before Mandela was freed in South Africa. Ben
was a tall, handsome Developer, which is unusual for a Black
man in America. He brought land projects for realtors.

At the time she lived in a co-op in Brooklyn. Ben invited
her to an elegant OAU reception at the United Nations. Dava
was stunning. Africans from several nations were there donned
in their African ceremonial attire. Colorful and stately, they all
looked like Kings to Dava. That was the moment she realized
she was destined to go to Africa one day.

Ben was twenty years older than she was, but Dava liked
being mentored and nurtured by him. Her parents divorced
when she was seven years old, and she missed her dad on an
everyday basis.

Ben had an ex-wife and three children by her and one child
by a Jewish woman. He told Dava that she was the first Black
woman he dated in twenty years even though he was black. In
fact, he continued to date white women when Dava was not

around. Sometimes he would even pick a fight with Dava when one of his other women was arriving and vice-versa.

Dava always maintained an excellent job in her field as a telecommunications engineer. Her job kept her busy enough that Ben became her only other interest. She loved to listen to him because he knew so much about the politics in Africa, despite the fact he had never been there.

Ben knew several of the important ambassadors from six West African countries on a personal level. He was invited to their mansions in New Rochelle and in Sutton Place in Manhattan. He would often take Dava with him and she made a great impression on them with her knowledge of computers. They would often suggest that she go to Africa someday and teach computer technology.

After three years of frequent dating, Ben asked Dava to move in with him. She decided to go for it. She rented her co-op furnished. Ben lived on 95th Street and Central Park West. Occasionally his children would stop by and stay overnight, and sometimes longer. This Dava also enjoyed because the two oldest were fun and the youngest girl, aged eleven, adored Dava.

Slowly Ben brought Dava into his world. They rarely did anything she once enjoyed, such as go to plays, movies, dances, clubbing, music concerts, and French Restaurants. He enjoyed going to political meetings, certain Chinese restaurants on Broadway, and bars. He always made the choices of what they would eat from the menu. Later she found out that he was a former Black Panther during the 1960s and was still riding that glory train. Ben felt that if anything happened to him while he was in a place such as a silly romantic or comedic movie or disco, he'd lose his credibility. Now and then he'd take her to three or four bars on the West Side of Manhattan, now and then, and that was it.

This soon got tired, but Dava was trapped, as she now lived with him and anything he said became the law. He even told her he wanted her to fix dinner every night for him and on Saturdays and Sunday he wanted breakfast, lunch, and dinner. He went so far as to say she was his slave.

Dava had a miscarriage after the last beating from Ben and he actually came to the hospital to visit her.

"I don't think this arrangement is working so well for me anymore," Dava calmly told him one evening while she watched his favorite TV shows in bed.

"I think I may have to move..."

Before she knew what happened he slapped her so hard that the skin broke next to her left eye. She lay there stunned and said, "My eye is bleeding!"

"You are a liar," he scowled at her. Dava got out of the bed and had to show him the blood before she could go to the bathroom and dress her wound.

She got dressed, grabbed her pocketbook, and ran out of the door as fast as she could. At first, she didn't know where to go and then remembered Cheyenne lived on 81st and Columbus Avenue near the police station.

When Cheyenne opened the door, she cried. Dava was bleeding and dressed in such a way that let her know her friend was running from someone.

"Don't tell me Ben did this to you," Cheyenne said comforting Dava and dousing her wound in Witch Hazel.

"Yes, he has gone crazy. As he gets on in his sixties, he gets meaner and meaner. You don't know what I've had to put up with. It was a big mistake moving in with him."

"You can stay here until you get settled. Don't worry about anything, Dava."

But day after day Ben called Cheyenne looking for Dava. He followed Dava to work and almost made it inside, but she had to tell the security guards not to let him in to see her. He was determined to get her back.

One day he saw her on Columbus and 81st Street and they got into a big argument. He grabbed her and tried to hit her, but she ducked. Suddenly his hands were wrapped tightly around her neck shoving her against an iron fence that led to a storage basement and passersby yelled at him to stop, and when he pulled up for an instant, Dava broke free from his hold on her and ran to the Police Station around the corner. She had a knot on her forehead the size of a fist for a week.

After several months he finally left her alone, but only after trying to pay certain people who didn't like her to arrange meetings where he would show up. Two people Dava trusted made this arrangement and when Ben showed up with them, she left. It was like having a contract on her life.

The only good thing that happened from that relationship was Dava meeting Queen Mother Moore at one of those international seminars. Dava introduced Cheyenne to her, and they connected immediately. Queen Mother Moore always liked young ambitious people around her that didn't have misconceptions and prejudices formed about her political standing.

Cheyenne started working with Dava toward Queen Mother Moore's dream of building an African Historical Monument to the fallen ancestors who had died. She wanted to install attractions that represented: African civilizations, the Middle Passage, and America fighting for our freedom. Queen Mother Moore was a freedom fighter and had friends like Fannie Mae Hamer and Malcolm X, who were among her notable activist friends. They all did their part to gain equality, equality we are still fighting for today. Her memoirs will be published someday they both had promised her.

Dava had not been the same since the harassment and only Cheyenne knew about her drama. Cheyenne constantly assured her that her life was not ruined by this one bad choice. Things would get better, and this was a learning experience. Cheyenne tried to coax Dava into dating again when she got her apartment back, but Dava was through with men for a while. She only went out in groups or with Leon and Cheyenne. Going to Africa was the best move she could make. It would help her to help others and clear her mind of her pain. Forgiveness was her only salvation.

★★★★★★★★★

When the video ended, Cheyenne informed everyone that her best friend, Dava Love, was going to Rwanda with them. Everybody cheered and clapped at this news. At least once a week one or both friends would write to someone in the group besides their parents. And if everybody stayed connected with one another someone would always know how Dava and Cheyenne were doing. Cheyenne secretly asked her friends to call her parents now and then so they wouldn't get too lonely for their eldest two daughters, as Dava, too, was considered.

Cheyenne knew it would be hardest on Dava's mother since she would be by herself without Dava. Dava had no sisters, except for their make-believe sisterhood. Since her father left when she was only seven her mother never had time to remarry. She had to care for Dava and maintain the house. As Cheyenne looked back, three of her friends also had single parents. Her parents, and other friends whose parents were together, were slowly losing their majority status. However, Cheyenne was thinking, now that Dava's mom was free and that she may still find romance. She was young looking and very pretty and had maintained her shape since high school.

As everybody started to listen closely to why they were going to Rwanda and what they planned to do when they got there, it was easy for the sad thoughts to creep into their friends' and family's minds. Cheyenne knew that her friends didn't want to see her go away for so long, but they knew that life was always separating them for one reason or another and always bringing them back together again. It was a hard sell, but she gave a good close.

"The members of the African Affairs Council are being sponsored by some African American companies and other individuals who thoroughly believe in our mission. These council members and their sponsors have the foresight to see Africans throughout the world leading themselves into financial wealth. Our goal is for the Africans to use their own natural resources for their own profit and use. Something that is not being done so much in Africa, today," she continued. Everyone knew Africa was the richest continent in the world with diamonds, rubies, oil, cobalt, coltan and other minerals and precious stones and metals, with the poorest people in the world.

As the next video showed how the AT&T Africa Telecommunications, *Africa Two*, project was going to be constructed and implemented in Rwanda and other African nations, Cheyenne thought, "They thought I'd be planting and digging." She reminisced about seeing her grandfather puttering about in his garden and the great tomatoes he grew at their country house in Sag Harbor.

"I am so lucky to have known both sets of grandparents.

My mom's father was a pioneer of the computer industry for the government as were his siblings. My father's parents were great leaders for two generations in Brooklyn. The Latours were well known and respected. My grandmother's sisters and brothers, all six of them, produced doctors, ministers and teachers who stayed in the neighborhood throughout the 1970s until things got too rough, then most of them moved to various places in New York, Washington D.C., and other areas throughout the U.S. My father's parents, especially GranNellie, knew a variety of great people through the friends she had. They both knew Lena Horne and her family, Eubie Blake, and Adam Clayton Powell and others who made great strides in America and the world."

When the house was still and quiet again, Shy's father told her more concerns about the unstable country and harsh life she was embarking on.

"Shy, who will be protecting all of you? Are there armed guards surrounding your location? Is the protection for the group on the same campus you are working?"

"Dad, we have ample protection. AT&T wouldn't be there with only the workers. We are protected and the people and government want us to bring cable to their country. They want this communication with the world.

I believe in this project and have faith that we are safe and protected. Just like we are here."

"Shy, I have to ask these questions, you know that." They hugged.

"Daddy, I love you and will always honor your words. I understand your fear, it is yours to feel. I have another way of being in this world. I cannot give up on love. It conquers fear. This has always worked for me."

"You risk your life for the cable optics? This is so uncertain, Shy."

"Life is uncertain. I know there are dangers everywhere. I don't dwell there; I believe in my heart and soul we are going to be safe and protected."

CHAPTER 6

‖‖‖‖‖‖‖‖‖‖‖‖‖‖‖‖‖‖‖‖‖‖‖‖‖‖‖‖‖‖‖‖‖‖‖‖‖‖‖

The Original African Affairs Council

"If thou criest, criest after Knowledge…"
KJV Proverbs 2:3

Aunt Wen presented pictures and discussed the African Affairs Council. She began with one of the stories GranNellie told her when GranNellie worked on the Amsterdam Newspaper in the 1940's and 1950's.

"It was about how Lena Horne was deeply involved in the moral fiber of this country's bigotry. Once while performing in Europe in 1945, Ms. Horne noticed that the European Nazi prisoners of war were seated at the front near the white American soldiers, while the Black soldiers were forced to sit and stand in the back. She didn't sing until the Black soldiers were mixed in with the white American soldiers in the front. In protest she plunged into politics and allied herself with Paul Robeson and others, which caused her to be blacklisted in the 1950s."

Shy's aunt loved to talk about her mother, "On the other hand GranNellie, had no interest in domestic matters much less gardening. In fact, GranNellie's social life with her close friends was the most important thing next to her family." The beginning of the slide show on the history of the Huntons and the Council began. Wen LaTour narrated.

"GranNellie was presently in this club of girlfriends she

had known since she was twelve years old. That was when she moved to N.Y. from Boston as a Higginbotham-Latour. GrandNellie was very worldly and concerned with human rights for all people especially Africans and African- Americans.

She joined the Council of African Affairs in the 1940's integrations and the1950s boycotts. GranNellie and Grandpa were involved with the early 1960s marches; she even took me to Washington D.C.. In 1960 GranNellie and I submitted to the United Nations peace contest the picture of children around the world holding hands.

"GrandNellie was involved with the Council of African Affairs, as it was called then, in the decades of 1930, 1940 and 1950. This was due to her friendship with Dr. Alphaeus and Dorothy Hunton, the co-founders of the Council of African Affairs," said Aunt Wen.

"In the early days of my parents' marriage, they shared a house with the Huntons on McDonough Street in Brooklyn. The Council of African Affairs was a powerful group that made progress for Black people in America and Africa. That is why Dava and Cheyenne, along with some powerful friends in Brooklyn, helped form a new Council and renamed it the African Affairs Council in respect and honor for Dr. Hunton's great work."

Memories of Dr. Alphaeus Hunton were only from the stories Shy's grandmother told her and the great pictures of those early days. Cheyenne's grandma told them, "Dr. Hunton was the most handsome man I could remember seeing, next to your grandad. He was mahogany brown skinned and had the softest looking silver hair ever so delicately mixed with jet black and topped by beautiful natural waves. He was at least six feet eight inches tall or so he seemed. He towered over everyone he stood next to; including grandad who I thought was the tallest man in the world, then. We were ten years younger than Dorothy and Alphaeus."

Aunt Wen continued with the slide show. "Mrs. Hunton on the other hand was petite. Her beauty was more exotic than GranNellie's other friends who were fair skinned for the most part. In fact, she looked like a full blooded Native American Indian. Mrs. Hunton wore her hair long and always pinned up in the same bun. She had high cheekbones. Her eyes slanted slightly, reminiscent of an Asian. Her smile was wide and lovely showing the prettiest white teeth. Her smooth honey-colored skin glowed with all the goodness she possessed inside," her aunt remembered. Cheyenne found out later that Mrs. Hunton was eating health foods and was a vegetarian since the 1920s. This was years, even decades, before it became fashionable.

"The Hunton's life together was hard from the day they met. Dr. Hunton was Dorothy's professor at Howard University. They corresponded after her graduation and fell in love through letters and brief visits due to his hectic schedule.

"In 1937 Dr, Hunton helped organize the Council of African Affairs with W.E.B. Dubois, Paul Robeson, and others. One of the Council's first awareness projects was to let the Black Americans know of the brutality going on in Kenya. Britain ruled Kenya and quickly killed any movement on the part of the Kenyans for self-rule. The Council supported The Kenya African Union headed by Jomo Kenyatta in 1944. Another of the Council's projects was it collected and sent funds and food to relieve the South African famine in 1946-47 this was two decades before African nations gained their independence from European colonizers in the decades of 1960 and 1970.

"However, at this time the U.S. government was on a campaign to stop anyone or group from showing that there were problems in the United States or Europe due to the swift rise in the communist movement around the world. McCarthyism spread like a disease, movie stars, writers and especially anyone who stood up against racism were branded as Un-American. In September 1950, Alphaeus organized a protest in front of Madison Square Garden to protest their refusal to permit the Council on African Affairs to hold a concert featuring Paul Robeson.

"The purpose of the event was twofold. First, it was to protest Paul Robeson's passport revocation by the U.S. government. The second purpose was to show support for W.E. B. Dubois. Dubois was facing a five-year prison sentence for refusal to register under the Foreign Agents Registration Act, since he was chair of the Peace Information Center.

"The Civil Rights Congress and the Council on African Affairs were on McCarthy's list and targeted as Un-American. The Council formed the Civil Rights Bail Fund with Dashiell Hammett, Frederick Vanderbilt Field, and Abner Greene. The Bail Fund was formed because private bonding companies refused to provide bail for progressives like Dubois, even though these white bail companies quickly gave bail money to gangsters, (mafia), thieves, and murderers, Dubois was denied.

"In July 1951, GranNellie went to court with Dorothy Hunton to hear Alphaeus's sentencing along with the other men that started the Civil Rights Bail Fund. The only friend Dorothy Hunton had that would stick by her was GranNellie, risking her job with the school system in N.Y. and her family's security, GranNellie stuck by her friend, and testified.

"Alphaeus was sentenced to six months for not revealing the names of contributors to the Civil Rights Bail Fund to the government. He served this time even though the 'Special Committee on Dr. W. A. Hunton', organized by W. E. B.

Dubois, petitioned the Attorney General of the U.S. to appeal his case.

"Alphaeus continued writing and when he was released, the Council on African Affairs became active in support of the Liberation movements in Tunisia and Morocco by picketing the French Consul in 1951. Then the Council on African Affairs raised and sent $2,500 to the Campaign of Defiance of unjust Laws in South Africa and picketed the South African Consulate and Delegation fighting against apartheid.

"In 1952 Jomo Kenyatta was arrested and thousands more Africans were arrested in their homeland, by Britain. Britain went to war with the Kenyan people because of the Mau Mau rebellion in which thirteen whites were killed by Kenyans and the Britons killed ten thousand Black Kenyan Africans. Alphaeus began the Aide to Kenyan Africans program, trying to help feed the devastated Kenyan people after the British burned and looted their crops and homes.

"The Council was expected to attend and make a presentation at the historic Asian-African Conference at Bandung, Indonesia in April 1955. But the Council was closed by the U.S. government. In October 1955, the Federal Grand Jury subpoenaed Alphaeus to appear and present all correspondence with: the African National Congress or ANC; the South African Indian Congress, and all other correspondence and records of funds sent to Africa; and all materials published or disseminated by the Council from 1946 to 1955. This was happening because the Justice Department wanted the Council to register with the U.S. government as a foreign agent.

"The need for supporting the Council by Black Americans waned as other groups were beginning to see the need to help the people of Africa. At the same time, Civil Rights demonstrations in America were beginning to take root with the 1954 boycott in the south, spurred by Rosa Parks' refusal to abide by Jim Crow Laws.

"In the early 1960s, Kwame Nkrumah, Ghana's first elected President after independence invited W.E.B. Dubois to head a project for the creation of an Encyclopedia Africana in Accra, Ghana. Dubois moved there with his wife and son. Alphaeus Hunton and Dorothy moved to Ghana. Alphaeus wrote a major part of this Encyclopedia in Ghana and tried to complete the encyclopedia after Dubois' death. He and Dorothy worked on it until his own death. Dorothy then moved back to Brooklyn with her sister, and wrote a book about Dr. Hunton's life titled, *"Unsung Valiant,"* Aunt Wen said.

Shy chimed in, "Because of the rich history of the Council on African Affairs, we joined an offshoot of the Council, renamed the African Affairs Council to honor this great and little-known group. The presiding belief was that if Africa could become a viable economic force, the natural resources that are being taken daily from the continent for Western consumption and profit, would eventually fall back into the hands of the Africans. This would promote equality and justice for all Africans throughout the world-The African Diaspora.

'In Brooklyn there were groups in place that had journeyed to Liberia and other places with investors but no sure plan. Unlike the Anglo- Euro people of the world who merely raided and looted Africa of her wealth, and going so far as to steal the people for slaves, the African Americans would work as partners. They would unite with their African brothers and sisters in building Africa and with their one commonality, race, would then take the best from each other's cultures," Shy was revealing her heart.

Mrs. Nellie Latour, Cheyenne's grandmother, engraved on her children's memories that all the people in the world are equal. She would stress to her children, especially to her daughter, that she was as great as or better than any other child. When Cheyenne's Aunt Wen was ten years old she contributed to the world a symbol for world unity that is still copied today. For a city-wide United Nations project in 1960, she drew the now popular picture of children of different racial and ethnic origins, in their native costumes, holding hands around the globe. She was recognized by National and International organizations. She received awards from B'nai B'rith, the United Nations Children Organization, and the NAACP.

The symbol of children holding hands around the world is famous. GranNellie's daughter never got the world recognition she deserved, since she was "just a Black child" from Bedford-Stuyvesant in 1960. This contribution of peace and harmony has been used sixty plus years after she drew it, she has had satisfaction and forgiveness.

★★★★★★★★★★

Cheyenne's life was about to take a major turn in going to Africa. She would miss everyone terribly. However, she was glad her best friend Dava was part of this dream. As an active council member, Dava was going with Cheyenne to Rwanda to teach and bring the 21st century to these people. The fact that they were going together relieved the pressure from both their parents. The two of them were together since elementary school and throughout high school at Brooklyn Tech. They separated briefly when Dava went to M.I.T. while Cheyenne went to Tufts. They were in the same state while in college, but for the first time since elementary school, there was a little distance between them. It was critical for them to be together for this big move, Cheyenne thought, as she looked at Dava.

Cheyenne wasn't about to leave Dava. She didn't trust Dava to manage her love life without advice. Although it sounds controlling, Dava's heartaches and problems began with her first boyfriend in high school. Somehow Dava's first love of her life was addicted to crack cocaine without her knowing it. Vito was always so happy and carefree. Even in high school he got by with his studies and graduated while all the time he was running up to Myrtle Avenue and smoking with the crackheads in their hidden crack dens. Later he told about how these people from Central America had government privileges and passes to sell crack in the neighborhood in the 1980s under Regan's Iran Contra.

Somehow Dava used up her money from her summer and after school jobs supporting Vito's habit, without realizing what she was doing. He always had a sad story for her and needed money he'd pay back, which he never did. He was a manipulative genius.

Cheyenne will never forget the last day in their senior year; they caught Dava's boyfriend smoking crack in the school behind the stage in the auditorium. Dava cried so much it took a trip to the Bahamas and parasailing after their graduation before she could get over it.

Cheyenne loved all her friends and family as much as they loved her. They never doubted her love and if they needed her for whatever, she would be there, and if necessary bring others to help. She did good things with her life and her friends always protected her innocence and realness. She would tell them the truth without holding back, but never with the intention to hurt anyone. They all told her they'd miss her laughter the most. She had a magnetic, contagious laughter, mainly because she made all kinds of funny noises. They could see constant unconditional love filter through her eyes right into their hearts. They'd never turn their backs on each other.

Cheyenne would be working with technological endeavors in Rwanda. The Council's legal department might be able to restore the ownership of mining to the Rwandese people while they were there. Their mission did not include any farming or working in the fields and digging wells. These things were done by the international Christian groups and the Peace Corps that preceded the Council. In fact, agriculture was growing so fast there that land was becoming a problem and not meeting the farmers' demands. The Rwandese were looking to industrialize, as were all the African Nations. Now the Rwandese were ready to move into the twentieth and twenty-first centuries, and more importantly they really wanted to advance.

Cheyenne thought about this, and the phrase came to her, "Give a man a fish and you feed one man; teach a man how to fish and you feed a nation."

As the slide show ended there was one fact of reality that brought everyone into accord with her that evening. This was the last piece that finally convinced both family and friends, especially her father and grandfather, that her move to Rwanda was OK.

Lastly came her big announcement, "The first thing is Leon Virgo will be in Egypt literally up the river from me if I need to get to safety." Shy gave Leon a wink and grabbed his hand. "Then, I want you all to know that if I wanted my job back, it would be waiting after no more than two years. This is in writing, signed by Mr. M.H, Duran and notarized, at even more money than I make now." There was actually applause. They all saw the document with their own eyes. This concern bothered others more than she had over a job.

73

She really knew her employment credentials were high on the ladder for business.

A cousin subleased her condominium with the backup cosignatory of her aunt and uncle after their house was renovated. Cheyenne put her dress clothes, fancy shoes and coats in cold storage, and she gave away a lot of things having mentally outgrown them. Her checking account was automated to pay all of her other bills which were made minimal. Her uncle took over payments of her car and was happy to take it as a second car for his wife.

Everything was set, except for one big dilemma. The only man she forever loved. The man both his parents and hers wanted for her. The man who stole her heart twenty years ago, Leon Virgo, was going to be four hours and fifty-four minutes and two thousand two hundred two miles from her. They had to have time for themselves before she left. Even though he'd be going to Egypt in a month they would be apart by three African countries and connected by the Nile River.

CHAPTER 7

Shy, Leon – Fare Thee Well

"Love points the way, and the Law of Nature
makes the way possible." By Ernest Holmes.

Falling in love and loving a person who can be your friend forever is the difference between a fling and a lasting relationship. As love grows constantly, unconditionally more, and deeper each day, life is filled with everlasting joy.

Cheyenne will always have special feelings for Leon. Driving through the old neighborhood for the last time, her mind fills with beautiful memories of Hancock Street in Brooklyn, N.Y.

She remembers the first moment she fell in love with Leon. It started one day in first grade, when the class bully hid in the wardrobe closet in class exposing himself. When he tried to grab Cheyenne and force her to take a close look, Leon, who was watching the scene unfold, gently pulled her away from him. After school Leon chased the boy home and told the boy's mother what he tried to do.

From that moment on Leon was Cheyenne's hero, and Leon knew that he would always want to protect her.

There would always be children around and Dava, Cheyenne, and Leon would always be right there in the middle of fun. Sometimes it would be the three of them walking after school behind whichever parent or sitter they would have that day.

Later when they could walk home from school by themselves, they would stay at the house across the street from

Cheyenne's grandparents which was run by a loving wonderful woman called Big Mama. This house was full of children and was the only house big enough to have a driveway and three garages on Hancock Street. This yard and driveway provided a safe natural playground for all of them.

At the age of seven Dava's mother and father separated and then sadly divorced a year later. At this time Dava would spend nights at Cheyenne's house and cry often. Sometimes Dava would have the same number of clothes in the washer as Cheyenne and separating them became an interesting task for both mothers. Leon loved Dava as a sister. There were no feelings of envy because they were all innocent children together.

In the sixth grade Leon and Cheyenne would write each other love notes in class and sometimes they'd get caught. One day in the latter part of May they wrote to each other to meet after school at the corner of Ralph Ave. with their bikes at three thirty.

As they were riding their bikes together in Highland Park in Brooklyn, a group of five or six white boys came out of the bushes from nowhere and told them to, "Get out of the park. We don't want no niggers here." Then they hit Leon with a bat across the side of his head and as Cheyenne started screaming the boys ran away. The two of them rode back to Cheyenne's house wounded physically and emotionally. She put an ice pack on his head and Leon told her not to tell her parents.

She naively obeyed him, and later found out she should have told her mother while he was still there, in case he had severe damage done to his head.

"Did you tell your parents yet?" Leon later asked Cheyenne on the phone. Cheyenne was young and unsuspecting and told him she had not.

"Well, I had to tell my parents when they saw that big red bruise on my head. They took me to the doctor and I had a concussion test, but I'm OK. Those thugs didn't do any damage to this hard head," said Leon.

"That was really scary, wasn't it, Shy?"

"Leon, I am so worried about you. I didn't feel right not telling my parents, so I'm glad you did. Nothing like this has ever happened before. I never heard anyone say nigger to me and I don't understand why it happened," she said crying.

"Shy, tell your parents what happened. I have to go now. My grandmother's calling me for dinner. Call me later if you want," Leon hung up.

She went downstairs, in time to help her grandmother. Her uncle Web was visiting, and he was milling around, while her two baby sisters were playing in their playpen in the backyard.

"GranNellie, today when Leon and I were riding in the park, six white boys stopped us and called us 'niggers' and told us to get out the park. Then they hit Leon with a bat," Shy blurted.

"Oh, my God, why didn't you tell us earlier. We would have gotten in the car and looked for them and turned them over to the police, or something," her grandmother said, totally taken aback by this tragedy.

Her grandfather asked, "Is Leon alright?"

"Yes, he had tests and all, he's OK," Shy said.

"I'll kill them," said Web, totally incensed that his little daughter had to be exposed to such vile hatred. He had gone to a southern college and knew the feeling of hatred for no other reason than for skin color.

"Calm down Web, we'll manage this. Shy whenever anything like that happens to you tell us immediately. This could have been worse than it was."

GrandNellie looked at granddad and they both thought the same thing. These two children could have been raped and or killed. She decided not to say anymore to avoid frightening Cheyenne further.

"Shy, don't go in that park again unless we all go and I don't think we all need ever go there, for a while." Her grandfather was visibly upset as he left the table.

She didn't ask any more questions and thought I'll call Leon again after dinner. The question of why those boys did that to them would linger in her mind long into adulthood. Forgiving and forgetting and moving on was impossible to process as this never happened in her own neighborhood, in Bed-Stuy.

During Junior High School days, Dava and her mother took all of them, of course, including Leon, to the Ice Capades. Since GranNellie was in the Jack and Jill group and her adult Brooklyn Girl Friends group, her children and grandchildren were automatic members. Leon and Dava were at all the functions as guests. Dava was also at GranNellie's summer home in Sag Harbor. Leon's parents owned their own summer house in Sag Harbor.

Dava, Leon and Cheyenne continued to Brooklyn Technical High School together. In their first year, Dava finally told Cheyenne what she knew for a while-that Cheyenne loved Leon. From a distance they could see each other grow into adulthood, Dava knew Cheyenne loved him more seriously than she thought.

"Dava," said Cheyenne, "is this love, or do I feel used to him because he's always there? I don't know any better. He is all I ever wanted or needed," Cheyenne continued, puzzled by this emotion. She loved to have fun with her friends but being kissed by Leon gave her an unfamiliar sensation. She tried not to fall in love with him because they were such good friends. She didn't want to break the friendship up.

"This is the best thing that could happen," Dava said. "My mother always says to be friends with your husband first, then fall in love. She fell in love with my father, she says, and when things got strained they didn't have that initial liking for each other to fall back on to fix it. I'm sure I will know what she's talking about someday. I continuously fall in love first and break up and fall in love again with someone else. But you Shy, I think you've got the real thing," Dava said sincerely to her.

"Dava I think I know what you are talking about, but right now I feel very good around the man," and she laughed and Dava did too

Years went by and Cheyenne found herself in many social groups and clubs chosen by her parents for her. She went along with their choices because she thought it was due to the incident in the park. Leon was invited to each event and soon people thought he also was a member of the same clubs in which Cheyenne was a member. Leon was like no other boy Shy knew.

They knew that if their friends, and especially their parents, suspected their love for each other, they would be molded into these boxes carved out for them and never be able to live their own lives the way they wanted. They wanted to wait a while before marrying each other and definitely wait before they had children. Friends tend to push you into marriage and showers and that kind of stuff. They wanted to live the only way their two natural, free spirits could love: unfettered, passionate, and private. After their separate college and graduate school experiences, they no longer hid their love.

One evening under the pale December skies in the upstate countryside of New York's Bear Mountains, Cheyenne and

Leon committed to one another. They vowed before the low lighting of the fire to always remember this feeling right here and right now.

Years later, August 28, 1993, seven months before their respective African journeys, Leon and Cheyenne were engaged right after Aunt Wen and Ted's Sag Harbor wedding. Sitting on beach towels in the sand, watching the small waves inch in from the Bay on Shelter Island after taking Leon's red motor boat across, their commitment to each other was sealed. They talked about the future of the world and their own future.

They didn't know it then, but this was to be their last summer together in the innocence of youth. Time had brought them into their twenties, but they were still kids when they were together. They were teenagers when they first discovered their true love for each other.

"No matter what we do, let's always be together, Leon. You are the only person in the entire world who really understands me. You are my future," Cheyenne whispered and then kissed his forehead.

She told him about her upcoming trip to Rwanda. She spoke of how the African Affairs Council proposed to install and train the people there in computer technology.

"Listen babe, I don't want you to feel you are leaving me or anything like that. I've always known the kind of woman you are and your incredible strength and focus. Our temporary separation will only make our love stronger like when we were separated in college. This will give us both an opportunity to venture out unhampered by any thoughts of losing each other. Remember, since Columbia School of Journalism is sending a bunch of us to Egypt I'll be up the Nile from you."

"I know Leon, and we'll phone when we can," whispered Cheyenne.

"I'll be getting on-the-job journalism training. It will be comforting to know you won't be wringing your hands worrying about me and I know you can handle yourself." Leon was looking straight into her eyes when he spoke. .

"I pray for strength every day, Leon. I am a little frightened by this whole prospect of a new life in Africa." Cheyenne gently leaned into his chest.

"Shy, I pray for the same thing. Let's pray together knowing each other's strength, safety, and success," Leon said as he held her hand and they closed their eyes.

After a while Leon felt her restlessness and grabbing both hands suggested, "Let's take a ride," as he piloted them back across to Asurest Beach.

They put on their shorts and headed for his car in the lot fifteen feet away. They rode down the newly paved roads, top down, toward their secret place by the ocean.

The wind whistled through her hair as they rode down the two-lane street and over a one lane bridge toward the ocean. They could see the mist and hear the roaring crests rise above the small embankment that separated the farms from the beach. They parked and embraced, then raced down the small hill to the beckoning waves of the sea.

Straight ahead to the east lay their destiny. They looked at each other and knew what the other was thinking.

Leon spoke first, "In a few months from now we both will be crossing this ocean to the land of our ancestors; you in Rwanda, and me in Egypt. I have the great Red Sea and you get to glimpse the Indian Ocean. Isn't it funny how the ocean always has meaning in our lives? We are intertwined and our past, present, and future are linked by the seas. I look out at this splendid creation of God's and am humbled again and thankful for you and everything in my life." Cheyenne fell back into Leon's arms.

He grasped her gently from behind and clasped his hands around my waist. She hugged his arms and turned her head upward for a kiss. It was hot and the ocean invited its sandy guests to enter and join in on the fun, so they jumped in. Playtime ensued; jumping waves, swimming parallel to the coast, diving under waves, sitting at the edge of the shore as waves rolled in, and at last they walked tiredly toward the blanket.

When they came out they slipped slowly upon the slope of the embankment and listened and watched the waves bound into the shore with thunderous delight. Marching in endless cadences, the next waves would tip-toe in and barely reach shore before it was swallowed up by the one underneath it. It was all so mysterious and all so exciting for them to take in and decipher. They had so much to look forward to and so much to enjoy now.

"Even though we will be far from each other soon, you will come to me in my dreams. If we both see the same picture it will be real and we can have each other every night," Cheyenne said with her eyes closed wondering what the dream looked like.

"I will and we will never have to tell one another what the dream is," Leon said, being so practical and sensitive to her feelings at the same time.

The anticipation of their respective trips was exciting, exhilarating and very frightening all at the same time. Thoughts of every kind ran through their minds as they lay there watching and listening to the sea. The sea was going to separate them yet bring them together on the continent of Africa. This beautiful and unforgettably special day, August 28, was to be an anniversary day for Shy and Leon, forever.

CHAPTER 8

The Trans-Atlantic Sojourn

"Fear is temporary, but regret is forever."
Unknown author

Their autumn together passed sweetly and colorfully and then winter came in like a lion and continued to roar throughout January and February. Cheyenne and Leon loved each other every day as if this might be the last day they would have in each other's embrace on earth. They didn't question this, and it did not make them sad. Somehow they knew that after these experiences in Africa they would be changed, not toward each other, but their spirits would be touched.

They clung to these last innocent moments in New York, "Each day was like Christmas and each night like New Year's Eve," as one of their favorite Sade songs went.

They were headed toward the point of no return. There would be no going back. They made their commitments to God, themselves, and each other. In this commitment they found the strength to overcome this milestone in their lives.

The next month after Cheyenne and Dava's big announcement about going to Rwanda at her grandparent's house, Leon drove Cheyenne to the airport. However, throughout those cold, snowy Brooklyn January nights the warmth of their love and commitment and the confidence they shared in the adventure that lay ahead could not freeze.

Leaving behind their family and friends was overwhelming. Toward the days leading to her departure date Cheyenne saw her parents every day and there was a kind of disbelief, and at times denial, in their actions. She was regretful for having made them unhappy, but she was so grateful that she only had a month of seeing them like that and not a moment longer. Cheyenne would never utterly understand their pain until she too had to say goodbye to a child of her own.

On February 10th, the day finally arrived. Amidst tearful goodbyes in N.Y.'s Kennedy airport, Cheyenne went to Leon. While holding her in his arms, Leon whispered, "Don't be afraid-I will be with you every step of the way. You have been in everybody's prayers so God will carry you through the tough parts. Be careful, honey, and write. I'll be in Egypt by this time next month; you already have some of your clothing at my address. Call me collect, and I will come down to Rwanda whenever you want. I miss you already. So long my love." They embraced and kissed for the first time in front of friends and family, and the final time for an unknown period.

"I'll miss you, too. You don't know how much," Cheyenne whispered back, "I love you."

When it came to his turn to say goodbye, her father found it hard to break his hug and she had to whisper, "I'm in God's mighty hands, now, daddy. You have to let me go. I love you,"

Their friends who came to the airport yelled out how fine Cheyenne and Dava looked as they walked to the plane. "You two will sure stop traffic or whatever they have there," they yelled trying to embarrass the travelers.

Cheyenne and Dava couldn't help but smile and as they boarded with their usual flair, Cheyenne knew that a few pieces of her wardrobe were inappropriate for the climate and duties in Rwanda. However, she could not help bringing along two designer business pieces. Eighty percent of her clothing was practical and she hoped to wear the attire the people in Rwanda don. But this one time she knew that when she deplaned in Rwanda she was going to be stunning. She wore a light indigo St. John's knit pants suit with black and brass buttons, and black silk buttonholes that highlighted the brass. Her shoes were a simple Ferragamo black pump. Dava sported her DKNY miniskirt suit with her usual high heels. She said she could not walk without them.

Half of the group was already on board when Cheyenne and Dava took their seats with the rest of the African Affairs Council in the coach section, each of them thinking of the solace of their destiny and the loved ones they were leaving behind. Fathers were leaving children and wives, four or five members were leaving parents and lovers, three were leaving all the above. But all had the promise of seeing their loved ones once again.

★★★★★★★★★★

Cheyenne and Dava shifted their thoughts to the airplane and the present situation. They looked to see who else and for what reason, these other passengers were headed to Rwanda. This was the only charter plane ever to go to Rwanda. They expected one stop at the coast for refueling, and then the plane was to fly over 1,000 miles of rainforest and jungle.

They looked forward to the stop. Mr. Duran arranged the entire flight for the Council. Mr. Duran sent two men, one white and one Black person, seated together in suits and ties, whispering in the first-class section. In front of them were casually dressed military men. They read pamphlets and spoke little. The other men sat in the other three seats separately nearer to the rear.

Cheyenne and Dava sat next to the first class section, near enough so that indiscreet conversations from the Council could be easily overheard. With seatbelts fastened, lift off took their breath away and swept this motley group air bound onward to the Motherland.

The Council members could be heard discussing all they had read about Rwanda and how similar their history was to the U.S. In African American relationships they were taught not to trust each other by the slave owner William Lynch who published papers on "How to Make a Slave." That had such a widespread effect that it permeated the waters to the pristine cultures of Africa.

Tombe, President of the African Affairs Council said, "Although the Rwandese, as the Tutsi, Hutu and Twa in Rwanda like to be called, were a divided people due to immigration sequences and language, this division had its roots before the European age of enlightenment. Then the Belgians separated the groups even more, creating more distrust, and gave some favored treatment to certain ones over others."

Discussions on the plane ensued on how the people in Europe, in the 17th century discovered that the civilized world lay beyond its boundaries, in Africa, China, India, and the Americas. They were forced to use barbaric means in conquering these people who defended their land and people with hand-to-hand weaponry for hundreds of years. The Europeans used the Chinese fire power in guns to divide and conquer as our Western history reveals.

"Imagine a quiet African village, with most of its residents in some way related to the chief of the village, living in peace and harmony with their own education and spiritual life, and along comes the European who captures some of the village people, while those that can run for their lives go into another village family.

"A natural leadership and land problem will result as these

two separate village families living on separate pieces of land, now must share. All at once forced to live together for their very existence and that is what the Tutsi had to do when they left the north of Africa arriving in Rwanda in the 15th century. They had to live in this new world causing division among the current residents who had their own principalities," said Tombe, who was also one of the engineers.

"The difference that kept them separate was the Watusi were cattle herders and the Hutu were farmers. This difference led to a system of barter that worked to an extent. The Watusi had new innovations and teachings that were not present in the small Hutu and Twa villages," another member said.

"As teachers, the Tutsi, the modern name for Watutsi, became dominators and chiefs, and the Hutu found themselves subservient. A Hutu who had cattle could, however, become a Tutsi. There was intermarriage between the Hutu and Tutsi; however, the Belgians instigated division between the ethnic groups from the end of the 19th century in Rwanda to today. Since they were outnumbered, the Belgians found it profitable to force the Tutsi to take control over the Hutu and Twa people. The Tutsi are tall with angular narrow noses, thin lips and long lean bodies and legs. The Hutu have wide noses and big lips and were smaller with shorter legs. The Twa also had thicker lips and nose and were extremely short," Joe would add. Everyone in the Council agreed that they had these same features themselves.

"With the military support of the Belgians, the Tutsi established a monarchy and treated the other people poorly. Tutsis were given luxuries, education, and privileges by the Belgians. 'They were less,' as the European says, 'Negroid' with Euro type features," Barry said.

"Twa people did not receive any privileges and were in

turn treated badly by the Hutu. Prejudice and hatred developed among these people. The rumors that the Tutsis were the ancient Nubian people from Egypt and had to leave their riches and pyramids when the Arabs invaded was one position believed. This, therefore, gave them the royal privilege to lord over the Hutus and Twa people. Since the Watutsi were so tall the Belgians had them in the front line of battle against the Germans in WWII. But when the Tutsis wanted independence from the Belgians and united with the Hutu and Twa against them, the Belgians turned against the Tutsis and poisoned the Hutu to hate all Tutsis."

"The Hutu were said to have come from the west as a part of a great migration of Bantu around 1,000 A.D. long before the European was enslaving and slaughtering Africans everywhere they went in Africa. The Arab nations ran them off their land," Tombe, an activist and the group's spokesperson, would continue.

"I read today that the Rwandese legend is one of unity for all three groups. They tell the story that the Tutsi, Hutu, and Twa have one mother. She gave birth to triplets, and one came out tall, one medium size and one small with their features, color hues, and characteristics all being different."

"In African American families this is a common occurrence in families with the same mother and father, the children can come out with all different features, colors, and shapes," Dava interjected.

The African Affairs Council and other members of this assemblage of engineers, computer scientists, and construction technicians ate, slept, and talked a lot more on this journey across the North Atlantic Ocean across the Equator to the South Atlantic Ocean. They prayed and meditated until they could see their ancestral homeland.

The first ascent and leveling of the plane brought a sigh of relief from the Council members as they looked forward to their new and exciting venture in the Motherland. Startled by the Council's joy, the military, and civilians of doom in the first-class section, jeered at the stupidity of the Council's naiveté. Two men in plain clothes stared and wondered how this world got so crazy and if they would survive their special mission.

CHAPTER 9

The Conspiracy Plot

"The Lord is my Shepherd; I shall not
want ...He preparest a table before me in the
presence of mine enemies, he anointeth my
head with oil..." KJV Psalm 23

On a beautiful day, as cherry blossoms began to peek through the cold in Washington, D.C., the steady drone of business as usual was heard at Naval Intelligence headquarters. Amidst the tumult of covert and overt military and national security operations, Admiral Havel Biggelo moved out of the war room unnoticed. He left in a private car and drove himself to a remote part of Maryland. It was 6:30 a.m. and the streets were still quiet.

In a park densely lined with trees, Admiral Biggelo peered out of his window into the blackened windows of the limousine across from him. He got out and was followed by a man in a black suit with an Arabic taqiyah on his head and carrying an attaché case.

"Greetings, Ashir," Admiral Biggelo said with a sarcastic air. He hated addressing these rich third world people with pronounced dignity, so courteously.

"Greetings, Biggelo," Amir Mahmoud Ashir held the same contempt for the Admiral as the Admiral held for him. Except for their common deadly purpose, these two would have never met, much less ever spoken to each other.

"Do you have the agreed-upon package?" the Admiral blurted.

"Here," he held up his attaché case. "We will not rest until all of our people are safe from the poisonous teachings of the Pope," said the Amir.

"Never mind all that, hand me the money!" Admiral Biggelo responded with coarse hatred.

"Yes," said Amir, "Here it is." As he handed the case over ever so slowly he wanted the Admiral to understand his reasons clearly. "The Catholic influence in this land has weakened the unity of the people. It will not be difficult to create the start of the Civil War in Rwanda and central Africa and rid them of their Catholic and Christian brainwashing. The people there have had differences for centuries. Even before slavery, they had to leave their own lands throughout Africa and squeeze together in the interior of the small countries of Rwanda, Burundi, Zaire, and the interior of Uganda. The Catholic missionaries did their job. They have Black Rwandese Bishops and priests and nuns feeding the people their doctrine. We will have no problem destroying the churches and hospitals made by these people."

"Good, then we shall proceed as planned. What a half dozen of those priests are doing to the nuns there, it is no wonder they are happy. The Hutu government is training the slaughter gangs as we speak. They have totally intimidated and used the vilest propaganda on the Hutu and have convinced the people into thinking that they are going to be rich and live good lives if they kill the Tutsi. They are also threatening them with death if they don't kill Tutsis. Our heavily armed mercenary troops will be deployed immediately. The Neo-Nazi's are leaving South Africa and going to Rwanda to add to the slaughter training. With all the arms the Organization is providing, bloodshed will begin within weeks of the untimely death of the President of Rwanda," Admiral Biggelo spoke with assurance.

"You can expect to see our terrorists infiltrate Rwanda in the next month or two, goodbye." As he turned his back, Ashir mumbled, "Wait until you see what we do in Sudan in the next millennium and the U.S., too," Ashir left Admiral Biggelo the attaché full of money and headed toward the door. His motive was contrary to Biggelo's but they both used the same vicious means.

"We have no more business to conduct, so I won't see you ever again." Admiral Biggelo smiled to himself. "If that pig thinks we'll let them take over Rwanda he's crazy."

He abruptly departed and it was as if they had never spoken with one another. They parted forever. Biggelo prepared to leave Washington, D.C., and head for New York. His purpose was to meet the top members of the Organization.

That very same night in a dark, malevolent, eerie setting, unidentifiable cars were parked beside a warehouse across the river from Manhattan. Facing the United Nations, a group of men gathered to discuss a deadly plot that would be the ruin of not only one African country, but the malicious contagion would spread throughout central Africa. In previous years, these Navy Yards were the home of peacekeeping vessels and men and women fighting to keep the world free from the malignancy of Nazism. Now a new hatred without a name or manifesto invaded the Yard, a hatred enveloped in greed, racism, and fanaticism.

Admiral Havelo Biggelo and Chairman Fossel Gatt presided over the clandestine Organization meeting. The members included various diplomats from around the world, east Europe and west Europe, South America, and the U.S., Asia, and

Russia. There were U.N. officers in charge of the protection of civilians, seven militia groups, and known mercenary officers also present. They were all in attendance tonight for one malevolent purpose. They were seated at a round table in dim light. Each took their turn reporting their onerous assignment and how it would be executed for the demise of Rwanda and eventually all of Africa.

"The assassination will take place very soon; a bomb will explode on the Rwanda President's plane. No one will know who did it and each ethnic faction will blame the other."

"Oui, pardon-yes, the mercenaries are already planted in Rwanda and have armed and trained the Hutu slaughter groups with machetes, axes, knives, a few automatic guns, and mortar provided by the Rwanda government's military. This way no one can say an outside group brought in arms and started the massacre," the contingency said.

"Drago Dupree, our best nigger boy, has infiltrated the Hutus. As soon as we kill their President, Dupree will begin agitating Tutsi and Hutu blaming each group for the assassination."

"Should we alert Dupree and the rest of our guys to get out?"

"No, they are expendable. They are misfits or blacks anyway. There are plenty more where they come from, besides, most of them know all about the perils of combat."

"Our businesspeople, who mine gold and diamonds in Africa, want to establish white dominated governments and protect European plantations on African soil. They want white run governments in Central Africa."

"We will have to keep these civil wars going for at least another twenty years to really affect that kind of change so blatantly. The Africans will surely notice a white President of their country. It's not like South Africa anymore."

"Africans do not matter in the universal quest for racial purity and world power. We have never been as close as we are now to our goal of eliminating non-whites altogether. Since we have methodically been deforesting the African, Indo-Polynesian, and South American rainforests leaving their land barren, we have already caused uncontrollable famine and displacement in these areas."

"On every turn we will promote civil war and internal military strife in these countries of color. They will kill each other with a small amount of agitation from us. There are more African nations at war with themselves or plagued by disease than there were in the 1960s. Cholera is so spreadable, and the guinea worm loves their unfiltered water. It is so easy. And since we did such an excellent job with the Agent Orange in Vietnam in the 1970s, our new strand is even less perceptible. When we use it in Africa they will never fully recover."

"We have virtually wiped-out hundreds of thousands by spreading the AIDS virus and Ebola virus, particularly in areas of the most undesirable people, the Black Africans. It will be much like The Black War between the British colonists and the Aboriginal Australians, and the extermination that took place in Tasmania in the 1800s. The island's Indigenous population was nearly annihilated. Australia is now considered a white country. Yes, indeed, our little Organization is going to dominate over the world with white supremacy."

"And nobody can stop our French members who supplied certain nations, Pakistan in particular, with nuclear warheads so that they could enter the nuclear age basically to fight neighboring India and other non-Muslim groups. The whole idea behind that was for these non-white countries to eventually destroy themselves."

"And our boys over here, our stateside members of the Organization, are still stockpiling land mines for those pickaninnies here in the states. Our leadership here refused to give up their use even upon the request of European nobility."

"Our Organization's sights are pointed on China giving up its hold on Hong Kong in 1999. Wait 'til you see the power and destruction to be wielded there, especially viruses in the port to all of Asia. Africa and Asia will soon be desperately seeking our help. This is when we take control under the guise of aid and peace."

★★★★★★★★★★

"Our power goes beyond the World Peacekeeping Organizations. With nuclear weapons still being tested around the world, NATO and the United Nations organizations are helpless trying to make peace anywhere."

"We should know, we are that force. In fact, we are weakening these peace and disarmament groups daily. I'd like to kick the United Nations with all their third world optimism with 'developing countries,' right out of here. At the same time, the Organization holds the major economic advantages since our people are responsible for the building of these weapons. The threat of nuclear war will still forever hang over these peacekeeping agencies. Soon those so-called Arab nations will crumble. The Organization will control the destiny of the world through fear."

"We have devised a geographic strategy to contaminate the rivers with the slaughtered Tutsi bodies. We will pollute as far north as Lake Victoria."

"The natural resources will be decimated by fires set to the crops. And when the fighting ceases they will starve to death or die of some unsanitary disease."

"Don't forget Ashir's men have planted firebombs that will take on the appearance of natural causes given the current circumstances."

"Our group is leaving Rwanda and has already spread the meningitis in Nigeria by placing the laboratory-made virus into the drinking water. It will not be stopped. There is no treatment and no cure, only sure death since it is in the drinking water."

"Other diseases will be spread in the West African nations like the river worm which they get when drinking their water. This gets inside and eats them from the inside. By introducing this worm to other river communities, it will spread disease in other parts of Africa. No one will suspect a thing. We are proud of this worm; it is a hybrid of the maggot in the waters of Brazil that eats all the flesh right off the bone. By the time anyone notices these diseases in Africa and elsewhere, we will have achieved our mission."

"We have more cholera and TB bacteria if we need it. Outbreaks can arise at any time at any place."

"And we have internal help. There will be no sanctuary given the Tutsi from the Catholic Church, as they are being massacred. Although 90% of them are Catholic we have word from very high up that some priests are in league with the Hutu murderers and some churches would be destroyed rather than have Tutsi men, women or children find sanctuary in them."

"Though the Tutsis used to have a prominent status in the world when there were more of them and they once stood as tall as eight feet, they lost most of their giant Watutsi tribe fighting with the allies during World War II. Now they have a shorter name, are not as statuesque anymore, and have mixed marriages with the Hutu, so therefore, the world will not notice or regret their demise."

"Good, then we can begin to carry out the destruction immediately."

"With our consolidated efforts we can eliminate the Christian influence and the Red Cross."

"We are ready except for one thing."

"What?"

"Will M.H. Duran get in our way again?"

"No, there is no way. This time he doesn't know what's going on in Rwanda. I am absolutely sure of this."

"I know that group of African Affair Council niggers don't have money or arms, but do you think they have the power to unite the people there?"

"No way in hell can one group of niggers unite another group of niggers. That's been branded on their brains since slavery."

"Let's get the details absolutely straight for the killing to begin, in a natural way."

"At precisely 3p.m. Wednesday April 4, 1994, the plane will explode with President Habyarimana of Rwanda and Prime Minister Cyprian Ntaryamira of Burundi on board. A spy in the President's commission assured me of this fact. By 3:30 p.m. our faction of terrorists and our trained mercenaries will lead a Hutu rebellion slaughtering Tutsi civilians wherever they are. There may be a faction of Tutsi rebels in the north and Uganda that may try to stop this war. But there is no way to help them stop the slaughter that we know of, so it will continue until the Tutsi are eliminated which will give our peacekeeping forces a reason to kill the Hutu. Our plan is to help get arms to the Hutus and prolong the war. There will be mass exodus by women and children, but we plan to have slaughter groups spread throughout the countryside waiting for these refugees by the borders. As we chase refugees into camps in Zaire, we will take over and have civil war there, too."

"By the fifth month of this mayhem and killing the population of Rwanda will be diminished by about five million and we can take over. There will be famine and disease as dead bodies will be everywhere and they will not have the facilities to clean them up."

"I have word that the United Nations and the U.S. will be too confused as to how to stop the massacres since the debacle in Eritrea and Somalia."

"We don't want to waste our time setting up a dictator who will not be bought or whose army we can't defeat without international retribution like in Zaire."

"At every turn an opposition leader will emerge, and the killing will start over and over again as long as we can keep the people divided and starving."

"And if we can stop those bleeding-heart liberals, like those Christian, Catholic and Red Cross groups from entering the scene and helping, we can keep things upset there for at least five months to a year. The population will shrink to maybe one hundred thousand Rwandans, and we will make them our gophers and servants and take over everything there. Gold, copper, iron ore, oil, coffee, tea, cobalt, and most importantly the coltan for computers will belong to each of us individually. It is all just waiting for us to take it. World opinion and history will read that we are on a mission to help restore civilization and keep peace."

"As with any takeover let us now decide how we will further split up this country so that we all have the share equal to our efforts. Of course, only a private business like McGrumur can claim a part of Rwanda for the U.S. Now that the U.S. democracy does not allow the slaughter of innocents openly anymore, we must hide behind business interests."

The group laughed and toasted to the success of their malicious mission.

"The neighboring countries of Burundi, Tanzania, Zaire and Uganda will be next for civil war. It must spread since the refugees are the Tutsis and Hutus mixed together. Once we have these countries under our rule with puppet governments, South Africa and West Africa will fall. Factions are already at work dividing the African people in South Africa. West Africa will be easy prey for total annihilation since civil war is rising and the people in north and east Africa are starving to death already. They will help us fight and do it in the name of the Muslim religion. By the year 2002, it will be doubtful if there will be any Indigenous Africans in Africa at all."

"There must be as much apathy toward the African race as possible. Stirring racial hatred won't be difficult to do in America. There's plenty there already. Europe already has its hate and neo-Nazis groups in operation, and those misguided Muslim terrorists are helping our cause unintentionally. They generate fear and the need for more military intervention, as much as any government could muster to stop their threat."

"Paris residents are always complaining of the Mali invaders in their streets, parading about the city, begging for help for their country and demanding permanent residency. The last thing we want is those Africans living with us in our country. It could grow to be almost as bad as those niggers in America who are almost living equally to the white people there and some better than whites."

"Almost living equally but will never be equal to us in America. Don't worry. We have an economic and political plan set aside for them, especially the ones who think they have made it. Our political puppets change the law every time they get ahead and cut Blacks off. Prominent Blacks will fall prey to their own popularity when disgraced."

"Yes, by the year 2010 white people will at last dominate the human population, unlike the population proportions now. With the white people giving multiple births and the average Black family in America having one or no children, we shall be in need of the new frontier, Africa, for more resources. Even the Chinese and Japanese have restrictions on the number of children their people can have."

"Along with the destruction of rainforests in the South Pacific Islands, in Asia and South America, brown people everywhere will die off; we plan to inhabit all the world's best land. It will be the same as when our ancestors killed the Indians here in America for their land. And this slow destruction of the people of color will look justified. We will send in troops to make it look like we are stopping the African, Asians and South Americans from killing each other. Our people will look like Peacekeepers; however, they will kill whoever is in the way of our special brand of peace."

"Plus, we have to make sure our boys identify amd kill those church officials who are going to help stop the war or help the injured and hide them from our people."

"Who's to stop us? Are the Africans going to stop killing each other? It is the same question we ask here in America. Are the black male teenagers going to stop killing each other in America? Are the poor Natives in any third world country from Afghanistan to Serbia ever going to stop killing each other? The answer is clear, gentlemen. They will destroy each other. Do we all agree? We begin Protocol 2000, now! make sure the opiates and heroin are pure to give to our killers."

"Yes," was heard from every voice in the room, but every

heart did not share the same sentiment. Something was wrong with this plan.

★★★★★★★★★★

There were five representatives from their respective American and European countries that had a change of heart when all was finally revealed to them. They cringed with the very thought of being in the same room as the members of this hate Organization. This was insanity. Power can be achieved without annihilation of all the people of color around the world.

All was not going exactly as planned for the Organization. It was clear not everyone saw the enemy as a person of color. Secrets were kept in this Organization built on hatred, fear, and mistrust, so it was to exist within as well as without its circumference.

As the Senator instructed the war lobbyist from the southern arms plant to send weapons directly to Rwanda in the guise of farm equipment, the members of the five countries who were not in agreement with the Organization got word to Duran about this covert operation. They must put an end to it.

Secretly an insider from one of the countries against the Organization supplied the Tutsi Patriotic Front with arms, while the Organization supplied the Hutus with simple weapons and machetes. An African friendly military, dressed in plain clothes, found the leaders of the Tutsi led Rwandan Patriotic Front and told them about the impending trouble and that they should start training for combat immediately. Word got to the United Nations, but the U.N. ignored the threat in Rwanda.

Another problem was that the Rwandan Patriotic Front no longer trusted the Belgians. The dilemma facing these five representatives was how they could allow a war to take place with no intention of stopping it before it starts. The Rwandese questioned how the French knew the Front would have to mobilize their forces and fight Hutu gangs who slaughtered their people before it even happened.

These renegade Organization members never thought about the thinking Rwandan, who would see both sides being armed and wonder who was controlling this war that did not yet happen. But clearly, they could see the preparations for armed struggle was coming from outside of Rwanda, not from within. Why all the training for war if it was not starting with the people who live in the country? Who was starting this war? Who or what was behind all the disruption?

Secretly, five renegade groups that were against the Organization decided to help the Tutsi after the war began. Hoping to cast less suspicion on themselves, they personally funded the peace.

Rwanda was a convenient place to start incipient ethnic cleansing. The people were trained to fear the power of a ruling government since their independence from Belgium. They didn't realize they would never have the economic power that was shared by the dictator and his military guards. They didn't realize that they still would not be able to get some of the rich land of the Volcanoes National Park for farming. They would be as poor as they were now even if all the Tutsis disappeared.

CHAPTER 10

⸻⸻⸻⸻⸻⸻⸻⸻⸻⸻⸻⸻⸻⸻⸻⸻

The Arrivals in Africa

"Now the Lord God had planted a garden in
the east, in Eden; and there he put the man he
had formed." KJV Gen. 2:8 -beginning of the
human race, Botswana.

After what seemed like millions of miles of ocean, the African
Affairs Council, the soldiers, and the mysterious men in suits
sensed a shift in direction as the plane began its slow and
gradual descent toward the airport.

Cheyenne's first glimpse of Africa was perceived from her
tiny airplane portal. They were told to look to the right at the
Cape Verde Islands off Morocco. They looked at each other
puzzled and could only imagine what must be on these islands
off the Senegal coastline. A review of the world map was in
order once they landed in Rwanda.

The first stop in Sierra Leone was a two-hour layover
where they refueled and checked the airplane. The passengers
were so anxious to deplane despite the restrictions to stay
within the airport loading area; they hardly noticed the name
of the town until someone asked why it was called Freetown.

Shaka, the historian, and African Studies mentor gave a
brief history of Sierra Leone.

"Following England's abolishment of the slave trade in
1772, it seems that because of three prominent men, Granville
Sharp, Thomas Clarkson, and William Wilberforce, who set up

a colony in Sierra Leone with British efforts to resettle formerly enslaved people in Africa.

"In 1787, the British government settled three hundred formerly enslaved people and seventy white prostitutes on the Sierra Leone peninsula in West Africa. Within two years, most members of this settlement had died from disease or warfare with the local Temne people.

"By 1790 the settlement was all but finished and then attacked by other Africans and dispersed totally. In 1791, a new colony was established by Granville Sharp and some European businesspeople for ex-slaves mostly to establish a government, a Council, and to bring traders and artificers.

"However, in 1792, a second attempt was made when 1,100 formerly enslaved people, were unhappy with their postwar resettlement in Canada and were sent to Sierra Leone. These enslaved Africans were mostly individuals who had supported Britain during the American Revolution and were punished by the new U.S. government and sent out of the U.S.

"In 1794 the colony was attacked and burnt down by the French.

Britain established a permanent Naval Patrol in order to stop the export of slaves. In 1807 it was illegal for British subjects to engage in the slave trade, and from 1808 to 1818 European countries outlawed the slave trade. This is why the British claimed Sierra Leone as a colony in 1818 and established a naval base. Freed Africans were brought here, and Freetown was born.

"If slaves were found on the ships leaving the West Coast of Africa they were taken to Sierra Leone for adjudication. The countries that made slavery illegal from 1810 to 1814 were Denmark, the United States, Sweden, and the Netherlands.

Portugal in 1815, Spain in 1817, France in 1818, Brazil in 1825, all outlawed slavery.

"So, the pirates, who are so romanticized in Western countries, became the slave traders.

"The sad part is that the illegal slave trade rose from approximately 85,000 Africans in 1810 to 135,000 by 1840. The shippers found a way to have papers stating their boats were not from the countries that agreed to the Reciprocal Search Treaty."

Discussions continued into the next hour about how and why enslavement increased at the rate that it did, especially after the laws were made to outlaw it. What a pirate actually was back then was the hot topic.

Their time on Sierra Leone soil gave them a new respect for this country. The added knowledge that South Carolina's coast is populated with direct descendants from Sierra Leone was of particular interest to Cheyenne and her associates.

Back on the plane, questions remained. The Council members considered themselves African by race, and American by nationality, and this short layover deepened their resolve to find answers.

The roar of the engines pulled them back into the present as the aircraft began its last leg of the journey.

★★★★★★★★★★

To the amazement of all aboard the plane, their second view of Africa was the orange torches of offshore oilrigs aflame near the coastline of Angola and Zaire. At once they felt a sudden pang of heartache with the knowledge that the oil did not belong to the Africans who lived there. In fact, the Africans had to import their oil from Brazil at great expense. The Brazilian refineries got their raw oil from Africa, refined it, then sent it back to Africa for sale.

"To the victor so goes the spoils," Tombe, the Council's president said. A lighthouse was visible, and the serenity prayer flashed across his mind momentarily.

It wasn't long before the plane began to descend far below the clouds. A road ran between mangroves and dwarf orange-berried palms on one side, and a long beach on the other; the beginning of Zaire's twenty-five miles of coastline. They flew over the river source where the ocean takes the river. Its islands and its fishing villages were behind barricades of mangrove.

"This was a most magnificent sight. Just like Michael Crichton describes in his book, Congo," said Shy.

"Welcome to Africa ladies and gentlemen," the pilot interrupted their thoughts. "Please look from both left and right windows and take in the glorious sight."

"Notice the magnificent ebony and mahogany trees as we leave the coast, giants in their splendor."

Starting the descent into central Africa, they saw how green the interior was. The trees were tremendous. Though they flew high above the ground, the coastal cities could be defined apart from the vast greenery of the forest and jungles filled with trees as tall as two hundred feet.

While flying closer to the interior of the land Cheyenne noticed the great vertical separation in the land below. The captain explained.

"This split spreads halfway up the middle of Africa. It's about thirty miles wide, for fifteen hundred miles. The split is a great lake that separates Zaire with a peninsula and comes between Zaire and Rwanda with Lake Kivu. It further splits to the north at Lake Edward in Uganda and splits Kenya and Tanzania with Lake Victoria; to the south the split continues from Lake Malawi to Northern Mozambique. Further research on this great land separation found that the eastern third of the continent had begun splitting off from the rest of the African landmass two hundred million years ago; for some reason, it stopped before the break was complete. This is called the Rift Valley. At one time Africa could have become two continents," the pilot told them. That bit of information made her imagination leap.

Thoughts of the earth's creation and the first human bones being found raced through Cheyenne's mind. In East Africa, the first human which scientists named "Lucy" was found to be two million years old. "If she populated only the Eastern section as she traveled north, because of the Rift Valley splitting, this would explain a lot. The Nile River flows northward up to Egypt. That would explain why Ethiopia and Egypt developed so quickly while the rest of the world slept. These countries had great empires and dynasties long before the Chinese developed their civilizations."

The pilot interrupted her thoughts again. "This split was occurring at the same time the continents separated. Africa and eastern and western Europe may have been four separate continents at one time."

Cheyenne could possibly conceive all of earth's land as one piece at the beginning of time. Life began in the middle of the world, where Africa is located.

She began to ponder the theory shared among geologists and scientists, that at one time South America, India, Asia, and Africa were united. She tried to remember what her geography teacher said about the continental drift that separated South America from Africa. This would totally explain how the pyramids were built in South America similar to the ones the

Black pharaohs built in Egypt. They were probably the same people-the original Africans.

The captain's voice filled the cabin, "We are now flying over a series of volcanoes, including the only active volcanoes in Africa at Virunga. The three volcanoes in the Virunga chain that are still active are; Mukenko, Mbuti, and Kanagarwi. They rise 11,000-15,000 feet above the Rift Valley to the east, and the Congo Basin to the west. You can see the two large volcanoes made famous by Dian Fossey, with her "Gorillas in the Mist." The first is Mount Bisoke which means, 'there where the herds go to drink' and Mount Karisimbi which is called 'white shell' because occasionally its crater is covered with snow."

Between Zaire and Rwanda, a great jungle of trees spread an enormous blanket of vegetation, concealing whatever lay beneath. From the air the Congo rainforest appeared as a vast and mysterious steaming hot house without the glass. Rivers fifty to a hundred feet wide were hidden beneath the green canopy. Cheyenne thought about the animals of the jungle. She also thought about how safe the people were that lived in the forests distanced from the European slaver.

"Ladies and gentlemen, what lies below and north of you is the largest rainforest in the world-The Congo. Winter or summer, the foliage remains the same. The untouched or virgin rainforest is called a primary jungle. You will see huge hardwood trees, mahogany, teak, and ebony. Underneath and unseen from above is a lower layer of ferns and palms, clinging to the ground. Primary jungles are dark and forbidding, but easy to move through since everything grows tall and big. The ground is clear of underbrush and thickets," the captain explained to the eager passengers.

"However," he continued, "If the primary jungle of the

rainforest was cleared by man and later abandoned, an entirely different secondary growth would take over. The dominant plants in the secondary jungle are softwoods and fast-growing trees, bamboo, and thorny tearing vines, which form dense and impenetrable barriers. Walking through a secondary jungle without a machete or bulldozer is not likely," the pilot laughed.

"The secondary jungle could be graded by age unlike the hardwood trees of the primary forest that live hundreds of years. The softwoods of the secondary jungle live only twenty years or so. Thus, as time goes on the secondary jungle is replaced by another form of secondary jungle, and this process repeats. Life in the rainforest never ceases to multiply," he continued.

Flying low over the great jungle was a flock of large birds. No more than ten hovered and seemed to buzz over and through the branches of the trees in a graceful dance. Flying above the birds and looking down on their wingspan was amazing.

"I've never seen birds flying under me before this close up," Cheyenne told Dava.

"Me neither," these were the first words Dava uttered since they came to the African continent

"We are coming to our destination. Below you is Rwanda," the captain majestically relayed.

"Look over there beyond the second curve of the river; see those bluish mountains sitting in that beautiful lake? It makes you want to just dive right in," Dava pointed out, and then laughed with excitement, finally out of wherever her mind temporarily took her.

"That must be the Lake Kivu beach resort on the lake ahead of us. It is gorgeous, and there it looks like hotels are right on the beach. Now I see why it's called the 'Riviera of Africa.' Those peninsulas and islands jut out into this river as it winds and curves following our route," Cheyenne said pointing down the river.

The plane flew low so that they could get a panoramic view of the land of Rwanda. Kivu Lake and the Volcanoes Mountains, both separated Zaire from Rwanda to the north.

Then they flew in and out of the green, neatly cultivated hilly land below. All up and down the mountains they saw geometrically cut out gardens. The hills showed perfectly furrowed lines of vegetation in concentric circles that rounded the hills to the valley below.

"In the high altitude of the hills are coffee berries growing on bushes, banana groves, and abundant trees and orchids," the pilot told them.

"Their tea and coffee are the best in the world."

The entire group in the plane gasped at the beauty of the hills and the river twisting and turning beneath them, in and out the valleys of these coffee and tea farms.

Cheyenne thought, "We don't even get Rwandan coffee in New York."

Bringing their attention to another crop, the captain said, "Looking down from the top of the hill to the right of the aircraft you'll see rows of tea leaves growing in straight vertical rows. Adjacent to the rows are neatly cut out squares of manioc and potatoes lined up and down the hillside."

"Like a good cornrow braided head," Cheyenne mused.

"Between the rows are furrows allowing the water from the top of the mountain to drain down easily into the first plateau. This plateau is leveled above the planting of the horizontally grown crop of vegetables. This crop goes in concentric circles around the mountain. The furrows catch the water so that the vegetation is not uprooted and thrown into an avalanche of vegetation down the hill," the pilot told them.

"Why do they take that risk? Why not plant on less steep land?" Dava asked innocently.

"The higher the altitude the tea and coffee is cultivated, the better the aroma. And look around, there is not much low land left for planting," he said closing the door to the cockpit.

"Now I see why this is called the land of a thousand hills," Cheyenne said to Dava, straining her neck to see out both sides of the plane.

"The greenery is overwhelming. I've never seen such lush thickets of trees and vegetation and such blue water," Dava told Shy.

Cheyenne's heart seemed to leap as she felt how the air seemed to give way beneath the plane as the landing gear lowered. The plane dropped once, twice, and then touched down at Gregoire Kayibanda de Kanombe International Airport, ten miles from Kigali. A cacophony of cheers and applause rose up from the coach passengers as they peered out the cabin windows

They emerged into heat, a welcome relief from the frost and icy cold February winds of New York. It was not as humid, nor was the aroma of soil as strong as expected. Instead, fresh chlorophyll and oxygenated air from the mountains energized them to an almost dizzying state. Everyone took a deep breath and those who had come to Africa for the first time touched the ground ceremoniously with both hands saying, "Ashe."

They walked the tarmac to the terminal building, a mass of officials, people claiming to be officials, and men and boys eager to carry bags greeted them. As they entered the crush, the U.S. Ambassador's assistant guided them to the right spot, just as the customs officials were about to demand their passports.

"My sisters and brothers, on behalf of the Rwanda Ambassador, we welcome you back to the motherland."

One-by-one he slid the passports through a narrow slit beneath a screen that should have been transparent glass but was opaque. This was Immigration. When it seemed as if the process was taking too long the Ambassador's assistant went inside behind the opaque wall and emerged with everyone's passport stamped and ready to go.

Regardless of anything else, Cheyenne knew her first duty while in the airport was to call home. When she finally reached her parents after some effort with the Rwandese and French operators, she told them how wonderfully they were received, and a big reception was awaiting their arrival.

"You know I will call as soon as I'm situated in my living area. I'll give you full details and where to write exactly and my phone number. I must go now, because there is a delegation about to present us with something," she told her parents, knowing they wanted to talk longer.

"O.K. sweetheart, you take good care of yourself. Please don't have us waiting too long for your call. I know you have to go to the reception, but right after that, as soon as you get to your new home, call us, regardless of the six hours ahead," said her mother with much urgency.

As Cheyenne placed the phone on the hook, after kissing her mom and dad goodbye, she noticed some Rwandese giving threatening looks at their entire group, and some other men were walking outside the terminal with weapons.

Her anxiety was heightened when she saw that she had been flying on the same plane with two obviously armed men, one white and one black. They watched her discreetly and looked around. Their eyes told her that they knew who she was, and as she was about to show concern and face them with some questions; they quickly leaped into a waiting car

However, her attention was then focused on something

going on in the terminal. There was another African American who seemed very agitated and uncomfortable as he entered the customs arena from their plane. Cheyenne heard a customs man say, "Thank you Colonel Dupree."

Also on the plane were several other men that were not part of the African Affairs Council. They moved quickly and in such a way that it would be difficult to identify them. Senator Gatt sent these professional crowd agitators and assassins who scattered into waiting unmarked cars.

CHAPTER 11

New Home, New Family

"Rich in possessions, rich in greed"
M.B. Paternostre De la Mairieu, Rwandan

After retrieving her baggage from the conveyor, she was no longer an ordinary person. They all got the royal treatment, and their luggage was carefully carried to the motorbus that would take them to their new homes for the next two years.

The moment she stepped onto the African earth; Cheyenne could feel her ancestors pull at her spirit. Even with all the beauty and colorful clothing of the people and greenland, her heart felt heavy with the thought of slavery, and what it must have been like to be ripped away from this wondrous land. She felt a blood affinity to this beautiful continent and people. But the radiant and charming smiles and welcoming arms of the people who came to greet them quickly changed her spirit from sad to glad.

After the motorbus's interior had been swept, their baggage was placed under the seats, and they quickly boarded. As they slowly moved away from the bustle of the airport, beyond the crowds, behind the maze of dark creeks and green landscapes, she saw a team of white and black soldiers riding horseback. This was not expected, and somewhat disheartening, yet oddly reassuring at the same time.

Noticeable immediately was how rich in orchids Rwanda was. Brilliant flowers all stood in serried rows to welcome foreign visitors to Kigali. Some were wild and some were cared for; the fragrance was almost intoxicating, Cheyenne nodded in silence to Dava, who read her mind.

Then as the motorbus slowed after miles of riding outside the airport, the sweetest sound arose. It was not the tender sound of a bird's song or the high notes of a melodic musical instrument, but a sound so perfect, it mesmerized them.

As they rode onto the green road, they saw one hundred children smiling and singing the Rwandese welcome song. It was so beautiful. The visitors' jaws hung open in total surprise. Their motorbus stopped and the Council exited in a trance-like gaze listening to this beautiful rhythmic song.

As they looked around there were hundreds of colorfully dressed Rwandese men, women, and military clad officials, who stood with open arms awaiting the much-anticipated arrival of their honored guests. The Ambassador of Rwanda then personally received each of the Council members with a handshake and genuine hug. The Council could not help but wipe the glistening drops from their eyes.

"Welcome to you all. I hope you liked our children's 'Thousand Hills Singers.' Dinner will be served at our Franco-Rwanda Cultural Center in our beautiful downtown, Kigali. Here you will enjoy our food, entertainment, and social talk with some of the people with whom you'll be working. But first let us escort you to your living quarters so that you may check in. You will get the full tour by our motorbus driver Francois. Francois and Miss Balzac will get you situated when you arrive at the hotel," said the Ambassador, as he and his assistant ushered the group back onto the motorbus shaking every hand as the passengers reboarded.

The motorbus driver introduced himself in French, which was somewhat lacking, "Mesdemoiselles et Messieurs, welcome to our beautiful city. My name is Francois."

Leading from the airport into central Kigali were bamboo and palm trees which spanned the road with branches nearly touching overhead. The open motorbus allowed the fragrances of porcelain roses, hibiscus, and bougainvillea to dazzle their senses. Orchids and exotic flowers were enjoyed by all for free on the road.

The trip took them along a path, near a tributary of the river. In the water surrounded by purple water hyacinth, women washed clothes on an upturned dugout and soaped them white; a man watered bean plants in his garden behind a palisade of twigs; a woman climbed the bank with a shining galvanized bucket full of water which nodded with her head as she greeted the motorbus as it passed.

As they entered Kigali, the Council members gasped in unison at the sight ahead. On a high plateau they could see a massive white brick hotel, sitting high above the city, surrounded by beautiful colors of gardens and greenery.

They rode the wide and narrow passages that began as streets and roads, then ended as paths unpaved, then back to streets. Further along they saw the lily of the Nile, African violets and orchids and the red-hot poker plant Cheyenne recognized from Brooklyn's Botanical Gardens; they were all growing everywhere free and naturally. Africa was after all the place of origin for all of the flora now grown everywhere around the world.

"As you noticed, from the hills you can see our beautiful countryside," said Francois. "The hotel on the high plateau ahead is the Hotel Rebero l'Horizon. On a clear night you can see the Volcanoes Mountains to the north from there."

"It is like a city in the countryside," Cheyenne remarked. "It seems like a beautiful garden with a few buildings sprinkled here and there that blend in without disturbing the essence of the garden."

As the motorbus turned on Rue Du Travel they slowed to a stop. Francois pointed out, "We are now at Logement Bon Accueil, your new home. As you notice you are near the bus station, which is good for you to get to the office building where you will be working. I hope you enjoyed your ride; Madame Balzac will assist you now." Francois took everyone's luggage off the motorbus with the help of the men inside the apartment office.

"Goodbye Francois," Mme. Balzac said as she helped the Council members get down from the motorbus.

"We have already made the arrangements so please follow me into the lobby. Your luggage will be brought to your rooms."

The building was surrounded by beautiful rose bushes and palm trees, and the garden was filled with every color. While walking into the lobby they could hear the birds chirping. It was a sound to which they would become familiar.

This residence was a mere five dollars a week, a fraction of the cost of a N.Y.C. apartment, but it was a win for both the landlord and tenant, because the owners of the residence knew they had a guaranteed income for the next two years.

"Shy, this is some deal," Dava whispered.

Each Council member then dispersed into his or her flat. The buildings were solid concrete with flowers everywhere. Cheyenne and Dava began to look around inside and noticed that it was basic yet exceptionally clean. It had the strong scent of cleaning detergent.

"This will do just fine for now, until something better comes around," Dava said.

They were aware that the job they came to do would be

lucrative after the completion of basic installations of computers and certain programs. It was inevitable that soon there would follow the manufacturing of products and the money producing cable operations.

However, they were resigned to a minimal salary while construction and installation was taking place.

"Well, I guess this will be like sharing a bedroom with a sister. Neither of us have had that experience. My two little sisters are so much younger than I am. And I was already in middle school when they were born. Dava, this will be a new experience for you without ever having any siblings to share with. Well, I guess we will have to be sisters for real now. Besides in this strange new country, it will be fun sharing quarters," Cheyenne told Dava.

No one really knew what kind of living conditions they would have until they arrived. A few Council members had been to West Africa twenty years prior to this trip, and were invited to live in one of the villages there. They described thatched roofs and mud huts with mats on the floor for sleeping. In another hut, there was a hole dug in the dirt floor a foot wide in diameter and with the bottom unseen, and a bucket of water nearby it. This was the bathroom. Eating was a communal event. There was one wash basin for cleansing their hands, and then each villager would dip their fingers in fufu and dunk a piece in a fish stew. The Council sighed deeply when Kwame told this story on the plane. So, their clean tiled floor boarding cottage was a refreshing, pleasant surprise in comparison.

Cheyenne could never fully express to Dava how much she appreciated being with her on this combined learning, business, pleasure journey into an unknown country. Dava believed enough in the work of the African Affairs Council that she shared Shy's dream. The two of them would try to right a wrong in the world by coming to Rwanda and giving back. Thoughts of this nature raced through Shy's mind as they both looked around their new home.

Cheyenne and Dava casually relaxed in the two lounge chairs that were especially provided for them. There was a small desk and chair facing the window. They smiled over the tiny kitchenette, which would barely hold the dishes Cheyenne packed. Overall, they were delighted with the apartment.

"Dava, what do you think?" her best friend asked, knowing the answer from her dancing eyes.

"This is wonderful! I'm really happy we are doing this." They smiled at one another. "This will be home in no time. Once we go shopping and place art and local crafts around, it will be beautiful."

"The people seem happy to see us. They certainly are colorful. The clothing of the singers and our greeters outside the airport blended in so strikingly with the landscape and openness of the country," Cheyenne pointed out as she unpacked and placed the small kitchen utensils, pots, and dishes in the kitchenette.

"You know I once camped out in a tent after reading 'Walden Pond' by H.D. Thoreau, the summer of my junior year in college. So, I can adjust to just about anything," Dava blurted, "Not that this is roughing it. I knew we couldn't afford the luxury tourist hotels for the two years we will be here. These quarters will be great. We have a shower and toilet and sink in the bathroom. We have two comfortable beds in a separate room and this large living area, two closets and a kitchenette. What more can we ask for?"

"That reminds me, I'm glad I packed some canned goods and crackers. Let's fix something quick to eat then look around," Cheyenne said, as she put her suitcase and other things on the bed.

"I'm down, girlfriend; we don't exactly know what the food will taste like at the Cultural Center. Even though we are familiar with all of it, it may be slightly different here in Rwanda. So, if we get a little nibble we won't starve. My mother said, 'never go anywhere hungry and act greedy.' Still, we won't be too full if the food is great, which I think it will be. Don't you think so, Shy?" Dava said in one breath.

Cheyenne nodded in the affirmative. Dava struggled with her overloaded suitcases, but was thrilled to see the larger than expected closet in the room. Cheyenne prepared crackers and tuna. The canned peaches were served in a bowl, and after the light meal, they freshened up and changed into more elegant dress for the evening.

CHAPTER 12

||||||||||||||||||||||||||||||||||||||||||||||

The Reception

"And he took the seven loaves and fishes, and
gave thanks, and broke them, and gave to his
disciples, and the disciples to the multitudes."
KJV Matt 15:36

Soon, the Rwandese welcome motorbus arrived with the
same young handsome driver who spoke little French and no
English. Each of the Council members had been given lessons
in Kinyarwanda, the language spoken by the Rwandese, and so
they were able to understand most of what the young, smiling
man said.

As he swept them off through the beautiful, flowered city
of Kigali again, Francois pointed out the busy, bustling Muslim
Quarter at the top of the hill overlooking layers of deep green
and tall thick trees. In former times Arab traders from the
Indian Ocean coast settled here.

"Is there Watusi music we can hear? I read about them five
years ago," said Dava innocently.

"There is no longer Watusi music. We have Rwandese
music, we have the same culture Tutsi, Hutu, Twa, and we
dance the same way. Our musicians go everywhere, Senegal,
Canada, Paris, Belgium, and all play traditional Rwandese
music. Rwandese dance has a meaning; we have a dance for
women and a dance for men.

"Men dance physically, dancing shows courage, they are
strong, and they dance with spears and shields. They make

faces to show they are fighting warriors. The women dance like a cow for the cow is a sign of wealth and gracefulness, the way it moves. They move them in a herd very graciously. These dances are danced for any occasion, weddings, church ceremonies, and baptisms. Children are baptized as babies.

"They introduced the dance in the church in 1993. We used to clap in the church throughout the ceremony and we used a bell. The priests, and church ministry use bells and the people clap.

"Islam is 1% of the population, the rest are Catholic 90%. There are well known dancing groups called the Rwandan National Ballet, a traditional women's dance group, and the Intore, a traditional men's group," Francois struggled happily with his French.

The African Affairs Council members were fascinated not only as New Yorkers who really didn't know anything about this rich Rwandese History, but as African Americans whose lives were being changed, at this moment by the sights they saw and the information they took in like sponges. They studied every sight that they passed by from the exotic flowers that grew in a wild, colorful array along the road, to the beautifully dressed women and men. From their perspective from their motorbus. seats, so far Rwanda looked like a happy, thriving place to live.

"Look at all the crafts; this is a sure bet for a return shopping visit," said Dava.

"There are so many beautiful flowers everywhere," Cheyenne said in her best French.

"In southwest Rwanda in Nyugere there are no less than one hundred species of orchid and two hundred-fifty species of trees along with the thousands of monkeys, chimps, and other animals," Francois surprisingly spoke in clear French, as if he memorized it for them.

"All homes have flowers, roses and other beautiful plants. We have many private and public gardens," he continued.

"Our national parks are protected as historic sites."

As they drove along the streets mostly in silence, it did not take them long to notice that the people were carrying everything on their heads except their children. Small children are always carried on their backs. Cheyenne nodded to a small woman who had a huge bundle on her head and a baby on her back, while holding the hand of another child. The woman smiled back as if she weren't carrying the weight of the world, or so it looked to Cheyenne, on her entire body.

Cheyenne thought, "I feel it when I overload my pocketbook at home. Maybe it's the way I carry it on my shoulder that makes it uncomfortable." She looked at the woman again in utter wonder and admiration.

They climbed the winding, beautifully sculpted street into the landscape itself as the driver pointed out special sites to them.

He told them, "This is Nyarugenge Hill; it is the city center and the location of government and administrative buildings, also commercial businesses and international banks are here in abundance. It is, how do you say, cosmopolitan due to the expatriates and because the United Nations Food and Agriculture Organization and the European Community have bases here." This was stunning news to the Council.

"Now, as we pass by this large traffic roundabout, right here, at the entrance to the Avenue de la Republique, our destination is arrived, the Franco-Rwanda Cultural Center." We smiled at Francois' attempt at English in the final part of his sentence.

As they entered they were greeted by President Habyarimana, ministers and head chiefs of the neighboring localities and distant regions. The Council members were served hors-d'oeuvres and non-alcohol cocktails by passing waiters.

The Ambassadors from several other African countries greeted them and asked that they visit their countries during their stay in Africa. Later that afternoon, after everyone in the African Affairs Council toured all of the Franco-Rwanda Cultural Center, the Intore Dancers performed in the music hall. The music from the initial drums and horns opened the show with unrestrained rhythms and vocals.

The guests were seated next to the Nigerian Ambassador. When the music began the President and his generals left unobtrusively. Cheyenne thought that was odd for him to leave when a beautiful symbol of Rwanda was about to perform.

The Nigerian Ambassador noticed her puzzled look and said in perfect English, "The drummers were recruited at exceedingly early ages and represent Rwanda at all major events, national and international. This group of young male dancers, chosen from the best of the country, is named the Intore, which means the best. Under the Watusi monarchs, wars were frequent, and the Intore were first and foremost elite warriors, organized into companies which practiced war and learned to fight with swords, spears and bows. The Intore carried all weapons during the war dances which were considered part of the martial arts, resulting from long apprenticeships in combat."

He went on intermittently as they danced different pieces, "With the arrival of the Europeans especially the Germans and Belgians in Rwanda, wars between kingdoms ended and the militia were dismantled as they were no match for the European guns that killed in mass. During the enslavement of the people of Rwanda, as with the rest of Africa, dances became simulated battles and the King's ballet corps left court only for ceremonies." The Nigerian Ambassador then signaled that he was called away on business and gave them a brochure of the Intore.

The Intore Warrior dancers wore white sarongs, with layered leopard or several skins over the sarong that fastened around their waists. Their headdresses were made of banana fibers or of sisal and flung silkily back and forth. Broad necklaces with the most beautiful geometric patterns of beading, in white and blue, or white and red or white and black adorned them and were wide enough to cover them from their neck to their shoulder. Their headdresses were held on by strings of the same beading that went under their chins. In one hand they held a spear and in the other a small shield that held the same or similar geometric pattern as the neck beading.

Cheyenne and Dava looked at each other with mutual excitement as the show continued. Then she whispered, "Three hundred years ago those European- made glass beads were bartered for our enslaved ancestors. I think these people originally polished and made their own beads or used the precious gems Rwanda is known to have. I hope they keep teaching the dances to the next generations."

While the dancers were performing their riveting and exhilarating moves, Shy and Dava tucked the beautiful brochure about the dancers carefully into their pocketbooks. They didn't want to miss a beat, and anticipated reliving this experience by reading about the dancers when they got home.

There was one war dance in which the dancers would spin their cornsilk manes in unison. This was a sight so spellbinding that vocals emanated from all corners of the audience.

The Master of Ceremonies of the performance said, "The show itself consists of a contest of agility, of resistance and art between the isocyaka "the rivals" and the indashyikurwa "the unsurpassables". The rivals are the Batwa, taught and led by the Mutusi, and the latter group are the extraordinaries.

"The Batwa begin the dances by executing the stage entrance and salutation theme. There is a pause during which the entire ballet corps sings the praises of ancient Batutsi heroes who, often enough, never existed. When the King claps his hands, the Batwa begin their dances again, miming 'Tattoo', 'The incomparable' and 'the most difficult case.'

"At this moment, the Intore dash into the arena, heads decorated with white colobus monkey fur, bodies enveloped in multicolored draperies or leopard skins, weapons in hand. The ensemble of their mimicry is called 'That puts an end to all discussion' and is composed of many dances: 'The Crested Crane', 'Lightning Flash', 'Invincible', and other meanings. All dances end with the exit and thank-you movements."

The group watched these long supple bodies, the rapid succession of acrobatic steps and leaps beyond belief. The shimmer of costumes slashed with color, the rhythm, sometimes violent, now caressing the music. The flashing weapons and long sticks decorated with thick fringes of raffia had the audience feel the pulsation deep inside the unreachable part of their bodies.

After the body throbbing experience of the Intore and the drummers, everyone was led into the dining area and seated. There was an eloquent libation made to the ancestors and then a Catholic prayer. The Council members were all treated like royalty. The dinner delighted the palate with beautifully prepared baked fish wrapped in leaves, spiced beans, and rice, fufu, sweet potatoes, banana beer and Fanta soda, sweets, and fruits.

The guests were cautioned about drinking too much banana

beer, so Cheyenne and Dava sipped one together and decided to split a Fanta orange instead. Other African Affair Council members sat with Ambassadors and some of the executives they would be working with at the plant.

After the main course was served there was an announcement, over dessert and coffee, that they would meet their comfort host family. The plan was for the Council members to match the color and pattern of the beautiful African print they were given to the cloth on the tables where their host family was seated. At this time, the Ambassadors and dignitaries were led off to another section to have their dessert and talk over matters they don't usually have time to discuss in person with one another.

The family that Cheyenne and Dava were assigned to was Mr. and Mrs. Henri Ntetesi and their three children. Each Council member was seated at a place setting with their name beautifully handwritten on a card. With their new seating arrangements in place, banana bread, sweets and fruit cakes were served with fresh coffee and tea. The tea was Rwanda's pride. As they learned, the high altitudes give it the best aroma. For the first time Shy and Dava didn't even put sugar in it.

It was remarkable to Cheyenne how pleasant the French language sounded to her ear when spoken by the Ntetesi family. There were a few differences in inflections and dialects, but for the most part what she learned in school was substantial for simple communication with the people here.

Of course, the family Cheyenne and Dava were going to be with spoke English and French as well as the Rwandese language. They were truly kind people. Marie d'Arc Ntetesi had a respectable job as secretary at the U.S. Embassy and her husband Henri Ntetesi was a science teacher at the secondary school which is equivalent to a junior college or community college in the U.S.

"I hope we can be of some major service to your country Mr. and Mrs. Ntetesi," Cheyenne and Dava said, "And please forgive our clumsy mispronunciation of your name, we hope to correct it!" The family smiled at the young Americans so lovingly that they were set at ease immediately.

Mr. Ntetesi leapt to his feet and extended his arms as his wife smiled and waited for Cheyenne and Dava's acknowledgement before she extended her arms to them. He was tall, dark, and handsome. His smile could light a tunnel, Cheyenne thought to herself.

"We have waited many generations for you my sisters," Mrs. Marie Ntetesi said as she clasped her arms around the both of them in turn. She had the most beautiful smile with the most perfectly white teeth.

These words of love sprang on their ears and hearts like butterflies. At that very moment the American song, "Black Butterfly," played and echoed through Cheyenne's head. The song of South Africa's freedom, in the 1970s, calls to African Americans across the sea.

The lyrics lullabied by Denise Williams fell gently on Cheyenne's ears and to the very core of her soul; it sent chills and shivers up and down her spine. The feeling of family reuniting permeated throughout the great hall, and they all fell silently into each other's arms once again as long-lost brothers and sisters. Cheyenne had known these people not for seconds, but years, decades; she knew them even centuries ago.

Tearfully Cheyenne and Dava looked with their hearts at their newfound sisters and brothers. Love coursed through that room like newly made river falls, cascading down a sloping mountain. Love was bursting from every corner, everywhere they looked in that great room.

The evening turned into a magical, spiritual experience.

More libations were made for appreciation to the ancestors for bringing the African Americans back home to them. Nearly everyone felt the warmth. The gathering ended with a free for all dance to the rhythm of the African drum and horn. They knew then that it was a night they would remember for the rest of their lives. This is one time Cheyenne was so happy she imitated her Dad dancing and took pictures to always remember the moment. Later everyone left with their comfort families.

Since it was still relatively early, the Ntetesi family walked Cheyenne and Dava about the city on a brief tour for half an hour before returning to the bus and returning home. Office buildings and stores seemed to sprout up from nowhere amidst bungalows and huts.

"From our vantage point here, at the top of Nyarugenge Hill, we can nearly see the entire city of Kigali," Marie told them. "Above the Cultural Center are two important buildings to Rwanda. One main building on the edge of this traffic roundabout, at the entrance to the grand Boulevard de la Revolution, is the ORTPN-the Office Rwandais du Tourisme et des Parcs Nationaux. This is where they are in charge of preserving and protecting the wildlife in our national parks. Next to that is the Hotel des Mille Collines, which is the hotel of a thousand hills, with one hundred twelve rooms, bar, restaurant, swimming pool and boutiques, built by the Belgian airline in association with the State of Rwanda."

From the main Avenue de la Republique they walked down small streets and saw the Commerce Bank of Rwanda, The Continental African Bank, the Rwanda Bank of Development, the Bank of Kigali, and the Caritas Bookstore.

"The Rwandese businesses seem to be very profitable with all these banks," said Dava very innocently. Cheyenne nudged her as if to say be quiet. These banks did not belong to the Rwandese; they were owned by European and other foreign enterprises. Money was taken out of the country and some was used to develop streets, sewage, and hotels mostly for the Europeans.

Cheyenne remembered the words when she had talked to an international student at the college where she was doing her Research. He had told her companies started here are tax exempt for ten years. Companies operating under the Free Zone Act producing exclusively for export are entitled to income tax exemption in perpetuity. This had to be the greatest place for a business. Little or no tax paid to the government forever, along with labor and land which was very inexpensive.

They briefly and carefully glided down to the Kigali Grand Market, also located on the Nyarugenge Hill. Henri said, "Here we see a preponderance of mangoes, pineapples, and manioc along with classic garden produce for Western tastes, such as cabbage, tomatoes, carrots, and lettuces that all grow in Rwanda due to the temperate high-altitude climate. Spices, condiments, traditional utensils, odds and ends, the Rwandese also sell arts, crafts, and souvenirs here," he said proudly.

Along the way there were bookstores and more boutiques and arts and crafts shops. Cheyenne had a strange sensation seeing these things of western and European lifestyles.

"I guess they wanted to show us all of the parts that make the whole of Rwanda," she thought. Except for the many white tourists in the open-air terraces of several of the elegant restaurants, as well as a few financial centers with futuristic architecture, there was no mistaking that they were in Africa.

Even with all of these edifices the greenery was still everywhere. These huge buildings still had huge trees and shrubs landscaping them perfectly. No matter where they walked there were beautiful flowers blooming in abundance. And always the Rwandese women walking with their multi-colored skirts, with children bundled in their waist sashes.

The huge baskets perched on their heads were balanced with such equilibrium that it caused one American biomechanical specialist to spend fifteen years of his life researching how these women did it. He wanted to know how these small delicate boned African women could carry up to 70% of their weight on their head without holding it or developing huge neck muscles.

Needless to say, he still hadn't gotten it; even when he had Marines, trained and stronger than these women, fail in their attempts at balancing these things on their heads. African women must find it amusing to think how much research, time and money white people spend studying them, Cheyenne thought.

Once again she was reminded of Maya Angelo's poem, Our Grandmothers in her line, "... my description cannot fit your tongue, for I have a certain way of being in this world, I shall not be moved."

After the great reception, the ladies noticed that some more militant members of their group were very disturbed at the dominance of the European presence. However, their guide assured everyone that the Rwanda people benefit from the tourism these businesses and tourists generate. Everyone, they are finding out, cannot farm the land and live untouched or unscathed by Western influence in Rwanda.

They wound their way back to the Cultural Center. "We will call you about 9 a.m.," Marie told Cheyenne. "We will have breakfast prepared for you tomorrow, OK?" Cheyenne planned with Francois, the motorbus driver, to visit their adopted families the next day. Everyone was incredibly pleased with everyone.

FORGIVE AND LIVE: RWANDA

On their way back to the apartment Cheyenne said to Dava, "The Rwandese are proud of us, and we are very proud of them. It seems like we hugged and kissed and shook hands all night."

They rode back cheerily to what would be their home for the next two years. "This was it, we are definitely committed now," Cheyenne thought.

When they arrived home not one council member went inside. Everyone had so much to say about the incredible Intore Dancers who they later found out were not only the Tutsi warriors, but Intore was comprised of the much-appreciated Twa warriors known for their fierceness as well as the Hutu.

They reminisced about the wonderful feeling when they all met their own, personal, host family and the tour of this beautiful city. They talked about the good African dinner, and vigorously discussed the walk and the European banks, businesses, and shops. They all agreed that the most wonderful part was each Council member individually knowing they had someone like family looking out for them.

This was definitely a great idea, having a family to call their own. It would make the adjustment to this new and foreign country that much easier. The family would help them learn the language and culture of Rwanda that much better. They would have the pleasure of going to a real home with people and families like the ones they left behind in America.

Later that night, two of the elders of the Council quickly visited Cheyenne and Dava to make sure everything was alright with them. Cheyenne and Dava were the youngest and only females who were qualified and brave enough to come on a trip such as this.

"So how are you two making it together so far? Is your

room large enough?" asked Tombe, the President of the African Affairs Council.

"We are so happy to be here, Tombe," Cheyenne said.

"Our room is fine for the two of us. Our host family is sweet and wonderful and tomorrow we are having breakfast with them," said Dava.

"This country is so beautiful, obviously anything can grow here," Cheyenne started, "But there is something I noticed that bothers me. It may not mean anything."

"What is that?" Tombe asked with some concern.

"When the Intore Dancers began the President of Rwanda, Juvenal Habyarimana, walked out with his officers, looking rather upset." Cheyenne was too straight forward to hold back now.

"Well, you know the Hutu and Tutsi have been having problems in this country for years. The President is Hutu and the Intore Dancers are mixed, but mostly Tutsi. However, there is a peace accord that President Habyarimana is upholding and hopefully will sign another in April of this year," Tombe said sadly. "They still are not one united people."

"They look too similar to one another for that kind of mess," said Dava.

"They have intermarried and mixed for generations," Cheyenne said. "They should see my family. We run the gamut from very dark and short to tall and some very fair. Some of the very fair members of my family left the U.S. and God only knows what they are passing for wherever they may be."

"Through you two we are able to show the Rwandese our beautiful African sisters," said Tombe who never used African American, always African.

"Maybe your working side by side with us and the African men here will allow them to see that they too can become

133

educated and work together for a common cause. We are showing them how women can excel in technology. This is not a man only project; this is for all of our people to learn together."

"Thank you Tombe," Cheyenne felt proud. "We feel so honored and privileged to be a part of this historical event. Here and now, we shall forever make a difference."

Everyone hugged and when the two men left Cheyenne and Dava fell out flat on their beds. Their heads were swimming with all that took place and all that will take place in the next few days. After Cheyenne phoned home, she and Dava talked until their eyes shut and neither one of them made any sense any longer. Tomorrow, Sunday, they would visit with the Ntetesi's for breakfast then a special local tour.

CHAPTER 13

||||||||||||||||||||||||||||||||||||||||||||||||||

Our Kin, Our History,
New Awakenings

"Children's children are the crown of old
men; and the glory of children are their
fathers." KJV Proverbs 17:6

The next morning, they prepared for their visit to Henri and
Marie's home. "Shy, do you think I should wear this shirt with
my tummy showing a little with these slacks?" Dava asked
innocently.

"I wouldn't if I were you. My aunt was telling me that
in 1972 when she went to Ghana, she wore a halter with her
tummy out and a Ghanaian woman told her 'we do not dress
like that over here.' So, if I were you I'd wear that blue sun
dress you packed," Cheyenne said as she slipped into her shirt
waist dress and canvas easy walkers.

"I hear Francois' horn beeping for us," Dava excitedly
exclaimed. "I'll go and tell him we're almost ready."

She ran out without her shoes to tell him they would only
be one minute. Cheyenne made one last peek into the mirror,
happy she cut her hair short for this trip, and headed out. Dava
on the other hand left hers long and made a quick ponytail,
while stepping into her shoes.

When they locked the door to their apartment and left in
Francois' cab, they had no idea so many eyes were on them.
Tombe and some Council members watched the cab and wrote

the license number for the ladies' protection. But there were other eyes following Cheyenne and Dava that had nothing to do with protection, from sources they would find out about much later in their trip.

On their way to the home of Henri and Marie Ntetesi, Francois drove them by the Oil refinery; this place took the crude oil from the coast of Africa and prepared it for consumption abroad.

Francois was so proud of his taxi, he bragged about how he obtained his own taxi/private car service.

"I made friends with the owner of the Hotel d'Colinas, and he bought me the motorbus and made me the driver for his maids. With the money I saved I bought the taxi," a proud Francois told us.

"I see," said Cheyenne, disappointed at first then thought of the logic in it.

"It's so very green everywhere in this city," Dava said wanting to hear about the city.

"It's very green, called the 'land of thousands hills.' Rwanda is perpetually green all year. With very high land it's also called the 'Switzerland of Africa' because of so many hills. In the evening it is a bit cool. It is not hot. When you go from east to west the country becomes higher and higher because the east is quite flat," he said.

Francois drove through the heart of the city and paused where a man and his son made hand carved stools, low with the seat carved in a rectangular curve. The father finished the shaping with a design in the center of the stand. His son hacked with a machete at a whole tree stump from which another stool was roughly emerging. The handsome ladies and inquisitive children watched the passengers as the passengers watched the carvers.

Francois' old but clean Berliet whizzed slowly past fish

hatcheries and out towards the oil torches that symbolize another foreign power. The sky looked heavy, but he was adamant that rain would not come. The drizzle that smudged dust on the windscreen and compelled him to use the wipers, simply did not exist. He denied the rain, even though this was the beginning of the rainy season for Rwanda.

He showed them the refinery, which was a bizarre example of international collaboration, designed to refine oil of a grade which did not come out of the ground here. They read about the international rip-off the oil companies perpetuated. Crude oil, from the seventy-odd private on shore wells off Zaire and some from Rwanda, was exported, and the refined oil compatible with the African oil was imported, mostly from Brazil. It was a simple equation which transformed oil wealth for Africa into oil deficit. Other countries became rich from taking oil out of Africa and selling Brazilian oil to Africa at triple the cost.

Fishermen walking after church stayed closely grouped, carrying machetes, pliant mangrove rods and spear-like paddles on their shoulders. They climbed a path from the creek and passed under tremendous arches formed by baobabs.

"They say that the devil, or God grown careless in the toils of creation, planted these mangrove trees with their roots in the air," said Francois.

Fruits, olive-green and velvet-covered like tree ornaments, hung from vegetable constructs. Where the car passed, these fruits and huge seeds fell into the ground and huge plants stuck up through the sand under them.

When they finally reached their destination Cheyenne and Dava were impressed with Marie and Henri's home. The two guests were greeted at the door by a housekeeper. She was all smiles and very happy to see the famous American women.

This naturally surprised them because it takes a lot of money in the United States to have a housekeeper, but not here.

After the French hugged and cheek kissed by the family, they went inside.

The home was brightly washed brick with an aluminum and bamboo roof. The floor was cement with beautifully colored hand-woven rugs covering each inch of floor space in the living room. The furniture was very comfortable. Some distinctly French pieces aroused Cheyenne's curiosity.

"Have you been to France often?" she asked.

"Yes, the whole family has been there many times. We have dual citizenship," said Henri.

"I have breakfast all ready for you," Marie said as she escorted them to the dining room, and they all sat down.

"You must be starving after the drive," Marie had a very motherly concern in her voice.

"I know Francois took you the scenic route past the oil refinery." Henri had paid Francois and they spoke briefly while he walked Francois to the car. Francois left happily knowing he would see the American women again.

The table was set, and a delicious spread of banana bread, coffee, mangos, oranges, and scrambled eggs and beef lay before them. Prayer was said by Henri and food was passed first to the guests, then the children, then Henri and Marie.

"We have planned your group's arrival for many months. Our plans for a more modern and self-sufficient Rwanda go hand in hand with your plans. We have been waiting for many years for our African American brethren to share their skills and knowledge with us," said Henri very proudly and happily.

"You don't know what this means to us, Mr. Ntetesi," Cheyenne said very carefully. "Our dreams have been your dreams. We were taken away, and your land was taken from you. Now we are both educated; we have the skills in Western technology, while you have the land and natural resources. Together we can do just about anything in the world. You have maintained the values and morals of our ancestors that were lost to us because of our western miseducation. We can learn the universe from you. The combination and exchange of knowledge will be awesome."

"It is a wonderful thing, and Shy please call us Marie and Henri, we are only in our forties you know." said Henri as he took a drink.

"Henri is so excited about the future and the prospect of our collaborating with you that he may reveal his dreams and overwhelm you," said Marie smiling.

"His dreams can't possibly be as dramatic as ours are. You should have heard the talk on the plane coming here. The Council discerned an unfathomable number of things that we as a people united for the first time in centuries can do together. You have something here we just don't have in America, land, and resources. It's a virtual gold mine!" Cheyenne exclaimed, trying not to let go of her natural excitement and enthusiasm.

She thought, "I don't want to scare them into thinking we were there to take over. Far be it from the truth. This was going to be the beginning of a great alliance and business venture. We are going to rock the world."

Trying not to show her thoughts, Cheyenne asked, "And your children are so well behaved, yesterday they seemed so fascinated by my foot wear?" as she winked to the children who were quietly eating.

At the Cultural Center the children had giggled and stared at her dress that hugged her form and fit her body like a glove and her red heels that to them seemed too high to walk in.

"Dominique and Eugenia and Iramineni, say hello and don't be so silly," Marie answered.

Dominique, a high school student, was obviously infatuated with the two guests. Proudly Marie said, "Dominique is in Ste. Famille Secondary School and wants to become a doctor. There is nothing to stop him now with America helping us."

Dominique and the girls bowed to Cheyenne and Dava then went over and kissed the hemline of their mother's long dress and bowed to their father. This they did every time they saw their parents. Of course, Dava and Cheyenne were floored by this ritual of respect and honor.

After breakfast the children were escorted to Sunday school by the housekeeper. They were Catholics and had already gone to 6am mass together as a family, before Cheyenne and Dava were even awake.

Then Henri and Marie escorted their guests to sit out on the screened porch where Henri pointed out the various trees while Cheyenne's mind drifted.

The bright fragrance and beautiful colors of the flowers and shrubs led her mind to wander. The romantic sounding French names and dialogue had her spellbound, and then she remembered the history of Rwanda.

The Belgians colonized Rwanda in 1916, after Germany had to give up its African possessions after WWI. The Belgians continued to heighten the separation between the Tutsi and the Hutu by blatantly favoring the Tutsis. Since they had angular features, beautiful smooth brown skin, and were tall and graceful, the Belgians thought them more appealing to their European sensibilities.

Cheyenne noticed how the French influence had reached into the personal lives of the Rwandese. But then again she thought, look at the English and Spanish influence all over the world with other people of color from the Philippines to Chile.

Their discussion led to the beginning of human life found

recently by archeologists in the Congo and Kenya regions. They talked about Lucy, the first human ancestor who walked upright more than one million years ago. Then Henri brought up the finding of a woman some scientists labeled Eve, and the million-year-old human found in Malawi.

"The scientists are looking for the evolutionary missing link between apes and humans. They recently discovered a new species which appears to be a direct descendant to the short human bones of Lucy found in Kenya. This recently discovered fossil named Eve was discovered in Ethiopia and is four point four million years old," Henri said.

They spoke of the vast anthropological riches found in Africa by the white explorers. Then Henri told the story of the Congo and the area of Rwanda where the Nile originates, called the Blue Nile.

"The ancient Black Egyptians on the upper Nile knew only that their river originated far to the south, in a region they called the Land of Trees. This was a mysterious place with forests so dense it was as dark as night in the middle of the day. They spoke of small people who lived in trees," Henri began as everyone relaxed and sat back, with anticipation of a fascinating story.

"As you can see some of the stories had some truth as the Twa people are small and live in the forests. Did you know the Twa, originally the Batwa people, are the original inhabitants of this region and in particular Rwanda? Their ancestors lived here 200,000 to 300,000 years ago, legend has it.

"Scientists have found genetic evidence that all men originated from the common ancestor, Lucy. Scientific research provides evidence that modern man - despite their racial and ethnic differences - all share the same basic genetic makeup. In 1991 a 2.5-million-year-old genus Homo jawbone was found

FORGIVE AND LIVE: RWANDA

in the East Rift Valley in Karonga, Malawi," Henri said, very happy to share his knowledge.

"As you can well imagine this has caused internal problems for the science community. Most scientists agree that humanity's earliest ancestors evolved in Africa, but there are conflicting theories on when and where humankind took its present form. From these human DNA sequences, it is concluded that humans are closely related. They realized that all humans have a more recent common ancestor.

"For nearly four thousand years afterward, the white man had never known the existence of the interior part of Africa. The Arabs came to North and East Africa in the seventh century A.D., in search of gold, ivory, spices, and slaves. But the Arabs were merchant seamen and did not venture inland. They called the interior the Land of the Blacks.

"The white Europeans were busy warring with each other, the Barbarians, Saxons, Celts and much later the King Arthur stories, to concern themselves with deepest Africa. The Romans sent Alexander to battle with such great Africans as Hannibal of Ethiopia and other African Kings, like Mansa Musa, for their lands. Hannibal and the Nubians, original Black Egyptians, fought to keep Europeans out of Africa for centuries; he even invaded Sicily with his ships of elephants and warriors.

"However, the Egyptians knew they had no chance of peace with the Romans. The Greeks on the other hand were friendly in the beginning and took all of the knowledge they could from the libraries of Kemet, the ancient name for Egypt. And a good thing they did take the knowledge with them, because Alexander later burned every library in Egypt and Northern Africa. His rage at Hannibal and the superior knowledge these Black people had was a great humiliation to the European, so he decided to destroy it.

CHAPTER 14

What Are You?

"…The Meek, … Shall Inherit the Earth."
KJV Matt 5.5

Henri had to continue his explanation of the Tutsi. "The reason for the migration of the Tutsi was due to the Arab slave trade and invasion of Ethiopia, Egypt, and other countries in northern Africa. It is in my humble opinion, Dava and Shy, that the Watusi were at one time the Nubian Pharaoh Kings and Queens of Egypt and Ethiopia. They once ruled as pharaohs centuries before the Arabs came into Egypt and destroyed the Nubian legacy.

"My belief is that they traveled southeast along the Upper Nile to the White Nile and down the Blue Nile River until they felt safe in a land away from the invading foreigners. So, they traveled further into the interior and south to southern Uganda, eastern Zaire, Rwanda, and Burundi.

"Here the Watutsis were able to continue their rule over the BaHutu and the Batwa people and maintain some of the rich customs and royal practices they had in Egypt, such as herding and the extravagant dress. The true descendants of the Pharaoh of ancient Egypt, in my opinion, were exiled to the south. They came to Rwanda and other locals during the Hyksos, Greek, Roman and Arab invasions of Egypt, and they are now called the Tutsi people.

"Where else did the giant seven- and eight-feet tall Watusis come from but from royal lineage? They started migrating in the 13th century fleeing further slaughter of the people of Egypt and the Arab takeover. I am sure the libraries told the truth of the true Nubian Pharaohs," Henri had longed to tell someone he could trust this belief of his. When he finished, peace and calm came over him like never before.

"Meanwhile the Arab and African explorers from every part of Africa, told stories of vast forests; stories of mountains that spewed fire and turned the sky black; stories of native villages overwhelmed by monkeys, which would have congress with the women; stories of great giants with hairy bodies and flat noses; stories of creatures half leopard, half man; stories of native markets where fattened carcasses of men were butchered and sold as a delicacy.

"Such stories were sufficiently forbidding keeping the Arabs on the coast, despite other stories equally alluring: mountains of shimmering gold, riverbeds beaming with diamonds, animals that spoke the language of men, great jungle civilizations of unimaginable splendor. In particular, one story was repeated again and again in early accounts; the story of the Lost City of the Black Man.

"According to legend, a city known to the Hebrews of Solomonic times had been a source of inconceivable wealth in diamonds. The arduous caravan routes were long since swallowed up by jungle, and the last trader who remembered the way had carried his secret with him to the grave many hundreds of years before.

"The inhabitants, who are black, once lived in wealth and luxury, and even their slaves decorated themselves with jewels and especially blue diamonds, for a great store of diamonds was supposed to be in the Congo. In 1292, a Persian stated that "a diamond the size of a man's clenched fist was exhibited in the streets of Zanzibar, and all stated it had come from the interior.

"The slave trade steered clear of Rwanda. The major trading routes used by the Arab slavers for Sultan Oman and Zanzibar extended from the coast of the Indian Ocean to Central Africa.

"More Arabs came looking for the diamonds in 1334 but did not succeed through the Congo. The Portuguese came in 1544 still looking but were turned back by the rapids of the Congo River. The English tried in 1644 but all of them died. It wasn't until the nineteenth century that the English got through that is when the famous meeting of Stanley and Livingston took place. Stanley, the missionary, camped out at what is now called Akagera Park, here in Rwanda," Henri was proud of his country for resisting, through utilizing the nature of the landscape and the fighting Congo inhabitants, who held the white invader off for so long.

Just then Dominique quietly rapped on the porch entrance. The children had been listening intently to their father by the door.

"Papa, may we sit and listen to you for a while, please?" Asked Dominique politely, as the oldest he spoke for the girls. Dava and Cheyenne were very impressed. In America a child usually didn't want to be around adults, especially a teenage boy, and if they did they would just sit down and listen unasked.

"Yes, my son, bring the girls too, we were speaking of how long it took the Europeans to come to the Congo region and Rwanda. The missionaries came first to convert the African from their belief in one God to the Christian belief in Jesus and one God. After them came the pirates who stole the riches out of Africa including the people.

"They had already plundered the north and West African nations and were looking for more loot. This was the time that the Tutsi came down from the northeastern countries into this area around the 13th century to also escape enslavement. All of the coastal Africans had to retreat into the interior or risk enslavement by the Arabs and pirates."

Cheyenne said to him with all sincerity, "I shall make it a point in my travels here in Africa to find out more about the Watutsi or Tutsi. It makes perfect sense that they came from Egypt. Their features are similar to the other North African groups. The huge Egyptian structures would only parallel the Watusi height, strength, and stature. Henri, I am sure you are right. Thank you for sharing this with us." She filed this away but knew that she would trace the lineage of the Watusi even if it meant traveling by car or train to Egypt.

"We, Rwandese, are part of all ethnic groups. For centuries we mixed. We share the same language and culture. That is the first thing the European analyzed in our country. We have been divided by foreign politicians and the arrival of the missionaries. When the missionaries arrived, the Tutsis were further appraised over the Hutu. The missionaries and foreigners used their own invented criteria to separate us.

"They assimilated one group with the Caucasian race and made that group superior. In doing that they also tried to implement their prejudice into our life. This created social imbalance and hatred between Rwandese. Last year we had genocide wars in Rwanda, and it was not the first time we had massacres here. In 1959 there was terrible killing.

"But, because we want unity so much, Rwandese people say Tutsi, Hutu, Twa were children of one mother. Just like any other African group, the children all come out differently. In theory it is true we all came from Eve or Lucy differently."

"So that means that all of the races and ethnic groups came from one common ancestor?" Shy hadn't read this new research and was thrilled.

"Yes!" said Henri emphatically.

"All of the wars people have been fighting over millennia have been against themselves, their own relatives!" Dava said disgustedly. "What a waste of time, money, and human sacrifice. By now we would have cured all diseases and could be living on other planets if people had realized this long ago."

"Perhaps," said Henri. "You must remember certain groups of humans are basically greedy. Look at all the wars fought amongst the so-called 'royal families' in Europe. From the Tudors to Richard III, they fought their own family members," Henri said with a bit of sadness. As a teacher he knew that knowledge was power, and the more people knew the more they would think first and act with reason.

"So it is that God created man in his own image. God created the original African man. Scientifically speaking, study of the hominids, who were the earliest said ancestor of man who walked upright, lived four million years ago in Africa.

"The first fossils of this species were found in Europe 1.9 and 1.5 million years ago. The Homo sapiens spread to China and Java in Indonesia two million years ago. He brought tools with him.

"Scientists have fenced the issue and never really developed good theories of where the Neanderthal people came from. They never really went into the derivation of the Neanderthal man who developed in Northern Europe one million years after the Homo sapiens developed in Africa." Henri let the guests ponder this phenomenon in silence.

"There is a missed step, a flaw that has led to the destruction of ancient African civilizations, vast wars throughout the world, and the oppression and slavery of people of color," Cheyenne said thinking out loud.

"Now hold on now," said Dava. "Can we have a moment

for a reality check, please? You have always been before your time, but this seems a bit much."

"I can affirm some of Henri's theories," Cheyenne said to Dava. "These theories are based on the scientific evidence that has been uncovered then hushed for obvious reasons. The last trip of the Homo sapiens was to Northern Europe. Homo sapiens had traveled throughout Africa, Polynesia, Asia, including the aborigines of Australia, North and South America centuries before going to Europe.

"Soon, as the books say, the Neanderthal became extinct. After the ice age the continents separated," Cheyenne said knowing this was going too far but she was too involved with this subject to hold back her thoughts.

"Later most traces of the Neanderthal disappeared or intermixed with the Homo sapiens in Europe. Does this mean anything? Are there any Neanderthal DNA traces that can be found in Modern man today? Is anyone investigating this, or do they really care to know? It all makes more sense now."

"The Bantu, or Batahutu, migration toward central, eastern and southern Africa brought the iron age to the Batwa people. Remains of smelting furnaces for iron were found in Rwanda from the 10th to 7th century B.C.," Henri said. "Thus, the modern age began and ended when the European and Arab intrusions and finally Stanley's penetration of the last African sanctuary, the Congo, happened.

"The Twa, the Hutu and the Tutsi always spoke the same Bantu language and shared the same culture, lived side by side even though they shared none of the same characteristics. The Twa, who were very few 1% or less of the population, were called pygmoids by the Europeans. They lived as hunter-gatherers in the forests or served as slaves to the King. The Hutu who made up the vast majority of the population, were peasants who cultivated the soil. They had the Bantu physique, flat noses, and full lips and were medium height and muscular. But the Tutsi were extremely tall, thin, and often displaying sharp, angular facial features; these were the cattle herders." Henri hesitated to go on, but his audience was spellbound.

"With the racially obsessed European in 1884-1885, European powers held a Berlin Conference to carve Africa up amongst them. The Germans got the allegiance of the Tutsi who were in power and retained the monarchy structure," Henri paused for cakes brought to him by the housekeeper.

★★★★★★★★★★

"The Germans were impressed and could not understand how a savage Negro could have such an elegant Kingship institution.

"In the Tutsi hierarchy, the Mwami, known as King, lived at the center of a large court, and was treated like a divine being. The nature of his power was sacred, and he physically embodied Rwanda. He was surrounded by elaborate rituals carried out by Abiru, the Royal Ritualists, and even the vocabulary relating to his daily life was special, with special words to mean 'the King's speech', 'the King's bed' and so on.

"His authority was symbolized by a sacred drum called the Kaliga on which nobody ever drummed; there were other ordinary drums for that purpose. Kaliga was decorated with the testicles of slain enemies and to dare revolt against the King was not only an outrage but a sacrilege.

"The King was the father and patriarch of his people, given to them by Imana, God. When he exercised his authority, he was impeccable, infallible. His decisions could not be questioned. The parents of a victim he unjustly struck would bring him presents so that he would not resent them for having been forced to cause them affliction. They still trusted him; he remained Nyagansani, the only Lord, superb and magnificent.

"Under the King were the chiefs, but of these there were three types: first, the mutwale wa buttaka, the 'chief of the landholdings' who took care of attributing land and of agricultural production, and taxation; then the mutwale wa ingabo, the 'chief of men' who ruled not the land but the bodies and, among other things, was in charge of recruiting fighters for the King's armies; and then the mutwale wa inka or mutawale wa igikingi, the 'chief of the pastures' who ruled over the grazing lands. The three functions could be concentrated in a single person for a certain area, but in a difficult or rebellious area, according to the principle of 'divide and rule', the King could separate all three positions and give them to different men.

"Most of the chiefs were Tutsi, although a number of the abatwale wa buttaka were Hutu since agriculture was their domain. And in order to make everything even more complicated which was something the King rather relished, the same man could be 'chief of men' and 'of grazing lands' on a certain musozi, the hill, and have to put up with being also mutwale wa inka on 'his' hill, while at the same time being also mutawale wa ingabo for a couple of different hills when the rest of the power was held by third parties." Henri stopped as Marie quietly served tea to the guests and milk to her children.

Cheyenne and Dava bowed their heads to Marie so as to not miss a word of this fascinating history.

"These chiefs, like all the administrators of all governments, were there basically to play two roles: controlling and extracting. The controlling varied; close to the central core of the kingdom, it was tight, but it became looser as one went towards the outer boundaries of the kingdom.

"The extracting duties were: maintaining the chiefly

enclosures called kwibuka inkike, working the land or gufata igihe, and minding the cattle or ubushumba bw'inka. There was a salary and taxes paid in kind since there was no money system before the European took over, and never did one individual have all the responsibility. The chiefs set work and pay practices for the umusozi or hill, and within each rugo or household people made their own arrangements to satisfy the government.

"After World War I the Belgians occupied Rwanda, Burundi, and other territories of eastern Africa that were formerly German. The Belgians destroyed and took over what was left of the Batusi army, land and pastures as the Tutsi were cattle herders. Thus, pushing the Tutsi or Watusi as they were then, further inland on land occupied by the Hutu. Like two families squeezing into the same house under force. That is what putting Tutsi on Hutu land was like."

"Was this the beginning of the disagreement between the Tutsi and the Hutu?" asked Dava innocently.

"Yes," said Henri, not really wanting to get into this difficult subject the first day.

He went on to say, "The later complaint against the Belgians was that they tightened up the chief's system excessively by making each and every able-bodied person pay and work on the European taxation model instead of retaining the softer form of African collective responsibility. By the late 19th century all peasants were forced to work called ubuletwa.

"This new word ubuletwa was not a Kinyarwanda word or practice, it was a Kiswahili word. The word and meaning were the new trading language brought by the coastal Swahili merchants from Zanzibar who now reached Rwanda. Of course, the people hated it. King Rwaburgiri spread it and the Belgians abused it."

"Henri, excuse me but it's getting chilly and soon the children must go to bed. Let's move into the parlor," Marie said.

They sat down in the comfortable chairs and sofa. The housekeeper poured water for the guests.

"In 1928 they repressed the Nyiraburumbuke movement and all other uprisings, that same year they fostered a famine. From 1946 to 1959 the whole of Africa and Rwanda struggled for independence from Europe. The Hutu massacred hundreds of Tutsi in 1959, as the Belgian were hostile to the Tutsis for wanting independence and gave promises to the Hutu that they'd be king.

"In 1961 the Parmehutu staged a tribal revolution: the monarchy was deposed, and the Belgian trusteeship was abolished with the declaration of an independent Rwandan Republic. In 1962 Rwanda was independent and separated from Burundi. In 1963 the Tutsi rebelled and there were massacres, with some Tutsi fleeing the country. In 1973 President Habyarimana became chief of state after his successful takeover of the Tutsi. In 1978 a new constitution was adapted, and in 1983 President Habyarimana was reelected. In 1990 Pope John Paul visited Rwanda since over 80% of us were Catholic at that time." Henri had a slight change in attitude as he talked about the Tutsi and Hutu violent exchange of power.

"So, the wars were over land and dominance?" Cheyenne asked.

"Yes," replied Henri. "The saddest part is the Tutsi really believed they brought a better quality of life to the Hutu and Twa people. The ubuhake was the point at which the Hutu and Tutsi ideologies differed. The ubuhake was a form of an unequal clientship contract entered into by two men, the shebuja (patron) and the mugaragu (client).

"A Tutsi patron gave a cow to his Hutu client. Since the Hutu were not really supposed to have cattle, which were a sign of wealth, power, and good breeding, it was not only an 'economic gift' but also a form of upward social mobility. For the cow could reproduce, and the future calves would be shared between shebuja and mugargu.

"This is the same as Europeans saying to you I forget that you are African sometimes. Forget what your ancestry is and just be like us. It might be a push to an upward social climb with herds of cattle the Hutu could be icyihuture, de-hutuised, or even better, tutsified. As you can see the Hutu looked at this as quasi-slavery and degrading their group even more while the Tutsi believed this was a great honor just as they thought intermarriage with a Hutu was uplifting the Hutu clan that joined them. The Rwandese family went the way of the father. If a Hutu man married a Tutsi girl their children were Hutu, unless the whole clan changed according to the icyihutur process.

"Worst of all was that outside of the King's domain there were Hutu principalities, with Hutu royalty. These were in the north, northwest and southwest of Rwanda. They resisted until the nineteenth century when the European arrived and incorporated them into the whole of Rwanda. Then the King's control extended over outlying principalities and the government became centralized and authoritarian with the help of the Europeans. Eventually all rebelling Hutu principalities were under the rule of the King," Henri stopped as Marie signaled to him.

★★★★★★★★★★

At this time another meal was to be served. They went back into the dining room for a simple late afternoon supper of rice and beans, fufu and mango juice. They all discussed the complicated life of royalty and saw that the democratic principles the European was establishing had to be learned by the people first and brought into existence by the government in order for them to work fully. However, it was not democratic to have governors selected by the Belgians rather than elected by the people.

The children were sent to their area as children were not really allowed to be in company of adults too often. Soon after, their mother went to the girls' room and asked Cheyenne and Dava to join her to say goodnight to them. It was late afternoon, and they were going to bed. Marie tucked them into bed with loving kisses as she sang the 'Cradle Song' in French and English:

Sleep
do not cry
tonight, the little animal watches
from under the warm cinders of the hearth

Sleep, do not cry
the little animal has four legs on its head
six arms on its stomach
two tails behind

Sleep, stay put
the little animal has turned into an elephant
his eyes are three, his tongues are ten
his legs carry him toward you on their own
I see his body with hair standing on end
like the quills on a porcupine

Sleep, wipe your tears away
put a mat over your head
and sleep well my little ones
I will kill this monster
who wants to touch your legs.

Cheyenne and Dava tiptoed out of the girls' bedroom having heard the lyrics, looked at each other and were glad their mothers did not lullaby them with such a scary song. Dominique was also excused, and the adults continued the conversation as Marie reentered the living room.

★★★★★★★★★★

Henri continued, "We are looking forward to seeing your computer expertise in operation here in our country. When our people can unite and start building things without importing so much, we will become more independent and less dependent on the Europeans.

"They export all of our natural resources then send products back to us to buy after we had dug them up as raw materials. Also, more jobs will mean less strife for our people, and maybe working side by side with everyone together we will be happier living with each other," believed Henri.

"Tomorrow we start in the building you have provided us," Cheyenne said. "AT&T has invested millions in getting the satellite connection to pursue wireless telecommunications services and opportunities in Rwanda. We have just enough to start drawing the plans and connecting the satellite to the computers needed to build these networks. The second building that we begin to work on six months down the road will be for the raw materials and products. We will be able to refine iron ore, rubber, and brown diamond necessary for making parts needed for tooling the machines," Cheyenne was naturally enthused with the prospects in store. They hugged and Henri gave a libation and prayer then drove their guests home.

"Yes, I hope we can do this great thing," Dava responded.

When they returned to their apartment, Cheyenne and Dava discussed how similar their adoptive families were to their own. The families selected for this partnership were handpicked because of this similarity.

Shy said, "The coordinators of this project didn't want anything to go wrong. This is Africa's big chance to finally try to catch up to the modern world economically. Sure, they dressed very westernized and had big government buildings and cars, but they had no industry or business of their own with which they could participate in world commerce and trade except Nigerian oil and mineral wealth. Now is the time and now is their chance. The Rwandese didn't think of competing for markets as much as being part of the world economic system."

Later that evening all of the Council members decided to walk to town together. The guys never let on, they were waiting all day for Cheyenne and Dava to return safely to them. They relaxed seeing Mr. Ntesesi.

"I feel so connected to the people here in Rwanda. It feels so natural for us to be cultivating the natural resources with our African brothers and sisters. Henri and the others are sure ready for the computer business and industrialization. I am so glad that they trust us. We will never let them down," Dava said as they walked together through Kigali. All of the Council members agreed.

As they walked down the various streets of Kigali they couldn't help noticing the blazing vermillion of blooming flamboyant, or royal poincianas, the molten purple of bougainvillea, the brilliant scarlet of hibiscus, and the ice-blue jacarandas, that all seemed to stand in serried rows of honor to welcome and thank them.

They also noticed that some flowers were cared for and nurtured by humans, and some grew wild and natural. They saw how the flora exploded in its entire splendor; so much so that during their haphazard stroll along the avenues of the capital every hotel had their own beautiful garden. Everything seemed to grow without restraint. Because the climate is neither too hot nor too dry, hardy plants flourish alongside the blossoms of more delicate flowers, such as the orchid.

They really loved it here. They had laughed and talked their way right back into their respective rooms, without even realizing it, totally exhausted as they went their separate ways to bed.

"I am so full and happy. This is the most important first step toward economic independence for Africa ever realized since the great Songhay empires in Mali, and the University in Timbuktu more than 1,000 years ago. This may not reach the heights our Nubian brothers and sisters and as King Keop did with the Pyramids and Sphinx 5,000 years ago, but it sure ain't a small hill of beans either," Cheyenne said with much enthusiasm as she prepared for bed.

"I know what you mean. You know it's almost frightening the impact we will make in Rwanda and in all of Africa after this notion catches on. We may even be written in history books," Dava laughs from her own bed.

"We are taking them to the new millennium with telecommunication systems. As Verge Magazine read, '90% of the people who live in the southern region of Africa have never even used a telephone, and of the 49 countries with the least developed phone systems, 35 are in sub-Saharan Africa'," Cheyenne said.

"That's right," said Dava. "The average wait of a phone line in Zimbabwe is five years. In Chad, 91 percent of calls don't go through. It's easier to call outside the continent than to another town in the same country."

They recalled seeing completely empty phone booths that were never hooked up for a phone along their drive to the city.

"Dava, on our plane ride over here, you didn't say a word. Do you want to talk about it?" Shy whispered.

"Shy, I just thought about how I am escaping a stalker in Manhattan, and perhaps I can know a real man here in Rwanda who doesn't abuse me or take drugs," Dava snickered.

"Amen, you are safe here, goodnight sis," Shy knew Dava was better off now than ever before in her life.

As she lay snuggled under her covers Cheyenne smiled to herself and felt proud to have this great opportunity. She closed her eyes and prepared mentally for the big day tomorrow. The first day of production that will bring the world to Africa and Africa into the computer age, at last.

CHAPTER 15

|||||||||||||||||||||||||||||||||||||||||||||||

Square One at Work, Comfort Family, Back Home

'Change Is the only constant in life'
Héraclitus.

The imponderable dream of dreams that enfolded all aspects of possibilities, is right here and right now! Cheyenne Latour is fascinated by the hope that is still very much alive in the hearts and souls of those she works with today. The enormous ships of promise reach their destination outside the perimeters of Africa carrying dreamers and technicians of all colors, as black men from Africa envision all aspects of what the massive cable will bring. They work side by side with the Europeans and Americans. Today they lay Africa's future in her great encompassing seas, the Indian, Mediterranean and the Atlantic Oceans, sealing her fate under these same seas that once tore her people from her arms.

That next morning before Cheyenne and Dava left to begin their workday, they shared a mutual excitement and a cup of Rwandese coffee fresh from the hills. They had never experienced such rich coffee. They took it black because sugar and cream would destroy its essence.

"Shy, I can't believe this is the day we begin the most important work of our lives," Dava said while finishing dressing for work.

"Dava, if this works the way I know it will, all of Africa will be looking to Rwanda to show them the way into the twenty-first century through Computer technology," Cheyenne said in between mouthfuls of banana bread and coffee.

"This bread is delicious. I am so happy the guys picked it up for us. We are sure lucky we have such great people with us, you know Dava?"

"Shy, that is one of the reasons my mother let me come here, besides being with you, of course, the fact that the African Affairs Council is made up of mature sensible men," Dava said, now having her breakfast with fresh fruit.

"That goes for me too, honey, don't kid yourself. You know how my father is," they both laughed lovingly at dad the 'sweet authoritarian'.

The rest of the Council members met Dava and Cheyenne outside their apartment and they boarded Francois' motorbus together. The group had established a regular transportation system with Francois and if any of them worked late into the night, Francois drove them home in his taxi. They knew that eventually everyone would be taking a turn working late at some point from now on.

"I can't get over how AT&T had already put up the satellite link for the computers at the Rwandese International building," said Tombe.

He continued, "For them to do something grand like this shows that there are some good businessmen in the world that know they must make up for the atrocities done by their predecessors. They know they fall when even one human falls. Peace comes when all have peace."

"All of the Rwandese people seem to be coming out of their large brick and small thatched homes this morning to see us," said Dava excitedly as they pass home after home on the way, waving to everyone.

"This ride is the most beautiful we have ever taken so far in Rwanda," Cheyenne noticed as the motorbus edged up the hills and through natural gardens of sweet aromas, and colorful visions of flowers.

"Bougainville, hibiscus, orchid," Francois rattled them off to the excited riders.

"Well, we are almost there, gang. This is history in the making. Do you realize we are the first African American group to work, subsidize and implement a fiber optic business for the Rwandese?" said Kojo.

"There will be great strides made in this country from here on. Nothing can stop them if they work together and keep this thing growing," Cheyenne said.

"I know our part will be 150%. We have all given up too much to do this thing any other way but perfectly," said Jamaal who just had a baby boy three months ago.

When they first arrived, they were led into an orientation meeting. The African Affairs Council, Rwandese and other African engineers and computer experts as well as many Europeans were sitting together to begin the first real integrated workforce. The involvement of the AT&T Corporation and other collaborative forces, including two African American companies, began with a vision and dream for equity for all people. They had representatives ready to begin this historic sojourn into the future of Africa.

"Good morning and welcome to Rwandese Communications, Inc. My name is Wayne Richjar," began the AT&T CEO. He was the African American that represented the interests of the stockholders and board members at AT&T.

"And I am Abdel Digne, your Senegalese liaison and President of Operations and Communications here at Rwandese International. Welcome." Mr. Digne greeted them with a broad smile, Dava and Cheyenne thought.

"As some of you know, AT&T wanted to come to Rwanda to start telecommunications in 1990-1992. The telephones were managed by the government. Beginning in 1994 they had to give the telephones to a joint company where the government would have some control and could sell them to a private company. My company from Senegal and AT&T are uniting with the government to make this project work," said Mr. Digne. He's so very scholarly and dignified, Cheyenne thought.

"Our first task is to assist the technicians in any way, along with training the Rwandese we are working with in this project. This phase, I assure you, you have never seen done before. For the most part this procedure is already in place. By the time you start working at your computer stations cable lines will be in place. I guarantee you this will be an absolute breakthrough in the new Africa since the liberation movements in the 1960s.

"As you know AT&T has already launched the satellite necessary for us to have the installation at the space center at MESA. This is a big head advantage. Our first phase now is to make assignments and work groups that will train as well as do their own jobs."

Mr. Richjar meticulously passed assignments and Cheyenne was thrilled to see she was Vice President of Communications and Tombe, Vice President of Operations.

"Cheyenne Latour, you are in charge of the communications department. You will be responsible for keeping lines up and operations going. You will have a staff of six to eight people in round-the-clock shifts. Their job is to monitor the data scopes. Data scopes allow a person to look at what would happen online. I'm responsible for writing software that will troubleshoot. By signaling when there is a disconnect it will then retract and redirect data when lines go down. Lines go down because of weather sometimes.

"Once they set up the software environment programs, these programs help them solve problems, signal, redirect and set up. Your group is responsible for operating and for improving communication and making it run faster. You will be providing cable service to businesses first. You set up cable lines to these businesses," said Mr. Richjar, showing Cheyenne the paper with the exclusive businesses first.

"Dava Love, you are the Director of Cable Operations. You will oversee the fiber optic lines that are already laid in the ground to various AT&T phone company sites in the country and neighboring connections that are made to other countries. This project was abandoned because of the warring ethnic groups in 1992 and general discouragement of the Rwandese people in the project originally," he continued.

"Mr. Digne, would you like to briefly tell everyone how things will work?"

"It is my pleasure, sir. We will have some AT&T technicians from America and some African technicians from South Africa, Cameroon, Kenya, Senegal, and Liberia to help the Rwandese technicians install a satellite transmission system in Kigali. The technicians in the African Affairs Council help supervise and teach the more intricate systems like the ones you worked on in New York City. Hardware is installed outside the building. On another level the fiber optic cable is laid in the ground to transmit the video and data back and forth to a central switching station," Mr. Digne explained.

Mr. Digne further explained, "All local cable lines terminate, that is, fiber optic cable, coaxial cable, outside Rwanda that goes from the central location to the satellite along coaxial cable poles. The cable company runs coaxial cable to and from central switching stations to whomever will get cable.

"The central switching stations are the terminals we will

operate from our computers. I will work as Vice President and supervisor of all Rwandese training and work orders. This was done to show the Rwandese two major factors: that Africa is becoming more open and there will be other Africans from other countries coming to train and work in Rwanda, and second, the look or ethnic group of a person is not important when you are working for a common goal," he said very plainly.

Later in the day after the initial preparations, all of the workers together watched as Mr. Digne taught some Rwandese technicians how the computer data could be transmitted from cable lines in French, thus bringing countries to the 21st century through international broadcasts.

"Most of Africa skipped the landline stage and will go directly to the internet and cell phones. The fiber cable industry is live market data using satellite transmissions to get intercommunications," one of the workers told Shy.

Cheyenne and Dava marveled at the technicians working on satellite transmissions. Everyone present saw how the satellite dish went up to connect with the satellite and how the coaxial cable was laid for the transmitter, receiver, computer chips, computer hardware, ethereal cable connections and how all of these things together make their job possible.

"Mr. Digne has a tall order to fill," Cheyenne said as she watched him show how a minicomputer based on the Pentium processor would be used to control satellite transmission-flow control and develop software and microcode.

Mr. Digne explained each step of the computer transmissions, " Microcode software that is burned into a chip can't be modified. It handles link level communications that link directly to physical lines to the hardware. One end would talk to the coaxial cord. The software detects, disconnects, and reconnects the computer to the line.

"The software provides a carrier system that allows data to flow. The low-level buffering gets a bunch of data. It then holds on to some amount of data until a computer clears the buffer. They control the computer on one end and a line plugged into another computer, then goes to the satellite dish.

"The satellite has a receiver and transmitter. Sometimes the satellite passes on too much data for the computer and the data is held in a low level buffer until it can process and receive it. Microcode operates this low-level buffer. High level software does many functions. Low level means it does one basic thing. Cheyenne's group handles both," Mr. Digne continued as he took individuals aside and spoke in French and English for them.

"Well group, there is no time like the present to get started. Who has worked with the hardware for communications?" Cheyenne asked her group..

"I have worked in charge of communications of all of the hardware, the receivers, coaxial cables, transmissions and data scopes," said Pierre, one of her group members. Cheyenne couldn't get over how all of the Rwandese had these simple French first names and these difficult, for her, last names.

"Pierre you will set up the data scopes for data line analysis. You can look at what is happening over a communication line. As you know our communication lines are any lines that have data coming over them. These lines have one terminal to the main computer and the other coaxial cable connects a TV to a cable switch box."

Her mind whirred into the job at hand; her pace heightened as she got deep into computer land.

This is her world, Cheyenne smiled as she managed Pierre, Jacques, Rudolph, and the rest of her group to swing into action, excited, happy, and making a difference for their country.

"I just want to say thank you again, Miss LaTour. You can't

imagine how much our country needs something like this to help us get together. I believe this project can cement past hatred and restore peace forever," said Jacques as he busily pressed on.

"You're welcome. It is my pleasure. I hope everyone in Rwanda feels like you do. We were told the fighting had subsided," Cheyenne hoped.

"Yes we hope," Jacques had tears in his eyes and this worried her plenty. Cheyenne knew then and there she had to find out some more about the problems here.

The first workday went well. They saw and felt the magnitude of many tasks before them and happily did what was required to make this whole project work. There was a little stress between the Hutu and Tutsi workers, but they seemed to be able to work together as long as no one group dominated the other.

At lunchtime Cheyenne took time out to go to the library. She noticed most of the books she was interested in were written in French, German or Belgian. But these had the anthropological information she needed. She was determined to struggle through them using her French and German dictionary and college textbook.

When she checked the books out she noticed a Black guy who looked American, for some reason watching her but trying not to let her know he was. She just figured he wanted to talk so she left with her books.

★★★★★★★★★★

When going home on the motorbus she had to ask her American companions what they knew about the Hutu/Tutsi conflict and what the chances were of another uprising.

"The last skirmish or slaughter was in January, yes, last month. But they promised us we were in no danger and that this project would foster peace if we can get it going and employ some of these people before anything else happens," Tombe confessed.

Pete added, "The pressure is on us to hurry with this construction so that we can employ the people who might otherwise be fighting each other."

"I feel confident that the people here will come together to better their country," said Dava with her innocent mind.

"We have to realize the ethnic problems of these two groups have been going on for centuries. When the European gave Rwanda her independence they also inspired favoritism for the Tutsi until the Tutsi wanted to break all European ties. Then the Europeans favored the Hutu and made sure they had an active role in the government. That is why the President is a Hutu. Yet much of his ministry is Tutsi. But his army is Hutu," Tombe said.

"That sounds like the beginnings of another impasse to me," Cheyenne said.

"Before we begin to speculate and assume, we should talk to someone in the government or military and see if all that we are working for is not in vain," said levelheaded Tombe.

They gathered and prayed that all would turn out for the best and that they returned safely to their loved ones when the work was over. Cheyenne secretly prayed for peace.

Later that night she called home. "Hello mom."

The voice on the other line was tearful with joy, "Baby, I have prayed for you. Thank God you called." Her Mom didn't get emotional, but this was major.

"The Council dispersed from a prayer and I thought about you guys. How are you guys doing up there? I know it's snowing like crazy since it's February," Cheyenne said trying to get less emotional, the weather always does it.

"You know it is; a winter wonderland. I am so happy to hear your voice. How is it there?" her mom asked.

"This is the most beautiful place I have ever seen. Even the U.S. south with its beautiful blossoms all year round cannot compare to this paradise of color.

"Everywhere you look, and I mean everywhere, there are gorgeous flowers, even orchids growing vividly all over. The gardens grow wild or are cultivated. It's no matter there are flowers and shrubs by the thousands. The hills and the river valleys make beautiful pictures no matter where you stand. Mom, have you talked to Leon up there?"

"Yes baby. Leon calls once a week to check on us. He is doing well in school and as you know is leaving for Egypt in a few weeks. Now your dad is waiting to say hi to you, hold on, baby."

"Hey girl, you OK over there. How's the job?" Dad asked excitedly.

"Dad, you would not believe what we are doing here. It is the best job I have ever had. I am Vice President in Charge of Communications, and Dava is Director of Cable Operations. We see everything starting from the first installation of the cable line to it literally connecting to our computers."

Cheyenne tried as best as she could to relay some of her excitement and joy to her folks and not give any hint that there may be a problem here.

"That sounds great. You sound like you are enjoying it. How are the people treating you?" Dad now had some concern in his voice.

She knew she had to give them a guarded yet common sense answer. "Our host family reminds me of you and my sisters. We are there on weekends if we don't have to work. We are beginning to notice the distrust between the Hutu and

Tutsi we work with regarding each other. We hope that as we get more involved with the project they will see that working together for the good of their country is the best thing to do. They treat all of us like royalty, yet, at the same time, as if we were so very naive."

"If there is any problem you use the money we gave you for emergencies and come right back home. I know you are grown and want the best for everyone, but you can't always change the tide, baby," Dad said with his authoritarian concern.

"We have decided to investigate with some government and military officials how the political climate is doing. Tombe watches over Dava and me like we were his children. You'd be very happy about that."

Cheyenne knew they hadn't heard from her since she arrived and called them from the airport, so she carefully began to tell them how Dava was getting along and how they were living together. Dava was like a daughter to her mom and dad and Cheyenne was the same with Dava's parents even after Dava's were separated.

Cheyenne had to tell how well the members of the council treated them, she thought her dad would like that in particular. She described the Ntetesi family which made her parents beam with joy to know that they were taken care of by such wonderful people. Cheyenne reassured them that they were well looked after and everything was great, but not too great to sound phony, but comfortable enough for them to be happy.

Dava spoke to Shy's parents then called her mom that same night. That night they all slept a little better with the memory of old times at home when they were all together.

CHAPTER 16

IIIIIIIIIIIIIIIIIIIIIIIIIIIIIIIIIIIIIIIIIIIIIIIIIIII

The Work

"And he shall be like a tree planted by the
rivers of water, that bringeth forth his fruit
in his season; his leaf shall not wither; and
whatsoever he doeth shall prosper."
KJV Psalm 1:3

Meanwhile, everyone worked night and day to make the final
internet connections possible. The first sign that a connection
would be made came on a dismal rainy March day. They were
attempting to dial in a network to get a response from someone,
anyone, on another computer in South Africa.

*Hello, this is Cheyenne from Rwanda. Can anyone read this
signal?*

As she completed the transmission, moments later, across
her otherwise blank screen came the response: *We are here,
welcome to the world, Rwanda, this is President Nelson Mandela here.*

Cheyenne screamed so loud everyone ran over to her
desk hooting and shouting and wanting to say something to
President Mandela for history's sake.

Tombe: *President Mandela, we brought the internet to Rwanda,
the African Affairs Council of N.Y., AT&T and Africans from
Senegal;* Mr. Digne typed: *My honorable King of South Africa;*
each officer had to type something. President Mandela cried
at the unity and transmitted back to them all: *You have changed
the people of Africa forever. Our hope is your hope for our people to*

thrive everywhere. This is a moment when nothing will ever be like it was. Thank God for all of you!

As with many miracles that happen in life, the love felt at that moment had everyone in tears of ecstasy. This is how the universe works in your favor. This was one happy day at Rwanda International, Inc. moving in the direction of all of their dreams.

Now the beginning of the rainy season unfolded, and Dava and Cheyenne started to feel the pangs of homesickness after many rainy days. They missed the ones they loved. Small talk became difficult. Their work, though exhilarating, was still all work and no play and quite dull, for these two young, charismatic, fun-loving ladies.

The other Council members attempted to entertain them with games of spades, chess and backgammon and shopping; however, these older men could not substitute for the company of their peers.

So, in short order, Cheyenne and Dava decided they'd start looking for what they desired the most. The problem was how to safely meet people in their twenties when they worked and lived with men mostly in their forties and fifties.

One day Mr. Digne came over to Shy's office and began talking about how he felt being in Rwanda. Shy immediately thought of what Queen Mother Moore had told her about this extremely tall, slim, dark, handsome man.

"Look at him," Queen Mother Moore would say, as she watched Preston walk near her, "One of our African kings." Queen Mother Moore believed that these tall black men were direct descendants of our ancient African Kings and Pharaohs. Shy could believe it looking at this wondrous man from Senegal coming toward her.

"May I have a moment of your time," he said in English

with a slight accent, which made the words soothing to her soul.

"Yes, of course Mr. Digne," Shy said, starting to rise and not really knowing what to do in his presence and how to address him.

"Please, Miss LaTour," he said motioning her to remain in her seat, "I have come because I have admired your work so much and your demeanor. I wish to befriend you and there is no one to give me an introduction on a less formal basis.

"I am so happy you came over to me, Mr. Digne. I was wondering how things were going with you. You are totally confusing the Rwandese. They don't know if you are a Tutsi or what. Right?"

"Oh, they know I am not one of them; they know I come from someplace else. But it is funny how they look at me. I do possess some of the similarities to the Tutsi. It is extremely important for our African brothers and sisters to know each other on the whole continent. We can't even get along with the same people in the same country. It makes me very sad sometimes."

"It makes me sad also," said Shy, feeling this man's pain. "When our Council members get together this Friday you must join us. All we do is talk and eat fufu and drink some banana beer. I personally am unable to indulge myself in that luxury again. But you are welcome. They would love to get your perspective on things here. Do you have many friends in Rwanda?"

"Actually no," he said. "I do talk with Mr. Richjar quite often as he is isolated, and we are both Black. The Europeans have a hold on the economy and most of the tourist places are geared for and by them exclusively. I don't see anything wrong with that; it is progress, and the most progressive people economically are white."

"I have had this same conversation many times. I know Africa is very rich. The diamond trade alone could quelch famine in the continent within a year. Yet the money goes to Europe. They did mine the diamonds and make them valuable on the market, but it seems so unfair that the people in the country from which the diamonds and gold have come are in poverty." Shy loved to share her views with someone as intelligent as Mr. Digne.

"If enough of us think this way and Rwanda gets into the World Wide Web as we are hoping, there may be a change for the better for all people. We have several problems in our own country that better communication could solve," he said eagerly now that he found someone from a different heritage who really understood the beauty and tragedy of Africa and its people.

"Rwandan gold coins are much valued internationally, yet the Rwandan Franc is not valued; it is a dilemma for sure," Cheyenne said, letting him know there were many unanswered questions.

"I will be looking forward to Friday to get together with everyone. Thank you so much for inviting me. See you then," he said as he shook her hand and started to leave.

"Anytime you feel the urge to talk to someone please come over to my office, sir," Shy was fascinated by him. "I hope I can do the same sometime."

"It would wholly be my pleasure if you would grace my office with your presence, thank you again, bye for now."

"Wow that was a pleasant surprise," Shy smiled and thought, "Once again you can't judge a book by its cover. He seemed so aloof and business-like at first, but it turns out he is the opposite. Then again who else does he have here? As with us, he will be going back to his own country when they train a Rwandese to take his place. He probably left seven wives and sixteen children in Senegal." Her focus drifted back to her work.

CHAPTER 17

IIIIIIIIIIIIIIIIIIIIIIIIIIIIIIIIIIIIIIIIIIIIIIIIIII

Adventure and Loved Ones

"Thou shalt love thy neighbor as thyself."
KJV Galatians 5:14

Cheyenne and Dava visited the Ntetesis almost every other day in the first month. Attending church with the Ntetesis was an unspoken rite Dava and Cheyenne fell into on Sundays. At church they were welcomed and some of the elder members of the Council also attended services with them. The two young women occasionally saw young professionals; however, language and custom kept them apart.

The Priest, though Catholic, reminded them so much of their southern Baptist ministers back home. He bellowed his sermon with fervor and praise. Four choirs competed in praise to God with complex rhythms and compelling harmonies in turn swaying, standing, sitting, and backed by an orchestra of drums, tambourines, double gongs, friction-drums, rattles, scrapers, and an antelope horn. The taking of the collection was in the form of a dance to the pulpit for children, women, and men in succession.

One of the best experiences they had was the time the Ntetesi's family invited Dava and Cheyenne along on a weekend trip to the Akagera National Park.

"This is the Africa one reads about; the animals in their natural habitat, the raft ride, and seeing where Stanley, of Stanley and Livingston fame, met. The beautiful, spectacular falls in Rusumo, at the southeast corner of Rwanda near southern Tanzania and northern Burundi are breathtaking," Henri described the trip to them.

They started out early in the morning for their two-hour trek in a well-equipped Land Rover that traveled a road that ran between mangroves and dwarf orange-berried palms on one side, and the long, long beach of the river on the other. Approaching the river area, they could feel the cool moist air against their bare arms as they rode along the sandy clay road.

Cheyenne inhaled the outdoor air of early winter and spring freshness. It reminded her of the meandering rivers and falls of upstate New York and in North Carolina Blue Mountain parks.

A beautiful, yet poorly dressed woman waved at their vehicle. The red plastic crate on her head contained huge chunks of dried elephant meat and fresh silver-pink fish; Dava was repulsed.

"How smelly the elephant carcass must be lying next to that fish the woman had on her head," Dava said as she stared out the window fascinated.

They both waved back at the woman as their vehicle rambled past her. Marie said, "Don't knock it till you have tried it," and they laughed..

Sandy streets appeared suddenly as they found themselves back on a savanna. Sturdy huts and houses were set within neatly divided land squares of swept earth hedged with shrubs.

Shy said, "On one of the Gullah Islands in South Carolina the people still sweep the sand flat in front of their homes."

They were proud of the fact that some of their African customs continued to hold strong in America long after all these many centuries and miles between the two continents had separated their cultures.

Henri said, "I am heartfelt happy to hear this great news of this African tradition in America."

Henri cautiously drove the truck around steep bends and over the rock-shelves and sand-beds of the plunging, climbing road. It was an exhilarating ride that included maneuvering between impenetrable treescapes of mahogany and balsa lined with tower-like trunks. Suddenly, the landscape dropped. It was as if they were riding on a roller coaster. The truck slowed down to a crawl as they reached the top, then seeing nothing below, the vehicle plummeted downward at rapid speed.

"Wheeee," Shy and Dava laughed, loving every second. The two little girls squealed and giggled.

They saw hills suddenly change to what were invisible valleys, presenting vista after shifting vista of treetops, on the unfolding hills, more heights beyond and, beyond those, hazy and wonderful mountains.

Then, the landscape changed into a sudden dense forest. "How far have we come? How long would it take? How many miles to go?" asked the children and to these old questions the answer was, "Not far now."

At the south entrance to the park, a guide took over the driving and just in time. For then suddenly, the hill exposed, regal and timeless, a lioness, motionless in high grass, her eyes fixed on a herd of impala. Dava and Cheyenne were stunned and overwhelmed as they drove by unnoticed.

Then they saw the heavily playful elephant from Lake Ihema, plunging its trunk up to gorge on bananas. It was as touching as beguiling to see this wild African animal, scampering off with her young ones, each with its tail straight up like a feather.

As they drove through the many plateaus and marshes a sight they could have done without was this big slimy-black mamba snake, slithering off into a burrow.

At almost every turn they'd get out of the vehicle and find a good vantage point at which time Cheyenne would photograph herds of zebra, antelopes, and hippopotamus all living in their natural African home.

"This is the most wonderful journey of my life," Shy said.

Unfriendly, to say the least, a buffalo poised under a grove, looked ready to charge intruders. Indeed, as they started toward the car the buffalo charged in their direction. They ran to the car, started the motor, and missed being pummeled under this fierce animal's hoofs. The children screamed and the ladies sat frozen in fear, searing in a memory that would stay with them forever.

Theirs was a safari unhindered by tourists and far different from what they heard about bumper-to-bumper traffic conditions on most of the Kenyan safaris.

Their eyes beheld such breathtaking scenery; it took Cheyenne back to a time in childhood of innocence and wonder. There are no monotonous savannas as in some countries in Africa. They were among hills, low and rounded or high and abrupt, which opened to wide valleys penetrated by lakes.

Once again they are reminded that Rwanda is the 'Country of a Thousand Hills.' There are high plateaus with many rivers, mainly the Akagera River which is about the most spectacular vision anyone could ever behold.

"This park has three distinct environments, open savanna dotted with acacia trees; this is then broken up by a chain of low mountains running the length of the park and the huge swampy areas running along the Tanzania border," said the French speaking guide.

As they drove further north off Lake Hago they saw a wide variety of animals. There was more screaming and pointing from all of them at the sight of these elephants, hippopotami, giraffes, rhinoceros, baboons, buffalo, roan antelope, warthogs, lions, leopards, hyenas, and crocodiles.

"Giraffes are so beautiful. Tall and graceful with spindly legs that appear so delicate until they sense danger and flash off at high speeds. They saw herds of zebra and impala, you may see twenty or more protected by one male," said the guide.

"Three types of antelopes over there," he pointed, "and one could really tell the difference between them and their predators, lions, and leopards. Look, the antelope are within feet of the lions and leopards."

"It is very scary to see the lions' dinner unaware and grazing contently, with the lion ready to attack," Shy said. "I am not ready to see that sight."

They drove faster and the guide said, "Twenty species of elephants and six giraffes were donated to this park by other parts of Africa and India

"Watch the baboons," Henri said. "Quickly, over there beautiful silver monkeys moving fast! The birds and the baboons are engaged in mutual grooming that seemed to communicate acceptance. It is amazing how readily they can tell if danger is near."

This safari took the entire day until the passengers settled for the night at the Hotel Akagera near Lake Ihema. Cheyenne counted her ten rolls of film left.

They awoke the next day, Saturday, ready to go but starving for breakfast. The fruit, bread, tea, and coffee would be enough to hold them until lunch

"The coffee here is from the highest hills. It is among the richest in the world," said Henri proudly.

"It's the best I have ever had," said Cheyenne.

Their next adventure was going to be a boating and hippopotami experience. Dava said, "I feel somewhat skeptical about riding in a small boat surrounded by hippos." But everyone assured her that they were very well protected.

As they boarded the boat and made their cameras ready for more pictures, hundreds of crabs emerged and retreated at the mouths of their holes in the sand. In what seemed like crazy choreography, the crabs stood high on their six legs and performed some kind of jig with one large claw and one small, before scuttling back into the dark. The motorboat is set up for twelve passengers, so the nine of them, including the captain, sat comfortably as the boat began its glide through Nile grass and water lilies.

The birds choired to them throughout the entire trip becoming more vocal through the papyrus forests. These were red and black birds, white shouldered birds, herons, and others no one recognized.

"Look at the large antelope that lives in this marshy land and can stand in mud without sinking. The antelopes can hide in the reeds with the tips of their muzzles sticking up above the water. Their hooves are shaped a certain way and they don't sink," said the guide.

They saw hippopotamus frolicking with their spouses then suddenly disappear into the murky waters below. Shy and Dava panicked.

The captain said, "The hippos hide when they sense danger, humans, and can stay emerged for five to six minutes and like submarines moving underwater find other locales to continue their activity." The snapshots Cheyenne took were great.

That afternoon they traveled by land to their last destination on Lakes Cyambwe and Rwampanga. Ranch Mpanga was comfortable with forty-two rooms. The food was good, and the resort had exactly what Dava and Cheyenne needed: two big beds and a private bath that included a hot shower. Sleep was quick to follow.

The next day they would arrive at the town of Rusumo after crossing all of eastern Rwanda and descending its greatest tributary, the Akagera River. The paved road to Rusumo from the great river traveled to a village where the people convened at a sacred baobab near the neck of the peninsula.

"Libations fill a hollow at the tree's roots. Prayers are offered to conjure catches of bountiful fish. The clans' chiefs stand back-to-back and each, moving to his own side, lies face-down on the mat. They represent schools of fish and, when the two clan-members return from the river, they rise. The ritual ends," said Henri.

Sunday morning the group was promised a swim for relief from the heat. They were on foot now. They dropped down from the main road onto a sandy track through woodland and then began the long steep descent between red boulders and white rocks, purple grass, and scrubby trees.

It was a challenging descent; rocks redoubled the sun's heat; the travelers paused to drink, admire the Akagera from afar, and dreamed of the white-sanded beaches. Down, down they went towards dwarf antique baobabs trees, and white-water cascading over emerald, green rock.

They are led down a path on foot to what seemed to be more forests. They clambered down to water level, to a fisherman's nets and his catch clinging to his liana rope.

Cheyenne asked, "Will we see the Akagera Falls from our swimming place?"

"Yes," said Henri, "You will see everything."

Below, the river stretched as far as the eye could see and they waded into the grass, with small boys who warned them against snakes, to their waiting vessel. The hiking boots were the dress for the day.

"Get into the boat carefully, no tipping the boat," smiled the boat pilot.

Dava, Cheyenne, the Ntetesis, and our driver, watched as Nilo, the boatman, fixed the motor into the slot in the rear lip of the dugout and loaded reserve tanks. The river appeared choppy. There were paddles nestled in the bottom of the canoe in case the motor failed. Soon after ten, they loaded their gear and, sitting in line on stools with Nilo standing astern, launched out into the river.

"At the river's edge some rhinoceros actually hold still and pose for pictures then go about their business," said Nilo.

They went upstream and heard the sound of rapids running back to the great falls below. Then they circled around downstream toward the Akagera Falls.

Shifting islands exposed water-hyacinth, reeds, grass, trees like incidental scenery in this world of water.

Now and then they could see whole settlements of huts on stilts, with tall frames for drying nets and fish and manioc, and, with men and women's clothes on rocks.

The wind dropped. Nilo cracked two coconuts together and drained them over the side. He split them in his hand with a keen machete and shared the succulent white flesh between the passengers. Refreshed, they seemed to be floating past a park, studded with great trees, and backed by hills. They left behind the tall white buoy that marks the end of the upriver islands, and saw their destination, Akagera Falls, spread out over the slopes.

The roar of the rapids filled the air.

They rode the river up to the point where instant death can overcome the novice rapids' rafter.

This was where they disembarked to get as close as possible to the falls. The small boat would have sunk immediately in the whirl and current as the water rushed down from the high peak, if they hadn't docked it on shore. They climbed the bridge that spans the Akagera, and in the foreground, was the view of the magnificent Akagera Falls.

They were at the far side of the mountains of Akagera at Rusumo, where the falls plummeted down over a thousand feet.

"This is the third highest falls in Africa. It splinters and rushes into Lake Akagera which marks the boundary between Rwanda and Tanzania shared with Zaire," said Henri.

It seemed as if thousands of intermingling rainbows appeared before their eyes overlapping the falls. They were humbled and dwindled to the size of ants in its presence. The ionic connection into the air resulted in an intoxicating walk toward the mountains for the group.

Whistling birds and the occasional roar reminded them of where they were. They passed a beautiful small waterfall that made a small rainbow exclusively for them.

The great trip to the falls ended as they walked back to the small boat nearby the beautiful sandy beach promised to them for their refreshing swim.

Twice, a little upriver Dava and Cheyenne had swum with Marie and the children. Up to their necks in soft water floating on their backs, they'd watch passing boat traffic. They baked in the sun watching an orchestra of weavers, sunbirds, waxbills, hoopoes, white-tailed flycatchers, yellow-vented bulbuls and three kinds of kingfisher working the water. The trees and the air fizzed with color. A pair of blue-headed coucals, with buff breasts and rust colored wings, mated on a branch, flaunting dark tails.

The day ended with laughter, awe inspired conversation, hot showers, and a sound sleep. Their last day was spent in an entirely different atmosphere. The driver who was experienced in showing his country's best took them to the far south.

Their journey from Rusumo deviated slightly as they swung over to the road leading to Kibungo. Before they got there they saw what appeared to be a bootcamp.

"Who are they training to fight against with knives and machetes, surely not the government?" Dava said innocently.

"I fear I don't know who they are training to fight. It looks more like they are training to kill," said Henri somewhat nervously.

Nilo ignores the English-speaking passengers, and mumbles "forest rangers, for poachers" in French.

They visited workshops along the road that dealt in cow dung art.

"This is only done by women," said Nilo. Cheyenne thought of this as a curiosity.

"... and is used to decorate walls and columns in homes. It is worked in patterned reliefs of spirals, diamonds, triangles, zigzags, herringbone, or checks. The walls are then painted in natural colors, ochre red, porcelain clay white, or animal black," continued Nilo.

"We will definitely have to investigate buying some of this, perhaps, Dava," said Shy, not quite sure she wanted cow dung hanging on her walls.

"We'll look into it in town; it is striking and rich looking," said Dava.

"I thought you might want to see where these paintings are made and the tradition behind them since we are down here in Rusumo," said Henri.

"Yes, thank you so much, we probably would never know

anything about it if you didn't show us. This is fascinating to see how the women make art from, well, cow poop," said Dava.

At night blue-black waters matched the blue-black sky with the brightest moon shimmering a path through the clouds across the water.

That evening Nilo carried some sweet manioc-modele mpako up to Marie and Henri's room. Henri was laying out a spread of fish-stew, kwanga - manioc-bread, mpondu-manioc leaves like spinach, likemba - fried plantain, rice, sweet potato, and pineapple. He was preparing a feast. This was their last meal on the road.

Before they set off back to Kigali to their homes, the Elders told them more about the river after dinner. "Rwanda's small stream, the Rukara, flows into the Mwogo River. The Mwogo flows into the Mbirurume which becomes Nyabarongo, the principal tributary of the Akagera. The Akagera is a tributary of Lake Victoria also known as the White Nile. The White Nile flows into the Blue Nile at Khartoum in Sudan. So, it is said the Nile River in Egypt begins in Rwanda."

At the end of the day, now at home, Cheyenne wrote Leon her heart's feelings about her first trip in Rwanda:

Dear Leon,

> *As I sit here in this distant land, far from home, far from you and everything I know, I miss you the most. I miss you in a special way. You have become part of me, more than my home, family, or friends. I love you so deeply, words can't express this feeling.*
>
> *My love, thank you for giving me this blissful emotion. I shall keep it within my heart forever. My happiness is in your love. I am filled with joy to know you love me too.*

Let me tell you about our river journey and the great Akagera National Park. Our adopted family the Ntetesis took us on one of our most exciting weekend trips. We went to one of the great national parks in Rwanda. The Akagera Lake is a tributary of Lake Victoria which has tributaries that flow into the Nile.

Imagine being able to take this river from the southeastern part of central Africa right up to the Pyramids! Lakes abound here and are surrounded by marshlands, reeds, and forests of papyrus. This great river splits into smaller tributaries that make great lakes all over Rwanda.

I fell in love easily with the bombastic, tea-brown river. I was in awe of the colorful vegetable patches of the banks, the tall trees that now and then stood proud of the many-textured, liana-threaded green.

At the end of our journey of nearly being swept into the rapids, we saw an old man before our final trip back to the Land Rover. The old man led us to his cave-dwelling for the fishermen

The Ntetesis were wonderful in taking us to the Akagera Falls and river rafting, and it felt like they were a part of the country's entire splendor. The only exception of this splendor was our final hike through the Kagera forest where we saw the government's military personnel training what seemed to be little boys and nomads how to use a machete. They demonstrated on each other as if they were preparing for hand-to-hand combat.

During the excursions we asked someone at the foot of the falls what was going on with the military. We were abruptly told that the military is training forest rangers against poachers and the like and that was the end of that. Somehow that didn't rest easily with us, but the day was so wonderful we tried to put that aside.

Even though you are far away I don't feel lonesome, just a little lonely now and then. Dava and I are making the best of it, but we are going to have to make some friends besides the Ntetesi family and the people from the Council and work.

At night is the most difficult time without you. I miss you but knowing we share a powerful love makes it not so painful. I can love you through words, spoken and written. I can love you because I can trust you with my heart.

I'm happy to have Dava here with me. She's a piece of home that keeps me sane. The others in the group are very dedicated. They are older and have more experience with diversity than we do. They guide and give us strength as we are the youngest and only females in the Council on this project.

Leon, please keep this letter if you can. If you have time, copy it and send it to mom for me, only the trip part. She would love to read the details of my trip.

God Bless and Keep You.
Love,
Shy

Shy posts the letter at the Post Office mailbox and prays that it will reach Leon within the week so that she can get his letter in return. She decides then and there that if she needs to she won't wait for his letters she will write and hope it won't be redundant for him.

Not surprisingly their respective parents sent Dava and Shy letters that arrived on the same day at the same time. It seems that mail arrives once a week all at one time. Shy's mother writes lovingly:

Dear Shy,

Hope all is going well there for you in the new country and new job. Do you get to see the other Council members often? I told them to look after you and Dava. We have planned to give Granpa and GranNellie a fifty-fifth wedding anniversary party. We are getting the names and addresses, of course, from GranNellie and Grandpa. In fact, they are planning the seating arrangement and the liquors. I am reserving the venue and the catering from our friends at Two Steps Down, here in Brooklyn. It looks to be a great event. We are going to videotape it. Hope you can return for a week in June and be here for the celebration.

Your sisters are going to Packer the private school on the Heights. They seem to love it. You know they enjoy their freedom which this school provides as opposed to the Public School in the neighborhood.

I know what you are thinking since GranNellie was a high school teacher. How could she teach these children and not send her own? I can see on a daily basis how the system is geared for failure. She had to group her children almost six ways for each subject. I preferred it when the class grouping was more homogenous. Sometimes you have to let the ones who excel stay together and separate them from the average who need to be separated from the below average who need to be separated from the slow who need to be separated from the behavior problems. Call me old fashioned, but she has in the system twenty- plus years and has seen the difference separation makes.

I will write to you at least twice a week to keep you abreast of the family. Please let us know how you are doing. We pray for you daily in a big family prayer, even your uncle joins us in prayer which you know is a big deal.

Love you so much,
God Bless you all,
Mom

Cheyenne decided to write to her immediately to get it done and calm her mother's fears.

Dear Mom,

We are doing great. It's so exciting here. I am enclosing pictures of our last trip. I wrote down all the details and Leon will send you a copy as soon as he can.

As you can imagine things are really buzzing at work. I like going to work. Dava and I look forward to work every day. It gives us a chance to use our skills to the limit and then some. We get to talk to the Rwandese as well as other African people all day long. Our first transmission was received by Nelson Mandela! I actually communicated with him personally. We love the style and non-hurry up to wait demeanor the people have here. No one tenses or gets stressed out if there is a glitch in the system, everyone knows this is in an experimental stage of development. What we do here will lead to world wide communication with each other.

Tell Aunt Wen I am doing my research quietly. I can see that my theories of Homo sapiens and Neanderthals would cause some alarm among the Europeans here who are very much separatists. They are very curious about our project. They know that if the Rwandese flourish, they will flourish even more.

You don't have to write twice a week. We get our mail only once a week so far. So, I read both of your letters at once. I will let you know if and when delivery improves. I am sending my undeveloped canisters of film in the letters to be developed in N.Y. Thanks, mom.

Love you much,
Shy

Rwanda and Burundi

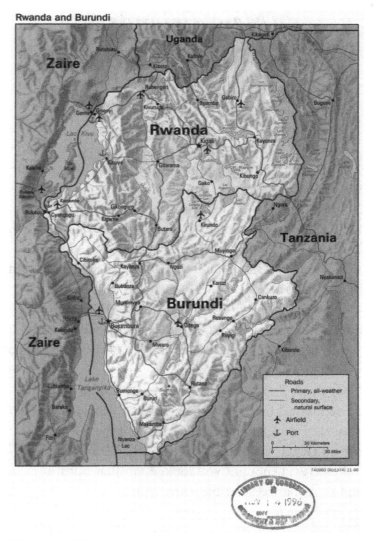

191

CHAPTER 18

||||||||||||||||||||||||||||||||||||||||||||||||||||

New Friends

"If it be possible, as much as lieth in you, live
peaceably with all men." KJV Romans 12:18

Shy and Dava and the Council members who were on her
work shift left together for home that evening. They gathered
together for their evening bench sitting, enjoyed after work
parlay, then all went in for their dinners and bed.

As Shy was cleaning up that night's meager meal there
was a knock at their door. Dava, being closest and most bored,
answered it immediately. Enter three young people who seemed
very familiar. They were the same age as Shy and Dava.

"Hello and greetings, I am Jeanne Habyarimana, the
President's daughter and these are my cousins, Paoul and
Antoin." She smiled brightly at the two Americans and signaled
her chauffeur that she was alright.

"We thought you might be getting a little lonesome for
your friends and family about now, so we thought we would
come by. Do you remember meeting us at the Cultural Center
when you first arrived in Rwanda?" asked Paoul.

"Well, yes. I thought you looked familiar but forgive us if
we didn't recognize you by name immediately," Dava stated
in perfect French.

"That is alright. We were trying to find a way to contact
you, without being intrusive, for less formal introductions. Too
bad you don't have a phone yet in your room. Do you know

you can get one?" Antoin, the handsome tall young black man stated.

"They told us that we'd have to use the phone in the office of the superintendent and that all our calls would come through there for the time being," replied Dava, smiling coyly.

"Well not so, you will have a phone tomorrow, Paoul make sure she is connected tomorrow. Anyway, we are here to take you girls on the town. Do you like to dance?" asked Jeanne, ready to have fun.

Shy and Dava slipped into their more casual clothes to match their hosts, and happily jumped at an opportunity to be with young people. First they told Tombe, who had been looking out his door since the group's arrival. He was the protectorate of their village.

They drove to a European disco called the Chez Lando. The music sounded like American and French mixed together. Shy and Dava noticed that the people there felt like France's rich and Manhattan's funky.

"This reminds me of the discos on the East side of Manhattan," Shy said, not wanting to be rude. "Do you come here often?"

"Not really," said Jeanne, "Only when we are taking people from out of town someplace. We thought this would remind you of home and you wouldn't feel so homesick," she continued very innocently.

They all danced with fun abandonment. Shy noticed Dava and Antoin hitting it off right away. She made a note to tell her about sex in Africa.

Later Shy and Dava said they wanted to go where the people were. They drove "over the hill" as the African area was called. They immediately finished their drinks and happily headed for the Eden Garden on Rue de Karisimbi. The smooth drive soon became rocky. They turned onto a paved street and went into the disco. It was a combination disco and restaurant where the Rwandese and of course some Europeans converged.

"Yeah, this is more like it," Dava said, moving to the mixed African and African American music.

Everyone wanted to dance with the two New Yorkers. But in Africa respect is shown for the entire group and people asked Antoin and Paoul occasionally if they could dance with the ladies. The two men asked Dava and Shy who declined to dance with others and danced all night with only Antoin and Paoul. Jeanne, who was very popular, had two of her friends join the party at their table.

They stayed there until 3 a.m. "Closing time for this Saturday night," Jeanne said. "We have one more place to go before we drop you home. It has excellent food and a special treat that will give you great dreams for the night."

They visited the bar by the Zone and sat under palm trees within high white walls. They drank banana beer, danced on a raised concrete floor, and watched the men, with slight and profound motions, signal their intentions towards bandumbas or femmes libres. Sometimes men danced with men, and sometimes by themselves, admiring their style in a full-length mirror hung on a pilar for that purpose.

There was talk at their table about the mores and acceptance of sex for sale. Antoin talked of the trade in femmes libres' "compulsory" venereal health certificates. The Rwandese men played along with their country's music by strumming the rough bottles with bottle tops. Then a surprise appearance by Francois-Xavier Munyarugerero sent great cheers from the crowd. He played the piano and sang his famous song 'Rayons et nuees" (Rays and Clouds) and the crowd went crazy.

"Slither/ Slithering grass-snake with fairy like fingers/ in the thin ether clouds/ with sparkling sprays/ to the rhythm of your angel wings/ which jump/ skip/ form a void to our half-open ear drums.

"The flute sows its melancholy sounds/ allied to the grave voice of the contralto/ our drums boom-booming/ and the trumpet makes the Milky Way smile;/ the guitar calls the moon/ timidly pressed against the back of the heavens/ here it is coming/ slowly like a queen at a gala evening/ under the vigilant eye of Prince Charming.

"Already the stars/ one by one/ are ceaselessly winking/ like jealous spectators/ the cymbals produced thunder, / the drumsticks lightning."

…The lyrics resonated with Dava as she pressed her head on Antoin's chest as they glided on air across the dance floor.

This atmosphere became much more relaxing, and the music was loud enough to dance to and talk over. Many people came to the table with this lively group of young people and showed their joy and enthusiasm for the promise the American group would bring. They all danced to the lively music of Zaire.

"Who is this singing?" asked Dava of Antoin.

"That is Kanda Bongo Man singing 'Zing Zong' a fun song," said Antoin as he moved Dava around on the dance floor to the fast beat. Antoin held Dava tightly as Kanda Bongo Man sang his love song, 'Isambe.' She melted into his arms, and he relaxed his arms around her body lovingly.

★★★★★★★★★

As they drank the delicious intoxicating banana beer an old man, hands blistered and twisted, from working in the land, told of the picturesque brewing of "banana beer," the much-appreciated national beverage of Rwanda.

"The banana trees provide beer, fruit and vegetables, and also provide the farmer with leaves used as plates, wrappings and umbrellas, as well as bark fibers which are primary material for a variety of crafts.

"One liter of banana beer costs the equivalent of one fifth to one half day's work. The farmer picks the green bunches before they are ripe, covers them with banana leaves and puts them to rot in his courtyard for two or three days. Still wrapped in leaves, the bunches are then placed in a ditch covered with banana stems and soil.

"This primitive oven is then fired, and after cooking, the bananas are removed and peeled, before being mixed with water of brassin, in a long wooden container in the form of a canoe. The cake thus formed is pressed and the juice filtered into calabashes. Mixed with a little sorghum flour, it is next heated in a large vat. After three days of fermentation, it is ready to be drunk, without too much delay, for within a few days it becomes acid and unpalatable." Everyone gave the man money as a reward for his storytelling.

The group cheerfully drank and danced and made many friends that night, few to be remembered the next day. Banana beer, unlike alcoholic drinks, makes people very friendly. There were no miserable people in the Zone that night.

As they began to leave, men loitered to talk in an open space outside the bar, which might have been large enough for a few football plays. Upon leaving the Bar the new friends walked a little with the chauffeur following. Since it was the crack of dawn and life was awakening in the marketplace,

Dava and Shy wanted to experience the early morning sights and sounds.

Old women in their forties crossed the road with loads on their heads: enamel basins stacked high with bread, bananas, or piles of manioc leaves like large green feathery hats.

Entering the market was like a maze; narrow alleys of thickly packed, densely stocked stalls where two people could hardly pass in shadows cast by corrugated-iron roofs; a stooping progress through a world of smells, while eyes and ears were drawn this way and that by goods held up for the group's inspection and consumption and rival cries, "Mademoiselle... venez., venez voir...bon marche... voila Mademoiselle... c'est un bon prix!...Achetez, achetez, achetez!"

Some women kept cautiously staring as if daring the group to affront their humanity by not buying her wares.

Cloths, gorgeous glowing waz-prints and cheaper cottons, jewelry, bright accessories, men laboring at sewing-machines, whole stalls of soap like long cheeses, onions, tomatoes, garlic, ginger, heaps of plastic sandals, hordes of silver, spiced fish and a special feature, caches of nails, screws, bolts, bicycle and car spares, tools, and welding gear, all imported from Angola and Zaire and displayed in abundance.

Dava bought a handful of bananas for five francs, about ten cents, and ducked out into the light of the street once more. Shy and Dava questioned why there were so many elaborate tools.

"In Belgian times, each town had its white residential area, its commercial area, and its Cite, or 'native quarter.' There were still immaculate Belgian houses, Portuguese villas, and high-walled compounds like Gulf Oil's, where generators throbbed all day and air-conditioning insulated the inhabitants from Africa. But only the rich could afford paint.

"The dust roads were smoothed by the oil companies'

earthmovers, though in the rains everything turned to mire," said Paoul.

"The main street, named like main streets everywhere, for the independence in 1963 was Boulevard de la Revolution, near the Tam-Tam Restaurant, which is where we will dine for breakfast."

After they ate and enjoyed each other's company some more, Jeanne called the driver to open the door and they nearly fell on the seats still laughing and feeling the effects of the banana beer. Dava slipped her arm through Antoin's to steady herself.

"Thank you," said Antoin, pleased with himself that she offered her arm to him, at which time he helped her into the car with great care. "We hope you enjoyed our slice of life with the real people, this evening?" Antoin said to Shy and Dava as they drove back to their apartment.

"There are no words, in fact, the way I'm feeling from this banana beer was the best night of my life," Dava said.

"Jeanne, you don't know how lonely we were becoming especially for someone to talk to who's our own age," Shy said beaming from the banana beer herself. They sat smiling and glowing in the dawn's orange-haze sun.

"You have made us very happy, also, by your wanting to enjoy our Rwandese culture. It means a lot to us when our African American brothers and sisters party with us and not only the Europeans," Jeanne answered as seriously as the effects of banana beer allowed her.

On the way back home the brightness of the sun was coming fast. They passed a nursing school, and crossed a narrow footbridge where women washed themselves in the stream and pounded clothes.

Across the road they found a crippled French-speaking boy

listening to a radio with an aerial rigged up to the roof of his hut. The news on the radio disturbed the new young friends of Shy and Dava, but they didn't say anything.

"We must get together very soon," Antoin blurted out, looking directly at Dava.

"I have planned a weekend trip for us to the Volcanoes National Park in two weekends from now," Jeanne said, quickly sensing embarrassment with her cousin's display of emotion.

They all hugged and departed each holding their own private contentment. For Dava and Shy the rest of that Sunday was pretty well spent resting and talking over their evening, and Dava discussing Antoin.

Antoin, Paoul and Jeanne made them feel at home. It was the feeling they had longed for like when they were hanging out with friends in N.Y. Maybe the likeness in age made the difference.

★★★★★★★★★★

Back at work that Monday, things seemed to take on a new flavor. Shy and Dava, having visited a local spot and drinking banana beer and dancing with the people, felt more like they belonged there. No one at work appeared to recognize them from the bar or said anything derogatory, but a familiar friendliness was felt and fostered from then on at work. They even noticed more smiles when they walked the streets of Kigali.

One week night after they had an informal dinner at Paoul's, Dava and Shy discussed the technical complexities of the job and how the people were reacting to this new technology.

"First you need to know what the internet is. It is like a TV network where signals are sent out, but the difference is the computer network is two way. Some computer networks consist of a central computer and a bunch of remote stations that report to it and some like the internet permit any computer on the network to communicate with any other, "Dava began.

"Like a telephone?" asked Jeanne.

"No, the telephone uses electrical signals to transfer your voice to sound, but the fiber optics uses light to send the message," said Shy.

"So, a television network sends the signal one way, and the internet is a network of networks sending messages back and forth," said Antoin, very proud of himself.

"Yes, exactly," said Dava, smiling the biggest smile she had for Antoin.

"It translates a digital message into electrical impulses that can travel through the phone wire," Shy was beginning to get wrapped up in her instruction.

" All of our offices are rewired for the network connections," Shy continued.

"Fiber optic cables that carry words, pictures and sound will connect homes, businesses, schools, and all aspects of society. This opens limitless opportunities for computer users.

"For entertainment, digital television, interactive programs that allow users to respond, and virtual reality which gives the allusion of participation, will revolutionize past-time activities. Digital theme parks and multimedia CDs offer even broader opportunities.

"In business the workplace information revolution started with electronic mail and in-house communications and gave way to email and video conferences between companies or different locations. Now, new software innovations allow tracking of inventory, customer relations, employee work flow, manufacturing, and marketing. Small and self-owned companies can benefit," Cheyenne blushed at her enthusiastic monologue.

"When I get my personal computer and internet hook-up please advise me as to which one is the fastest, but not now. I don't think I could retain that information right now," said Jeanne, fascinated by these two young women her own age with so much knowledge. Jeanne made a decision secretly to follow a course of study on computer technology herself.

"Yes, it took me four years of college and two years of grad school to really get this," Dava said still smiling.

"I will probably use this in my medical practice when I finish my residency here on Rue de l'Hopital," said Antoin, looking at Dava and thinking of them happily together.

"I think I've had about all the technical input I can take into my little computer here," said Paoul pointing to his head.

They laughed and talked again about their night out at the Rwandese bar and the people they met and the fun they had. They laughed about the effects of the banana beer. They exchanged stories about growing up and how parents and elders are the same everywhere with their eternal words of wisdom usually not acknowledged seriously by their children until adulthood.

Antoin drove Shy and Dava back home. Shy went inside while Antoin and Dava talked outside in front of the apartment on a bench in the garden.

Meanwhile, the telephone connection depended on wiring above ground and it took weeks for the installation. Shy and Leon wrote to each other every other week hoping for a reply to each other's letters soon.

Shy found a letter from Leon waiting for her and glad for the privacy to read her beloved's words:

My Dearest Love,

I hope you finally find some people your age to befriend. You know everyone in this journalism program in Egypt is our age so that is not a problem for me. And they all seem to be from New York or the southeast. We are having a ball here. Some of them brought their wives, and they are anxious to meet you when you come to visit.

I can hardly contain the excitement I feel being in the lands of our ancestors. Although the Arabs had taken over for centuries you can still see the marks of our Nubian forefathers whose great monuments to humanity can never be destroyed. There is a definite coverup going on as to the original builders of the pyramids and of course Karmac. However, they don't even entertain the idea of an alien source for the pyramid building as do the American movie makers and tour guides who tell tourists this myth.

There is so much to tell you I could write a newspaper article every day. What I am doing is keeping a detailed diary I hope to share with you of the frenzy and population explosion of Cairo and on the other hand, the absolute stillness and sanctuary of the Pyramids and Karmac.

I mention Karmac so often because this is definitely a piece of the Egyptian Pharaoh's legacy. I can't wait for you to come here, and I can tell you the story. However, I will tell you this much, every Pharaoh from the 18th dynasty to the 7th century AD went to Karmac to perform a secret ritual to rebirth himself with his wife, I should say their Queens.

There are bathing facilities, and each Pharoah added an obelisk or addition to the temple in some way. Amen the God that the Pharaohs believed created life from nothing gave birth to himself and mankind by taking the seed from his phallus in his hand and giving it to his Queen orally who then gave birth to mankind. Probably why there is an obelisk everywhere in the world. This is a familiar story of virgin birth, right? If I could only show you this at the ruins of Karmac, you'd see it is detailed in the most picturesque hieroglyphics.

There is some disturbing history here in Egypt that involves Israel and the Palestinians. I remember the Camp David agreement where Egypt would demilitarize the Sinai Peninsula and allow freedom of movement in the Suez Canal. More on that later,

From the sound of your letter the Ntetesis are taking very good care of you. Tell them hello for me. The Akagera Park and Rusumo Falls trip sounds fantastic. Seeing all those wild animals up close must have been exciting. From your letter I can see you felt protected and safe. I still am concerned, but I guess the Ntetesis wouldn't put their own children in danger either.

I must tell you I have further concern for your safety in Kigali. There are reports of secret military operations getting ready to hatch major offenses in many key places in Africa, especially Liberia, Somalia, and Rwanda. When I get more details I will get them to you. As we say in N.Y. "keep your awareness up!"

I miss you and love you so much. I am so proud of you and all of the African Affairs Council for the work you are doing there. This is the beginning of a beautiful friendship: Africans of the world uniting instead of fighting. Boy, what a blow to racism that would be.

As they say, in the struggle no one can really get ahead if there is any one class being oppressed. Makes more work for the oppressor, too. They have to find more ways to keep the people down and out, too much negative energy and resources wasted.

There are some things going on here in Egypt that Mubarak is sanctioning in conjunction with our government concerning terrorism. I don't know exactly what is happening yet, but I'll keep you informed.

Well, I want you to enjoy your stay and remember to keep your awareness up. I love you so much.

Yours forever,
Leon

After reading his letter again Shy immediately wrote back to him while Dava was still outside with Antoin. Shy can very faintly hear them whispering and laughing. She knew these signs of affection very well and felt inspired to write Leon.

CHAPTER 19

||||||||||||||||||||||||||||||||||||||||||||||||||

Heart Songs

"God is Love, Whoever lives in love, lives in God and God lives in them." KJV 1 John 4:16

Hello My Love,

I read your letter and can't wait to join you for at least a week in Egypt. I know some of the ancestor's history there but to see it would really be mind-blowing. Except for Dava and the Council members you are the only other person I can talk to in English. I love French, but it is a second language. I am so tempted to speak in English so that I think people can better understand me, especially with the technical stuff.

Yes, Dava and I have finally met some people our age. And guess what? Three of our newest acquaintances happen to be the President's daughter and his two nephews! Dava seems to be getting interested in one of the guys already. He is very nice, and I can't blame her. I'm so happy I have you, so I don't have to worry about such mundane things, ha ha.

Dava's friend's name is Antoin. He's tall and black and handsome. He's a med intern and in Doctors Without Borders. He comes with great credentials. He seems to really care for Dava. I hope he's sincere. You know she can't take any more pain after that last jerk she had in New York.

I look at them together and wish you were near to me. I love the scent of you and the warmth of your nature. I miss you, but the busyness of work helps distract me from the emptiness I sometimes feel.

One day while Dava and I were walking to Henri and Marie's house after work, we saw a man in an orange shirt sit on one of the capstans, with his naked three year old daughter between his knees; he soaped her from head to foot with water from a bucket; he made her blow her nose into his hand and flicked the snot into the dirt; he washed his hands and cleaned her nose and ears with his little finger; he rinsed her and hugged her dry with a cloth; he dressed her and greased her hair with his palms, over and over; he took the comb from his hair and teased hers; he held her head between his big hands as she clutched a little chrome-framed mirror and examined herself; she smiled and glanced up at me, large-eyed. I smiled and winked at her. I fell in love with this ceremony. The people here have an innocence that can't compare to any other people I know that inhabit this planet of ours.

I told the Ntetesis about this and they said bathing a child is a ritual. It is spiritual and a religious rite. The cleansing of the body is not just a grooming habit here. It is something you do to prepare for God to enter. It's something like you were telling me of the Pharaohs and their wives at Karmac.

I told them all about you and showed them your picture and told them what you are doing in Egypt *from the Columbia Graduate School of Journalism. They can't wait to meet you, too, Leon.*

Have to tell you about the time our new friends took us out dancing and bar hopping Rwandese style. I have been introduced to banana beer. It's so good and strong. We had a great time. The music here is wonderfully melodic and hypnotic. I am getting used to the food. One thing for sure, I am eating organic, natural food for the most part.

The people are faced with the need to cultivate farmland because of the population growth and increased longevity of the people. So, they destroy many trees and forests. In the process of losing forests, is the fact that the trees no longer absorb nor slow the water poured down by the rains. The Arabic soil is then washed away and pulled down the slopes. This soil needed to make the teas and coffees rich and exclusive, is lost forever at the bottom of the hill.

Rwandans must struggle heroically to keep the soil in place. All Rwandans, including administrators are urged to work together to fight against erosion, planting as many trees as possible, digging ditches and trenches, raising parapets, caring for hedges and terraces on the sloping fields. This is what gives the hills those contoured lines which dissect the hills and lend the scenery a slightly Asian touch.

In this land where more than 90% of the population live from agriculture and work in the fields, as a tourist we have the impression of being on a long country holiday. As we climb it is even more so in the mountains, we get the most out of a health cure of chlorophyll and fresh air near the summits. There is a

FORGIVE AND LIVE: RWANDA

little lesson to be learned every step of the way on the subject of tropical botany.

The colors of flowers, the ancient skyscraper trees and thousands of hills weaving in and out of the city and the peninsula laden with lakes, make this place seem like a paradise. Being new here and not a native Rwandan, I can really appreciate the beauty of this country. If the people were only treated with equality in the sharing of profits of their country's natural resources, God would be so much happier.

Well, Dava is back, and I know she wants to talk about Antoin so, my love, bye for now. I love you so. I will continue to keep you in my prayers and thanks for keeping me in yours.

Yours completely,
Shy

✶✶✶✶✶✶✶✶✶✶

"Shy, I am so happy when I am with Antoin, but you know I am still scared to death of a relationship," Dava confided in her best friend as she flopped on the couch.

"I know your fear, and I think it will work for you in the long run. It is always better not to let go of your emotions immediately when you first meet someone. Stay friends with him. Come here and get a hug," Shy said, extending her arms to her friend.

"I believe he really cares for me. But words seem so shallow sometimes. Yet he treats me so special. I feel confused since I am not totally healed, spiritually, emotionally, physically, and psychologically from you know who. I can't even say his name yet and it's been a year and a half," as Dava let herself relax in Shy's arms.

"I wish I knew how to help you mend, but only time and perhaps Antoin can help," Shy said. They both have a cup of sleepy time tea and dream of their men.

★★★★★★★★★★

That Sunday they went to church with the Ntetesis which seemed to be a way of life. Afterward they sat, ate, listened to Henri, and discussed their progress at work. The children were always eager to hear of the electronics and technical aspects of their jobs.

Shy and Dava continued to enjoy the home and warm family relationship they had with the Ntetesis, but Dava also had someone else she was getting close to, Antoin. They called each other on the phone daily now that the ladies had their own personal phone. One evening, before Antoin came by the apartment to take Dava on an early evening after work date, Shy had a serious talk with Dava.

"I am so happy for you my friend. I know you really like Antoin and Lord knows he's fine. Did he say anything yet?"

'Well, he told me I am the most beautiful woman he has ever seen in his life and that he loves me. But I think African men can say that so easily to a woman they hardly know. He looks at me as if he is expecting me to say I love him too, but I can't. That is definitely not New York style," Dava laughed with her friend.

"And you know that. On the serious side I must remind you of the sub-Sahara statistics on AIDS," Shy said as she brought out newspaper articles her mother sent her on AIDS in Africa.

"According to this article, thirty different strains of the virus have been identified that cannot be detected in the blood by conventional AIDs tests. This Belgian researcher has isolated new strains found in Cameroon and other parts of Central Africa. The saddest part of this story is that most of the world's proportion of AIDs is found in Sub Saharan Africa. Here's the statistics: 860,000 in North America, 310,000 in the Caribbean, 1,300,000 in Latin America, 480,000 in Western Europe, 190,000 in Eastern Europe and Central Asia, 210,000 in North Africa and Middle East, 5,800,000 in South and Southeast Asia, 12,000 in Australia and New Zealand, and 21,000,000 in Sub-Saharan Africa. That is where we are now in 1994."

Cheyenne continued, "It's odd how this disease was conceived in Western Europe and is more prevalent in countries where people of color live."

"I do appreciate you telling me this, but we are not at that point yet and I do have some self-control. I have had it for over a year since I broke up with that crazy Ben."

"I don't want you to think I'm getting in your business, but I love you, and I don't want anything to happen to you or see anyone hurt you again like Ben did. I couldn't bear it.

Remember I was there through every terrible week."

"Let's not revisit that incident again, but thanks, Shy," they hugged each other and Shy gave Dava her condoms. "You sure come prepared don't you?" Dava took them and smiled at her friend.

"Well, you know Leon is up the Nile a piece from here?" Shy laughed and they both hugged again when they heard the knock on the door.

"He's here," as Dava ripped the door open.

"Good evening my queen, good evening Shy," Antoin bowed slightly as he greeted the two women.

Dava escorted him to a chair and the two sat around him. They loved his French and his accent. Even Shy was smitten by those white pearls of teeth against that smooth black skin. He lit up a room each time he smiled.

"How was your day, Antoin?" Dava asked always interested in whatever he says.

"Things are getting quite bad, I'm afraid. President Habyarimana is between pleasing his Hutu military leadership and the U.N. in negotiating and sharing the responsibilities of the government with Tutsi leadership according to the ARUSHA Accord. We must have peace and harmony. I am half Tutsi and half Hutu myself as most of us are. There is a dangerous element afoot, and I don't know where or how to cope," said Antoin, alone in his political world. He worked for his uncle the Hutu President and yet he loved his mother, a beautiful Tutsi woman whose family also was in government leadership for years.

Dava and Antoin left, and a package arrived. It was from Leon, Shy read the letter first:

★★★★★★★★★★

Dear Enchantress Cheyenne,

Some people give such a giant share of themselves to humanity, while others among us give none. And I wonder how this comes about. What prompts a person to risk his or her future, to divorce self from the American life because what one sees in the shadows is all too real; what one hears is the crying of hungry children in the ghetto, desperate people's minds struggling to be free; silence from the aged who sit and wait for life's ultimate end. These are some reasons which reach the heart and strike pain and sadness. And the sharpness of it all sends love flowing, releases energy to help; to really help regardless of traditions, rules, or time. This is you, my Queen.

We speak of love, of concern but where is the love, where is this concern? We only speak of it, it does not exist, for when one amongst us has it, we crush it, we imprison the bearer, and we send him into exile. But somehow my dearest, the spirit lingers, and it lies dormant within us - but its presence is continually felt, and if by chance we uncover the needed strength, we become like the Bobby Seales', the David Harrises, Malcolm's, and King's - hoping for a better world, working to create a heaven on earth, perhaps, being smothered in the process. There is a quiet rebellion here against the torture of souls who may be innocent. I am uncertain of all of the information. The government keeps it all top secret. I feel no animosity here since our government and this government have an agreement.

So, I give to you this symbol of the struggle, I give to you a part of myself with it.

I hope you like the enclosed gift to you. It is for you to remember me and for your protection. Do not hesitate to use it for your defense. It was blessed with the waters of the Nile and by a Nubian priest who I believe is a descendant of a Pharaoh.

I hope you and your two new little sisters love the bracelets I send you all. They are replicas of one of Queen Nefertari's wedding bracelets. I hope that Iraminani and Eugenia like them.

I love you with all my heart and soul. I think of you night and day, except when I am in the middle of some grueling job. You would not believe the excavations that go on here in a day. There is a

constant bevy of international journalists in and out of
Cairo focused on reporting the finds of their country's
representative archaeologist. It is disgusting. They
have no regard for the place of honor of the hidden
sanctuaries the dead Kings and Queens tried in vain
to hide in ancient times.

Now they claim to have found Alexander's tomb
in the western desert. So, what! After he plundered
and burned the African's libraries he wanted to be
buried here. Imagine the nerve! Sometimes I get
so angry with these people. They dig and dig not
thinking of preserving; just taking out never adding
wealth to the indigenous people here.

That is one thing I must give the current Arab
inhabitants of Egypt; they do try to preserve the
ancient tombs. If the Nubians were still in their
original habitat things would be different; however,
with the flooding of the Valley of the Dead and the
great dam, they had to move.

There has been great loss of historical treasure due
to excavations abandoned and the harsh sun and sand
erasing the exposed hieroglyphics and wall paintings
left by the Egyptians. There have been floods that
have wiped away entire tomb walls. The current
Egyptians do try to restore and protect the Nubian
tombs, but it takes the money spent by the European
archaeologists to do the job properly. Millions are spent
by them to take, take, take. Don't they realize there
is no natural balance in just taking without preserving.

I am sorry to go on like this, but when you come
here you will experience it for yourself. The most
amazing people and cultures dwell here together in

peace. Christians as well as mostly Muslims. However, I met and helped save a Sufi Jew. I can't wait to see you again to tell you about him.

I have been getting reports of a drought spreading your way. Presently Sudan has five million people affected. Some of the journalists in my class are there now. My mentors seem to be enjoying my slant on the excavations here so I will probably stay here for the entire year and a half.

The countries involved in the drought are Ethiopia, Somalia, Eritrea, Rwanda, Burundi, Uganda, Tanzania, Djibouti, and Kenya. Donor countries are alerted, and the Agency for International Developments is staying informed to avoid mass famine and malnutrition.

On another note, I am glad you have finally found some young people you can hang with as it's so important when you call a place home for a while. Watch out for my little play sister, Dava. I don't want her to be eaten up by the wolf again. I miss your face, your smell. I miss everything.

I will always pray for you -God Bless you. I will love you forever and always.

Leon Virgo

Enclosed in the package Shy found three beautiful bracelets and pulled out a sword inscribed with Egyptian Hieroglyphics which read, " Ma'at are the ancient virtues our ancestors died for, I too shall fight to the death for the honor of my people."

"Wow," exhaled Shy as she thought how deep her lover is. "Leave it to Leon to give me a little sword and these great words to inspire and encourage me." Shy placed the sword on a shelf near her books in the living room.

"For some reason I feel the need to have this thing handy," she said to herself as she felt the weight of this magnificent gift.

She put on her bracelet and called Francois and she took the other two bracelets to Eugenia and Iraminani Ntetesi.

When she gave them to the young girls they put them on and kissed and hugged Shy's face for a good five minutes, laughed and showed off the precious jewels to their family. They had a party and invited their friends to show off their bracelets. They were silver with gold and platinum hieroglyphics which legend had it means the wearer will have eternal protection by God's hand.

CHAPTER 20

Exploring and Gorillas

"Be strong and courageous. Do not be afraid
for the Lord, your God will be with you
wherever you go." KJV Joshua 1:9

The following Saturday, Antoin and Paoul arrived as planned for their trip to the Volcanoes National Park. This was a long-awaited trip for Shy and Dava since they saw the movie, "Gorillas in the Mist" a few years ago.

"Where is Jeanne?" asked Shy.

"She's been sent back to school in Paris," was all Paolo gave in a grim mood.

They packed enough for two days and two nights since it was such a long way and they wanted to fully experience the trip. Paoul did the driving so that Antoin could tell all about everything they passed. They drove along the tar-paved road parallel to the Akanyaru River. Antoin pointed out along the river bank among ferns and tall grass, water-hyacinths, and pale violet flowers.

"These water hyacinths are one of the few things brought to Africa from America," he said, not wanting to offend his American friends by simply stating facts. "That is until you all arrived with your gifts of knowledge and wisdom," Antoin said, smiling proudly at Shy and Dava.

Antoin was very knowledgeable in the animal and plant life along the rivers and the Congo. He was a student of zoology and biology in preparation for medical school.

"Look, there are some hippos bathing and three pelicans feeding. Look also at the beautiful Egyptian ibis, black body with white wings, flying overhead," He said as Dava and Shy poked their heads out the window and craned their necks to see everything he said that was there to see.

Suddenly Antoin said, "Watch this," and pointed to the river. They turned and saw obviously white tourists on their yacht being chased then lassoed by several small boats with African men and women. As they attached to the yacht in the most peculiar ways they spread their wares on their decks and began trying to out-talk each other.

"On the small decks are onions, ginger root, chili peppers, heaps of rice, salt and sugar, and kerosene lamps made from recycled tins. They will start to barter with the tourists who usually do buy with money.

"Tourists know they are pretty safe here so there was no need to throw the ropes off the sides of the yacht. I bet you thought they were being mugged right?" Antoin teased.

"Well, I have to admit I was a little perplexed when I saw how they paddled so hard to catch the yacht. I really didn't know what to expect," said Shy.

As the water hyacinth and papyrus sailed by along the river the sky darkened, and showers pounded the car. On the shore they saw a man carry a huge bundle of the beautiful purple flowers of the water hyacinth on his head. The broadening river became choppy, and lightning roared down. The sky became the darkest of gray. Distant beaches were imperceptible under the dark sky. Lightening flared upwards from the river. They saw boats and barges nestled beneath trees.

"Why don't they keep going? Don't they have shelter on the boats?" Dava asked innocently.

"They would if it were not for the huge rocks that lay

ahead of them. Without total visibility a boat can easily crash and sink by the sharp edges of the big boulders." Paoul, who had been quiet, spoke with experience. A few miles further the sun shone again.

They passed small hills with vegetation and streams near wooded country. They passed women with children, baskets of wood, palm-nuts, calabashes and liana hoops, and hunters with locally made guns. Palm and banana groves became lusher. A cantaloupe dangled from a branch; stacks of charcoal stood by the road.

Fired brick houses, as trees, became taller and thicker, and the earth redder, more and more were built of lapped plants. The town of Ruhengeri appeared, which is at the foot of the Virunga Volcanic chain, before plunging into the nearby denser forest.

As they drove past the fork where the river glides to the south, they rode to Kinigi entering a beautiful, winding trail to the first stop, the information reception center of the park.

Here they confirmed their tour guide which is mandatory for the protection of visitors and the natural habitat to many species of animal and flora.

"Swimming, boating and water sports are enjoyed every season especially on Lake Kivu to the east where the sun is more intense," said Anton.

As they picked up speed it looked like the people were flowing in colorful cloth in huts of straw near stumps of trees and their smoldering trunks.

They saw palm and banana trees marking villages; houses painted with stripes, zigzags, checkerboards, plants, with roofs in white, black, and light-yellow to deep orange to red grass. Bridges took them over waterways where people washed between green growths of grass and reeds. They turned left, off the road which led past Lake Ruhondo and in view were the Volcanoes Mountains in the Virunga National Park. They stopped in a small village. The car settled.

They got out into the lake's sunlit, wet air. The State set up rest-houses in these villages simply furnished and supplied with eggs, fowls, and flour by arrangement with the chefs. The caretaker and his wife welcomed them effusively with water for washing and a gift of oranges. They warmed up, were refreshed and everyone gasped at what had been at their back, the splendor of the Volcanoes Mountains rising six thousand feet. High up, waterfalls sparkled off into Lake Kivu which marks the boundary between Zaire and Rwanda.

The journey began. At one river toward the lake fishing was allowed. With bladed hand cutting tools, they saw men carve and hollow out canoes of white wood. Others launched one into the breakers. Groups heaved on ropes and hauled in large nets; two men walked in the surf spinning out small ropes.

Every inch of this trip seemed filled with wonders and delights. Unexplored territory lay ahead of them like a beckoning child wanting his playmates to enjoy the frivolities of life with him.

As they walked they heard monkeys and the constant sound of birds which let them know they were in no danger of ferocious beasts or killing. It was whisper quiet when predators were nearby.

They went on trudging through brown water covering their entire shoe. They felt like ants next to the huge trees as they were dwarfed by giant hardwoods. Evenings in the mountain region of west and north Rwanda were cooler than Kigali. Each person donned a sweater or jacket against the sudden chill.

The next morning, they were greeted by the tourist guide

who Jeanne wisely booked two weeks ago for this great trip. Dava and Shy anxiously asked if they would see the gorillas from Dian Fossey's "The Gorillas of the Mist," based on the Virunga gorillas.

"Yes, if we are lucky. We are on the side of the mountain where they live. On the Zaire side of the Volcanoes mountains there are still some active volcanoes like the Nyamuragira, which last erupted in 1976 and the Nyiragongo in January 1977, "said the guide.

"Ahead of us are the five volcanoes. The jagged one is 'father of teeth', it is the oldest; next is the smallest one called, 'mountain of cultivation', and to the east is the one that shelters a small lake called, 'the one who shows the way," the guide told the group.

On the way in at the gate they were given brochures with the Kinyarwanda names they couldn't pronounce and were grateful for the translations.

Then turning west, they see the final two large volcanoes made famous by Dian Fossey, covered in clouds. This is where she lived on Mount Bisoke or Bushokoro and Mount Karisimbi, the highest summit of the chain of all Rwanda.

The guide then explained, "The first mountain is translated to' where the herds go to drink', because of its lakes, and the second is called 'white shell', because the crater is occasionally covered in snow."

Walking sticks in hand they ascended into the volcanoes at the crack of dawn. They were separated from other tourists so there were only five to eight in a group to meet the gorillas. The steep slippery paths offered a challenge to the healthy young group on their adventure.

"The gorillas are not to be approached closer than four yards. Please speak in a low voice. No flash photography.

Do not run if the gorilla becomes threatening but take a submissive position. Do not overstay your welcome. Gorillas become nervous when strangers hang around for over an hour. They begin to groan, fight with each other, enough to signal aggression that could easily turn against us," said the guide.

"This is not a zoo. Remember, this is the natural ungated habitat of the gorillas. This is my first time also," said Paolo who for the first time loved his country for all its beauty. He had been quiet. truly appreciating everything around him.

Strung out in single file behind the guide who hacked away, opening a trail with a machete through the immense forests of giant bamboo, they still, occasionally, sank to mid-calf in the swamps. Then they waded through a sea of wild grass and nettles. They climbed and kept climbing.

After two to three hours of making their own way through an obstacle course of vegetation, the first gorilla droppings were spotted, still fresh. Abruptly a crest is crossed. From here all the way to the horizon there was nothing but more hills and valleys with dense forest.

"This is the nest of a gorilla and is still warm from its presence," said the guide as he looked closely at the gorilla droppings..

All of a sudden they heard a loud human type noise.

"SHHHH, look. It's an enormous adult gorilla," said the guide. The gorilla pulled on a tree shrub, bending the branches downward to get at the leaves for easier eating. His back was turned to them, nine yards away. They walked nearby without his showing the slightest reaction.

"If he beats his chest that is a sign of danger and he may snarl at us," said our guide quietly and calmly.

"Then what do we do," Dava whispered back.

"Just bow your head and walk away from him," he continued in a less than urgent voice.

They continued on and everyone was watching the big gorillas for a sign of danger. It was exciting and frightening beyond their expectations.

Lower down, resting in the grass were half-a-dozen gorillas with their young ones, sunbathing. The young gorillas, full of mischief, rolled over the backs of their mothers, climbed the trees, played dead, fought, separated, scrambled towards the tourists, and ran back, turning somersaults. They were about the size of chimpanzees, with a furry coat as disheveled and soft as a stuffed bear.

"Their parents' fur is blacker and longer, covering a good part of the face, giving the gorilla that fierce, scowling look. They look at the sky, sleep, eat leaves or sit," said the guide softly.

Further down, a silverback - dominant male of the group - didn't bother even to turn around as the group approached. The whole lower part of his back was covered with white hairs, a sign of his advanced years.

"No one really knows the lifespan of gorillas. Even though we have this preserve, they still die of attacks by poachers rather than of old age. They die of illness more frequently, pulmonary, and gastric illnesses. They are very susceptible to germs, so we try to keep sick tourists away," whispered the guide.

"Listen hard and you can hear the 'burping vocalizations,' as Fossey called the stomach gurgles. The adults spend nearly an hour trying to find the best position for sleeping on their backs. Watch the children endlessly play, frolic, and do gymnastics," said the guide as everyone had a smile on their lips.

"Some of the colobus monkeys become food for the

baboons. So, if we hear horrible squealing that is likely what it is."

"As we continue to descend to Kinigi, there is constant sound in the forest, crickets, tons of birds, monkeys, and the sounds of water, falling, foaming as white water, splashing, dripping from the steam produced by the heat on the leaves or bubbling. There is never silence in the forest," Antoin said.

"I'm glad we wore our spiked hiking boots," said Dava as she slipped a little on the soggy terrain. They made this climb in the rainy season which made it even more adventurous than usual.

That evening they talked and ate heartily. The thrill of being that close to the gorillas and being that high in the mountains knocked the city girls out cold. They slept well looking forward to the sun and fun of the next day on Africa's Riviera, as Europeans called Lake Kivu.

The next morning, they got in their vehicle and took the coastal trail that connects Gisenyi, to the north, with Cyangugu, and to the south passing through Kibuye. There were hundreds of bends that inspire the driver to take complicated and perilous twists and turns with the car.

"This is as dangerous as climbing that mountain yesterday," Shy said, holding on for dear life. "We are high on this mountain with only inches separating us from the never-ending ravine below. What a view!"

"Hold on! We are about to pass the Onatracom bus," said the driver. At this point everyone momentarily closed their eyes and held their breath. There was hardly enough room for the Land Rover and a bus full of people.

The Land Rover got its workout for the next three hours as it crossed the Zaire-Nile crest. This was a large barrier of mountains and high hills which cut the west of Rwanda from top to bottom.

Finally, after viewing the most beautiful panorama of their lives the young group arrived at Kibuye. Lake Kivu jutted into peninsulas with mountainous islets covered with patches of forest and plantations of brilliant greenery and color.

A guest house had already been built with a mini port for pleasure boats. This was truly a lakeside resort. They immediately changed into their bathing attire and stretched out on deck chairs looking at the lake while eating their European type lunch.

After they ate they spent the rest of the morning and afternoon swimming, playing, windsurfing, water skiing, and watching boats as they sang and talked by the beautiful Lake with its backdrop of mountains. They stayed well past their banquet style dinner and headed back to Kigali an hour and a half away from Kibuye. They said they would come back to this resort. It was worth every turn and bump they had to encounter to get there.

When they returned home Shy and Dava couldn't thank Antoin and Paolo enough for taking them on this wonderful weekend. Everyone had fun and kissed and hugged and said how knocked out they were, but it felt so good!

CHAPTER 21

||||||||||||||||||||||||||||||||||||||||||||||||

The Beginning of the End

"But I say to you, love your enemies and pray
for those who persecute you." KJV Matt. 5:44

The next day at work the host names were distributed and
at last Rwanda could use its two-letter geographical zone
name-RW. There is an international standard list of two-letter
country codes, which is used almost but not quite unmodified
as the list of two-letter zones. Shy's code was chey.commu.rw.
She never had her own personal code in a business before. She
immediately called Dava at her code name and they chatted
about how great this was.

Suddenly and without warning a message came across Shy's
monitor. Shy couldn't figure out how she was already the
recipient of a host's network unless it was passed forth from an
unknown forwarding host.

The message was sinister: You will die by tomorrow, your
life and the life of the other schwarzers are in jeopardy unless
they stop what they were doing and leave." Shy traced the
connection and alerted the officials at AT&T.

Still at work Shy told her fears to Henri who was a Tutsi
and he immediately understood. Before she could turn around
all of the men were off huddling and moving out.

"Obviously we have neo-Nazis here as well as South Africa.
It's not like we don't have enough on our minds without this."
Shy said. She thought it would be better for Henri to send the

warning out and not tell her fellow workers unless this became a more threatening issue.

After working in the computer lab teaching and helping set up the information superhighway infrastructure, Shy and Dava returned home hungry and exhausted, but very satisfied.

"I don't think I have completely recuperated from that mountain climb and the gorillas," Shy told Dava as they prepared dinner.

"I know what you mean," Dava said as she turned on the radio. They had found a radio station that played not only Rwandese music, but music from other neighboring countries.

"Isn't it great to hear and know this music now? They are playing all of the Bhundu Boys music, from Zimbabwe. This is my favorite 'Wonderful World.' Remember when Antoin told us that it is about how God created a world of beauty; mankind created apartheid," Dava said, turning the volume up.

Then they both danced to the 'Chitaunhike.' "This song is about the village elders thanking the ancestors while the young people dance to it, to celebrate the good fortune of Chitaunhike's family. They hear 'Vana,' the Children.

"Antoin told me this is dedicated to those who fought and died in the Zimbabwean war of independence, and 'Bye Bye Stembi' a musician plans to go to work in the city. His wife says she's leaving him, too. He's losing all his values but wishes Stembilne good luck," smiled Dava at the words.

"After listening to this beautiful music and knowing what the meaning is, it will be hard to go back to hip hop," Dava laughed.

"No problem, it's not my first choice of music anyway," Shy said in some Jamaican/African accent.

The night settles down and the music signs off with the

'Ladysmith Black Mambazo' a group from South Africa that performed in Zimbabwe on Paul Simon's Graceland tour.

Shy mused nonchalantly as the two got ready for bed, "Today at work I had a little trouble getting the packet which carries the addresses of its sender and its receiver on a message I received."

"Shy, did you check the bridges, routers and gateways? The three things that pass packets from one network to another."

"I think the packet was garbled on a communication line and the IP threw the packet away. Even though the TCP numbers each packet, and the TCP, Transmission Control Protocol, software on the two communicating hosts track the packet numbers it doesn't track an intermediate host. I think that is what I am dealing with here," Shy said, trying not to show concern.

"Is there something wrong?" Dava asked knowing her good friend too well to let this go.

"Well maybe. But I'm not going to bother you or get rankled by this, so forget it, OK?" Shy said, doing her best to put it behind her.

"Done deal, my friend and with that I bid
you goodnight," Dava said as she pulled the covers over her head. The week ahead was going to be innervating.

"Goodnight," Shy fell off to sleep immediately.

Friday arrived and the Council members met their new honoree member Dr. Abdel Digne, whom everyone now called Abdel. Francois delivered him to their home.

"Well Abdel, do you think the African countries will respect Rwanda in a new light now that telecommunications are in place here?" Tombe asked.

"There is great progress made and the Rwandese people seem to be happy with the new telecommunication lines they now have to the rest of the world. We transmit mostly to Europe since few nations in Africa are connected yet. We can email now and then, which makes our communication almost a daily venture."

The evening progressed and light refreshments were served with tea and coffee, as they discussed how Africa went from zero phones to the internet overnight.

Saturday, Shy returned to work for a few hours with some other members of her Communications department to fix a few bugs in the system. She also had in mind emailing Leon as pre arranged by the two of them. She told him how much the girls, and she, loved the bracelets. She also told him about her trip.

Meanwhile, Dava met Antoin at his hospital. He was called to work with Doctors Without Borders, a devoted staff of European and Rwandese professionals who were working feverishly on curing the children. A terrible outbreak of meningitis had occurred in Nigeria and there were more questions than answers

"As you can see, I am not quite finished. The Doctors Without Borders wants my advice about this strain of meningitis. They can't figure out where it's coming from. I will only be there another hour. Can you meet me at the French Cafe down the street? I promise I will be right there," Antoin kissed her lightly on the cheek.

"Of course, I'll wait for you. This meningitis sounds serious, and it is very contagious. Solve the problem first and foremost. If you can't make it, please get word to me and I'll see you when I can. I want to know more about Doctors Without Borders. They sound like a very noble group of human beings," Dava smiled, disappointed but glad for the chance to see him if only for a moment.

"I will tell you everything in one hour. I will be there," he kissed her swiftly and headed off back to the laboratory.

Dava went into the restaurant and felt as if she walked out of Africa and into Paris. There was French music, French people and Belgian people. She couldn't tell the difference, yet, French food, French posters on the wall, and French Bistro tablecloths on small round tables and unmatching chairs.

Gratefully there were two landscape paintings by the Rwandese artist, Umugabo Mukaga. A beautiful painting of the lion, crocodile and great mountains and hills hung proudly under spotlights.

Then she looked out the window and saw the women carrying their wares on their heads and their babies securely fastened to their backs. She thought about the hard work these women do and what the work these Europeans must do to be able to sit in here on a Saturday afternoon. Then she thought, *like I am doing. What the heck,* she sighs.

The hour passed quickly before Antoin rushed to her and kissed her hand so gently and humbly. "Forgive me my queen," he said as he sat with her.

"Antoin you took less than an hour. Did you complete your research or whatever you were doing?" Dava felt a pang of guilt pulling him away from his vital work.

"No, my dear, we don't have the children here, no one is sick. This is research, all test tube work. I can finish it tomorrow," he said. He ordered a bottle of the red wine she was drinking.

"Do you like this place?" he said wanting to talk about more pleasant things.

"Very much so," Dava said. "But please one last thing. Please tell me all you know about Doctors Without Borders. It's the first time I've heard of this group."

"It is an organization of medical personnel from around the world. Almost every country including India, both Americas, Europe, China, everywhere, has a representative in the organization. They usually travel to places no one else will, arriving well before the Red Cross or WHO, if those organizations choose to go at all. Doctors Without Borders can be found in the middle of disasters from Africa to Asia to the Pacific Islands. They are the true humanitarians. Anytime they ask me I am always willing to help. Sometimes they will go into a country that has an epidemic of some kind. They isolate the virus area, take the sample to a proper facility for analysis and find an antidote that will cure it. These doctors found out we have a world-famous meningitis expert visiting our hospital and they wanted to get data from his expertise." Antoin was happy to tell her of something he was proud to be a part of in his work.

"That is fascinating," Dava said. "I have a whole new level of respect for the medical profession now.

"I've been admiring this painting," Dava said, nodding to it.

"This painting was submitted in a nationwide ArtFest that was held in the United Kingdom. More than three hundred artists from fifty African nations participated. They used all mediums, dance, film, literature, fashion, painting, etc., and it was broadcast on British TV via satellite to the African countries that had a satellite connection," Antoin said.

"Well, next time they broadcast the Artsfest, Rwanda will definitely be able to see it on TV now that we have the internet," Dava added proudly.

They completed their wine, bread, fruit, and cheese and took in the beautiful sights of Kigali. They found themselves at the top of a hill overlooking the city. Dava was falling in love with the city too.

The next day, after Sunday church with the Netetesis, Shy and Marie talked with the two little girls, Iraminani and Eugenia. The men were not present, and Marie seemed agitated. Marie fears that which remained unspoken. Shy reads the fear on Marie's face.

The work week went quickly, and Shy and Dava looked forward to the weekend and another sightseeing adventure with Antoin and Paolo, but only Dava is called on by Antoin this time. The plan was for the four of them to visit the National Museum of Butare.

"Hey Antoin, I really have to talk to Marie today. Since Paolo isn't here, you two go and enjoy the weekend together, OK?" Shy said diplomatically.

Dava and Antoin anxiously got in the car and immediately fell in love with the beautiful music coming from the car radio.

"Please turn that up, how wonderful that sound is," Dava rejoiced.

"That is one of the older songs that was remade and became popular recently," said Antoin as he slowly drove. He was pensive and slightly quieter than usual.

"I guess we don't have the pleasure of Paolo's company for this trip," Dava stated this obvious fact.

"Something is happening. He got into trouble. They sent him back to France to go to school there for a while. He hates France. Something really bad must have happened," Antoin said, looking at Dava as if he knew more. He tried to change the subject.

"It is a brilliant day. Golden and green leaves lie crisp in the gutters. Spring is so bright in Rwanda. Nothing really dies during the rainy season which is our winter. It grows better," Antoin laughed uneasily.

Dava said nothing. She couldn't imagine their friend being shipped off to France under protest. But then again he was the President's nephew and there must be a certain duty to one's station in life in that position.

For the next few hours, they traveled the paved road to the Butare-Gitarama. There the green earth had been removed and the landscape became a barren desert of brownish/red soil. Yellow bulldozers scraped at the vegetation. No one could or would say what the site was for. That sound, that smell of unearthed fresh soil and the overcast sky made Dava homesick for New York.

"We have a philosopher so to speak that gives us many proverbs," Antoin said, thinking of Dava's sad look.

"Tell them to me, I love proverbs especially the ones in the Bible," said Dava, anxious to get off the subject of loneliness.

"His name is M.B. Paternostre, and I quote, 'No matter how early a traveler sets out he never arrives at a place far from those he loves,'" Antoin thought about this one and seeing Dava's smile told him she understood

"Please, more," Dava said.

"'A rapid stream wears itself out,' 'Rich in possessions, rich in greed,' 'Hearsay is questionable', 'The witless appreciate each other,' 'As a tree leans, so it falls,'" Antoin told as many of them that he could remember.

As they drove they discussed the meaning of each one and had many references from their own lives' experiences. They enjoyed the lively knowledgeable conversation.

"There is one that reminds me of my beloved Rwanda," he said.

"Please don't hold back," said Dava.

"It is 'The river flows, and where it flows there follow the rocks,'" Antoin said then became pensive again.

Antoin knew what this meant and said something in Kinyarwanda in a dialect he knew Dava wouldn't understand. Antoin turned to her and smiled. "Remember Paternostre also said, 'Another's pain is bearable.'"

In the city of Butare they passed carpenters and tinsmiths in workshops. They produced high-quality utensils, such as buckets, watering-cans, and brilliant tools. Low-technology machines made wood wheels, bicycles, wheeled plows, weeders, seed-drills for maize and soya, pedaled rice-threshers, and winnowers, and hullers for soya and peanuts.

As they drove up to the machinery shop, a the shopkeeper told them, "Such a huller transforms two days' labor into a one or two-hour job. We are very modern with thermostatically controlled, paraffin-heated incubators to aid village chicken-breeding, screw-thread mills for mpondu, manioc leaves, popular among Butare flat-dwellers where pounding was unpopular."

Antoin and Dava were inspired by all this creative energy, but the prevailing attitude was one of realistic pessimism tempered by a little hope.

"History is hard. Problems of theft, clannishness which undermines wider co-operation, corruption, and the sense that despite all the motivation and innovation for good, one might not leave anything behind. It could end. All trouble can't always be blamed on the white man coming to Africa taking, taking, and never giving back," The shopkeeper yelled as Antoin blasted the music on the radio as he drove off.

Suddenly the music ended, and an angry voice said over and over in his native language, "Kill the cockroach!"

"This is not good news." Antoin's face dropped and he immediately turned the radio off.

At that moment, Antoin recognized an art professor from the university, and they parked to sit with him, "Dava, I would like to introduce you to Professor Nsengimana."

"It is my pleasure, mademoiselle," said the professor as he stood. He was very political and spoke freely about the disproportionate education in Rwanda,

"It is a rural life. Adults and young children begin working the land early in the morning around 5 a.m. or 6 a.m. before it is light. There is no lunch break, no stopping until the end of the day. At the age of seven, children must go to school."

"That sounds very good," said Dava innocently. "In America they start at five or earlier, if they go to preschool."

"Yes it starts good. However, after they do primary school, if they manage to succeed there is a special exam for high school. It is very hard and then the most difficult is to go to the University because there is very limited space in our National University, so you apply for a scholarship. Some groups are favored over another. It is very corrupt. These are things that we are trying to change we are doing our best to change in a new direction.

"The school reform started by President Habyarimana in 1980 and was initiated by France. We wanted to increase the Rwandese lesson and provide more skills so people could become more specialized in craft manual labor. If they were unable to go beyond the University they could do some craft work and learn industrial skills to work.

"This reform was a failure because most of these skills were not useful. The fact that they used one language over another was difficult for the children. They had to learn more skills in French. So, it was difficult to translate some subjects into

Rwandese like the scientific subjects. And this retarded the process of learning. In fact some of the people from this reform speak very poor French."

"Was there any mechanism in place to teach the children skills in Kinyarwanda?" asked Dava.

"No, because the French technicians did not learn our language," Antoin said sadly.

"The lack of education and lack of enough land are the two great obstacles that continue to separate Rwandese people," said Professor Nsengimana. "Poverty runs rampant."

"Our people do share government responsibilities together," Antoin cuts in.

"President Habyarimana was pressured by the international community to sign an accord for power sharing in an agreement in which all groups share equally." Antoin surprisingly let out in almost one breath as if he were making a political statement. The conversation became slightly tense, and the men's focus turned back to Dava. They resumed lunch and the light hearted atmosphere shared all morning returned.

"Here is the National Pedagogical Institute, the National Institute of Scientific Research, and the School of Agriculture," said the professor proudly. They passed other institutions as well. "This city lost to Kigali by a hair for the capital of Rwanda," the professor stated boldly.

They said goodbye to the professor and drove to the National Museum. Upon their arrival they saw a woman making pottery of clay.

"It is said that the Kinyarwandese language spread because the people of the forest came to the river for this pottery," said Antoin.

Antoin parked the car, and a man was outside assembling shards of pottery from an archaeological dig. Curved roofs, sheer concrete and stoneface walls sheltered well-ordered exhibits.

They bought tickets and a guidebook and joined the tour of Central African history and prehistory.

"The museum is composed of pavilions with pointed roofs, as in the Rwandan countryside. It is an architectural building incorporating sun dried clay bricks like those manufactured by Rwandan farmers and herders.

"As you see in the entrance hall several display cases are set aside for temporary exhibits - toys of Rwandan children, for example - or for the presentation of scholarly works on the history and archaeology of Rwanda which are on sale along with examples of local crafts: wooden milk-jugs, straw baskets, etc.

"Here in the second small square space, Room Two, is presented the geological and geographic context in the world, and in Africa, of Rwanda. The Rift Valley is the famous long fault line which runs from the Red Sea to the south of Lake Malawi," he said.

In the third room display cases showed agriculture, food gathering, cattle raising, fishing, transportation, and hunting. "Hunting by the monarchs and upper-class Rwandans was for sport near Kigali.

"Cattle raising was a sign of wealth and more for meat consumption than milk. Certain cows were considered sacred. These black cows with long, semi-circular horns were destined only for royal parades.

"If someone tried to steal one of these cows they would be impaled," the guide never hesitated to tell them things that he thought all tourists wanted to hear.

They moved on to room four and five. "This is a reconstructed royal hut made in real life dimensions."

"This is great," Dava thought, "What do they need bricks and stone for when thatched will do?"

The guide strides before them in an almost majestic fashion. "Here is room six these are consecrated weapons and headdresses, jewelry, sports, colorful cloths, and dance apparel worn by the Intore Dancers," again the pride was evident in the guide.

The last room, seven, he told the tourists of the prehistory of Rwanda with stone Age tools, weapons, and cave engravings.

"These remind me of the unearthed artifacts in museums at home," said Dava.

"The Bronze and Iron Age are not distinct; the Iron/Copper Age saw the rise of agriculture, metallurgy, and ceramics. Skeletons in graves of the eight to sixteenth centuries are accompanied by knives, spades, copper bracelets, ivory beads, shell currency and richly decorated pots with elaborate rims, lips, and handles," the guide smiled at Dava knowing this culture was so much older than American culture. He pointed to a sign next to the artifacts.

A notice spelled out the message: "Beyond death and beyond forgetting may our exhumed treasures bring hope and pride."

The museum's thick walls kept them and the exhibits cool.

They spoke in length with the guide about the art of the Rwandese people.

"Are Rwandese people cognizant of the value of their art?" asked one of the Europeans.

"Our art is what we use in everyday activities. As you see the designs on our pottery tells what the pot should be used for: water or ceremonial blood of sacrifice, never will the two be confused. In that respect the distinction is made to the Rwandese people. Our ceremonial robes and headdress are specially made and prayed over by the spiritual chiefs in the village. These things that you have seen are the beliefs and religious traditions of our people. They would die for the sanctity of them, but they could not put a dollar value on these things," said our guide so eloquently. He was a great student of both Tutsi and Arab heritages.

"Now let us move on to the gift shop where some of the arts and crafts of the Rwandese people are sold with half the profit going directly back to the Rwandese artist and half to the museum," the guide said.

"Antoin, I am so impressed by our guide. I can see how intelligence, justice and honesty can win any argument over emotion," said Dava, so impressed.

The tour ended outside.

Later they explored this fascinating city of old and new. At a flower-strewn table, in a tropical garden, they ate nsusu, chicken cooked in mwamba, palm-oil, with chips.

In the small zoo, a melancholy baboon, a frustrated lynx, a comatose crocodile, and verbose parrots were displayed. The military posed self-consciously beneath giant bamboos, or in the woodland fringe, for "jungle" photographs.

★★★★★★★★★

The next day in the early afternoon Dava and Antoin traveled westward. The city gave way to onion fields on the right and the Catholic missions to the left.

After their scenic drive, they found themselves at the entrance to another safari adventure, this time into the Nyungwe Natural Forest.

In the natural forest of Nyungwe alone, in this southwest portion of Rwanda, there were no less than one hundred identified species of orchid.

"This is a terrestrial paradise for the flower lover or gardener," said Antoin. He was also amazed and loved his country more and more.

The fantasy walk was suddenly made real by the tour

guide pointing up to the swinging vines a mere tourist would overlook. There chatting away and looking back at them were the celebrated colobus monkeys. They were beautiful and looked painted into their white whiskers and black shiny royal coats. They really did look like magistrates, and they even seemed to carry an air of superiority as if they knew who they were. These monkeys peered down from their tree limbs at the humans as if to say, "Look, another group who expect us to perform." They passed fruit to one another and engaged in small polite chatter as the tourist watched.

Dava and Antoin rode home weary but enlightened, full of Rwandese culture and history and Dava needed to know more about how the people felt.

On the radio children sang the song of the ancestors, answering all questions, removing all doubt. Porter's song of 1888, Antoin interprets for Dava.

"O mother, how unfortunate we are!...
The white man has made us work,
We are so happy before the white man came,
We'd like to kill the white man who has made us work,
But the whites have a fetish more powerful than ours,
The white man is stronger than the black man,
But the sun will kill the white man,
But the moon will kill the white man,
But the tiger will kill the white man,
But the crocodile will kill the white man,
But the elephant will kill the white man,
But the river will kill the white man."

They laughed all the way home. However, upon their arrival, they were suddenly aware that Shy was missing.

CHAPTER 22

‖‖‖‖‖‖‖‖‖‖‖‖‖‖‖‖‖‖‖‖‖‖‖‖‖‖‖‖‖‖‖‖‖‖‖‖‖‖‖

Conspiracy and Treachery

"Another's pain is bearable."
M.B. Paternostre de la Mairieu

Meanwhile, the mercenaries sent by the Organization began to agitate the crowds again into the all but faded Hutu-Tutsi hate cycle. When the Tutsi instigated Rwandan independence from Belgium in 1959, it caused the majority Hutu to overthrow the old Tutsi monarchy, the French and Belgian presence was still always felt.

Things between the Hutu and Tutsi had calmed down considerably since the war in Uganda, a neighboring country which invaded Rwanda in 1990, fighting ended within thirty miles of the capital. They forced President Juvenal Habyarimana, a Hutu, to negotiate with the Tutsi rebels and come to terms for multiparty elections starting in 1995. These enemies of Rwanda, especially the Organization, were determined that this would never come about - by any means necessary.

Chairman Gatt's personal agitators and assassins spread rumors among the poor Hutu farmers that the Belgians were going to help the Tutsi get back their power and reclaim parts of the country the Hutu had made into farmland.

Chairman Gatt knew his plan would work. He only had to infiltrate the Hutu military and lead them to believe the Tutsi were taking control and the military would do the rest. One thing concerned the Chairman, his assassins told him about the conversation the African Affairs Council had concerning the great plans of collaboration between African American skills and African land. This horrified him. He made the call to signal action.

"Is that damned bunch of niggers gonna upset our plans in any way?" Gatt questioned the French mercenary from the Organization.

"No, Monsieur Gatt, they will be targeted for death and eliminated on the second day of killing," reported the soldier of fortune in Rwanda.

"What about that bitch who keeps getting those anthropology books on the beginning of mankind? Is she going to write a book and expose things we've known about for centuries and hidden? We can't be exposed now. We must suppress any information about white and black roots. If her story gets out, it will erase all of our superiority tirades."

"We are looking at her carefully. Our boy Drago is getting all her information and giving it back to us. She will be destroyed anyway as soon as the fighting begins."

"The international community is leaning toward a hands-off approach to Africa's turmoil since they got smashed in the Somalian trouble. It would be a damn shame if this group of blacks have any kind of influence or power to stop the killing," Gatt huffed.

"You can consider them gone already," the mercenary soldier said.

"Very well, you better be damn right," Chairman Gatt said and slammed down the phone.

"I must do something about the Black Americans," the soldier said. "I didn't realize they posed any kind of threat whatsoever." He prepared to gather a small band of men to watch the African Affairs Council from this moment on.

King Ashir and his terrorists also began to prepare and train their hit squad - the Zero Network. They were supported by the Hutu military and trained to frighten the Rwandese into killing Tutsi and any Hutu sympathizers. These Hutu hardliners were hell bent on keeping the Tutsi out of their country and planned to totally eliminate them viciously and without warning. Destroying Catholicism in Rwanda was the Zero Network's main mission.

The Organization's hired militia was to arm the Zero Network with semi-automatic weapons, but mostly they were to be trained to maim and kill by beating a person with a mallet, ripping a person to pieces with knives, hacking them with machetes and making for a slow painful death. They were also given mortar fire power and told how to deploy fire bombs.

Admiral Havelo Biggelo visited the camp and was pleased at the ease in which these African people wanted to kill each other. He thought, "If they only knew that united they could have all of Africa again for themselves. Our plan is the only solution to get what we want!"

"Captain," yelled Admiral Biggelo.

"Yes sir," the Captain, a white mercenary from South Africa, saluted.

"I want these animals Hutu, to go house to house and force the Hutu men, women and children to kill the Tutsi. I want our men to scare the Hutu into killing each other if it is necessary. I want them to be so scared they will kill their wives, mothers, husbands or fathers if they refuse to kill the Tutsi or Hutu sympathizers."

The militia gathered everybody together near a big hole. Hutu were weeping, even men. Days and days before the killing they were weeping in fear. Shooting dissidents, the army supplied village after village with the necessary killing tools and oversaw the slaughter.

★★★★★★★★★★

"Marie, I know my theory seems strange but when I put all the pieces together evidence shows that African giants once ruled not only Egypt, but I think all of Africa," Shy said trying to make a statement that was not so Tutsi sided.

"We like to think we are all alike, however, since I am mostly Tutsi, it does not offend me to hear you say such things. But this and other theories have been pulling my country apart," said Marie sweetly.

Shy and Marie walked along for a while, in the dark near her house. The air had a tenseness about it, and something was lurking in the shadows that was perilous to all. Shy wanted to continue this conversation.

"O.K. I know that promoting any Tutsi superiority over the Hutu is politically incorrect, but I had to think of the Tutsis becoming extinct without anyone truly finding out their true historical heritage. I was reading in Genesis 6:4 (KJV) that when man started multiplying on the earth there were giants on earth. They lived until they were 120 years old. This fits in precisely with the time 50,000 years ago when the Sangoan man left Uganda and the 50,000 years ago the Homo sapiens settled Egypt.

"Am I the only person on earth to see this connection between the eight-foot Tutsi and the builders of ancient Egypt? Living for 120 years one has time to see Pyramids built and kingdoms established such as Karnak. Please humor me and tell me there could be something to this. That it's worth exploring."

"I know what you are talking about. Did you also know that in Numbers 13:31–33 (KJV) they also speak of the giants in Canaan? The Israelis were afraid because the giants were strong in stature, and they were the sons of Arnak. David and Goliath is another story of giants. Shy, it takes money to prove such things as this. You know Alexander the Great conquered

Egypt and burned the libraries, millions of books that could have told us the truth were lost forever. Unless there is sufficient proof we have to live with this, forgive, and move on with our lives," Marie said sadly.

"I was taught in Black History that you must know your past to understand the future, the word for it is 'Sankofa.' If our people were the great rulers of history and the Bible tells us we were, then what happened? We are mentioned in the Bible as the lost tribe of Israel! When do we proclaim our rightful place in the world?"

As Marie and Shy leave Marie's house and walk together, Shy was ready to jump up high on her soapbox the way her aunt's generation did in the 1960s. "I thought maybe this was my quiet mission in life to find out the truth. Maybe, I was not to find it in Rwanda. I know that the mention of the Tutsi as anything other than another ethnic group in Rwanda, or for that matter in any part of Central Africa, was taboo."

★★★★★★★★★

"Hello Shy?" Dava, surprised by the sound, picked up the phone receiver on the first ring.

"Hello, Dava," Leon said, "Isn't Shy with you?

"Leon, no she's not. We've been told to prepare to leave. Shy told us about the sword and Ma'at. She took it with her, Leon."

"Where is she, Dava?" he asked with growing concern.

"She went to Marie's when Antoin and I went to the National Museum."

Leon was quiet.

"What do you know, Leon?"

"I am currently in Cairo, Egypt. My work in journalism allows me to hear all sorts of things. Part of the problem right now is that my investigative news snooping has led me to the discovery of some terrorist groups. If what I heard is true, your life can be in serious danger."

"Leon, what are you talking about? Things are going so smoothly. We are actually connecting to other African countries and establishing a basis for business transactions. African people have all the skills they need right on the continent. They don't have to go anywhere else to start using their own natural resources. We are training the Rwandese to use technical equipment and computers, and profits of sales are expected to increase for them. How can you tell me my life is in danger?"

"Dava, you know I wouldn't tell you something that I could not backup. You should know I traced this source of information, and it stands up. In fact, I'm on the trail of a monster of a conspiracy between a Muslim faction here and a group of butchers called the Zero Network in Rwanda inspired by a Neo-Nazi group out of South Africa and Europe. Dava, I want you to try to leave there as soon as possible."

"That seems a bit drastic. I just got here just two months ago. Leon, is there any way this can be stopped before it starts?" Dava knew he was right. She could sometimes feel the tension between the Tutsi and Hutu while working side-by-side with them in the computer lab.

"No, but have you noticed any foreign diplomats or businessmen flying out of Rwanda recently? Look, this is the beginning of April. I suspect that within the next few days some dreadful things are going to happen to the people there. I am frightened for all of you." Leon didn't see any other way than to fly down there and get them out himself one way or another.

"You know, Leon, when I first arrived I noticed several very suspicious looking people getting off our plane. I didn't pay much attention to them at first, but I did notice how they hurried off in a black unlicensed vehicle. It was peculiar. Leon, you have seriously heightened my awareness. Now I see some of these same men running around in the streets with drunk teenage boys looking as if they want to start a fight."

"Right now, some of the most dangerous terrorists and mercenaries in the world are training Hutus in Rwanda. Some very powerful groups do not want the people of Rwanda to stop the tribal fighting, nor do they want the Rwandese to get any kind of commerce and trade going that is independent of the West's commerce. And there appears to be a concerted effort to actually physically destroy both tribes."

"Leon, I am taking your advice, and I will set into motion a major move within the next few days. I promise."

"I know you can look after yourself. Do whatever it takes to leave as quickly as possible. What they predict from this side is absolutely unthinkable." Leon knew he had to tell her something to keep her strong at this point.

"Stay strong and follow the orders of the rescuers."

As soon as Leon hung up, Dava called Marie's house. There was no answer.

Early the next morning, Dava got a very unexpected call from her former boss, Mr. Duran.

"Mr. Duran, what a surprise! How did you get my num.." she began to say, genuinely shocked to hear his voice.

"Dava, how are you doing? Is Shy with you?" asked Mr. Duran with polite abruptness. He desperately needed to tell Dava something. It was a matter of life and death. Yet, he didn't want to send her into a frenzy.

"Mr. Duran, I'm fine, but Shy is not here. You would not believe the progress we have made in so short a time. The communications networks are connected and...."

Mr. Duran had to cut her off, "Look Dava, I know anything you get involved with has to be a great success. But as you may have guessed this is not a business call."

"Yes sir." Deep down she understood the severity and urgency of the conversation and listened with tensed silence.

"There are two men down there who have been working for me. They were on the plane with you, and they reported that you noticed their weapons. They are there to protect you and others who are doing business with me. They have access to my helicopter hidden in a safe place. This will be needed to get you out when the trouble starts. My sources inform me that within the next two days blood will run in the streets of Kigali, Rwanda." He had no idea she had heard this before from Leon, but she trusted Mr. Duran and knew he would tell her the truth, she was assured of this.

"These two men you saw on the plane will take you and the Council to a safe place until the helicopter comes. They will be wearing blue denim shirts and blue head bandannas. Go with them and do as they say. If violence is at hand, you and the Council couldn't be in better hands. They will contact you tomorrow. Do you understand?'

Dava took a big gulp and whimpered, "Yes sir." Click... as fast as it started the conversation ended. Dava had to warn people. But she had to do it in a way that would not provoke attention to herself otherwise if something bad happened she could be charged as a conspirator. She also pondered the two men sent by Mr. Duran. Had he known there would be trouble before she left the U.S.A.?

CHAPTER 23

Help

Know Yourself, Save Others

That same night Admiral Havelo Biggelo called Drago Dupree from Uganda, headquarters for the Organization.

"Dupree, are the militias continuing their training of the Hutu sav...uh peasants across Rwanda?" Biggelo said with disdain.

"Yes sir," Drago said to his commander as a soldier following orders. He knew Biggelo would have said savages to any white soldier.

"We are paying the government's military too much not to get the job done right," Admiral Biggelo continued, "Make sure you keep your eye on that trouble making group called the African Affairs Council. Research has shown that they were a pinko organization from the 1930s to the 1950s when the government forced them to quit helping African nations. They were part of the reason the Africans got the courage to become independent from Europe in the 1960s. This group is trouble, and they have too much to say about the way things are over there. If you must, and if they are in the way, destroy them. You hear me bo.. Drago?" Admiral Biggelo almost slipped.

"I believe I heard you better than you think I did." He had no more to say to this racist.

"Over and out," Biggelo snorted unaware that he let slip information that was contrary to what Drago was taught in the military and the intelligence agency he worked for now.

Drago had also had his eye on one particular member of the African Affairs Council, Shy LaTour. The Organization sent him over there to start the killing and destruction of the Rwandese people, not to kill a beautiful African-American woman. He liked her and they had somehow had a friendly exchange when they saw each other.

The next day Drago spotted Shy walking toward her apartment and followed her nonchalantly. Shy was returning after helping Marie and the two girls find shelter in a secret hiding place.

The business district had two sides to it. The huge banks and exquisite hotels in one area, and further along near the Muslim section were the wooden structures that housed Rwandese crafts made and sold by the Rwandese. It was eerily quiet today, absent were the usual merchants in their stalls showing their crafts. The boutique hotels appeared empty and lifeless.

There was no chatter or hawking, no children playing with their handmade toys, no lorries and very few cars passed.

The artisan hurriedly packed her dung swirls and geometric drawings. "Times are getting bad in Rwanda," she said to Shy.

"Everyone senses something foul in the air," Shy tacitly concurred.

Shy was disturbed by a man who was staring at her. They made eye contact. She wished he would stop looking her way.

"Hello there, I hope I'm not offending you by speaking. But since we have flown over here on the same plane and have acknowledged each other's presence on numerous occasions, I felt it only courteous for me to speak now," Drago Dupree spoke in a calm, cool and collected manner.

"Yes, hello," said Shy, totally taken by surprise. She didn't want to talk to him. She had too much to do and no time to do it.

"I don't usually bother people like this but there is something about you. Have you ever lived in Brooklyn?" Drago knew darn well she was from Brooklyn; he was a spy after all.

"Why yes, how did you know?" Shy had to catch herself for at once she became suspicious.

"You actually look like a distant relative of mine who lives there, let me think ...yes, they lived in Bed-Stuy as I recall. It was a relative from marriage, of course, and..."

Shy had to interrupt and she didn't care if he was a hired assassin or not. This wasn't time for games.

"Just cut the crap mister. I don't know what exactly your part is over here, but I know you know entirely too much about me, pretending to be someone you're not. I really have to get away from you."

"OK, OK you got me. I guess I am a little rusty with my rap. I am sorry for going there. But I urgently need to talk with you. it is a matter of life and death and I know after what I just did this really sounds like a line."

"No, believe it or not, It doesn't. What do you know? And who and what are you? You have nothing to lose now that you have blown your cover with me, so let's get right to the point."

She looked into his deep brown eyes. Drago Dupree was a hardened, trained former naval intelligence officer empowered by the U.S. Government, but he was compelled to be straight with her.

"Rwandan Tutsi are under attack," Drago blurted.

"Please tell me why this awful thing is about to happen to these people? And what is your name?"

"I go by Drago Dupree. I am a soldier and the philosophy of our government is still dictated by the edicts of the Cold War. Maybe communism is no longer taking over the world now, but within military intelligence there is always a threat lodged on the people of the U.S., especially after certain terrorists actions took place in the U.S., like, the bombing of the World Trade Building basement in 1993, the Federal building in Oklahoma, along with several other events. As a soldier, when I am given an order and with my special training, I have no choice but to obey my commanding officer. They tell us the U.S. is threatened by some faction of people in Rwanda and we must go to battle. I follow orders. Men like me usually don't look toward retirement. We wonder which bullet will be ours."

"Drago, you're gonna stand there and tell me you think these people are a threat to our country? Are you and your boss mad? Who is he or them or whatever? Are the reasons given, the stories you're told worth destroying innocent people? Do you really believe it?"

"Miss Latour, I have already put my life and yours in jeopardy telling you who I am. Listen to me. Immediate danger is upon us. The mission will be executed tomorrow, and I refuse to let you get hurt. If you get out of this alive I know I can trust you to be discreet about my warning. Wherever and whenever you see me from this moment on you will know there is trouble brewing on the spot, and wherever it is, run away as fast as you can. Head for Lake Cyohoha. A Hutu good Samaritan smuggles Tutsi refugees to Burundi to safety. Peace be with you, goodbye."

Drago Dupree disappeared into the streets of Rwanda. Shy first went to Jeanne Habyarimana's house to warn the family. There was no one home, so she carefully wrote a quick note that read as a timid warning of impending danger, then rushed to find Dava.

The men following in Shy's footsteps found the critical note she left inside the Habyarimana home and destroyed it and left the Habyarimana home empty.

Cheyenne moved through the city quickly under cover

now. She started to reminisce about what her mother's friend Mrs. Hunton recently said about the ethnic problems in Africa. "You can't do anything about it." Mrs. Hunton recalled the memory, much to her dismay, in Ghana, at the inner strife among the ethnic groups there.

"These people have been fighting for centuries over the control of land since the West, Arabs, and other exploiters enslaved them and took their riches, thus forcing them to other lands."

Finally arriving back at the apartment, Shy found Dava gone and a note that read: *Get Out, NOW!*

Immediately, Shy ran to the other apartments searching for Council members. Everyone was gone. She was left alone. Scared, she headed for the Lake.

That Wednesday, Leon flew to Uganda to be closer to Shy. He was not allowed in Rwanda. Once there he contacted the press and learned of the refugee camps in Uganda and Burundi. He alerted his fellow journalist to look out for Black Americans and especially his love.

He was told that the plane carrying the President Juvenal Habyarimana of Rwanda and the President Cyprian Ntaryamira of Burundi had crashed, killing them both. No one was saying anything else except there was some gun fire at the airport. Leon prayed that his love would survive the mayhem. He could not imagine in his worst nightmare the slaughter that would soon start.

★★★★★★★★★★

Admiral Biggelo's intelligence force made sure the first grenades would destroy the Kigali weapons-secure area established Dec. 24, 1993. Brigadier-General R. Dallaire, Canada, the UNAMIR commander from the U.N., had set up a demilitarized zone that was operational by Nov.1,1993.

This was Admiral Biggelo's main target in Kigali. This was where the governmental power was located. This was where the U.N. had secured the Arusha Peace Agreement between the Hutu and the Tutsi. This was where President Habyarimana was sworn in to office, Jan. 5, 1994, for the 4th time. This was the place Biggelo hated the most.

The military weaponry was dispensed to the Hutu men and boys who were given liquor and told what they were doing was for the good of the poor, common people. They were told, "You will liberate Rwanda from the oppressive Tutsi upper class. The only alternative is to die yourselves. Kill or be killed.

The foreign trained agitators, sent by the Organization, proclaimed, "This is the start of the freedom revolution." The agitators mixed this message in with the inflammatory radio messages over the government radio station the Hutu listened to and it was the only station operating.

They heard over and over, "The enemy of the Hutu and the government is the Tutsi. All Tutsi must die." The agitators yelled and screamed and whipped the crowd into a frenzied froth of venom and hate. Hate for their countrymen, the Tutsi. The Tutsi were also fooled by the Belgians into thinking they were superior and that they were better than the Hutu because the Tutsi were tall.

Now the paid military will be used again to destroy their own. Over the years, there had been so much blending, it was difficult to tell some Hutus and Tutsi apart.

Before his demise, President Habyarimana had armed militias to keep peace and tried to accept terms of the Arusha Accord he signed at the same time.

Meanwhile, militias operating in their own villages, pulled out lists of Tutsis and anti-government Hutus and began separating women, men and children and killing them.

CHAPTER 24

|||||||||||||||||||||||||||||||||||||||||||||||||||

Genocidal War

"Would that I could be the peacemaker in
your soul, that I might turn the discord and
the rivalry of your elements into oneness and
melody." The Prophet by Kahlil Gibran

A few miles outside Kigali, Mr. Gasmama invited selected
neighbors into his home. He told them he was hiding them
from the killing gangs. The Tutsi neighbors believed him since
he was a prominent businessman. When they all arrived, the
village killers came in and the slaughter began.

"We are friends," one of the men cried out on their knees,
as the deadly blows repeated, rapidly and finally on his skull.

"We shared the same classroom..." another man yelled as
he fell to his death as the machete cut down from his shoulder
into his heart.

"Oh, no, we are the same people, we are your neighbors,"
they begged as they saw their friends die so brutally before
them.

"Instead of hiding us you are killing us," screamed each
man dying from the hand of his friend and other neighbors,
not believing their friend could betray them like that, without
mercy. Since they were mixed Hutu and Tutsi they looked alike
and lived in the same community together.

While the killing machines pounded the skulls of their
neighbors with bats, hacked them open with their machetes,
chopped at them with axes, and sliced them with their knives,

the Hutu women were going to the homes of these men to kill their women and children.

Some of the killers led the looting party while the others bludgeoned the stunned children of their neighbors with large sticks. The children didn't cry because they knew and trusted these women. They made big eyes, then fell dead at their neighbor's feet.

Mr. Gasmama's wife was killed by a neighbor because she refused to join the Interahamwe. He did not cry as he feared they would kill him as a sympathizer.

★★★★★★★★★★★★★

On the government radio station in Kigali, Hutu soldiers were telling the slaughter gangs to kill Tutsis no matter how young or how old.

"They are evil and will take over your life. If this is not done you would be killed as sympathizers."

"Kill," the message repeated, "Kill," over and over. "Hutus have a duty to kill the Tutsi. Take anything you have handy and beat them in the head with it, until they are dead."

As Shy heard the screams of death coming from house after house in Kigali, she ran in terror as the cries of anguish followed her. She had only the clothes on her back, two sweaters and a small sword. She prayed to God that she didn't have to use it on a human being.

After searching for Dava, Shy returned to the Ntetesi's house hoping to get them to safety, only to find Dominique, their son, waiting outside his home looking for his family.

"When the people that kill came, everyone ran out of the house. My father went off into the woods to join with the rebel force. I tried to go with him, but he told me to stay with my mother and my sisters. I don't know where they are. I am here waiting to die because I am tall," he sobbed in Shy's arms.

"Run for your life," Shy pulled at him. "We can find sanctuary with the missionaries. There are government guards minding the main entrance," she naively told him.

They ran past the crying and screaming. Past the burning and looting. Hiding in the shadows and foliage that once was beautiful days ago, now a refuge and cover. Dominique cried for his life and for his country. Shy had no reference for this and was unable to relate, so she prayed for Spirit to lead her, to help her, to do something, anything to get her through this.

Dominique ran into Ste. Famille Roman Catholic Church where nuns have welcomed about 1,500 Tutsi. These Rwandese refugees were waiting for 'the ones that kill' to allow them to stay alive in this sanctuary.

Shy moved on through the bushes. She became panic stricken as she watched government guards who were supposed to protect those inside the church open the doors to let in Hutu militia - seeking victims - sometimes the educated, often the young men, but always the Tutsi. A terrible blast penetrated her ears. The roof of the church was holed from an explosion.

She felt there was no place of safety in the open. She must hide. She looked like an African American and if they hated their neighbors so much they surely despised foreigners. Never before did she feel so alienated, so terrified, and depressed. This was no time for tears she must run, run, and hide.

Along the way Shy stepped over pools of blood oozing from the broken bodies of those who tried to run away from the murderous gangs. In front of the Red Cross storage facility were bodies of hacked to death women and children, now laying lifeless in puddles of blood, without the dignity of family or friend to mourn their death. Nothing but the breath of death engulfed the night with screams of women and children echoing in Shy's ears.

She passed a church orphanage and saw the Hutu threatening to kill all the children in the orphanage if the Tutsi children were not pointed out. The church staffers tearfully handed over the Tutsi children who were led outside and clubbed, stabbed, and hacked to death. Shy realized this war was not really against the Tutsi if the Hutu killers can't even tell Tutsi apart from other Hutu. This was prompted by political power which infuriated her more than saddened her, though her tears fell ceaselessly for the dead children.

She passed a mass grave and avoided stepping in the blood from bodies that were under blood-soaked sheets and dirt. She could not believe her eyes when she saw a little hand moving. The hand had one of the bracelets she gave to Eugenia and Iramania. To her shock and disgust the two girls were buried alive beneath the dead bodies. Shy didn't hesitate to uncover them; however, she didn't have the heart to see if her friends, Henri, and Marie were there, also.

She pulled the girls out from the pit of massacred bodies. They could hardly breathe because they were buried all day in the dirt with the dead. Eugenia's head was soft as a peach, from blows she received during the attack. Both were frightened and huddled close to Shy with their dirt-filled, blood-soaked dresses. They could not speak to Shy, but they recognized her.

Shy half carried and half ran with them to the outskirts of Kigali. Eugenia and Iramania were weak, but they stayed with Shy only crying for their parents now and then. As the three traveled, Shy gave them each her sweaters she brought for herself. The evenings got cool since this was only the beginning of April.

Shy took the girls toward a safe spot, and though they were

beyond the city limits of Kigali they could still hear the screams of men, women, and children in the night. They could see families crouched in fear listening helplessly to their neighbors' dreadful wails. The three passed invisibly through the thickets out of town. Shy only sensed the direction in the darkness, but she knew it was spirit that guided them to Burundi.

They reached Kayumba, six-teen miles from Kigali, a place where teal wall baskets and sisal and sweetgrass baskets were once made. It was now decimated. In the day it took to get there by foot Shy's exhaustion was replaced by adrenaline surges. She learned to eat wild mango and roasted manioc on an open fire during the daylight only, with the smoke blending in with the many fires from burning homes spread across the land. They could not drink the water for every river and tributary had a red tinge to it – the blood of innocent Rwandese civilians caught in this blood drenched nightmare.

Shy was alone with the two girls counting on her, oblivious to the fact that troops were sent in Saturday after she left Kigali to protect and evacuate foreign nationals from Rwanda. Now, at this point Shy's resolve was set. She would not leave the girls to die.

A few nuns from the Belgian Sisters of the Visitation told Shy a force of four hundred French soldiers took control of the Kigali airport and evacuated French, American and European citizens. Two hundred and fifty-five Americans, mostly aid workers and missionaries evacuated by car convoy to Burundi. Three hundred other Americans and Europeans arrived in Bujumbura.

The U.S. sent three hundred Marines and seven aircraft into Burundi to protect American citizens. Belgium dispatched eight hundred troops and plane loads of equipment.

The Sisters await Belgium Marines to rescue them. Shy

had chosen to stay in Rwanda. She had these two babies she felt completely responsible for. After being fed and clothed in warmer frocks the girls gained strength and courage for what lay ahead. Shy never told them she could be free and safe if not for them.

Meanwhile, Shy could hear mortar fire and shelling. Somebody was fighting back. Maybe this nightmare would end soon if the U.N. troops and other foreign troops helped stop the massacres. She felt sure they would help.

She did not know there would be no outside intervention. The only resistance to the Presidential Guard of civilian and military slaughterers was the Rwandan Patriotic Front made up of Rwandese men determined to have a united country. They consisted mostly of Tutsi but mixed with Hutu sympathizers.

The two little girls, now growing weak and sick, and Shy, doing her best to stay strong, were on their way to Lake Cyohoha. Shy's heart broke as she passed a hospital and witnessed the beaten and bleeding patients dragged out of their beds and hacked with machetes and knives and clubbed to death. Red Cross nurses and Doctors Without Borders 'staff begged the drunken marauding Hutu gangs not to kill their patients. Their pleas fell on deaf ears. The killers went back inside the hospital and murdered dozens more helplessly trapped in their beds.

The girls and Shy hid when they saw a group of men advancing toward Kigali. They were short and tall and didn't seem drunk.

"If I only knew for sure who they were. If only I knew for sure they were the Tutsi soldiers," Shy said to herself.

The two little girls saw the men too and began to shiver and cry silently knowing the danger of being seen. They stared and then jumped as if they could hardly believe their own eyes. In their weak voices used for the first time in days they cried out, "Papa, papa," in only a tone a child can utter.

One soldier turned and looked and fell to his knees as the two little girls wobbled unsteadily to their father's arms. He kissed and hugged them and cried on them. Then he saw Shy and kissed and hugged her, too. Shy was numb with surprise.

"God bless you, Shy, for looking after my babies, I know you could have saved yourself with the other foreigners. My wife and son...," he said hesitantly, not wanting to know, "Are they with you?"

She couldn't stop the tears as she moved him away from the girls quietly telling him about Dominique..

"I don't know where Marie is, I'm sorry, Henri. We are headed to Burundi. Can you help us?"

"The Rwandan Patriotic Front has secured the Lake to Burundi. We are headed to Kigali to join the forces there. We hope to take over Kigali in a few days. The rest of the country is too sad," Henri said looking down, shaking his head at the horrors he saw. "They are ruining everything. They are killing women and children. They are burning whole villages. They don't care who they kill. They don't even know the difference between Hutus and Tutsis. They are young boys in the Hutu gangs drunk and high with weapons," Henri was visibly angry and hurt.

"Will we be alright if we continue to travel along this route?" Shy wanted to get out of Rwanda. And she knew Henri was not coming with them.

"Eugenia and Iramania, you are daddy's brave little girls," he said in a firm fatherly manner. "I want you to behave yourselves and listen to Shy and do everything she tells you to do. Do you understand?" Henri said with his heart breaking before Shy's eyes.

The two girls nodded in agreement. They could no longer speak from the sadness that had made them weak. Henri gave them big hugs and kissed and cried at the softness of their heads, and their bloodied bodies. He didn't want to know what they went through, and his heart wouldn't allow him to ask. They were alive. He had a reason to stay alive, for them.

"Shy, go with God. I must fight to save my people and my country. Something greater than we think is behind this. There is more to it than drunken boys and men killing innocent women and children," Henri said with a glare in his eye she had never seen before.

"Yes, I know. I will pray for you all, God Bless you, Henri," Shy said as she and the girls slowly started off. The two little girls looked at their father in total disbelief that he could leave them again.

"I will spare one soldier to go with you. He knows the forests and he is a brave young man. He is Kelele. He escaped death but saw his family die. He is thirteen but a man in his heart," Henri told the boy to go with them and protect his family.

"Thank you, Henri," she kissed him, and Henri disappeared with his troops toward Kigali. She gathered the two little girls and continued on with this boy-man soldier beside her.

"Walking to freedom, like my ancestors," Shy thought with renewed hope and faith. "This must be similar to the feeling the Africans who were able to escape from slavery felt as they headed north in America to freedom."

With renewed courage Shy led on with Eugenia in her arms and Iramania in Kelele's arms.

"Kelele, tell me how you escaped," Shy asked, trying to keep herself going.

"At night my father woke me and stuffed me into the wood

pile cuttings outside our door when he heard the people that kill come. I was hidden and told to be quiet no matter what I heard. They came and as I heard my mother and father scream I heard the cruel swish of machetes take life from each of them. I cried quietly, still afraid of disobeying my father."

They traveled on the paved road during the night but during the day walked between the shrubbery out of sight. Shy remembered how she traveled most of Rwanda with the Ntetesi's and Dava, then with Antoin, Paolo, and Jeanne, but never went toward Burundi. Suspecting trouble, Jeanne's father made her leave the country abruptly. That hunch and her obedient response saved her life.

The trip was made worse by the vision of shot and stabbed cattle ravaged by the buzzards and flies. Fires could be seen at night from the road and the smell of burning flesh and blood was everywhere. The little girls were trying to be brave. They couldn't talk and their bodies were beaten so badly the pain of walking prompted them to stop as often as they could.

Kelele, the young teenage soldier, knew his way in the forest lake because of the safety - rites of passage ritual he had in the forest. He tells Shy, "Teenage boys undergo a rite of passage – libeli – in the forest; they live in a sacred enclosure for three months; scared and scarred by dramatization of the ancestors' power, they submit to the elders and to circumcision; skins painted with chalk and ruddy clay, they wear parrot's feathers and cloths spotted like the leopard." Kelele told them proudly. Shy was grateful for his youthful, innocent story. Her mind was free from pain for a moment.

Kelele picked a tri-orbed fruit covered in stiff spines and demonstrated its use as a comb. He finds a tree, whose fruit had finer spines, whose fibers were used as thread for fishing-nets until 'les Blancs' brought nylon. Kelele gave a little laugh and explained, "A man must not speak when he harvests the thread; he must not even greet anyone on the path. After cutting the sticks he must wash, take water into his mouth, and spit it out, praying to the ancestors to make his fishing fruitful. Then he can talk. Nylon has done away with this custom, but men still keep silent when they cut wood for floats."

A great fruit tree had fallen. A mound of roots and poor soil thirty- feet high made a hill in the forest. They picked brown fruits and peeled them and ate them.

The stream flowed out into light. The sun shone through as they saw a boat on the lake, a boat that would take them to freedom.

The boatman saw them, and he and Kelele helped Shy and the girls on board. As they were motored across the lake, Kelele said, "The coffee fields are still intact. I guess the Hutu know they will be back to cultivate their crops soon. This would have been an hour ride in a car. But it's going to take longer by boat." The boat's motor lulled them into a trance.

While deboarding, Shy saw it; off the road straight ahead there was an orphanage. She went inside to get help and counted fifteen small children the size and age of Eugenia and Iramania alone, crying, hungry and scared. In the corner was a nun with her throat cut, dead staring blankly. Shy covered the lifeless body with nearby sheets, found some canned food, and using her knife to pry open the tops, fed the children, Kelele and herself.

"Well old girl this is no time to be weak," Shy wanted to burst out in uncontrollable sobs, but refused the urge. There were children staring at her for help. "My God give me strength," Shy begged on her knees.

CHAPTER 25

Burundi Camp

"For I know the plans I have for you...to give
you a future with hope."
NASB Jer. 29:11

As Kelele and Shy gathered what food there was to be found,
they gathered the children together, prodded about finding
what clothing they could to cover those half-naked bodies
with for the journey to the refugee camp up from the lake. Shy
recited the 23 Psalm: "The Lord is my Shepherd; I shall not
want. He maketh me to lie down in green pastures; He leadeth
me beside the still waters; He restoreth my soul; He leadeth me
in the paths of righteousness for His name sake; Yea though I
walk through the valley of the shadow of death; I will fear no
evil; for thou art with me; thy rod and thy staff they comfort
me..." She kept repeating these last few words unconsciously
until she realized what she said. "For thou art with me; thy rod
and thy staff will comfort me," Shy said aloud. "Yes, she was
going to be alright, and the children will be safe."

Her thoughts drifted to home as she watched the struggling
children walk slowly down the road toward some unseen safety
and shelter. She particularly thought of Mr. Duran. 'He knew
this was coming, he knew and didn't warn me. That's why he
told me, '... each struggle, each defeat, sharpens your skills, and
strengthens your courage and your endurance, your ability, and
your confidence and thus each obstacle is a comrade forcing
you to become better or quit.'

"If I quit, I die along with these children. When I get back, he has some explaining to do," she laughed at the irony. Here she was thousands of miles away from not only Fifth Avenue in geographic terms, but in terms of life and death situations as well.

Now, even harder, she pushed on and half carried every child for that last, long mile. These children had become so important to her now. There was no way she'd even think of leaving one behind. With determination they finally made it to the rescue camp. They made it to safety and received the medical attention they desperately needed.

The children were all so sad. They weren't like children that age should be. They were silent and wide eyed, in shock and scared. But Shy began to earn their trust when those children saw how Eugenia and Iramania clung to and trusted her.

They soaked in her kindness and nurturing. They ate whatever Shy gave them and were genuinely grateful. Shy was moved to tears in the realization that hate and malice had taken over their world. Cruelty and pain were their breakfast, death and blood were their lunch, broken bodies and minds were dinner. Their own country had starved them. This poisonous food could not build them up, it could only destroy them. Slow death by disease or starvation was the alternative to swift painful hacking or bludgeoning. How in God's name can these children grow to be healthy thinking adults? What they have seen would drive the strongest soldier to drinking, drugs and then insanity.

They needed nourishment. But she knew if this was the food the aid workers were offering, then these meals would satisfy them.

But the children were so quiet, Shy thought, as she fed them and bedded them down with the help of a few staff members of

Doctors Without Borders and volunteers. The children huddled under Shy for the night and Kelele didn't leave her side. They were safe and protected for the night.

★★★★★★★★★★

Miles away a BBC reporter announces: "Tens of thousands are killed in Rwanda on this third day of slaughter. Eight thousand in Kigali so far. The Kigali hospital cannot cope. The Red Cross morgue had to appeal to people to bury the bodies piled to overflowing. The wards are packed full of people with horrific open wounds from knives and machetes. Prisoners were ordered to dig graves."

Dava and Antoin overheard this and openly sobbed in the foreigner's evacuation shelter in Burundi. "My God, how will we ever know if Shy got out in time? If anything happened to her and I wasn't there to help her I don't know what I'll do. Those men that saved us were supposed to look after her too. Why couldn't they find her? Why, why?" Dava sobbed into Antoin's arms. "My family ... I don't know anything...," Antoin tried to talk, but the horror of it all was too much for him. All he could do was hold Dava and weep.

Over the radio, Dava heard the heartbreaking part, that the Belgian and French U.N. ambassadors were ordered to evacuate only foreigners. She worried that some of the African Affairs Council members did not look European or like any other foreigners. Unless they had time to open their mouths and speak American, they would be left behind with all of the innocent Rwandese begging to be taken with the evacuees, Dava thought.

To her amazement Dava saw members of the African Affairs Council. She rushed toward them, and they went toward her, each one thinking Shy was with the other. They hugged and cried and no one questioned the fact these grown men were crying, everyone was crying.

"I'm so glad to see you all are safe. Is Shy with you?" Dava couldn't wait to ask them.

"No, we were thinking when we saw you, she was with you. No one has seen her. We looked for the two of you when they were evacuating us. They almost left some of us since we look so African. We all had to speak and show proof we were not African. It was terrifying. I had to leave some Rwandese friends behind in the airport and I could hear them begging. They begged the soldiers to shoot them because they didn't want to be bludgeoned to death," Tombe said, visibly shaken and like the rest shocked by the horrors he saw.

"As the aircraft rose above the airport the passengers saw the onslaught of the Hutu killers slowly approaching the people at the airport as the landscape splashed to red. The passengers gagged and cried tears of disbelief and terror beyond their worst nightmare."

Everyone huddled together in silence waiting to hear something. The radio kept telling them of the slaughter. The song of Hutu pride and killing plays endlessly between the orders to slaughter Tutsi:

"'I hate these Hutus, these de-Hutuised Hutu, who have renounced their identity, dear comrades. I hate these Hutus, these Hutus who march blindly, like imbeciles.

"'This species of naive Hutus who join a war without knowing its cause. I hate these Hutus who cannot be brought to kill and who, I swear to you, kill Hutus, dear comrades. And if I hate them, so much the better.'"

Dava, Antoin and the Council members listened as Radio France International reported, "The Rwandan Patriotic Front, made of Tutsi rebels, have advanced within ten miles of Kigali.

They wanted to reinforce their approximate numbers of six hundred before they did battle with the Hutu Presidential Guard and militias that were killing Tutsi civilians in Kigali,"

"The Rwandan Patriotic Front exchanged fire with Hutu army troops in Byumba thirty miles north of Kigali," the broadcast continued.

"Thank God there are people trying to stop the killing. Too bad they have to stop it by killing more," another Council member said.

"I guess rebel is a good word today," Dava said to Antoin, who really couldn't hear her. He was deep in thought for his family and friends and patients.

On the radio they heard, "In the home of the first woman Prime Minister appointed by President Habyarimana, Uwilingiyimana Agathe, a small group of ten Belgian soldiers were supposed to be protecting her. She was a member of Habyarimana's opposition party, to whom he gave minor powers, not truly honoring the Arusha Accord, as a token of peace.

"The Belgian troops gave her away to the Hutu militia. They tortured her in front of them. As she was pregnant, they stood by as the killers took her baby from her stomach and killed it slowly. Then they cut off her breasts and other parts of her body while she was still alive until she died the most painful death anyone could die. The soldiers thought they would live since they gave her to the militia. But they were killed immediately after Prime Minister Agathe took her last breath."

★★★★★★★★★

Inside a secret meeting at the end of the first week of fighting in Rwanda, the Organization leaders listened to

French and Belgian agents who were visibly upset. They report, "The Hutu military have targeted Belgian soldiers to kill and call them friends of Tutsi. They are also beginning to suspect the Belgians of putting down President Habyarimana's plane.

"We are being pointed to by the Tutsi as well," said a French agent. "They have found out the French Legion was helping the former government of Habyarimana resist the Rwandan Patriotic Front, the Tutsi rebels. Then a French journalist was found at the French Embassy's Mission of Defense shredding evidence about how the French trained the Hutu militia, and gave them arms for fighting," he said anxiously. "This can be a slight embarrassment later when the International Tribunal wakes up."

"We have people on the Tribunal. The militia we hired and personally trained will be hidden and protected so that they would never talk. Don't fear, the International community will care less about these black savages killing each other off way over here," spoke Chairman Gatt.

In Kigali after many days the Tutsi who survived gathered at the Kigali airport for refuge under the protection of the U.N. control. The second flight of U.N. food and medicine arrived but was barely enough for the twelve thousand Rwandese at the airport and an additional nine thousand who were being protected by five hundred Bangladeshi troops from the U.N. who were at the stadium.

★★★★★★★★★★

Back in Kigali Drago Dupree communicated via radio with Admiral Bigelow about the progress of the killing.

"Admiral, the people are running out toward the Burundi borders by the hundreds of thousands in a slow river of human misery that stretches over five miles. They travel with only the clothes on their back, women look back searching for families they will never see again. Sweat, blood and tears cover these soon to be refugees. The Hutu dominated the national army and looting thugs joined armed gangs to slaughter what Tutsi, clergy, aid workers and even the patients left in their hospital beds."

"Well done, but I have reports that the Tutsi rebels are trying to take control of the capital, so the job is not done there," said Admiral Biggelo with disdain.

"The large rebel force that came down from the north joined with the Kigali rebels and the Hutu killers fell in the streets with machetes, clubs, hatchets, and spears still bloodied from the civilian's blood on their hands," reported Dupree becoming disgusted with the whole assignment.

"The U.N. commander is not sending in a peace keeping force so there is no stopping of the killing in sight," cheerfully said the Admiral.

"The killing has spread as you planned over all of Rwanda except in the north where rebel troops have been able to secure the area. Admiral, I feel that the Tutsi rebels will soon control Kigali. These Hutu gangs are untrained and drunk. The few military that are here from the Presidential guard are firing mortar and grenades for the most part at the airport. The Tutsi rebels are about to control the airport," said Dupree, looking toward an end soon.

"Don't worry about them, we have more death squads killing elsewhere. Hundreds of Tutsi were hacked to death by armed Hutu in a church in Gisenyi. In Butare refugees from the countryside were run from their homes by gangs setting fires to villages and hacking residents to death with machetes," said Admiral Biggelo.

"Admiral, nine thousand people were under U.N. protection

at Kigali's National Stadium and at the King Faisal Hospital. Last Saturday the first C -130 transport arrived with aid and food for them. But this U.N. force was lightly armed and did not have the resources to cope with the refugees. No place is safe from the killers," Drago said sadly.

"Listen, things are going according to the plan," Admiral Biggelo tried to sound concerned. "This is going to be for the good of all," he lied.

"I must sign off now Admiral, things are getting a bit quiet and that is not good right now," said Dupree.

"Good work, over and out," smirked Admiral Biggelo. "And soon the mercenaries will be sent to kill you, you half breed spear chucker," he laughed after completing his communication with Dupree.

CHAPTER 26

||||||||||||||||||||||||||||||||||||||||||||||||||||||||||

The World Watches Helplessly

"Rejoice in hope, be patient in suffering,
persevere in prayer." NRSV Rom. 12:12

Drago Dupree watched as food had run out, drinking water
was scarce and contaminated and the streets of this capital city,
Kigali, became empty of residents. He watched as women and
children ran, some running straight into the obstacle course of
drunken marauding gangs, armed with everything but guns
and dressed in a patchwork of uniforms, that killed them. Hutu
children carried hand grenades.

He watched the Hutu military in yellow trucks yell and
wave weapons at the foreigners in cars still trying to escape
the city they once loved. The interim Hutu government fled
thirty miles southwest of Kigali to Gitarama. Rebel troops said
their attack on Kigali was to end the chaos and bloodshed in
the capital. The Hutu murderers feared retaliation and fled the
city when the Tutsi rebels came.

He saw tens of thousands of refugees leaving Kigali heading
to Burundi, The only foreigners left in the city were the
International Red Cross with the rebel Tutsi truckers who
together removed the bodies from the streets.

Bodies piled on top of each other with feet of adults and
children barely hidden under blankets. This made it look even
more morbid to Dupree, because he could see lumps of parts
of the bodies through blood-soaked blankets. Then there were
the uncovered bodies lying in the street. Men, women, and

children brutally hacked or bashed to death. Pools of blood gathering and joining into tributaries of blood flowing down the cracks in the road. Some of the smaller children and infant bodies were covered, but some tiny feet and arms came from under the cover in a rigor mortis pose of absolute terror. The smell of death permeated the once flower sweet air of Kigali. The decaying bodies and desolation finally nauseated even this soldier, this strong Navy Seal.

In his heart he knew this was wrong.

Drago found himself at the Red Cross helping to distribute the thirty tons of food given them by the U.N. to feed thousands of people. Both Hutu and Tutsi had hidden themselves in the city starving to death in their hideouts waiting. They were more afraid of being slaughtered than watching each other's life drift away from a week of not eating. Thousands remained hiding, starving to death in their own homes. Many babies succumbed in their mother's arms. Hospitals were no longer open.

Drago wanted to kill the perpetrators of this madness. As European soldiers prepared to leave the city, the army and rebels agreed to make the airport a neutral zone so that food and supplies could be brought in. Mortar spray and a gun battle started in the city. Eight hundred Belgian paratroopers and four hundred twenty Belgian U.N. peacekeepers were handing over control of the airport to about four hundred Ghanaian soldiers as well as many Polish, Bangladesh, and Senegalese peacekeepers totaling two thousand one hundred altogether. These peacekeepers were ordered not to interfere with the killing because that could endanger their fragile efforts to help survivors. So, they watched as innocent women and children were slaughtered helplessly. Five hundred Bengalese troops shared their meager military rations with nine thousand

Tutsi refugees. Without European cover, Drago Dupree was a marked man.

★★★★★★★★★

Now Shy and the volunteers and staff took the children to find families or by a miracle their own mothers and fathers at the refugee camp. She woke with the sun and gathered the children together for their final lap to what she hoped was victory. She heard the familiar song in her head of Sade.

Shy cried silently understanding these lyrics more than ever before as she guided the children into a safe haven and out of the killing hands of their countrymen.

A few miles away from Shy, all Dava could do, after she called N.Y., and while listening to the government radio in Burundi, was help Antoin bandage, cleanse, and sparingly apply the medicines given by the Red Cross to help mend the gaping wounds of the refugees. The problems arose when after mending one, the patient would go off to seek a Hutu or Tutsi to fight with while in the refugee camp and then they came back worse off than before. She listened for any word that might give her a lead as to Shy's whereabouts. But only more distressing news is heard:

"On Wednesday a column of Belgian troops rescued eighteen foreigners from the Ndere Psychiatric Hospital north of the Kigali airport. As they arrived five hundred Tutsi refugees camped in one of the compound's buildings, rushed out begging the Belgians not to leave them behind. Along with them were two hundred mentally ill Rwandans living at the hospital. As the foreigners rode off they knew their friends and those left behind would be slaughtered.

Moctar Gueye, a U.N. spokesman stated,

"Tutsi rebels blew up the government radio station in Kigali that incited Hutus to slaughter Tutsis.

"In Uganda, the Rwandan Patriotic Front officially met with Rwanda's ambassador and agreed a cease fire agreement should be made, but they did not sign one without a Hutu representative present.

"The settlements in Tanzania, Uganda and Zaire have a food problem and the problem is that the men, women and children of Hutu and Tutsi backgrounds can't be put together.

"Thousands of corpses littering the streets is about to lead to an epidemic," Gueye continued from Kigali.

"Aid workers ask: What's the use? Doctors saw one hundred of their patients murdered in their hospital beds. Missionaries who went to teach Christianity saw twenty-two priests and young novice nuns executed. Aid workers who went to Rwanda to help them out of poverty asked what they can do in a land of such vicious and longstanding ethnic hatred," said a CARE worker in the forestry, agriculture, and water project in Rwanda.

The Pastor Litrick told a German paper, "At a church in Musha, twenty-five miles east of Kigali, one thousand two hundred Tutsis, mostly children were massacred when at six thirty Wednesday morning.

"The killers suddenly came into our church. They kicked in the door and immediately opened fire with semi-automatic weapons and threw grenades. Afterward they attacked the defenseless people with knives, bats, and spears. Only a few could have survived the massacre. There were one thousand eight hundred bodies in my church, six hundred and fifty were children."

A missionary said, "Polish missionaries said they could hear the slashing of machetes and calls for help when marauders slaughtered about eighty Tutsis at a Roman Catholic Church in Kigali Saturday. A gang returned Tuesday and began searching for survivors in the church. Since they could not get into the chapel, they set it ablaze, killing dozens more people including two mothers with two young children.

"Despite the danger, CARE, the International Committee of the Red Cross and Doctors Without Borders sent two surgical teams and tons of medical supplies into Kigali Wednesday."

"Thank God for them," said Dava as she tried to block out the rest of the news unsuccessfully.

CHAPTER 27

Hope, Faith, Existence

Animals abandoned their habitats and the
birds stopped singing. Nature cried blood as
bodies crushed the flora and turned the lakes
from blue to red. The sky darkened and the
hills bowed to the stench of bodies heaped on
each other lying ready for a mass grave in the
once holy ground.

Meanwhile, Shy successfully guided the children to refugee
mothers, whose own children were no longer with them. They
cared for them and fed them and cried for them as they tried
to caress away the pain.

As Shy was leaving the orphanage section of the camp she
saw and heard a woman lamenting how she once had a husband
and two little girls and a son, and in the panic of the war her
husband joined the Patriotic Front, and she was also separated
from her children. They were on their way to Byumba where
they were told the rebels had a hold. Along the way, the people
that kill came after them. She hid in rocks and crannies and paid
bribes as she trekked by herself up to Lake Cyohoha through
villages and forests, crisscrossing the paved road to Burundi.

This woman looked at Shy, who herself was dirty and
in tattered clothes, but Shy could still recognize something
familiar there. Shy wanted to believe her eyes, but this woman
didn't look like the stately Tutsi woman she spent so many
days with in her home. This woman looked despondent and

exhausted in her bloody, torn clothing, now only rags covered her dignity.

These two women silently stare their tired, pained eyes into each other's. They walked toward each other slowly, cautiously not trying to see a kind face, a friend, a sister in each for fear of more heartbreak they could not endure. Tears welled up in Shy's eyes and she let out "Marie!" and the woman fell into her arms sobbing uncontrollably.

"My God, thank God, Marie you are alive. Marie, they are here. I brought them here with fifteen other children. Your babies are here with us," Shy cried, speaking ever so slowly and gently to the woman in her tired arms.

"Oh no! Please dear God! What are you telling me? I can't understand you. God don't drive me crazy. Let me hear you," she pleaded, trying not to become absorbed in this untold joy.

"Come with me, now. We'll go to them. They are hurt, but they will be alright once they are with you by their side now. We'll all try to get better, together," and Shy walked her friend to the place where the children were resting, some were sound asleep after their good meals. Much of the terror was behind them now.

Shy cried at the sight of all the children. When Marie saw her two bloodied little girls she shrieked in horror and gladness and ran to them.

The children were all crying and whimpering pitifully in their half sleep. Unable to open their mouths and holler out like they should, they suffered their tiredness away. Shy chose to leave them for the moment and collect herself.

"My umwana, my bike umukobwa," Marie fell to her knees clutching her little girls. They opened their eyes wide, ever so slowly, still afraid of seeing more killing, and found themselves in their mother's arms, with loving eyes staring down at them.

"Mama, mama, mama," they barely whispered with their broken little voices.

Marie ceaselessly kissed and hugged them. They cried and tried to smile and tried to believe this dream was true after their tiny lives were broken with nightmares.

Shy, unable to deal with this, succumbed to the ordeal and joined the three of them. Marie put Shy's head on her lap and all of them held on to each other and rocked into a sleep like haze for hours.

Shy half opened her eyes squinting by the light of a flashlight shining at her. The two men in suits she saw on the plane tell her they were with her from the beginning.

"Duran sent us. We have been with you at every turn throughout your journey. We are taking you to Leon where he has been waiting for you." They let Kelele know who they were and for him to tell Marie Shy was safe.

They picked her up and Shy smiled and surrendered in the arms of these men as they put her on the helicopter. Light came slowly as they flew north to Uganda.

★★★★★★★★★★

Every day in New York, Mr. and Mrs. LaTour quietly and with great fear read the coverage of the war in Rwanda in the newspapers: First the Presidents of Rwanda and Burundi are mysteriously killed in an explosion on his plane and then the Rwanda first daughter went missing.

The first reports were sent across the United Press International to the Times:

"Descent into Mayhem -Tribal slaughter erupts in Rwanda, trapping foreigners and forcing the U.S. to send troops to the region. "We are lying prone on the floor,' Christian Goelette,

an aid worker for Oxfam managed to phone back to the British
aid group's headquarters on Thursday.

"Every window in the house has been shattered by shrapnel
and machine gun fire and soldiers are attacking the house next
door with grenades. The fighting is really bad."

Shy's parents could barely read another line: "Thousands
killed in less than three days; the murder of ten Belgian
peacekeepers and groups of Catholic priests. And it would
be Saturday before French air force could land at Rwanda's
Kigali airport and most of the country's two hundred fifty-
five Americans could be reported among them joining three
hundred thirty Marines in the relative safety of neighboring
Burundi,"

They read. "In two small Central African nations of
Rwanda and Burundi where politics is still dominated by the
ancient rivalry between the predominant Hutu and minority
Tutsi tribes, pure tribal enmity was behind the bloodshed.

"What happened was not an accident, but an assassination,"
said John Damascene Bizimana, Rwanda's Ambassador to the
U.N. "The two leaders were returning from a conference
in Tanzania. Its topic: the ending of decades of Hutu-Tutsi
savagery."

"After three years of fighting, Habyarimana's regime
in Rwanda, made up largely of fellow Hutus, had reached
a peace accord with the mainly Tutsi Rwandan Patriotic
Front last August. But Habyarimana failed to form an interim
government to last until new elections could be conducted.
Burundi's Ntaryamira had been elected President in January
by the National Assembly after the assassination of fellow
Hutu Melchior Ndave in a bloody coup attempt last October.
With Burundi's army still under the control of the Tutsis,
however, Ntaryamira had been unable to stop the rash of ethnic

clashes that have killed tens of thousands and made refugees of hundreds of thousands.

"Representatives of the church and aid organizations promoting human rights and the peace process in Rwanda also suffered. Five priests and twelve young women gathered for a retreat in a Jesuit monastery near the airport were massacred. All were Rwandan; most were Tutsi. The guards and regular troops of the mainly Hutu rebellion army reportedly killed Rwandan staff members or severely tortured them while expatriates were forced to look on at gunpoint.

"On Friday U.N. officials in New York City convened with commander Brigadier General Romeo Ubaliaire who brokered a partial ceasefire and that an interim government was then named. But within 24 hours, militia leaders receiving knowledge of the agreement, began attacking Tutsis and murdering any member of the political opposition they could find."

Mr. and Mrs. LaTour called the consulate and U.N. for more information, but that line remained busy for a solid week. They wrote Washington D.C. Senators and Congress members. Desperately looking for their daughter they phoned everyone they knew in high government positions. There was no fast cure. They continued to suffer the pain of not knowing if she was dead or alive. They didn't want to think the worst.

They didn't want to read anymore, but they might find her name or something. So, they went through every paper in New York and read story after tragic story:

"Rwandans packed into Kigali's hotels, huddling in the dark hallways without food or beds, hoping the few foreigners there would protect them. Their terror only increased as the foreigners slipped away." said hospital administrator, Gerard Van Selst as he boarded an armored Belgian convoy. "A huge number will be killed. One American sheltered a fugitive opposition politician and helped him to safety. But there were too many others he could not help. 'I saw scenes that will haunt me for the rest of my life.' he said. 'Bodies. piles of bodies, women, and children. Just piles of them.'

The narration continued, "The numbing stacks of corpses were the grisly hallmark of a horrifying intimate style of slaughter, literal hand-to-hand combat. The predominantly Tutsi forces of the Rwandan Patriotic Front and the Hutu-dominated army and presidential guard battled each other with mortars, machine guns and hand grenades. But what kept people shuddering in the darkest corners of their homes were the machete armed gangs of Hutu men on a wild killing spree, often drunk and dressed in startling fashions looted from abandoned stores and houses of the dead. Swaggering Hutu men and boys paraded through the city, loaded with weapons and cheap liquor. The army can't control them.'"

Another horrific story told them, "After France, Belgium, Italy, and the U.S. flew military rescue units, most of the two thousand eight hundred and fifty terrified foreign diplomats, aid workers and missionaries were evacuated. Some wept with guilt over the fate of Rwandan friends left behind. Theresa Scimani, an American teacher at the International school in Kigali, recalled the horror before she and her husband and two young daughters were rescued. "'We heard each of the houses near us attacked in turn. There would be firing, screams, then silence,'" she said, safe in Nairobi. "'Then a few minutes later the men would move to the next house, and it would start all over again and again'".

The API continued to sadden the LaTours, "On Saturday, however, both sides allowed food and medicine to be flown into the capital."

The newspaper reports didn't help, nor did they mention any other names of Americans rescued. Mrs. LaTour continued to seek information day after day with a heavy breaking heart.

★★★★★★★★★

As Shy waited in the long line of Americans, Europeans, and Africans for the international phone, she pondered the reasons such a thing could happen.

"Right now, I feel the pain my ancestors suffered. I close my eyes and drift into a past nightmare of captivity and humiliation. I am in the midst of another forced migration. I want to understand why. I don't want to forgive, I cannot hate. I see the Hutu as scared and dying as the Tutsi. What makes people so sensitive to the suffering of others? What makes us want to help strangers even though they may blatantly exhibit hate toward us? My mind drifts across the ocean and I walk the earth with my African ancestors' spirits who tell me the truth. They tell me how we are made of God and are meant to always be Godlike and love everyone no matter how they treat us.

"We are the true spirits of the creator. We are Yahweh. I shudder with disbelief. I don't want to believe this. I want to be able to get revenge for anyone hurting me or mine. I want to strike back at someone who hurts me. I don't want to love them. Then the voice says, 'You are made of God. Africa is the source of human life as we know it today. The great civilizations of the world were first built in Africa. All philosophy and language was created in Africa. All others are from you. They are your children. Have compassion for them. You are their strength. You can love them as a mother loves her sick child.' I know it is true. I know there is a force in nature stronger than any other I can imagine from the spirit of God.

I am empowered by that spirit to carry on the creed of love. Love is the only answer."

★★★★★★★

"Hello, mom? It's me, Shy," the words almost sent Mrs. LaTour into a head spin. Her husband grabbed her and the phone as both were heading for the floor.

"Hello, who is this?" he yelled.

"Daddy it's me, Shy. I'm safe. I'm OK. What happened to mommy?"

"Oh my God," he gasped then quickly said, "Thank God, Shy it's you. We didn't know for a week if you were alive or dead. Hold on, let me tell your mother," he said, but mother grabbed the phone before he could get started reviving her.

"Shy, baby, are you alright? What happened? Come home now! Please sweetheart, you don't know what we've been going through looking for you! We were scared..." Her mother was on the brink of hysteria, so her father got on the phone again.

"Shy, we are so happy you are alive and safe. We were about to give up, especially when Dava called and didn't know anything about where you were or what happened to you," her father started rattling on. Both of them had never acted like this before.

"Dava is safe, thank God. I'm so relieved. Daddy, I can't talk for too long because there are a few hundred other people needing to contact loved ones in Europe and the states. I promise I will stay safe. I am in Burundi, and I will be headed to Uganda soon to meet Leon. I will write to you and call you as soon as I can. I love you so much," she said tearfully.

"Shy, find Dava and Antoin, they are with the Doctors Without Borders in a refugee camp in Burundi," said her father.

"Thanks Dad, I will,"

"We love you so much baby. Stay safe, here's your mother, write to us soon. I love you." her father said.

"Shy, please let us know when you are out of Burundi. Contact us again as soon as you can. Write so we know this is not a dream. We'll contact where Dava is and let her know you are safe and where you are. Thank you for calling," her mother collapsed into a pile of tears.

"I love you mom, I'll call as soon as I get to Uganda, bye for now," Shy hung up the phone, overwhelmed with emotion, but she was not completely out of danger, yet.

Her parents dropped to their knees simultaneously without a word and thanked God again and again. Later Shy's Aunt Wen called everyone in New York including Mr. Duran to let them know she was alive and safe. Everyone asks why this horror happened. Duran appreciated the call even though he knew she was safe.

Duran explained part of the problem to Shy's aunt, "It was a conspiracy that began long before slavery. During the times the Arabs were taking over Egypt, the Nubians were exiled first to Southern Egypt then out of the country. They traveled south in Africa, always in the east following the Nile River, in any case they could never go back home. This was about the time Europe became enlightened, and Alexander plumaged and killed what the original Nubian Egyptian pharaohs left behind."

"I know that part, but who are the Tutsi people?" Wen asked.

"The same time the Arabs started invading Egypt and claiming it as their own, the Watusis inhabited the Congo region, specifically Rwanda and Burundi. This took place around the 13th century. Before that the Arabs were vested heavily in the trade of enslaved Africans to different parts of the

285

world. It is believed the Watusi were the original descendants of the Nubian royalty of Egypt," Duran went on.

"Yes I can see that, as their stature and their mode of cattle herding were reminiscent of Egyptian wealth and status," said Wen.

"The seven- to eight-foot-tall Watusis herded cattle, while the Hutu and Twa farmed. This would have been a perfect economic balance; a community that could have continued a barter system of fruits, tea, and vegetables for meat and poultry. The Tutsi kings ruled and at times wealth spread to Hutus. Some of the Hutus became Tutsis. But the influence of the European sickened the hearts of the cattle herders to feel they should lord over the farmers and peasants of the land. So, they did. The sadness of being driven away from their homes hardened the hearts of the Tutsi to fight to stay in their new land. They became monarchs and lords over the Hutu, like the Hutu lorded over the Twa, now.

"Whatever the cycle of oppression and hatred was between the three groups, it was spurred on to extremes by the conquering Germans, then the Belgians. Even though the European aggressors wanted them to eternally be at war, the three groups of Africans intermarried and all three, Tutsi, Hutu and Twa now spoke one Kinyarwanda language. Today you can barely tell a Hutu from a Tutsi and vice versa. They go to the same schools together. They live as neighbors side-by-side, but that isn't enough. What formula could stop the hatred between them? What else could be done other than have a Hutu President and military working side-by-side with a Tutsi Ministry and Parliament?

"Hutu militias were trained a year prior to the massacre which is claiming hundreds of thousands of Tutsi lives. Secret Hutu civilian armies the government claimed were being trained as park rangers were the creation of Hutu President Juvenal Habyarimana who armed them as he negotiated peace with the Tutsi, the designated enemy. In 1990, the Tutsi slaughtered hundreds of Hutus in a vicious raid of vengeance."

"One of the opposition Social Democrats Habyarimana was forced to put in his cabinet was Finance Minister Marc Rugenera. He was heard to say, 'We warned the international community that this was happening, that these people were being trained to kill great numbers of people.'

"The Government army armed and trained these gangs. Opposition figures said they complained nearly a year before the killing at Kagera National Park in the Northeast and the town of Gisenyi. Hutu extremists were being trained near the Zairean Border. Sporadic killing of Tutsi by terrorist's gangs broke out in mid-1993 and escalated in January 1994 to massacre hundreds," Duran couldn't help himself. He knew he said too much but had to tell someone.

"Mr. Duran I respect you for your knowledge, but I must say if you knew this before the Council left with my niece, how could you send them?"

"I had Shy and the Council under armed protection from the time they got off the plane to today."

★★★★★★★★★★★★

Meanwhile in Kigali, Drago Dupree realized his life was now in danger because he was taking sides. He no longer helped with the killing. He thought it was going to be a military war, not a civilian blood fest with raping, looting, and burning of innocent lives. He was sick of it all.

He saw Belgian troops stationed at the airport, unable to reach more than a dozen western journalists stranded in a hotel at the center of Kigali. On Thursday, a convoy of abandoned cars assembled by the journalists and escorted by an armed U.N. military vehicle made its way through roadblocks to the airport. The convoy was not fired upon, but the airport was hit at least ten times by mortar rounds. The journalists flew out to Nairobi on a C-130 transport with about forty Rwandan refugees. Five journalists remained in Kigali, but the U.N. military helped move them to a hotel away from the heaviest fighting. The U.N. troops witnessed massacres but did not intervene stating they were only there to monitor a broken peace agreement between the Tutsi rebels and the Hutu government. They were not on a peacekeeping mission.

In Burundi, Dava and Antoin worked feverishly to exhaustion trying to care for the thousands of refugees when they were ordered to stop. The International committee of the Red Cross temporarily suspended humanitarian operations on Thursday when gunmen stopped one of its trucks carrying six wounded Rwandans, pulled them out and killed them. Earlier they found fifteen bodies hacked to death in front of a religious school. The place where the Tutsis fled for safety had no food or water, they died of hunger, and cholera mysteriously broke out. Dava and Antoin were petrified and soon abandoned their work with the Red Cross. Trust was not high. They found a small hospital run by the Catholic Church and helped there for a while.

CHAPTER 28

IIIIIIIIIIIIIIIIIIIIIIIIIIIIIIIIIIIIIIIIIIIIIIIII

Love Conquers All

Oh, my people, see the beauty and the
heritage our ancestors have left us. Dwell in
the richness of our own culture, don't perish
in the image of the Western culture.

Cheyenne was taken to the American Rescue Mission
attachment at the Ugandan Heliport near the airport. She was
still badly damaged physically, emotionally, and mentally.

Leon saw his lovely sweetheart disembark tattered, worn
and still bandaged. He wept silently, uncontrollably. He mustn't
be weak; on the contrary, he must be the strength she needed
now. He felt faint, but stood firm and sought her eyes from
behind the metal fence. Their eyes locked for a moment as she
was gently seated in a wheelchair and taken to the terminal.

When Leon and Shy locked eyes for the first time in
Uganda, he smiled, but she could see that his heart ached
at her appearance. He knew she suffered mortal pain, blood
stained, and dirty. Shy looked so miserable. She saw him and
sobbed and shivered not from cold, but something even more
dreadful than fear and the unbelievable relief from it that his
presence offered her.

"Oh babe! What have they done to you? From now on I
won't let you leave my sight. I will be at your side forever, Shy.
I'm so sorry you had to go through what you did," Leon said,
trying to be strong for her, but his heart breaking and tears
welling up in his eyes all at once.

"Just hold me and talk to me softly. I need you so much, Leon you'll never know. You don't know, don't know," Shy began muttering to herself barely audible.

When Shy finally was able to sink into Leon's waiting, loving arms she let go of the pent-up emotions she held for Dominique, the children, Marie, and the lives she saw destroyed. The sound Shy emitted from her belly to her heart that exploded in a resounding deep gut sigh, stirred the internal sensitivity of all who heard that sound of pure relinquish.

Shy would not release Leon from his embrace for minutes in that heliport. She held on for dear life. Leon could not let her go and wasn't sure either one of them could stand erect by themselves.

Having gathered his composure, Leon whisked Shy into a waiting taxi to his hotel room. Alone, he bathed his lover, treated her wounds, and wrapped her in a soft fluffy covering. She took in the hot soup and tea, her tired body craved. Then Leon embraced her and talked her gently into sleep. Shy fell asleep in his arms for the first time in days she let go. She slept through the night. Leon woke her only once to give her water.

While Shy slept, Leon got to communicate with a broadcasting station in Uganda. He asked the U.S. and the international community to please send more troops to stop the gangs from killing innocent woman and children. Surely they could see these people were not in the war.

The answer he received was disheartening. The response to his plea was ignored. Then he heard from his friend Nyati, Director of Center for African Studies in Johannesburg who said, "The outside world seems to have been made weary by so much African misery and is intent only on getting out as fast as possible.

"Right now, the thing is ugly in the short term. The

solution is to militarize, to stabilize the situation, then follow this up with political initiatives. But there is no international will."

Leon called upon another associate who said, "This is a coup d'état," said Omar, a coordinator of London based Africa Rights. "You have to look at the people who were killed in the rioting that followed the crash. It was Hutu and Tutsi, and the ones targeted were the intellectuals and those pushing to open up the political system."

Shy and Leon were arranging to leave Uganda after Shy rested and felt strong enough to travel to Leon's apartment in Egypt. However, they wanted to remember the beauty of central Africa, the "Thousands Hills, the waterfall, the beautiful Lake Kivu, and Lake Victoria. However, when they reached the overlook they were nauseated by the color of Lake Victoria. They saw the red well up in the lake.

Lake Victoria in Uganda was now polluted with dead bodies of slaughtered Tutsis floating over the watery border grave.

They left speechless for the airport. When they arrived at Entebbe International Airport, there was a mural with words that nearly bowled Shy over. It read:

"The Beginning of the Nile, Uganda, and Kenya, where God Hapi dwells at the foot hill of the mountain of the Moon which is Kilimanjaro in Kenya and Rwenzori in Uganda.' From the Papyrus of Hunnefer, Egypt Originators".

This was perplexing and clarifying all at once in Shy's mind. Shy's heart leapt with anticipation through the bewilderment of reading that her research had led her to the original people of Egypt, in Uganda. The ancient WaTutsi went back home to their country of origin, she thought

This was her dream come true. Proof of her theories and talks about the original builders of the Pyramids and monuments. Maybe she could have some hope for peace and study again.

But, before they left Uganda, Shy and Leon met a genocide survivor at the airport who explained why the war spread so fast. He started talking quickly.

"'Every time there was a massacre in the country there was a mass exodus of Rwandese. Here the Rwandese stayed in Uganda for thirty or forty years. Some of them had been integrated in the Ugandan society, some were given some key posts in the Ugandan government. And as time went by they became harassed by all the regimes that succeeded themselves in Uganda.

"In 1982 some Rwandese were chased from Uganda back to Rwanda, and Habyarimana, who was President then, refused to take them in the country. And as time went on these people lived in the 'Polit natioanle couf,' as refugees in their own country. Rwanda was supposed to be their country of origin. This created a lot of frustration and anger for the Rwandese diaspora.

"They found it impossible to go back to Uganda where some of them were killed and some of them tried to legalize themselves, but some of them were determined to come back to Rwanda by any means necessary. Uganda was used as a territory for their comeback because most of them were refugees and they were somewhat integrated with the Ugandan National Resistance Army. Some of them were helped by the Ugandan Government to go back to Rwanda because Uganda did not want these Rwandese in their army or want them as prisoners in Uganda. So, Uganda recognized their right to go back to their own country.

"But when the time came to give the message they had to come back to Rwanda, Habyarimana sent them to Burundi.

And now our request must be heard with the sound of force and guns, but we are willing to negotiate with the government. Then someone in Rwanda made the first concession but they were not sincere especially with the arrival of the Arusha Accord which was a compilation of all the accords from when we met in the past during the war in 1959 very unsuccessfully. That war lasted for approximately twenty years. This was the final accord in which all these accords and agreements were to be united in one called the Arusha Accord.

"But Habyarimana failed to sign it because he had all this pressure from his own groups who were not authorized in the government and had threatened to kill him if he signed this accord. He was under tremendous political pressure to not sign, however, he decided to sign the accord hours before his plane was shot down.

"That is when the genocide crisis erupted and was difficult to control because the new government came to power right after Habyarimana's military decided to begin the slaughter. I would even say that genocide had been carefully studied fifteen months before it began. The international community had been warned of impending danger. They were told by the local political party in Rwanda, in written letters and documents to various governments including the U.S. telling them about the planning and preparation of the genocide in Rwanda. But no response was coming from the international community. In fact, when the genocide crisis began the Security Council decided to leave the U.N., leaving the Rwandese people vulnerable and on their own. The U.S. and others admit to ignoring the warning, but have not apologized for what happened. They could have prevented it, why didn't they? They made a very bad decision.

"They now have in Rwanda an association of survivors of genocide called 'Survival.' From time to time, the survivors make a demonstration against the U.N. peacekeeping headquarters. They also demonstrated in front of the French Embassy because they had complicity with the Habyarimana regime and gave training to the former militia. The French trained the former militia that did the genocide in Rwanda.

"The president started a school made of soldiers. The United Nations Assistance Mission for Rwanda (UNAMIR) did not protect them. The UNAMIR could kill the gangs with guns instead of the government sponsored militia killing the Tutsis with machetes."

"These survivors of genocide wanted to take the U.N. to the International Tribune. The French especially had too much to do with the split in Rwanda, This game of changing sides generated the first massacre in 1959. Hutus and the Belgians called it social revolution – compared it to the French Revolution. They could say it was the justice of the poor, overthrowing the monarchy. War of the oppressed except in Rwanda there was no class system except the white were economically in power.

"When the Hutu came to power with the help of the Belgians, they initiated a new government where the Hutu were privileged in 1962 and the Tutsi representations in the government was abolished. Even in 1968 the few political parties in which the Tutsis were represented were abolished. Rwanda became more and more radical. In 1973, the government was overthrown by Habyarimana.

"He was the savior of the Rwandan people as the man who would bring a peaceful solution to the ethnic conflict. So, his goal was unity and justice. He was not able to do this, because he legitimized the ethnic VIP mission. Tutsi Identification papers were required and mentioned ethnic criteria, and then quotas were established. Tutsi were given less than 9% representation, 90% Hutu and 1% Twa.

"Tutsi were segregated and not treated as equals. Out of hundreds no more than three Tutsi were in government. Before 1962 the Tutsis were in power

After Habyarimana's plane crashed there was a provisional government. This group of Hutus organized the government in a few minutes and the elements that master minded the genocide were included in this provisional government. It was a very radical, corrupt government. The head of this provisional government the new president himself said to the people on the radio who commit mass murders in the city of Butari south of Rwanda to come to Kigali, Rwanda. This was a member of the family of Habyarimana who became President. He was the president of the parliament, and ten officials of the former army were in league with each other and invested him as president.

"The military and government officials never left when the genocide began. These government officials knew what was going to happen and were already in the country of Rwanda."

This information brought back the grief Shy had been feeling. The survivor's voice lamented in homesick tones.

She sat very still and quiet under the protection of Leon's strong arm. He spoke softly to her while the mayhem of the airport helped settle her mind

"We'll grab a bite to eat then get on our flight to Egypt," Leon said, helping her get to her feet.

Within two hours, they were on a plane to Egypt.

However, her body was now beginning to feel the pains and aches of her wounds, and miles of walking, carrying children, and seeing harrowing human affliction and desolation. The agony of the week broke her body. Leon could only gently hold her as they flew to Egypt.

Still reports came back through the Associated Press and Ridder-Knight that about 170 staff and patients were slaughtered Sunday at a hospital in Butare. Shy remembers the trip there Dava and Antoin took the last time she saw her best friend. She got that sense of dread and hopelessness again when she thought of Dava. She blamed herself for being separated from her friend. How could she let that happen? It was like any other day. They were going to meet at their home, but were separated. A cryptic note and she had to run and suddenly gun fire was heard and blood everywhere.

Dava and Antoin attended the funeral of Burundi's President Cyprian Ntaryamira. He was buried ten days after he and President Habyarimana died in the crash at Kigali's airport. Habyarimana's body was not interred in the form and fashion he deserved, it was secretly done, no one knows where.

CHAPTER 29

Temporary Peace in Egypt, Africa

"The Hard and Stiff will be broken. The Soft and Supple will prevail." Tao Ching

Shy was in the land of the Pharaohs. Not just one sensibility or emotion could describe what she felt as the plane passed over the Pyramids near the landing strip in Cairo. The Pyramids stood high and tall in the sun. Looking exquisite after thousands of years waiting for her to view, this moment in time was for her.

They landed on the tarmac and beheld the beautiful earth-colored people, so true to living harmoniously in nature, in this land. In Egypt, the spirit of Africa brought semi-sweet thoughts to Shy even with the turmoil and devastation she had lived through

"Take me to your apartment. I want to see a little of Egypt before I am deported. The refugee visa flight passes will not last too much longer," said Shy, ready to move on. There was more to Egypt than she ever even imagined.

"Shy, don't worry about that. I have contacts who can give you a visa and passport by next week," Leon told her confidently.

Shy was so grateful to Leon. His presence gave her security and comfort. Shy was glad for a small bag of her personal items and some clothing in his apartment. She bathed and dressed in a familiarity she had missed while struggling in the war. It had seemed like years to her, but she was in Rwanda for less than three months.

Leon didn't press Shy for information about the war and what happened to her. He only wanted to soothe and calm her.

"You know we will have a formal ceremony of our love in Karmac. That's where the Nubian Pharaohs performed a secret rebirth ceremony with their wives, the Queens of Egypt," said Leon as he held Shy on his lap as she closed her eyes and pictured what he was saying.

"The land of Egypt has a sacredness about it. You can feel the spirit of the ancestors call out for you to reclaim our inheritance. Our greatness will shine again. All the world will praise our work and we will see equality and justice in all the world, Ma'at," Leon said, knowing what Shy needed to hear now. His words gently put her to sleep with a smile on her face. She slept until the sun rose the next day. Leon sat by and watched over Shy every minute of that time.

"Hello sleepy head," Leon said, hugging Shy into wakefulness as he saw she was trying to wake up.

"I feel so good, especially in your arms, Leon. Did I sleep for many hours?" She said innocently.

"Yes, my love you slept for a while," Leon knew she didn't know the day of the week or time of day. It didn't matter if he told Shy she slept through to the next day.

"I love you, Leon. I'm suddenly very very hungry and thirsty. I know you fed me before I went to sleep," Shy said snuggling up to him.

"Get dressed and let's get out in the fresh air and find some food," Leon said cheerfully, knowing she didn't want to leave the safety of the apartment.

"Don't worry it is completely safe where we are. There is

peace here, Shy," Leon said, giving her confidence to see the world again.

"I am so happy we are in Egypt, Leon. I really need to love Africa again. It's like riding a bike – when you fall off you must immediately get back on it," Shy said sure of the quote.

"Actually, it's if you fall off a horse get back on, but whatever, don't ever give up," Leon hugged her close, as they prepared to leave for the restaurant.

"Leon apart from the truly horrible things I witnessed and experienced in Rwanda I have come away with a final and ultimate purpose in my life besides keeping my faith and loving you," Shy said to him as she held his hand and looked upon his face.

"And what can this be for a woman who has done just about everything, including risking your life to save Marie's two girls and fifteen children during a barbaric war?" Leon smiled at her admiringly.

"Leon, in some way I am going to help children. Maybe I will eventually teach, but I feel that the children of the world need a chance to live better. Why must they continue to hate and kill people who their parents and ancestors say are bad and are enemies to them? Do you realize that children from Brazil to Bosnia, from China to Ireland, from Israel to America, will be taught to hate a group of people they haven't met yet, that haven't even been born yet? Much less many nations in Africa which teach tribal or ethnic hatred for no reason, along with the racists attitudes in Europe and the United States, innocent children will be subjected to the inferior or superior and self-hate attitudes of their sick parents. I need to do something even if it is for a few children somewhere. I need them to see the beauty in the world and in all people, especially those that are different from themselves. It just makes me feel so bad sometimes," Shy told him with tears in her eyes.

"Yes Shy, I can see you doing something like that. And I will support you in any way I can. I believe like you do, if the children of the world had a chance not to hate anyone even the natural circumstances that happen in childhood like bullies or abusers, the world would have peace. But the war mongers and hate groups won't let it happen. Maybe in a small way it can happen, a piece of this world can be saved from hatred and senseless killing," Leon spoke softly, holding Shy's hand to his heart.

They both knew deep inside this was the beginning of a new conscious determination. An idea that could change everything. In order to have real peace there must be total upheaval first. From Burundi to Uganda to Zaire and Tanganyika, rebel troops with Tutsi sympathies would take over eventually. Now, both the Tutsi and Hutu would work together once and for all. Through intermarriage and modern technology life for these people will go on to a higher level, but not before there is much suffering.

Leon took Shy to one of his favorite comfortable cafes. At the Café di Roma in his Zamalek neighborhood, they found a table in a quiet place in the restaurant and enjoyed a loving moment of peace together.

After dinner Shy called her parents from Leon's apartment. Their relief was quelled when Shy told them Leon procured a specialist from the American Embassy that helped Americans work through their trauma. He is going to talk to Shy next week.

"Mom, I cannot tell you what happened, but I was never injured physically. Mr. Duran had assigned two armed men to protect all of the African Affairs Council every moment we were there. None of us knew anything about it. He knew all the time about the danger, mom," Shy said unbelievingly.

"Wen spoke to him about you. I still can't understand why he didn't stop you if he knew you would be in danger," her mother said angrily. "But you know what, now that I know you are safe and with Leon, I am forgiving Duran. I hope you don't work for him again."

"Mom, I was just telling Leon I would like to do something with children. I haven't decided exactly what, but it will be with children," Shy told her mother, turning the conversation to a lighter note.

"Shy, your pictures came back and they are stunning. Do you want me to mail them to you or are you coming home soon?"

"I knew we'd get to this question sooner or later. I do plan to come home, but I want and need to spend some time with Leon. He told me he has a special event for me soon. Mom I know you are still worried about me and I am also concerned about how I will function in our country, knowing what I know. I am not the same person I was three months ago. I need some time to process and recover. Please give Dava my phone number here and you can have Tombe and Aunt Wen call me if they want to hear my voice.

"OK Shy. You know yourself better than anyone else. By the way, Dava is in Burundi with Antoin. Her mother is not happy. I will call you if I have to hear your voice again, also. Please call us and your grandparents when you are able to. I love you, take care. Kiss Leon for us. Bye for now," Shy's mother hung up the phone and rocked herself while hugging her arms. She felt better, but not good yet. She held back Shy's grandparents' health news. She remembered Ralph Waldo Emerson's quote, "The first wealth is health."

"Leon," Shy asked after she hung up from her mother, "Is there any way you can find out about Marie and the girls? Dava will be calling me here when mom gives her your number. I want to know if they all are OK."

"Shy, babe, Marie must contact us. Tell Dava to get the number to her. I wish I could tell you everyone is OK, but I can't right now," Leon wanted to help her feel at ease. " I trust Dava to avoid trouble and what you tell me about Antoin, he sounds like a responsible person."

Leon shops for food while Shy stays in the apartment. She still cries at the horror she witnessed. She is not able to grasp her interpretation of the war.

When the counselor from the Embassy sees Shy, he tells her that she must vocalize the pain. The only way to relieve the burden is to get it out in the open. See it for what it is. Reveal its power over her.

Shy told Leon what the counselor told her to do. Leon braced himself for what his love was about to tell him of what happened to her.

Leon had been worrying about Shy since the phone call to Dava when she told him, "Shy is missing."

They both took deep breaths as Shy told him about Dominique alone and afraid in his empty house and leading him to his death, hiding, hearing the screams and sounds of killing with machetes, and finding the girls under the dead bodies. This was too much for both of them and they sobbed quietly within and Shy let out another gut-wrenching sound. Leon hugged Shy and carried her to bed. They rested their sad hearts crying.

The next morning Leon brought Shy breakfast in bed. A croissant, coffee with whipped cream, figs, and yogurt. Shy sat up and kissed him. He drank coffee while he watched her eat.

"The counselor was right. I had to let it go out of me. I had to release that horrible part. But finding the girls alive helped me so much."

"Shy you must understand that you were leading Dominque to safety not his death," Leon said quietly to his love. He cried thinking of her pain as she walked away and heard the cries and explosion behind her.

"I know Leon, but the sounds are in my head. I heard his voice cry out, 'mama, mama.' I think some music today will be good. I don't want to talk right now about it."

"Funny you should say that. My new friend Mec is coming by today to help you purify your heart with a Sufi ritual song," said Leon with a big smile.

"What! A Sufi like the Dervish in Turkey is coming here? Does he dance in a circle, too?" Shy asked, astonished.

"No, not exactly. The Sufi Whirling Dervish are Islamic. Mec is a Jewish Sufi. He is unique. Sufi is mysticism and Egypt is home of Sufism," Leon explained.

"Leon, this is the best thing you could have done for me. What does he sing? Is he a Rumi follower?" Shy was transformed.

"Sufism is Mystical. They dance, sing, rock, pray all for remembrance to commit to God. 'God is real. God is all there is.' Unity and the oneness of God is their belief. What I love about it is there are no books on how to be a Sufi. They have a mystical, tasting of knowledge, a direct intuitive experience of God."

"OMG, Leon. You sure know me so well. You know I'd love this knowledge. I can't wait to meet him."

They get dressed in anticipation of Mec. They make space for him to move or dance as he sings.

"Mec is coming because I helped him when I was filming a

Sufi ritual in a village in the Nile delta. They were celebrating the birthday of the Prophet Muhammad for two and a half hours. They were Islamic Sufis and didn't want Mec and I was there watching them. I explained the West's fascination with Rumi and the Dervish Dancing Sufis and more interest about them is a way of gaining more interest and respect for who they are worldwide."

"What happened?" Shy was enthralled.

"Well, they let us go and sent us away with blessings!" Leon said, surprising himself. "They are completely peaceful beings."

Shy and Leon hear a tambourine and soft singing coming toward them in the hall. They opened the door and watched him rock and walk to them.

There was Mec singing his hypnotic utterance and shaking the tambourine in a slow melodic rhythm.

They let him in the living and watched this tall thin robed man float into their apartment and start rock walking in a circle around them both.

Shy and Leon rocked side to side and closed their eyes. Knowing what he was, they thought of God. Mec synchronized their rocking and soon they were one. After some time went by, Mec stopped the tambourine and sat on the floor. Leon and Shy joined him on the floor.

"Mec, thank you. That was so uplifting. I feel completely light hearted," Leon said in his best Egyptian.

"I am pleased. She looks lighter also,' Mec said looking at Shy.

Shy waited patiently for Leon to tell her what they were saying. He told her.

"Please tell Mec thank you for this wonderful feeling he gave us. I think some of my heaviness in my heart is lifted,"

Shy said with her first smile since arriving in Egypt. Leon's face smiled and he took her hand. He told Mec what she said.

"My joy to give. Please take time to meditate when I leave. Enrich your soul with love and let God lift your spirits," Mec said as he rose to leave and shut the door behind him.

Leon and Shy continued to sit on the floor and meditated. When they were done they went to bed and slept peacefully for an hour.

At work Leon was pressed by his supervisor to get his girlfriend to give them her story. He had to placate them and exaggerate Shy's emotional state. He wanted her to rest and relax while he prepared her big surprise.

Leon's American and European co-workers and their spouses were interested in meeting Shy. The women wanted to show her Egypt. They need to meet Shy before the big event.

While in Egypt, Leon tried to get hold of everything written on the war besides the daily paper. The API and the UKP reported the same news from similar sources as the Knight-Ridder Newspapers state: "Upheaval is not unique to Rwanda. Zambia, Kenya, and Angola also have problems. The West, after its humiliation in Somalia, seems willing to do little more in Rwanda than evacuate foreign nationals and let the killing continue. It's too easy for the outside world to blame centuries' old tribal conflict and not do anything."

CHAPTER 30

Progress in Rwanda

"...The Truth shall make you free!"
KJV John 8:22

When Rwandans learned an Organization of foreigners made the plot to kill them off, their hatred for each other subsided somewhat. They found out that to hate a hidden, powerful, and invisible enemy is not practical. They dedicated themselves to building a strong country, so it could never happen to them again. They fought together, to become one people, strong and forgiving enough to move on.

"Henri please come home with us," Marie begged as all Tutsi refugees were released from the refugee camps to go home.

"I cannot leave now. The Hutu are coming to the refugee camps, and we must start arrests. Everyman is needed. Don't you want the men who killed our son to pay?"

"I want you with us more than revenge. We are alive, we love and need you. The people who kill are suffering. Their suffering will be long and agonizing. Our son is in a peaceful place now, he's free. Yes, I am angry, but I cannot let it consume me, and I need you more," Marie pleaded to her husband.

"I will be home many times between the capture of the killers and see you very often, I promise," Henri said misty eyed looking at his hurt and bruised little girls with tears in his eyes. His heart was full of revenge for his son and daughters, and loving wife of twenty years. The family kissed their father good-bye, sadly, but ready to move on.

The camp truck took the Tutsi refugees back to Kigali which now reeked of smoke and death. Marie and Kelele found her home intact, except the inside was ravaged. Kelele left to find his home. "I'll be back," he promised Marie.

Marie sorted through the smashed and foul home that smelled of killing and urine. She began the cleansing and clearing of pain left by the ones that kill.

The girls ran to their room as if all was well, this was the familiar; they were home again. They were tired of living in dirt. They looked in their closets and everything was there like before, they got dressed. Marie went to the kitchen and fell into a routine of preparing dinner of what was left in the pantry.

After she and the girls cleaned up, Marie looked at her neighbor's house and knew Joseph, a Hutu, was part of the band of the men that killed. A fear so blinding passed over her, she became frozen and nauseous. A knock on the door sent a scream from the pit of her bowels and stopped in her throat. She opened the door and Tweena, her friend hugged her and both women allowed tears of relief to melt into their own. They kissed each other on the cheeks several times and cried some more; a friend amongst enemies, a calm refuge after the storm. Peace and a harmonious comfort, at last, blended anew in her heart.

"Oh, my friend, I feared for you and your family. I ran away to the north and stayed with friends who hid some of us in his bathroom. It was so miserable and horrifying. But I don't want to talk of that now. Tell me how the girls are?" Tweena said, hugging her friend for dear life.

"They seem to be OK. The doctor in the camp examined them and they suffered concussions when they ..." tears filled Marie's eyes at the thought of her girls being hurt.

"I understand. They are safe now. The Patriotic Front is protecting us now. Henri is there with them right?"

"Yes Tweena, and I miss him. There is so much to be done. Our country cries from the wounds of injustice and hate. I pray every night to God to find forgiveness and a way to live without fear."

"Marie, I don't know how to do it. The men still call me names and threaten me. I hate them and want to shoot them," Tweena said as she showed her gun to Marie.

"I can understand, but if you continue to hate it will take over your life. I can't kill. I need to know why my life was saved, Tweena. How come I survived, and my son was killed in a church then burned with hundreds of our people in the same church? I need to know why my daughters lived buried in a ditch of carcasses where the stench alone could put a grown man into a coma," Marie cried.

"I don't know, but how can you not have hatred in your heart? My family is gone, everyone, dead," Tweena said with anger. " I fear if I don't get them they will get me. They don't take me because they know I have a gun. Do you want one?"

"No, Tweena. There is nothing I can do with one. I need to believe these men who kill are free of hate and fear, so they can become our neighbors again because I know we can all change."

On the radio they hear a new voice. A voice of hope, security, and safety.

"Oh, yes! The truth sets Rwanda free. We now have a new leader of Rwanda, Phil Mamega, military leader in the Rwandan Patriotic Front and de facto President of Rwanda. He is a true mixture of all ethnic groups and a lover of all his people. He is tall and elegant as a Tutsi, with the features of the Twa, and the spirit of a Hutu," said Tweena to her friend Marie. They listened to the radio quietly.

"With the coming of this new millennium, we will be prepared, my people. In the next three to four years, we must educate ourselves. The vicious hatred we had for one another must be transmuted into empowerment through knowledge and love," Mamega said. "We will clean up corruption, develop the economy, and ban all divisionist talk." He ruled with an iron hand, and his countrymen have fallen in line.

Tears come to his eyes as his heart speaks, "Let us be able to talk face to face with our European counterpart, not with eyes cast downward, in shame. Let us no longer be the slave, but the freeman that will join with them as equal partners in this great world from now on. We no longer will be subservient underlings with our hands out-stretched for crumbs. We will have a slice of pie. Not by force, but by merit. First we must mend ourselves. Heal old wounds from the last 1000 years. I am looking at the year 2000 as our greatest moment in history. We came from the creators of civilization. Africa had the first university and library in the world. The Black man of the Nile made the great pyramids of Egypt and the Sphinx. We had one God while the rest of mankind lived as pagans and barbarians, in caves to the north of Africa.

"But because we did not want to conquer the world as our European brother did, we were conquered, lied about and ultimately lost our history and prestige.

"We did not travel to the Far east from Europe and see only dark people. We did not cross the great oceans of the world and be frightened by the realization of being the only white people on the planet.

"We as Africans had already been there, everywhere populating and mixing in the world. That is why there were people who looked like us. The European panicked when he saw no other white people in the entire world and began to suppress and rule all people who did not look like them throughout the world from India to Fiji, from the Americas to Africa and China in his Renaissance from the Dark Ages of his warring.

"It is time for our white brother to realize that we are all God's children made in his image.

"This new millennium will find us once again as great as our ancestors of old, before 1000 A.D.. From 1000 to 1994 A. D. the African around the world has suffered mightily. It is a time for change. Let's start with ourselves. Know the true perpetrator of our miseries, read, study history, and move on from there. Know our true enemy and love ourselves. Love your blood brother and sister. Ask yourself why the Europeans study us, and we don't study ourselves.

"Let's bring cures to the world's physical, emotional, and spiritual diseases. All the cures are in nature. In our jungles and forests and rivers and oceans and our people are the answers to the scientists' questions. Every white doctor and man of science knows the cures are in mother earth-herbs. Let's work together for all of mankind. Let's turn this world around and bring love into it, not hate, and paranoia.

"Change must come, my people, and it must start with you and me. It must start here with us now! We are the ones at the bottom and have no place else to go then up. So, rise you mighty people, Rise and show the world love and forgiveness. We must get rid of all African dictators who just take like the European. We must cleanse our land of the viper that kills our forested land, and waters. We must unite and start anew. Join the rebels and let's get our land back now!"

'The people rise and shout and cry and hug each other. No

longer enemies but brothers and sisters united in a common cause. The making of a New Africa for the Africans and all people,' the news commentator said tearfully after Mamega's speech.

CHAPTER 31

|||||||||||||||||||||||||||||||||||||||||||||||||||||

Safe, and Becoming Sound

"Your joy is your sorrow unmasked"
The Prophet by Kahlil Gibran

Shy and Leon found peace in Egypt. Dava and the African Affairs Council have returned to their homes in the U.S.

Leon found out that China had been connecting the fiber optics and setting up the internet connections. They were not training the Rwandese how to set up the internet. Rwandese could not take over, so the Chinese continued to be in charge and not leave Rwanda.

His journalist colleagues told him it was leaked that someone in Chairman Gatt's office informed M.H. Duran and therefore, all of the African Affairs Council escaped the slaughter and were brought to safety.

As the African Affairs Council members flew home, tears, and fears of unfathomable quantities rip at their brains. After many discussions of why the great turn the people took and why they weren't protected by the Rwandan people both Tutsi and Hutu, they came to realize in a calmer, peaceful demeanor as they neared the end of their twenty-hour ride, that they did not approach the situation in the African way.

"The culture of Africa is based on trust. This trust comes from the elders. There is an African code or chain of command. Every village and even every African American community has their leaders or elders.

"In these elders the people put their trust and obedience.

Noone, neither from AT&T or the African Affairs Council, really had a sit down and ceremonial rites of Passage consultation with the elders in the manner in which the Rwandese were accustomed.

"The African principles and law were disturbed as were the natural forces between the Hutu and Tutsi. In Tao culture, the Native and African Americans should never jump to the extreme. Life is a small wave or ripple that continues from birth to death. When extreme measures or lifestyles are introduced this makes sharp valleys and high waves, usually insurmountable in a fashion to which the individual is not used to dealing with in life. You never fully recover from extremes. They can never be made up. The best thing is not to make extreme waves in the life cycle," Tombe made his statement to all.

Tombe led his group in Brooklyn in meditations. He learned that a group of Radiant Transcendental Meditators were in Rwanda constantly meditating for peace. He had some of the Council members talk to psychologists at the Veterans Administration. Most of the members went to their former jobs and continued their home lives. Leon kept in touch with Tombe and some of the others.

"Tombe, I know you may not be ready, but it's been three months now since we left Rwanda and Shy and I want as many of the Council members to come to our wedding in Egypt this August," said Leon excitedly.

"Yes, Leon, we need a happy occasion. I know the war has ended in Rwanda, but now has spread to Burundi and Zaire. We need to face our fears and forgive and live again. We have had Post Traumatic Growth specialists help us out of the despair we suffered. I will talk to the men and see who is able to return to Africa," Tombe said ready to move-on.

"Great, Tombe, Dava and Shy's family are coming. Egypt

is a fascinating place and I have met some incredible people here both in the news business and socially. You will love it."

"Send all the details and arrangements and I'll get back to you with who is coming," Tombe said. "Antoin and Dava were able to send some of our personal items from the job site. We are so happy for them both. We'll all be together again. See you soon my brother."

"Bye for now, Tombe." They both felt the spirit of a new episode awaking in their bodies. An awareness of never quitting, rising above, and moving on was now springing up in their minds.

Shy was on the phone with Dava as she and Antoin were already married in Burundi and soon to be starting a life together in Egypt with Shy and Leon.

CHAPTER 32

Betrayal and The Bottom Line

"Money Talks – BS Walks."
Keefe Brasselle

One day when Adm. Biggelo visited the office of Chairman Gatt he told him he wanted to talk to Woodrow Falt. Chairman Gatt called Woody into his office. When Woody arrived Biggelo lit a cigarette then shook Woody's hand. He put his other hand with the cigarette on Woody's shoulder and acted as if he was congratulating him for a good job helping his old friend Chairman Gatt. As soon as Woody stepped away he collapsed and died immediately. Biggelo carefully snuffed out the cigarette and stuffed it into his pocket. Doctors rushed in immediately. They pronounced Woodrow Falt dead of a heart attack. Biggelo had a cigarette with poisonous smoke that when inhaled produced a heart attack. He received this from one of his former KGB partners in Russia.

Chairman Gatt is perturbed but understood there were always casualties in combat, civilian and otherwise. The Admiral and the Chairman plot how to get rid of the colored people as they liked to refer to them in the United States as well as the Caribbean, South Pacific Islands and South America.

"Those Dag – blasted nigger type people are everywhere. If there was one way we could blast them to hell, I wouldn't say nothing. The French tried to blast them in the South Pacific with their nuclear testing, but they weren't able to do any real damage," growled Chairman Gatt.

"Well, our children's children will benefit when those people are completely deranged and deformed from the fallout, ha ha," They both laughed their hateful laughs at Adm. Biggelo's so-called joke.

"What is the next step in the Organization's plot for world domination?" Chairman Gatt asked his friend.

"Well, you know I can't make it official, but we are arming some of the militias in our own country to defend themselves against the enemy. In time we will tell them the enemy is colored. Right now, we are having a little trouble convincing them the entire government is not so nigger loving as all the Presidents and House of Representatives seem to be now," replied Adm. Biggelo.

"You know, we good old boys have never stopped putting the pressure on the coloreds down south. Somebody started back with burning the Black churches, I hear, ha ha, " They both chuckled again this time at the Chairman's so-called joke with his bad grammar.

"Ain't it great to be superior with all the power and just pick who we will hate and kill, and nobody cares about them," Biggelo says.

"Well, we are still mad at them niggers for leaving the plantation and not working as slaves for us. Now they want to be equal as real human beings," says Chairman Gatt.

"Well, I think 'bout the time we really get into this hate thing in the USA people will have had enough of them.

"Why even those Righteous Christians groups hate them down here in the south," Chairman Gatt smiles maliciously.

"But we still have enough of those worldly do gooders who will always stand up for them and try to convince our lunatics that everybody should love one another, and peace should reign in the world or some such garbage," says Adm. Biggelo angrily, as he thinks how peace would put him out of work.

"Let's call a meeting real soon before the enthusiasm wears off over our Rwanda victory. They got to feel good about the rest of Africa falling apart. We can build on that and take it from there," Chairman Gatt continued and the two of them nodded malevolently and proceeded to plan hatred.

"We still have to make sure the mining for coltan and other minerals are taken out of Zaire for our technology. Certain international military forces will keep the war in Zaire going for twenty years or more." Said the Admiral.

★★★★★★★★★★★

The U.S. and France were battling in Rwanda. The French backed the Hutus led government and the U.S. supported the Tutsi Rwandan Patriotic Front.

As fate would have it, the Rwanda crisis spread throughout the central part of Africa from the Indian Ocean to the Atlantic. Noone could not have imagined the results would be so horrific that Zaire would overthrow their dictator and rename the country The Democratic Republic of the Congo.

"The peaceful soul after a blessed life will
finally rest in heaven" Quran

"Rwanda Tutsi fled to many camps during the 1994 massacre, when the Tutsi-led Rwandan Patriotic Front ousted the hard-liner Hutu regime that promoted the massacres. This occurrence fostered a reversal in refugees that took place. The Tutsi returned home, and the Hutu fled their homes to the refugee camp, The Hutus now feared revenge killings by the Tutsi minority.

"Rwanda's new government has been trying to close the camps for months, saying the areas have become hiding places for Hutus who took part in the genocide. Soldiers encircled Kibeho to screen inhabitants before sending them out of the camp.".(API)

"Henri, we have been fighting for three months now. It is time to go home. The Patriotic Front has grown strong and is fighting in Zaire and Burundi. I fight only for Rwanda," one of Henri's comrades told him.

"I have a wife and daughters who wait for me in our home. Before the war we lived in harmony with our neighbors. Now they fear us. I am going home also. Burundi has enough soldiers and in Zaire there is a different force perpetuating the war. There is something more going on than Tutsi - Hutu differences," Henri said.

The men head back to their homes in Rwanda to support their new President and raise their children in some semblance of normalcy.

CHAPTER 33

The Happy, Holy Reunion

> We have the power and authority to change
> any condition we are experiencing or attitude
> we are feeling.

After three months of therapy and loving care, Shy and Leon prepare for their long-awaited reunion with family and friends. The American journalist families take her in and help guide her into a more normal life in Egypt.

Shy is taken to a therapist twice a week and a meditation center three times a week.

"Growing up in the 1960's has made you a survivor and you have the ability of being resilient. You were born when the United States was still mourning the assassination of a much-loved young President of the United States. You were in Washington D.C. when a major Civil Rights March took place. You heard of Black Panthers, a community protection organization, who were killed and imprisoned by the FBI. Martin L King, Jr., Attorney General Robert Kennedy, and Malcolm X were gunned down in broad daylight. You watched on TV as your Aunt Wen's school was surrounded by armed National Guards while she was in the administration building. You saw your aunt's friends die in Vietnam and in 1971, a college student was shot by the National Guard in a peaceful protest. I say this to tell you how your life prepared you for some harsh and cruel realities. Just before you came to Rwanda in 1993 the World Trade Center's basement was bombed.

However, seeing people massacred in front of you is different. This will take care and time to mend in your heart, but you are a survivor," the psychologist explained to Shy.

"Doctor, I have been able to tell my story of what happened to the people of Rwanda and me. I look in the mirror and I see a different woman. I see stress in my face and feel myself tremble unconsciously at times," said Shy sadly. "My Buddhist guide talks to me daily and has me turn toward my demons." Shy's tears well up in her eyes as she sees her truth.

"I am a hopeless romantic, as my mother used to call me. I can see good in others and love the earth. I shut - off the horror people do to each other, and find it difficult to judge. My fear is avoidance of the negative, so that I don't have to feel it. Life has shown me that expressing any emotion, crying, laughing just feeling is the human experience. Just don't go to extremes."

Before preparations are made for the big day, Dava and Cheyenne go back to the U.S. They go to an African Affairs Council meeting and learn that two of the men suffered severe PTSD and had to be hospitalized when they got back home. One of their friends in the Council had a heart attack and died of a broken heart.

Cheyenne's grandparents are no longer able to care for themselves and the Hancock house is rented. So much had happened in the three months they were away that Dava and Shy decided to leave as soon as possible and return to Egypt and their lovers. Dava's mother found a boyfriend who loves the ground on which she walks.

Antoin and Leon find out about the Rendition against terrorists and their torture in Egypt. They find out the U.S. has a hand in this. The Nubians are removed from their homes as Mubarak floods the Nile Valley of the Kings and the Aswan Dam submerges ancient dynasties and coalesced the Nubian heritage into the Anglo - Pharoah. The Nubian population moved between the Sudan and southwest borders.

Antoin continued his work in Cairo with Doctors Without Borders and was sent into dangerous places: Lebanon-Syria; Iran; the Gulf War; Iraq-Kuwait-Saudi Arabia; Somalia and even Cyprus and Turkey. The world seemed to be in crisis. Antoin could only do so much.

Then the day of light and love approached for Leon and Cheyenne as the RSVP's came in and the rooms were rented for their guests. Dava and Antoin stayed in their hotel in Cairo at the Great Pyramid Inn with breathtaking views of the Pyramids. Marie, Henri, their lovely daughters, Iramania, and Eugenia stayed in Karmac at the B &B on the Nile, and Cheyenne and Leon's parents stayed and enjoyed Le Passage Cairo and Casino near the airport. Some Council members came with their families along with Tombe and his wife.

The Journalists and their wives had prepared Shy a wedding feast and regalia fit for a Queen. They all entered the Felucca with grand style and set sail up the Nile to the Karnak Temples in Luxor, Egypt.

It is here that the great Pharaohs of Egypt brought their Queens to have their sacred ceremonies and it is here Leon and Cheyenne did the Ritual of the Scarab Beetle as a Grand Celestial Alignment anointed their Holy Bond for eternity.

The End

THE APPENDIX

Historic Facts taken from the Associated Press,
Kidder and the Associated Press International
1994

"Between Tuesday and Thursday, 32 people were killed, either trampled in stampedes or shot by soldiers.

Along with those killed Saturday afternoon, more than 200 were injured," relief workers said.

"We couldn't get to many of the wounded because of the gunfire." said Capt. Carol Evans, a doctor with Australian Medical Corps who helped evacuate wounded Rwandans. "It's like a chicken shoot. About four soldiers run after one guy and then shoot him. It's horrible."

–June 30, 1994, French official warns troops in Rwanda of impending troubles. French Defense Minister Francois Leotard believes that troubles from the genocidal war in Rwanda are yet to come for the troops who so far have not had much trouble. The recent fighting between Hutu-led government army and rebel Tutsi is 2 miles from Gishyita near Lake Kivu which is just 30 miles from the Hutu owned government land. API

For 100 days from April 6, 1994 to July 1994.

–April 9, 1994 the 2nd relief flight reaches Rwanda as fights erupt. More than 12,000 Rwandans who had gathered at sites guarded by the United Nations awaited food and medicine Sunday as fighting between rebels and soldiers flared again. This second relief flight under UN control hoped that the violence would subside for more relief flights to land. Rebels and soldiers traded small arms fire and efforts for a cease fire seem unlikely.

-Most of the victims slaughtered were Tutsi minority slaughtered by Hutu gang members and Hutu dominated government forces. The rebels who pushed into Kigali on Tuesday are predominantly Tutsi.

-Abdul Kabila, director of the UN peacekeeping mission in Rwanda, said the UN sent more convoys of armored vehicles to parts of the city to evacuate people fearing for their lives. Marauding gangs, many with machetes, have terrorized the city, randomly looting and hacking thousands of people to death.

-Some of the more than 4000 foreigners evacuated from Kigali and elsewhere have reported massacres in different parts of Rwanda.

"Now the Hutu government considers France a friend since France intervened to prevent a rebel assault in 1990. The Rwandan Patriotic Front remains suspicious of the French because of that intervention. The French encountered no violence during their four missions into Rwanda Saturday. API

-July 19, 1994, More than 100,000 Hutu refugees flee into Zaire with no end in sight. The Red Cross and French soldiers are on the Zaire border town of Bukavu feeding the refugees and protecting the Hutu from the Rwandan Patriotic Front who have successfully put an end to the murder of over 500,000 Tutsi civilians. The Hutu started leaving the Rwandan town of Cyangugu 1000 at a time. The town was considered a safe haven against Tutsi led rebels who defeated the Hutu government.

-July 20,1994 Rwandan rebels install leaders, promise peace. The victorious Tutsi led rebels set up their new government and called for a halt to the fleeing of Hutu refugees from Rwanda. Faustin Twagiramungu was sworn in as prime minister and Pasteur Bizimuingu was sworn in as president. Both are moderate Hutus. The rebel military commander Maj. Gen. Paul Kagame was named vice president and defense minister. But in the southwestern corner of Rwanda 400,000 refugees have crossed into Kamannyola, Zaire and 300,000 crossed into the border farther north. Nearly 1,000,000 Hutu civilians and soldiers fled into Goma Zaire last week as refugees. API

-Friday July 22,1994 Number of dead just growing and growing. Nearby two boys no older than ten tugged at a filthy gray blanket to cover the thin corpse of another boy. Not far away, a girl, younger yet, silently sobbed by her father's limp body. An infant sat, wailing weakly by her mother's lifeless form in a pile of volcanic rocks.

-Up the road a French front-end loader dug a long trench near a grove of banana trees. Workers tossed body after body into the pit; each tumbled down to join the jumble of torsos, limbs, and rags. At least 500 corpses were in the mass grave, officials said. Behind them, a bulldozer pushed dirt over the searing Holocaust like scene.

-Three miles north at Mungi, physicians from Doctors Without Borders and other aid groups worked a makeshift triage ward on an open field strewn with jagged lava rocks and the bodies of the dead and dying.

"Yesterday morning we had 10 dead," said Dr. Isabelle Pardieu. "Last night we had 100. Now it is just growing and growing."

-A handful of still-living people had intravenous drips hooked up. But most simply waited for the agony to end. Groans of pain and children's cries filled the still air. A corner of the field was reserved for the dead; fresh corpses arrived in a steady stream at midday.

"Is he dead yet?" shouted Kevin Noone, from the Irish aid group GOAL. Pointing at the limp body of a man facedown.

"Not yet! Not yet," a colleague answered. "Soon".

Without pausing they returned to their grisly work; spraying a dozen bodies with disinfectant and loading them, sagging into a brown pickup truck. More bodies arrived as fast as these were carted off, 60 in an hour, 300 by nightfall.

"It's literally like a conveyor belt," Noone said as he worked. "They bring them in, and we load them on the truck."

Noone said he had rented a 40-foot trailer truck to carry bodies today, an indication of the horrors expected ahead.

Doctors predict that cholera-which causes severe diarrhea, vomiting and sometimes death within five hours- is likely to infect 10,000 to 50,000 refugees. Untreated half will probably die. "You cannot stop it at the moment." warned Henchaerts. API

Cholera initially spreads in contaminated water, but then can be passed directly from person to person. Corpses are especially contagious, so quick burial is critical.

The chief treatment for those infected is immediate rehydration with special solutions to replace lost fluids. And the only reliable prevention is chlorinated drinking water. But both the solutions and clean water are in short supply. API

-The first air shipment of 10,000 liters of solution arrived Thursday, but most had been used by nightfall. Another shipment was expected today, but the airport is already operating at near capacity.

"We only got one runway, and you can't just pop it and pound it or you'll have to close it." said Paul Gilham, in charge of the airlift. Moreover, only six planes can be parked and unloaded one time-fewer if they are large cargo planes.

The epidemic is the latest tragedy of Rwanda's four-month civil war and slaughter that has caused an estimated 1.2 million

Hutu refugees to flee for fear of retribution from victorious Tutsi-led rebels in Rwanda.

-The predominantly Tutsi Rwandan Patriotic Front now in Gitarama is linking up with the Tutsi in Biserero due east of Gishyita. This will improve their position in the area against the Hutu government. This has put fear in the Hutus living around Lake Kivu. API

-France has been mandated by the UN to give an even-handed policy in Rwanda. This is the problem since the French have backed the Hutu dominated government of the killed President Habyarimana, and the past has raised doubt about France's being neutral. Habyarimana's death April 6 in a plane crash, allegedly caused by two missiles, triggered a renewal of the Rwandan civil war and led to the slaying of hundreds of thousands of the minority Tutsi slaughtered by government led militias made up of Hutus. API

-The rebels have accused the French of wanting to intervene to help the Hutus under cover of humanitarian aid. The French in an effort to mollify the rebels, have said they will step aside and not get involved in the civil war. France's Operation Turquoise must separate protecting the civilians from further killing and taking sides. API

-The rebels radio repeatedly has called on Tutsi survivors of the massacres to gather at Mount Karongi in the Biserero area some 12 miles away suggesting that the region constitutes a safe haven from continuing Hutu violence because it is under rebel control. API

-1994 Refugees pour into Zaire.

Hundreds of thousands Hutu Rwandans flee Tutsi led Rwandan Patriotic Front rebel group. At the rate of 10,000 an hour overran the one guard after Zairian officials closed the little crossing at Goma.

-Millions of people were seen on a 25-mile stretch of road from Ruhengeri to Gisenyi. Gisenyi in western Rwanda was the stronghold of Rwanda's interim government made up of its Hutu majority. API

-Civil war with the remaining Hutu government army and the Tutsi led Rwanda Patriotic Front. Rebels were advancing to Ruhengeri but stalled at Mukunge River because they had a problem going across the river. The Hutu, Twagiramungu, was named prime minister in 1993, August at the peace accord to end the three-year civil war started in 1990. He was to lead the transitional government for 18 months paving the way for multiparty elections. His arrival back into Rwanda from Entebbe, Uganda would bring a cease fire to the civil war. He was to name cabinet members and Hutu leaders of the massacres against Tutsis were apprehended. He said his government would include Hutus and Tutsis.

-The Tutsi Chairman of the Rwanda Patriotic Front, Alexis Kanyarengwe said indications were high that high ranking army officials were prepared to turn over government officials implicated in the massacres. API

America the Beautiful and Bloody Peace

"The holiest of all the spots on earth is where an ancient hatred has become a present love." ACIM T-26.X.6:1

-Sat. July 2, 1994 French face dual hostility in Rwanda -The French rescued Tutsi refugees escaping from the massacre by the Hutu and evacuated to a base camp in Zaire. The French face hostility from both sides. The Hutu feel the French should stop the Tutsi rebels who have so far captured two thirds of Rwanda and the

Tutsi don't trust the French because of the aid and favoritism they showed the Hutu in the past. API

Hundreds of thousands Hutus in the south are fleeing advancing Patriotic Front Tutsi-led rebels. The French deployed into that region Friday. The main region of concern is between Gikongoro and Butare, Tutsi rebels were advancing on Butare where a French detachment of marines set up an aid post for refugees. This post could be seen as the French protecting the Hutu government.

The Hutu rebels have threatened to engage any French troops it met on the battlefield but would not attack as long as the French stayed within the limits of their aid mission.

The French based Doctors without Borders said a low flying Rwanda helicopter fired on a clearly marked aid vehicle, but no one was hurt.

The French airlifted 21 badly wounded Tutsi 30 miles outside of Goma and 50 French commandos had moved in to safeguard evacuees of seriously wounded Tutsi. They also uploaded 40 boxes of high protein biscuits, water, and medicine.

-July 23, 1994, President Clinton orders a massive increase

in aid. Gen. John Shalikashvili, chairman of the Joint Chiefs of Staff, Brian Atwood, director of the Agency for International Development, Lake of the UN and Deutch, briefed reporters at the White House with the following:

-The US military will establish and manage an airlift hub at Entebbe, Uganda, which will be used as a staging area for round-the clock relief shipments to refugee camps. Consultations with Uganda are underway.

-Expand airlift operations at smaller airfields closer for refugee camps in Goma and Bukavu in Zaire.

-Increase the capacity at those three airlifts, and potentially others, to receive transfer and distribute food, medicine, and other supplies.

-Establish a safe water supply and distribute water.

Clinton also said 20 million oral rehydration therapy packages were to be delivered. These can save a person by replenishing body salts within three hours.

-At the Goma camp 1300 refugees had cholera among the 1 million refugees 130 deaths are attributed to cholera and 770 were related to dehydration
and related diseases.

-Doctors Without Borders report up to 50,000 cholera cases will appear and half that number could die from the disease.

-Two C-141 transport planes are due to arrive today at Goma, Deutch said. One with medical supplies and the dehydration packets and the other with 10-ton forklifts to speed up unloading of supplies.

-Today 42 more flights will ship 1400 tons in food supplies.

-Peacekeepers mostly from African countries and the US will secure the safety of returning refugees into Rwanda. The goal is peaceful political reconciliation secured initially by the

UN. Rwandese will return home to harvest their crops and resume normalcy. API

-July 29,1994 Rwandans plight spurs gifts, offers of assistance

-US relief organizations have received more than $4.5 million in the last two weeks from individuals, according to InterAction, a coalition for humanitarian and relief agencies. Corporate gifts have amounted to $35 million.

-"The response has been unbelievable," said Michael Kierman, a spokesman for InterAction.

-Donations have come from across the country and in amounts large and small. Churches are taking up special collections, while children are sponsoring yard sales or dipping into banks for money.

-In Fairbanks, Alaska, patrons at a bar passed around a hat and raised $5000 for Doctors without Borders. They phoned in the contribution on someone's credit card.

-In Philadelphia, a mother on welfare called Doctors Without Borders to see if she could contribute half of her food stamps to the relief agency. It politely declined.

-At a housing complex for senior citizens near Boston, a woman recruited 10 of her neighbors to chip in a dollar apiece to send to Oxfam America a private charity relief group. The group sent a check, signed by each of them.

-Six-year-old Ariana of Reading Mass, sent this handwritten message with her donation to Oxfam. "Here is six dollars that my best friend Krista and me made selling pictures. We want to help the hungry people."

-In addition to cash contributions, relief groups and the US government have been bombarded by offers from people who want to volunteer their services.

-Todd Schaeffer, 34 a former Peace Corps volunteer in Africa and now an analyst with an economic think tank, called the US Agency for International Development to offer his services. He was stationed in Zaire for two years and has experience planning water and sanitation systems.

"What I have to offer is so, so, so small," said Schaefer, who speaks French and Lingala, one of the languages spoken in Zaire. "The problem is too big for a guy like me. But a thousand guys like me might be able to do something."

-Many volunteers, however, are being turned away.

The State Department is discouraging offers from people without special technical skills—such as medical services—experience in disaster relief in underdeveloped nations.

"A lot of people are seeing this on TV and want to do something like adopt a child or go to Rwanda themselves," said Suzanne Brooks, who works for the disaster information Center for Volunteers in Technical Assistance, private organization in Arlington VA. "We have to tell them if you don't have technical experience we don't discourage you to go out on your own because you could be more work than help."

-Friday July 29,1994

Troops and civilians get water flowing and the UN tries to reduce crowding.

-In a refugee camp near Lake Kivu where water is polluted with corpses, clean water was pumped by army engineers through a hose from a water treatment plant. Germany, Holland, and Britain announced they were rushing medics, water-purification plants and engineers and a field hospital to the region. UN troops were hauling tens of thousands of gallons to refugees farther off in camps where pestilence, mostly cholera has killed 20,000 Rwandans. They suffer from the dehydration caused from the cholera. The UN tried to clear this border town of refugees trying to eliminate the epidemic but the very sick needed a truck in order to move. These were Rwanda Tutsi who fled for their lives during the Hutu massacre.

-The UN brought 8000 gallons to 20 miles north of Goma to 300,000 refugees to Kibumba refugee camp. Days later the UN delivered 25,000 gallons of water to the camp. 18 Air Force specialists arrived in Goma to improve the unloading of aid [planes organization of plane parking and goods and storage and air traffic control. API

-1994 UN helps raid camp in Rwanda.

Kigali UN forces joined government troops on Wednesday to raid a refugee camp in the southwest seizing 200 machetes and some grenades and arresting 12 people.

This was an effort by the Rwanda government to persuade 350,000 refugees in the southwest to return to their villages. Most were Hutu who fled their homes during the civil war that brought a Tutsi dominated government to power in July.

1994 Quick trials urged in Rwanda war.

It can take more than three years for the UN to organize a tribunal and people will think we are playing around here." Twagiramungu he said.

The Prime Minister says the country won't wait long in war crimes cases; others [point to problems in approach.

Kigali Prime Minister Faustin Twagiramungu called for genocide trials as soon as possible against Hutu officials who planned, ordered, and executed the killings of hundreds of thousands of Rwandans from the Tutsi minority during the nation's civil war.

The UN is opposed to these trials of men, women, and children because they feel it would only prolong the ethnic hatreds between the Hutu and Tutsi. "You could be talking about 200,000 people shot for genocidal crimes".

Twagiramungu rejected the argument, "I don't know what happened in France after the war or in Germany, he said," but those nations pushed national unity while still trying war criminals. Why did it happen there, and it can't happen here?"

1995

–Jan 1995 Shooting in Rwanda camp kills at least 12.

36 other people are wounded in refugee camp violence

The shooting took place at a camp 2 miles southeast of Remera near Rwanda's border with Burundi. Six Rwandans were flown to a hospital run by Australian military in Kigali. Random violence is rampant in the refugee camps inhabited by mostly Hutus. It is mostly directed to the Hutu refugees who want to return home or individuals suspected of spying for the Tutsi-dominated government in Rwanda.

–Relief agencies say Zairean camps, with a population estimating 1.2 million are a powder keg because of the presence of the defeated Hutu army and an estimated 10,000 militiamen.

–1995 Burundi– Burundi president moves to prevent ethnic violence.

–Trying to diminish ethnic violence, Burundi's president has banned all political meetings, imposed censorship, and asked the nation's parliament for power to rule by decree until October.

The National Assembly met in a special session Monday to consider President Silvestre Ntibantunganya's request.

Burundi's Hutus and Tutsis have been slaughtering each other over political supremacy since the country gained independence from Belgium in 1962.

–July 1995 Civil War reaches gorilla habitat

Rwanda– Shards of glass litter the forest floor in Virunga Forest where 320 mountain gorillas lived and observed for research by the Karisoke Research Center. All of the employees fled as Tutsi rebels advanced and are now in Zaire. Dian Fossey whose movie, "Gorilla's in the Mist" was killed at this center in 1985 and now her cabin where her workers still worked was ramshackle. It might have been poachers and not soldiers as they were her worst enemy killing gorillas and antelope. Rwanda's government is encouraging the trackers to return and find the missing gorillas and help return the growing tourism that came after the movie.

However, with armies of both sides around the forest the future of the camp is unknown.

-July 1995 Tutsi leaders to control French zone

Rwanda's Tutsi led government said it would extend its control over the former French protection zone where more than 1 million frightened Hutu sought refuge.

About 70,000 Hutu refugees fled after the French left.

Zaire and the new government are discussing repatriation, but the UN High Commissioner Ray Wilkinson said there could be no quick repatriation without backing from the former government which has not been invited.

-March 26, 1995, Rwanda still struggling a year after civil war; a Roman Catholic church in Nyarubuye where Tutsi were being chased by Hutu killers sought refuge in the catholic church and the reverend gave them up to the Hutus and the Tutsi men, women, and children were massacred. After a year the corpses and bones of the massacred lay in the church but slowly one by one they have been collected secretly by friends and relatives who buried them. These people did it in secret because they did not want to bring attention to themselves and ask openly for permission to take the bodies. The fear between the Tutsi and Hutus still goes on even after the civil war abated.

-Rwanda's banks have been looted, tens of thousands of children are orphaned, its jails overflowing with accused mass murderers, and its justice system and other vital government functions paralyzed.

-April 1995 More than a half million Hutu still refuse to

return home. They are mostly in Goma, Zaire where they constitute one of the largest refugee camps in history.

Some are planning to plot insurrection against the Tutsi, and some don't come home for fear of retribution.

A 30-year-old Tutsi man can't even grieve for the loss of his family and so many many friends in the massacre. He says, "What hurts is not having the power to punish those who killed. What happened in Rwanda you just can't believe humans did it. It was like an exceptional event." API

-Recalling the massacres. Tutsi men are relaxing on a Sunday afternoon drinking banana beer from a calabash. It is a bitter brew that tastes neither like bananas nor beer. "When the Hutu killers came the 138 families of the Nyarubuye village where eucalyptus and banana groves thrive, ran to the Roman Catholic church for sanctuary and protection. Many others from neighboring villages also ran to the church totaling 6000 or more," A survivor tells of the massacre. "Nearly all were slaughtered except 8. The Hutu attacked first with machetes and crude weapons, after being repulsed, returned with soldiers with machine guns and rifle-propelled grenades to kill the remaining Tutsi." Some of the survivors recognized the Hutus killers as former friends and neighbors. "After the Tutsi were slaughtered many Hutu fled. At night, their camp fires can be seen 5 miles away, just across the Kagera River in Tanzania. Not all Hutus refugees are killers, but many surely are. Even the innocent have reason to fear retribution if they return home. Some say they have no reason to return, many of their homes and shops have been taken over by Tutsi."

-Nyarubuye is just bush now. Mud homes are crumbling now, and gardens and fields of corn and greens are overgrown with weeds.

-At the Kibumba refugee camp in Zaire, population

200,000 Hutu leader Alphonse Butsingiri calls the shots. He once worked for Rwanda's old government but now holds court in a cinder-block house at the edge of the settlement.

Asked when the crisis might end and refugees go home, he barked," We already gave our condition for going back. There must be power-sharing with the old Hutu leaders. In other words, Rwanda's new prime minister, Faustin Twagiramungu must go. He calls for the old Hutu leaders to return, and they will be arrested and tried for genocide."

Foreign diplomats can see Twagiramungu's point. And yet, without dialogue, a solution to the ethnic conflict seems impossible.

The old Hutu regime still commands an army of possibly 20,000 troops. Rumors persist that those troops are being trained and reequipped in the refugee camps. Aid workers say they have witnessed such training.

The new government made up of Tutsi and moderate Hutu, has vowed to protect innocent Hutu who return. It also has promised to remove Tutsi who occupy Hutu homes illegally.

But the new government also says it must punish those who did the killing. Otherwise, its leaders say, Rwanda's culture of ethnic violence will only continue. API

-Friday April 7, 1995, Six Hutus, including teens, are on trial in Rwanda for slaughter. Kigali, Rwanda, a year after the Rwandan slaughter of 500,000 Tutsi and some moderate Hutu, five men and one teenage boy went on trial Thursday.

Dressed in dirty pink prison clothes, their faces were etched with fear as prosecutor Silas Munyagishali read the murder charges against them. They are among 30,000 people, mostly majority Hutus, the government has imprisoned on suspicion of systematic acts of genocide against the minority Tutsi people.

Those blamed for organizing the slaughter have not yet been brought to trial.

The adults are facing life in prison or death and the youngest, a 17-year-old, is charged with killing six people and throwing them into a river in his hometown of Gitarama. UNICEF is defending the boy with a Tutsi lawyer representing the boy in the name of justice..

-Friday October 6, 1995, White French mercenary gives himself up after failed coup with Comorian soldiers against the government in this small island country off the coast of Mozambique. Bob Denard still in the days of when the Belgian Congo, now Zaire, Nigeria, Angola, Zimbabwe were white ruled as well as Rhodesia now Benin, and the Comoros were under colonial apartheid rule. API

-May 1995 another group of refugees sent home. Kibeho, Rwanda about 300 refugees some suspected of participating in massacres last year were released to their homes Saturday. With a warning to avoid further bloodshed. The Hutu men danced for joy then set out to join their families. The men had been jailed for two weeks in Kigoma in a school. API

1995 Jailed for massacres child prisoners from 5-14 years old line up to be moved out of the Kigali Prison in Rwanda on Saturday. The group of 77 children, accused of taking part in last year's massacres in Rwanda were being transferred to a newly opened rehabilitation center. More than 1,000 Rwanda children have been jailed with adult prisoners since the 1994 mass killings.

- Leaders approve plan for Rwanda refugees' return to their homes in Rwanda. In Cairo, Egypt leaders from five African countries agreed Wednesday on a plan to provide for the safe and voluntary return of nearly 2 million refugees who fled

Rwanda after a mass slaughter of minority Tutsis by majority Hutus last year.

"The agreement announced after a two-day meeting of leaders from Rwanda, Burundi, Zaire, Uganda, and Tanzania, does not provide a timetable for the refugees return but envisions a rate of 10,000 a day within a short time."

"I believe the refugees will return in large numbers when they believe that they will be safe," said former Jimmy Carter who brokered the agreement. API

-April 24, 1995, Refugees flee massacre scene in Butare, Rwanda. A UN truck separates Hutu and Tutsi refugees at camp. Tens of thousands Rwandan refugees escaped down rain slicked roads and into the hills in full panic Sunday after the army shut down their camps inside Rwanda leaving an estimated 200 shot, butchered, and trampled to death. API

-The army ordered the refugees to return to their former homes, promising them peace. These were Tutsi soldiers asking Hutu refugees to go to their homes. Many of those that tried to go home were pelted with stones and attacked.

-This was the first violence of this magnitude since the war ended in July 1994. At least 250 children were abandoned in the chaos and collected by relief workers; About 650 people were treated for injuries and wounds; Rwandan soldiers, assisted by UN troops buried most of the dead in hastily dug mass graves.

In the process, Rwanda's emerging efforts at national reconciliation suffered a tragic reversal-perhaps foreshadowing even worse consequences for its suffering people in the months ahead.

The death toll from three days of conflict at a refugee camp in southwest Rwanda remained a gruesome guessing game. Throughout the day Sunday, UN said its field reports indicated that 4000 may have died- the result of soldiers firing on refugees with machetes and of people being crushed by stampedes.

But late in the day UN military commander for Rwanda Maj. Gen. Guy Tousignant said the earlier estimate had been inflated as a result of confusion.

Rwanda President Pasteur Bizimuingu toured the Kibeho refugee camp Sunday and insisted that only 300 had died.

He defended the army's attack on the mass of refugees Saturday saying, "Radicals among the refugees had instituted the killings. People in the camp had arms and were violent. It's a pity that people died."

A week ago, the hillside camp was the semi-permanent home to 80,000 to 100,000 Hutus. On Sunday fewer than 1000 remained.

-Several thousand refugees fled to the city of Butare, where they took shelter in a stadium. The UN reported that 10,000 more have massed at various midpoints in the region. As for the rest, some tried to return to their homes in the nearby countryside and many thousands melted into the banana groves and cane fields.

-Those who tried to go home were not treated well. They were stoned by other as well as attacked and abused.

A year ago, the majority Hutus controlled Rwanda's elected government. Slaughter, however, did not stop a rebel Tutsi led army from taking control of the country and driving the Hutus into an exodus.

April 23,1995 Secretary of State Warren Christopher proposed to South African President Nelson Mandela that Europe can no longer feel that African countries are under their domain. He pointed out Mali as a French controlled country and pluralized the French. He also proposed that there be a military commission that can go into African nations that have civil strife and help the governments maintain peace. He said this would be sponsored by America and some Asian countries. Mandela said this would not be backed by Africans if they feel America is sending troops to their countries. He proposed the United Nations spear head this initiative and deploy troops. Mr. Christopher agreed.

-Arusha, Tanzania Oct 12, 1995, Burundi embargo upheld. African leaders from Cameroon, Ethiopia, Kenya, Rwanda, Uganda, Zaire, and Zambia have not been doing business with Burundi since the civil war there between the Hutus and the Tutsis. The Tutsi ruler, Pierre Buyoya said he was committed to unconditional negotiations with Hutu rebels. The summit agreed to take measures against any party that did not partake in the negotiations. Mr. Christopher suggested that some sanctions be lifted because of some progress toward national reconciliation.

April 13, 1995, In Burundi peace for the children came in the form of the puppet show put on by UNICEF and Disney. Burundi is close to the Ugandan Hutu nation and strongly influenced by Uganda. During the war in Rwanda many Tutsi tried to leave as well as Hutus escaping the murders on each side. The puppet show showed how after a cat and dog had a fight they made up and became friends again.

-April 25,1995 In a refugee camp in Kigali, Rwanda, Tutsi soldiers fired shots at 80,000 Hutu refugees in the refugee camp killing 2,000. World leaders decided to hold back on aide to this country in deciding unrest still prevails in Rwanda even though The Tutsi led soldiers and government want a reconciliation between the Hutu and Tutsi Rwandans. The Rwanda Patriotic Front wants the Hutus to return to their homes and even placed some Hutus in key government positions. World leaders feel that this new violence shows that the violence has not stopped, and they are unwilling to continue aide until it stops.

-1995 Rwanda video campaign. The UN aimed to lure refugees to return home. The refugees in Mugona camp saw a video of their home town with familiar faces telling them it's OK to return in their language. More than 1000 watched the 27-inch screen and cheered and laughed and waved at friends and relatives that called them to come back. The UN high commission used this as a tool to encourage refugees to return home. The aim is to counter disinformation and rumors spread by Hutu extremist who have intimidated refugees from returning home by claiming they will be killed in retaliation for last year's genocide.

-Dec,13,1995 Eight were charged with genocide in Rwanda.

-Arusha, Tanzania. An international tribunal announced Tuesday that it had issued its first indictments in connection with last year's ethnic slaughter in Rwanda, charging eight people with genocide and crimes against humanity.

The eight were charged with the murders of tens of thousands of people at four massacre sites part of the ethnic violence that killed some 500,000 people.

Justice Richard Goldstone of the International Tribunal for Rwanda said the defendants will not be identified until they are arrested. He also would not say where they were believed to be.

None charged were among the Hutu leaders in Rwanda who were accused of orchestrating the killings.

The first indictments issued November 27 and 28 in the Hague Netherlands focused on people who planned and carried out four massacres near Kibuye in western Rwanda.

-1995 Zaire stops expulsions of Rwanda refugees.

Goma, Zaire- Zairean soldiers halted their forced repatriation of Rwanda refugees Thursday, after a five-day campaign in which about 15,000 people were expelled from camps and more than 100,000 fled into the hills.

-UN officials in Goma said it was unclear whether Zaire's government has permanently stopped its effort to expel 1.5 million Rwanda refugees- including about 730,000 in the northeastern border region. The UN high commission for repatriation will assume a voluntary repatriation to Rwanda.

-The operation stopped in April after thousands of refugees were shot and killed in a stampede when the Rwanda army shut the Kibeho camp in Rwanda.

The voluntary refugees most of them Hutu fled to Zaire last summer following a civil war in their tiny Central African nation.

UN officials have been unsuccessful in getting refugees mostly Hutu, to return after the Rwandan Tutsi led army over threw the Hutu government. Some camps hold as many as 200,000 refugees. UN authorities said camp inhabitants sent letters in which they said they are willing to return home. They appear to be more afraid of the Zairean soldiers than they are of going to Rwanda.

UN representatives have criticized the forced repatriation effort which began a day after the UN security council lifted an embargo on Rwanda and implied Zaire officials had helped to rearm former Rwanda Hutu soldiers and militia members in the refugee camps.

-January 1996 Zaire says Rwandans will be returned gradually. The one million Rwandan refugees living in camps in eastern Zaire for one- and one-half years will be sent home gradually. Said Deputy Interior Minister Gustave Malumba Mbangula after a call from Rwanda's vice president asked that the refugees come home and start rebuilding their nation.

-UNHCR camp worker says the videos have been one of

the most effective tools and people want to look and see them. A visit that allows refugees to travel to their home area for a day to see whether life has returned to normal. Hutu intimidation is common at camps in Zaire and Tanzania most of the 24,000 refugees in Burundi still fear arrest and imprisonment for their crimes.

–They complain about the constant presence of Rwandan troops in the countryside. Foreigners at the Burundi camp tell them it is safe. "Foreigners never leave the main roads; they do not know what happens in the countryside where real life is," said one refugee.

1996

-1996 Burundi civil war begins

-The refugees have a desperate desire for more information. They want to know whether it is safe to go home. What has happened to other refugees who returned home. They want assurances from the Rwandan government.

-The UNHCR knows it will take a long time to replace the violent memories of Rwanda.

-February 28,1996 Rwanda report: world ignored hints of genocide. Paris-Outside world ignored early warnings of genocide and then botched its vast relief efforts. Blamed the vacillation of world leaders for encouraging genocide and triggering a mass exodus from Rwanda. Many relief workers and organizations did what they could, but poor coordination, rivalries and waste caused needless deaths. Timely international action would have made the relief action unnecessary.

-1996 Memorial dedicated to Rwanda slaying victims established in the southwestern town of Gikongoro where the remains of the victims of the 1994 genocide lay in a mass grave.

President Bizimuingu sealed the base of a pedestal that will support a monument to the memory of the victims. "We dedicate this in honor of those who lost their lives in the genocide." A candle light vigil was also held in Kigali stadium where thousands sought refuge from the killing.

-February 1996 Hutu leaders lobby for role in Rwanda

Kigali, Exiled Rwandan leaders blamed for orchestrating ethnic massacres want to participate in the rebel installed government that overthrew them before they will allow Hutu refugees to return home.

Hutu leaders in neighboring Zaire told UN sponsored task force on repatriation there can be no massive return of refugees until a power-sharing deal is cut, the deputy commander of UN peacekeepers in Rwanda, Bri. Gen Henry Anyidoho of Ghana said Tuesday.

Anyidoho returned Monday from visiting refugee camps in Zaire, where he met with Hutu leaders, including former chief of military staff Augustin Bizimuingu.

-Aug. 4, 1996, Hutu rebels take war into Burundi. They shelled the capital Bujumbura and three mortar shells hit the University there. They are fighting Tutsi soldiers who overthrew the government. More than150,000 people in Burundi have been killed since 1993 when the Tutsi paratroopers assassinated the first democratically elected Hutu president.

1996 Mara Group was established. They made the first smartphone phone produced in Africa. It was made by the Mara Group in Rwanda, and is extremely affordable.

-Rwanda refugee leaders arrested for intimidation. Hutu refugees intimidated Rwanda refugees who want to go home so the Zairean government has arrested eight Rwanda leaders in the last two weeks. One of the leaders was Francois Karera who the former mayor of Kigali. He is believed to be one of the leading forces in the massacre of 500,000 Tutsi in 1994.

-By video Clinton urges Burundi peace. Negotiators in Tanzania supported efforts to resolve the civil war in Burundi where fighting between Hutu rebels and the Tutsi dominated army has killed more than 200,000 people and uprooted 1.2 million since 1993.

Clinton spoke at the invitation of Nelson Mandela who took over as mediator last month.

-Oct. 1996 Rwandan troops invaded former Zaire now the Democratic Republic of the Congo, and the United States has been aiding Rwanda with military as well as health and food aid. Now with the invasion into DR Congo the US is withholding military aid as this poses a diplomatic [problem in the UN and African nations].

Congo rebels reportedly captured a power transformer in the western Congo Thursday, pitching the capital into darkness and cutting off the state's stream of propaganda. The action fueled speculation of an imminent takeover of Kinshasha.

Western diplomats and rebel spokesmen said rebel fighters had captured the town of Inga, about 135 miles southwest of the capital, where the primary power transformer for Kinshasha is situated.

Heavy fighting was also reported in Matadi, about 30 miles south of Inga, where authorities had earlier warned people to stay indoors.

A commander in the rebel stronghold of Goma, in eastern Congo, said his forces had captured the Matadi airport and the Inga power plant. The rebels also said some of their troops had advanced as far as Kalangala, 18 miles southwest of the capital.

-In 1996 The mass grave in Kibuye was exhumed for identification of the bodies. The smell of the dead bodies hangs in the air around the stone walls of the Kibuye Roman Catholic church, which is just above Lake Kivu.

Doctors and anthropologists extract more skeletons from the gray crush of bodies in the clay graves and record the telltale marks of horrible deaths. He has one tagged #467. The bodies are carried up to autopsy tables where pathologist reconstruct shattered skulls and severed bones. They then put the remnants of the victims clothes in shopping bags for survivors to identify.

A Seattle doctor in forensic anthropology states how these autopsies tell of the inhuman massacre these people suffered. The graves are of the Tutsi who lived along Lake Kibuye in the west. For 100 days in 1994, Tutsi were hacked to death by members of the Hutu majority. Investigators believe there are hundreds of graves like this one across the country. They hold at least 500,000 victims.

-October 27,1996 A Hutu refugee camp in Zaire is attacked and gun shots from the Tutsi led Rwanda Patriotic Front setting off a stampede of 80,000 Hutu refugees that still after two years refuse to go back to Rwanda. Some Hutus who have mobilized in the camp have been using the refugee camp in Zaire as bases for cross-border raids into Rwanda.

-Monday May 19, 1997, Zaire rebels take charge, for revenge Laurent Kabila seems to be using the same tactics as Mobutu as he comes closer to taking over the capital in Kinshasa. Kabila was trained with revolutionary Che Guevara in Cuba. Some fear he will be another dictator. The new name Democratic Rep of Congo has not had its flag flown yet nor its name officially changed, nor its President sworn into office. But violence surrounds the capital as executions of Mobutu officials and loyalist happens in the streets by Kabila soldiers.

Mobutu is in permanent exile. Nearly 200 bodies have been collected in the capital city and up to 5000 rebel troops arrived Sunday greeted by hundreds of residents waving branches and offering them food. "These are happy days," says Jean Mbwame, 26, a nurse. "These soldiers are our liberators."

"We control Kinshasha now," said an exuberant Bizima Karaha, Kabila's foreign minister.

Kabila has had an almost bloodless seven-month march into Kinshasha since Mobutu fled and didn't organize any resistance only left his officials and soldiers to die.

Kabila remains in in his headquarters in the southern mining city of Lumumbashi sent top aides to set up a local government in Kinshasha to assess the city's needs. The people were happy and burned the flag of Zaire after 32 years of despotic rule of Mobutu.

US officials began to treat Kabila more as a political leader and less of a guerrilla fighter as US ambassador Daniel

US Ambassador to the UN Bill Richardson stressed to Kabila a peaceful transition was very important to the United States. And future relations would be very dependent on his actions in the next few weeks."

Despite Western diplomatic pressure Kabila has banned all parties except the Alliance of Democratic Forces, from operating here. That is the same thing Mobutu did in 1965 said Rev. Gilbert of St. Andre's Catholic Church., a human rights leader here. We don't know him and what we see scares US."

South Africa recognized the government Sunday. The US could attempt to withhold financial support from the World Bank and the International Monetary Fund if Kabila fails to hold democratic elections.

1997

-In 1997 Hutu death agents are starving and watching their children die as they wait for food in a clearing in the jungle in Zaire. Now they are victims of the civil war there which broke out because of Tutsi rule in Rwanda and Zaire. API

-Hutu refugees cry out how" God is punishing us, " but they won't admit to their slaughtering innocent Tutsi men, women, and children. The Hutu refugees are starving and watch the skeletons of their children protrude their thin skin as they starve waiting for food packages from United Nations workers to arrive. Cholera has broken out as well as lack of water and supplies. Men eat before their starving children which makes the scene even more disturbing. Then they run back into the jungle for fear of their lives. They are afraid to return to Rwanda even though the Tutsi in Rwanda have emphasized they want the Hutu refugees to return home to achieve reconciliation. Tutsi rebels in Zaire have allowed Hutu refugees to fly out of Kisangani Zaire .

-Many innocent women and children are in the refugee camp in Zaire and are afraid of the violence they feel is still going on in Rwanda because of the genocide in 1994. It has been three years, but fear of revenge still keeps them away from their homes. Since they randomly killed Tutsi men, women, and children, they fear the Tutsi will do the same. The Tutsi deny any such vengeance and await the war crime tribunal promised them by the UN.

-A huge airlift is being arranged by the UN to transport these refugees back to Rwanda in the next few weeks. The problem is the Hutu refugees were under the control if the Hutu militia, many of whom were responsible for the massacre. These refugees had to listen to the political propaganda of these militia men and how to lay land mines. When they return to Rwanda they will be under Tutsi rule. API

-The big problem is the mindset of the Hutu refugees who some innocent had to flee their homes. They believe that the Tutsi were to blame for their misery and some think that the massacre never took place. They say that some Tutsi were murdered but many Hutu were killed also. These are some educated Hutus that claim the Tutsi never tell the truth they always lie.

-May 15, 1997, Mobuto stashed billions in the 1980s. The international Monetary Fund IMF reported that Zaire was endemically corrupt. Mobutu Sese Seko took out loans from the IMF for 3.9 billion dollars between 1982 and 1991.

Mobutu plundered the natural resources of Zaire by ordering Zaire's copper and cobalt mining company to deposit its 1978 export earning into a presidential account.

In 1978 the collapse of copper prices a key to Zairean export had Mobuto paying his patronage ion American dollars rather that Zairean currency. He was forced to pay Bosnian mercenaries serval millions of dollars to fight against rebel forces.

Mobutu has nine properties in and around Brussels and Belgium and in Portugal, Spain, and Switzerland. He also has property in South Africa. He has stock in German and Swiss companies and much liquid cash.

After 32 years Mobutu's regime is about to collapse, and he is sick with cancer. In seven months, rebels led by Laurent Kabila have overrun three-quarters of the central African nation which is rich in copper, cobalt, diamond, and timber and Kabila is within 30 miles of the capital Kinshasa.

-Dec. 1997 UN team in Congo starts long stalled probe.

Kinshasa members of the UN investigating team accused Laurent Kabila's forces of massacring Rwandan refugees.

-UN leader Kofi Annan reportedly knew of genocide plans. The New Yorker magazine has a copy of a fax that shows the UN was not to intervene in the planned governmental attacks on the Tutsis in Rwanda. The fax was ordered by Kofi Annan now the UN secretary general.

French, Belgian and US officials have denied they had any warning of a government orchestrated massacre.

Annan was the head of the UN peacekeeping operations on Jan 11, 1994, when the commander of UN forces in Rwanda Gen Romeo Dallaire warned the world body that the Kigali government was planning to slaughter Tutsis and called for intervention.

In a fax sent to UN headquarters in NY Dallaire quoted a senior Rwanda security official as saying he had been ordered to register all Tutsis in Kigali for the purpose he suspected of "their extermination".

In reply, "Annan 's office ordered Dallaire not to protect the informant or follow through on plans to confiscate illegal arms stockpiles. Annan was aware of the order, said his aide, Iqbal Riza, who signed the response.

"I was responsible," Riza told the New Yorker when shown a copy of the order. "This is not to say that Mr. Annan was oblivious of what was going on. No. Part of my responsibility was to keep him informed."

UN officials previously have blocked probes to determine who saw the fax and who ordered Dallaire to abandon his plan to intervene.

In a letter to the Belgian government last year, Annan refused to let Dallaire testify before a Belgian panel investigating the events in Rwanda because he did not believe it was "in the interest of the organization."

In a copy of the response the order was labeled as being sent from Annan. The order told him to assume the late Rwanda President Juvenal Habyarimana was not involved in planning the genocide-despite the informant's claims.

-Wednesday May 21, 1997, As Zaire gets new name proclamation, the easy part, getting the rest of the world to go along with Laurent Kabila's plan was not so easy.

As of Saturday, the former Zaire became the Democratic Republic of the Congo. The US state department recognized the new name immediately, but the UN did not. The UN claims it has received no formal notification of the new name and with no government, foreign ministry, or UN mission it's still legally Zaire.

The US had difficulty notifying other government agencies of the name change legally.

-Rwanda violence in Mukamira military camp report blamed the Rwandan Patriotic Army for increase in government sanctioned killings. Troops killed 62 in May, 124 in April and 226 in July. The government claims that many of the killings occurred when people tried to escape questioning.

-1998 Rwanda refugee camps emptied; 14 die in villages

The last of Rwanda's refugee camps was emptied Sunday as thousands of people were trucked back to their villages. Fourteen people were reported beaten and stoned to death when they returned home.

In the driving rain, a column of trucks filled with people left the Ndere camp outside Kigali and headed for villages. Fernando Del Mundo of the UN High Commission for Refugees said 3,400 people left Ndere Sunday the; last refugee center in the African country.

While camps are cleared, however, the problem of resettling people in villages where many are accused of war crimes is far from solved. Most of those in the camps were Hutus who fled to camps when the Tutsi-led government came to power.

The killings of thousands of refugees at one camp April 22-23 has put pressure on Rwanda's government to improve protection for refugees, and UN special envoy Aldo Aiello indicated a stronger UN role might help.

The mandate is up for review June 9 by the UN Security Council which could toughen it to let UN troops fire in situations other than just self-defense.

1998

-1998 The UN Investigated refugee complaints in Rwanda. 1998 Paul Kagame is elected Chairman of the Rwanda Patriotic Front and a partner in the Government Of National Unity.

-Even though the government in Rwanda has claimed security, the violence wracked city saw fourteen people in Taba and three others in Kayenzi were slain by Hutu rebels who hacked them as they were returning home from the refugee camp in an effort to destabilize the new Tutsi led government. These refugees were Hutus. Vice president and minister of defense, Maj. Gen. Paul Kagame stopped these attacks and said security has been returned and denied that Tutsi had anything to do with slayings.

Meanwhile in Butare criminal court found 330 guilty and sentenced 88 to death for the 1994 slaughter of 500,000 Tutsis. More than 22 are to executed in front of a firing squad immediately. More than 125,000 people are awaiting trial. The UN is conducting separate trials in Arusha, Tanzania- the prime minister who led Rwanda Hutus to slaughter -pleaded guilty to genocide and would testify against others who took part in the bloodbath.

. After three years in refugee camps in eastern Zaire they were sent on the most recent flight when Rwanda Tutsi attacked the camps, and a civil war broke out in Zaire. Now after reaching safety in the neighboring Congo Republic, these refugees face a future that may be as perilous as the past they have tried to flee.

UN officials said before the month is out they will begin repatriating the refugees to their homes in Rwanda. The Congo government said the refugees had to be out of the country by the end of the month. Under the UN high Commission for refugees only voluntary repatriation is acceptable. The overwhelming majority of Hutu refugees mostly young men, fear they will be killed or thrown in jail suspected of having been involved in the killing of Tutsi in 1994.

During their odyssey across an area as large as the United states east of the Mississippi the refugees were besieged by hunger and disease.

"We crossed a lot of water," said Nyarwango's 18-year-old granddaughter, Alice Benadamu. "Sometimes up to here," she said, raising her hand to her neck. Many people drowned.

But it was the guns "crying" that was the most frightening, said Josepha Mukaburanja, whose 12-year-old son was the only other member of her family of 11 to survive.

The refugees have been hunted for the last seven months by Tutsi soldiers in the rebel army of Laurent Kabila, who since his rebel army's victory has become president and re-adopted Zaire's original name, Congo. Allegations persist that thousands were killed.

"I ran over dead bodies," said 47-year-old Therese Nyarampaduka, standing with two daughters four and five, who made it; their father did not. "I was sure I would die."

Last month when the refugees reached Mbandaka, they were only a canoe ride from refuge in the Congo Republic.

"We were resting in Mbandaka," said Jean Nsingayumva, a 24-year-old peasant from Butare, Rwanda, "The Red Cross helped us. They gave us rice."

Then the town fell to rebels; the Zairean army fled without a fight.

"After we heard the guns crying, we began to run away," Nsingayumva said. He and his wife ran to the river with their two small children.

As Nsingayumva was running he turned around," I saw the body of my wife in the river with blood." he said. "My son was with her."

He said he also saw the rebels knife two men to death. That was on May 27–the day hundreds of men, women and children were clubbed, bayoneted, or shot by Kabila's forces, the Boston Globe reported last week.

The government in Kinshasha had long denied that its soldiers killed any unarmed civilians. But last week, it backed down, acknowledging some may have been killed in cross fire.

1999

-Thurs. July 1, 1999

UN panel investigates Rwandan genocide

Five years after the Rwanda genocide, a three-member panel began work on June 21 to answer the question that has perplexed UN officials: Did the world body do enough to prevent the massacres of as many as one million people?

Former Swedish Prime Minister Ingvar Carlsson, leader of the three-member team that includes delegates from South Korea and Nigeria said:" We will have full access to all materials. We hope to draw a conclusion about why this could happen."

Several nations including France and Belgium have conducted their own inquiries about the UN and other force's response to the massacres April 6, 1994-July .

"This new team is an independent panel not tied to one country," said former Korean Foreign Minister Han Sung-Joo, a member of the body.

The panel-which also includes Nigerian Gen. Rufus Kupolati- is scheduled to report to UN Secretary General Kofi Annan by the end of the year.

-Thursday, Aug 17,1999, Rwanda, and Uganda to meet in Congo. Both countries have stationed troops in the Congo as part of their effort to support rebels fighting to overthrow the President Laurent Kabila. But now the tow allies have moved apart backing rebel factions and disagreeing over how to conduct the war and more recent efforts for peace.

-1999 Clergy accused of genocide in Rwanda war.

First church leaders to be prosecuted at UN war crimes. Arusha Tanzania five clergy members will be tried here on charges that have shaken the trust of many Christens in the region. Their cases have drawn less attention than the turbulence over sexual abuse by priests in the US and other countries, but the accusations are more serious.

The five men are accused of genocide. The first catholic priest accused of helping to kill about 2,000 people who took refuge in his church, by ordering bulldozers to crush the building. The second Catholic priest is charged with playing a key role when a group of Hutus attacked and killed refugees in the college where he was rector. A third priest an army chaplain and the Anglican were aware and sided with the Hutus in the massacre against the Tutsi before the slayings began. At least 300 clergy members and nuns were slain themselves in the violence because they were Tutsi, or they were helping others. There is much evidence of refugees seeking protection in the churches, trapped, and killed after church workers called in armed mobs.

Friday December 17, 1999, Probe faults UN and US for genocide in Rwanda. According to the report the US failed to give the UN the political and material support it needed to prevent the genocide of nearly 800,000 Rwandans.

Annan and Riza of the UN ignored a UN commander in Africa Lt, Gen Romeo Dallaire of Canada who had repeatedly warned that mass murder was being planned Dallaire sought authorization from the UN to use force to disarm the plotters. But Annan and Riza informed the commander that he had neither the mandate nor means to use force.

As armed groups moved against ethnic Tutsi civilians the report says, UN peacekeepers were either unwilling or unable to defend the Rwandans or in some instances, themselves. Ten Belgian peace keepers were killed

Some UN peacekeeper helped but some Bangladesh forces left other refugees unprotected at a technical school in defiance of instructions from UN commanders.

Annan says he was deprived of means to stop the slaughter. The UN force was neither mandated nor equipped for the kind of forceful action which would prevent or halt the genocide.

The wrote of the report Carlsson former Swedish Prime Minster said the Clinton administration's explanation that the loss of 18 American soldiers in Somalia in October 1993 scared the US off peacekeeping for domestic political reasons, particularly peacekeeping in Africa

-Aug 17, 1999, Rwanda, and Uganda to Meet on Congo Uganda and Rwanda have troops in the Congo supporting the rebels aimed at overthrowing Laurent Kabila. But in recent months the two allies have moved apart backing rival rebel factions and disagreeing over how to conduct the war and more recent efforts for peace. This conflict escalated into fighting over Kisangani's main airport artillery and mortar fire continued until the evening meeting. More than 50 people have died many of them civilians in Kisangani. Women and children were trapped inside health center where artillery fire caused them to stop work. The UN condemned the fighting

The accord was aimed at ending the fighting between Rwanda, Uganda, and the rebels on one side and Mr. Kabila, Zimbabwe, Angola, and Namibia on the other. The US top official for African Affairs in the National Security Council met separately then together with Ugandan President Yoweri Museveni, President Pasteur Bizimuingu and Vice President Paul Kagame of Rwanda. John Nagendra, a senior advisor for the Ugandan President, felt the conflict between Uganda and Rwanda must stop for the ultimate goal of overthrowing Mr. Kabila. Fighting resumed later that evening at the Kisangani airport between Ugandan and Rwandan forces. Last year when the rebellion began both countries were on the same side supporting the same rebel forces, the Congolese Rally for Democracy. The CRD split and Uganda supported the original leader Ernest Wamba Dia Wamba and Rwanda supported Dr. Emile Ilunga a longtime opposition leader in the Congo.

2000-2010

On 17 April 2000-Paul Kagame was unanimously voted President of the Republic of Rwanda by the Transitional National Assembly, He took the Oath of Office on 22 April 2000.

In recent days Rwandan soldiers and Tutsi rebels have captured several eastern cities in their campaign against Kabila's government.

While Kabila was blamed, neighboring Rwandan rebel leader has called 'the fighting a struggle of the Congolese people."

-2001 Rebels in Congo capture strategic lakeside port

Kigali, Rwanda -Congolese rebels captured a strategic eastern lakeside port Sat. From government forces and their allies after a night of fierce fighting, the rebel commander said. The fall of the city of Moliro was a sign that a UN-mediated truce in the Congo has broken down.

-Thurs April 4, 2002, Ex-prime minister says education will pull Africa out of chaos The former prime minister of Rwanda urged international involvement to curb chaos and break up dictatorships in Africa.

Faustin Twagiramungu spoke to 100 students at the U of Louisville's Brandeis School of Law on Wed. He lives in Belgium now helped negotiate a failed peace accord and became prime minister shortly after 500,000 were killed in a government-orchestrated genocide in 1994.

"To have a bright future, you have to educate people," he said in a 30-minute speech. "Always keep in mind that Africa can develop."

The continent, ravaged by AIDS, wars and other forms

of civil unrest, is home to the bulk of the world's 50 poorest nations.

Many of the accused ringleaders in the genocide of 1994 are now on trial before a UN tribunal in Tanzania. But Twagiramungu said the tribunal would take "hundreds of years" to convict all the perpetrators.

On Wed., Twagiramungu criticized the UN as he has before, of standing idly by while the mass killings occurred.

"For three months, people were being killed while the international community was watching." he said. This week the first feature film on the three-month genocide, "100 Days," made its debut in Kigali, Rwanda.

Twagiramungu also said the UN has focused so much attention on the AIDS crisis in Africa, that it's overlooking education.

"The problem for Africa is not only the AIDS crisis, but a brain crisis," He said, "African children are so hungry they want to learn."

Twagiramungu said children are taught French as a second language in many countries, though he said many children have told him they would prefer to learn English, so they can "communicate with the world."

Twagiramungu came to prominence when he helped negotiate a peace agreement for Rwanda in 1993. The accord failed when Rwandan President Juvenal Habyarimana's plane was shot down the next year. What followed were mass killings by an extremist Hutu government, which targeted Tutsis and moderate Hutus.

After a year as prime minister, Twagiramungu and a group of his followers moved to Belgium and formed the Union of Rwandese Democratic Forces.

Twagiramungu 's appearances at U of L was sponsored by

The Muhammad Ali Institute for Peacekeeping and Conflict Resolution, a center that is planned for downtown Louisville. -April 21, 2002, Talks to stop Congo war end with no deal. Kinshasa Eight weeks of talks to end the four-year war in Congo halted Friday with no agreement on how the government and a rebel group can share power in an interim government. A key sticking point: Rebels refused to accept President Joseph Kabila as the leader of an interim government.

Fighting between government troops and Rwandan-backed rebels has flared recently in a mineral rich region in southeastern Congo. On Thursday a UN helicopter came under fire around the site if the recent clashes, near Lake Tanganyika.

-Thursday July 11,2002 African Union Developed in Durban South Africa. The AU is creating a Peace and Security Council that shall be a collective security and early warning arrangement to facilitate timely and efficient response to conflict and crisis situations in Africa. Among other possibilities, it will be responsible for following up " progress towards the promotion of democratic practices, good governance, the rule of law, protection of human rights and fundamental freedoms by member states. "The charter allows the AU to get involved in the domestic affairs of member states to prevent genocide and crimes against humanity the Peace and Security /Council of the AU is a powerful instrument on the continent It will be made of 15 elected countries, five of which will hold long-term seats. Nigeria, South Africa, Egypt, and Algeria-countries already committed to -NEPAD (New Partnership for African Development)-will be the front runners. NEPAD began in Sept. 1999 and mandated Pres. Mbeki of South Africa and Pres. Bouteflika of Algeria engage Africa's creditors on the total cancellation of Africa's external debt. NEPAD's primary objective is to eradicate poverty in Africa.

Already there is discord among the nations. Kenya and Libya have problems with NEPAD. Some of the wealthier African countries will now have their resources split among the whole continent instead of a few countries which some countries see as a threat to their receiving the aid they are used to receiving. South Africa is trying to keep NEPAD half in and half out of the AU.

-Thursday July11, 2002, Kenya sued over land grants Kenyan environmentalist sue the government that plans to give away 170,000 acres of public forest. The environmentalist that includes East Africa Wildlife Society and Kenya Forest Working Group says the government acted illegally by issuing title deeds before announcing its intention to give out the 167,000 acres of public land.

-Sat. Mar.15, 2003 Congo: Rwanda says it may send troops back. Rwanda is threatening to send its troops back into the Congo if Uganda does not withdraw soldiers that it recently deployed in the chaotic Iturbi region. "The United Nations must demand and obtain the total and immediate withdrawal of Ugandan troops." Rwanda's Foreign Ministry said in a statement, adding that it would be "legitimate" for Rwanda to send troops back into the Congo. Uganda said its 1,000 or so troops were there to stabilize the Congolese town of Bunia, near Uganda's western border. Rwanda withdrew its troops last year under an accord aimed at ending a war that drew in several African countries.

-Sunday June 15, 2003, Brutality of Congo war increases as machetes give way to firearms Wave of shooting, grenade attacks follows influx of weapons

Bunia, Congo -the civil war between the Hemas, who are traditionally herders and traders, and the Lendus, who are farmers started in 1966 but led to bloodshed in June 1999. The two groups lived peacefully side by side since the 17th century, but in the 19th century Belgian colonizers favored the Hemas, using them to run local government offices and manage Lendu workers in plantations and in mines.

–2006–Burundi civil war ends

–In 2006 NEPAD became a mandated initiative of the African Union.

2006 Rwanda broke diplomatic ties with France after a French judge issued international arrest warrants for several of Kagame's close associates and called for Kagame to face trial at the International Criminal Tribunal for Rwanda (established by the United Nations Security Council to try those involved in the 1994 genocide), alleging that Kagame and other FPR leaders had ordered the rocket attack that caused the 1994 plane crash that killed Habyarimana. Kagame vehemently denied the accusation and in turn claimed that France had armed and advised the rebels responsible for the genocide. In 2007 the Rwandan government launched a formal investigation into the 1994 plane crash. The results, released in 2010, indicated that Hutu extremist soldiers were responsible for shooting down the plane, in an effort to derail Habyarimana's peace negotiations with the Tutsi rebels.

- Under Paul Kagame, Rwanda's economy has grown five to nine percent a year. And one of his key drives is tourism, particularly around the magnificent gorilla reserves along the mountainous border. In 2007, 39,000 travelers visited Rwanda- a 26 percent increase over 2006. (From Conde Nast Traveler magazine, May 17, 2008).

–In 2010 Kagame sought reelection. In the run-up to the August presidential election, some opposition media outlets were repressed, and several individuals, including an independent journalist and an opposition party leader, were murdered—although Kagame vowed that neither he nor his regime were involved in the killings. Because of this environment, several opposition parties were unable to field candidates; some candidates faced arrest, others fled, and some were excluded from participation. The three candidates who eventually stood against Kagame posed little challenge. Official results indicated that Kagame had been reelected with 93 percent of the vote, and voter turnout was reported as more than 95 percent.

H.E. PAUL KAGAME PRESIDENT OF THE REPUBLIC OF RWANDA

His Excellency Paul Kagame was sworn in as President of the Republic of Rwanda for a seven-term mandate on 12 September 2003 after being elected in the first ever democratically contested multiparty elections help August 2003.

Paul Kagame was born in October 1957 in Ruhango, Southern Province, to Deogratius and Asteria Rutagambwa.

In 1960, he fled persecution and ethnic pogroms that were to characterize Rwanda in subsequent decades and became a refugee in Uganda.

Paul Kagame was among the first 27 men who, together with Yoweri Kaguta Museveni, launched a five-year liberation war in Uganda in 1980.

He served as a senior officer in the Ugandan army between 1986 and 1990 during which he attended a staff and command course at Lort Leavenworth, Kansas, USA.

On October 1990,Paul Kagame returned to Rwanda after 30 years in exile to lead the Rwanda Patriotic Army (RPA) in the struggle for the liberation of Rwanda, from Belgum.

On July 19,1994, he was appointed Vice-President and Minister for Defense in the Government of National Unity.

In 1998, he was elected Chairman of the Rwanda Patriotic Front (RPF),a partner in
The Government of National Unity.

On 17 April 2000, Paul Kagame was unanimously elected President of the Republic of Rwanda by the Transitional National Assembly. He took the Oath of Office on 22 April 2000.

President Kagame was awarded the 2003 Global Leadership Award by the Young Presidents Organization (YPO), in recognition of his role in uniting and reconciling Rwandans and in promoting peaceful solutions to the conflicts in the region.

In July 2003, President Kagame was elected 1st Vice President of the African Union during the African Union Heads of State and Government held in Maputo, Mozambique.

In April 2005, President Kagame was awarded an Honorary Degree Doctor of Laws by the University of the Pacific in the USA.

In September 2005, President Kagame was awarded the Andrew Young Medal for Capitalism and Social Progress by Georgia State University in the USA; and in the same month received the African National Achievement Award by the Africa America Institute in the USA.

In April 2006, President Kagame was awarded an Honorary Doctorate by Oklahoma Christian University in the USA.

President Kagame was presented the ICT Africa Award in 2006 and in 2007 – an award which recognizes organizations and individuals that have demonstrated excellence in promoting the use of ICTs for the overall development of the African continent.

President Kagame was the recipient of the 2007 African Gender Award presented by Femmes Africa Solidarite in recognition of outstanding achievement in furthering gender mainstreaming in the economic and public spheres, as well as addressing social and cultural barriers that impede the involvement and advancement of women in national affairs.

In August 2007, President Kagame received "The Abolitionist of the Year 2007" Award after Rwanda abolished the death penalty. The award was presented by Hands Off Cain to recognize the person, who, above all others, has demonstrated an extraordinary commitment in the struggle for a moratorium on executions and the abolition of the death penalty.

President Kagame has been married to Jeannette Nyiramongi since 1989. They have four children.

President Kagame is a keen tennis player and football fan.

Official Website for H. E. Paul Kagame 12/12/2008

FUTURE

AS the dawning of the world, as we know it, had its inception in the belly of Africa, so is the genesis of the next phase of civilization to begin, in Africa. Finally, we are no longer held hostage by oil companies or countries. Peace in the world can be attained in our lifetime. The fight and control of a needed source of energy is free to all.

Relaxing and enjoying the soothing wind and beautiful water landscape surrounding Lake Kivu, silently and invisibly the precious silent gold is pumped to the Central African region once deplete of hope. Now fresh and alive the hills and towns in Rwanda sing with the air of prosperity, love, peace, and harmony. Strife and discord are no more. The country is one with nature itself as all the people benefit from the sacred Lake Kivu with its endless supply of methane gas.

Cheyenne looks around at the happy faces of the waiters, the hotel owners, and the taxi drivers as they all prosper from the government of Rwanda's foresight in realizing the potential under the lake.

"Hello Henri, how is the government functioning this morning?" Cheyenne asks knowing the answer.

"Things are great, we are implementing an education system that tracks a child's ambition or career choice from elementary school through to college. We want to see that the dreams of our people are met from their earliest age when they still hear spirit speak to them directly. Babies of three to six years old hear the talk about the best life possible for them, and how to get it all the way to college life. Our goal is to guide the child in all aspects of their life, with free choice, to accomplishing their spirit's dream," Henri was so proud of the progress of his country and Central Africa.

"Henri, when is this taking place? I'll transfer my great-grandchild from the US here when that system is in place. What a wonderful concept to fulfill dreams of a child when they first know their purpose on this earth before life happens after four years of age." Cheyenne was excited by this new concept.

"Imagine when you are a child, someone asks you what you want to be when you grow up. Of course, a child knows, because they see with pure eyes the reason, they chose their parents and for being here," Henri explains. "If the child responds with President of the country. He is then put into classes, clubs and around the elements of law and political endeavors where he can see the workings of government and see venues for change and improvement.

"At every level of their education their ideas for the improvement of some function of the government are recorded. These are all stored on a unit key and when he makes his decision for a college career this information is given to him from kindergarten to his high school year. Imagine the impact of this on an individual. They have the choice to follow this dream or go after another. I would imagine if the individual hadn't changed their mind through high school, they would pursue the law or political science major that could lead them into politics," Henri enthusiastically said.

Cheyenne, Leon, Marie, Anton, and his wife Dava, listened as if this were a hallucination. They couldn't imagine in their wildest ideas, think that Rwanda could be the country with the most highly developed system of education for the 21st century and beyond. Children have the greatest imaginations ever. Their spirits are clear and unhampered by the decisions and choices adults must make daily to survive. A child unafraid of discouragement or disparagement freely telling his teacher or parent his vision for the future, accurately informs them of his or her true goal for being here now on earth.

"This is a miracle. After what we have all been through to realize a point in time today that is a true visualization of Rwanda's future, starting here and now as a world class country, is such a blessing. Let's not forget where we came from only to never go there again, but we must put the past way behind us and never go back. Rwanda is a forward-looking country, and we must only look forward and enjoy the journey here and now. Friends let us raise our drinks and toast the future and present Rwanda," Anton said as they all clicked glasses.

Celebration of this most happy time for all of them is long suffered. The New Year, 2030, has come in with great wisdom and hope. Having the right President in the US since President Obama and the promise has instantly brought peace and hope to the world. Honesty prevails. All greed and deceit of former administrations exposed through is dissipated and now only the determination for equality for all people. Once again, the world can rely on the strong nations lifting the weaker ones.

The Angels won. All around the world people, being still and silent, remember who they are.

The promise of one united Africa soars with the invisible gold ascending freely out of the Lake the Rwandans and Zairians used for their daily survival, now glimmers with hope. The same lake that was bloodied in 1994 by the senseless genocide that took place in both countries and spread to Burundi, Uganda, Tanzania, and Angola and then later from the west coast of Africa to the east and north. Now the poorest are the richest; The Blackest are the purest. Once they lived putrid lives now the people of Central Africa live in probity.

The remarkable times we live in now come not only from doing the right things, but also learning and acting from the thoughts and traits that were of the highest and greatest good in our natural history. Therein lies the solution.

We are at a significant place in history that all that preceded it seems a dream. The world has been swept into a consciousness, an awakening as to what and who we are. We remove the blocks to love that is within US all. Knowledge cannot be eradicated. Truth is the light in which our souls seek love.

"The blood of hatred fades to let the grass grow green again and let the flowers be all white and sparkling in the summer sun. What was a place of death has now become a living temple in a world of Light."

A Course In Miracles Text-26.X.3:1-2

FORGIVE AND LIVE

Five Steps to Restore Peace of Mind and Evolve to Better Everything

The world is designed to upset us at any moment. Learn how to take personal responsibility for your reactions and restore your peace of mind. Respond with your highest and embody the power that awaits.

1. Reveal It. First see the opportunity in the suffering to respond in saying I forgive you. At first it doesn't seem possible, just say it. When you realize you will not sink into utter and incomprehensible depression, grieving, and suicide you have something to do. When the suffering is directly aimed like a shooting gun, assault on you or close to you, or starving, there is only adrenaline pumped to fight, flight or freeze in fear, otherwise it is in your head to control. The thing to do is reveal the deep-down fear/hurt that is encompassing the suffering. What fear is revealed?

2. Feel It. Bring in to consciousness the need to see the fear clearly. When fear is active, the ego has thought of some future disgrace or detrimental action that will never actually happen, and it is time to ask why. Ask: How is this working in my favor? What am I learning from this? Think deeply about an insult, fight, rejection or disappointment of any kind as something to get over as soon as possible. Reveal the feelings associated with the hurt. Next feel the feelings that go with this hurt. Cry, shout, tell somebody how victimized you feel, reveal the why it makes you feel this way. Let the true feeling and truth be exposed. Journal,

write, or dictate these feelings and fears of what you think is in the future. Then write the opposite feelings.

3. Deal With It. Feel the hurt either alone or with someone who cares. When alone know the exact reason why you hurt and are suffering. Most of our suffering is either for the past or future events associated with the hurt, unless it is a crisis as stated in the first paragraph. Not forgiving keeps you in the past and freezes opportunity in the present and stops action. Open your eyes to your surroundings and be in the present. As soon as you have stopped the negative emotional chatter, deal with it. Get professional help if there was trauma which is more serious then daily drama. Eckhart Tolle once said, "Stop thinking." Projecting, over worrying, are meaningless energies; stop leaving you present moment. We have the power to control our thoughts and thereby control our lives. An emotional outlet is beneficial to the human system in keeping the production of cortisol down. Cortisol is a poison we discharge in our bodies and can cause cancer and other serious diseases. Stress causes many ill effects in the body. Acting out of stress results in desperation and that is always disastrous.

4. Find gratitude for life. Gratitude in the Now. There would be a lot less violence if more gratitude were given for the present moment. Actually, in real time, count your blessings. Deal with where you are in the present moment. It is not likely we can live in this world without getting upset at some of the things we see, hear, experience, or even eat in a day. Our job is to reveal it as soon as possible, feel it, experience the emotion, or vocalize it to get it finished. By fixing it, cleaning it up, buying something that can deal with it, you may feel better, and the sooner the better. If you don't deal with it as it comes whatever it was, it is

guaranteed to return to you maybe even worse. Leaving upsets to linger and agitate is harmful to our bodies. Fear is temporary, but regret is a lifetime. When you forgive you actually forget it long enough to move on.

5. Heal It. Now it is time to heal the upset. Stay in the present moment as much as possible. If driving, pay attention to the other cars and where you are, always. For example, if someone will cut you off in traffic, yell with windows up, blow the horn, feel it. Exhale slowly, say, "Ahhh," if possible forgive them. The upset is now unimportant. Relax and breathe. You can once again continue with your drive or attend to your child again in an appreciative light. Think of all the beautiful things associated with these things you are doing. The upset is now unimportant. Tapping, meditation twice a day, talking to someone you trust are some remedies for life's hurts. Forget blame, shame and game.

Move-on. Once healed you can move on to the matters at hand in the present without distraction. The past is over, never to return, the future is somewhat unpredictable unless you are moving toward your peace in love. At which time the universe will aid and move in your direction and handle things in your way. Make your life happen.

Printed in the United States
by Baker & Taylor Publisher Services